THE KIDNAPPING OF SARAH EASTON

Also by Erik Goddard

Requiem Series

THE KIDNAPPING OF SARAH EASTON

Erik Goddard

The Kidnapping of Sarah Easton by Erik Goddard

Published by Tension Press

www.erikgoddard.com/fiction

Copyright © 2021 Erik Goddard

ISBN: 978-0-9828327-0-7 (print)

Printed in United States

First Edition

CHAPTER 1

The Seattle streets were wet with morning rain, but the lingering clouds over Elliott Bay were fading. The early March air coming through the open window felt warm and gave Sarah an optimism about the day. She almost contemplated turning around and skipping the appointment with Levin.

Would it matter?

It would be like playing hooky. Levin wouldn't feel deprived. He'd get paid anyway. And he got paid a lot. So many things she could do with her day that didn't involve being in that office, him sitting in that wingback chair, saying just tell me about the way you and Tracy used to play when you were little, the memories you have of Tracy, the times you felt angry or happy when Tracy did something.

She pulled into the basement parking ramp of the office building on Mercer Island where Levin had his office. She knew she had to go. She'd feel guilty later if she didn't, and that could be worse than not dealing with the problem she was there to resolve. She took off her sunglasses and drove through the ramp. She wondered what he'd say if she just asked him what medication he thought would work. Wasn't that the inevitable outcome? Looking stuff up in the manual and matching the symptoms with a pill?

She parked her Audi in her usual space. A few people in suits came and went, talking on phones, looking at watches. In the lobby, she pressed the button on the wall and waited. She looked at her own watch, but realized she didn't have it on. She must have forgotten. She'd had it out on her dresser. She'd been going to wear the watch from the matching set that Brandon had bought for them when they were in Switzerland.

In the lobby, a few people came and went. A woman was sitting in a chair, talking on her phone. Ding. The elevator opened. When she got off on the fifth floor and went to Levin's office, she saw a thirty-something man in a crisp, dark suit at the front desk. Thick rims on his dark glasses, bright blue eyes, mustache, darkish hair parted. He was just putting down the phone.

He smiled when she approached. "Good morning."

"Morning, I'm here for my appointment."

"And your name?"

"Sarah Easton."

As he scanned the screen in front of him, the door opened and a woman walked in. It was the woman she'd seen in the lobby just now.

"Just to let you know, Sarah, we had some sudden issues come up with the building, and we're kind of having to juggle people and schedules. Ah, here you are. Just a moment." He acknowledged the new woman. "Hello, are you checking in?"

"Yes. Reynolds—10:30."

"Got it. So I might as well mention it to both of you. We've had some maintenance issues come up. We don't know much yet, but looks like water damage."

The woman looked exasperated and glanced at her watch, then between him and Sarah. "Okay?" She said impatiently.

"It looks like they'll have to close up for awhile to get it inspected. In the meantime we're trying to let people know that Dr. Levin and Dr. Reynolds are seeing clients out of their office in Queen Anne, just until this gets resolved."

"I didn't get a call," the woman said.

"We just started calling people—I'm really sorry about this. We're trying to let everyone know but we just found out ourselves."

Sarah felt minor irritation. "So there's another office in Queen Anne?"

"Yes." He handed her a card with the address on it. "If you're able to go there, I'll just call them and let them know to expect you."

The woman looked at the clock on the wall, then at Sarah. "What time's your appointment?"

"10:30," Sarah said. "With Levin."

"Me too, with Reynolds."

"We got something Tuesday night from maintenance," the man said. "Sounds like whatever they were doing turned into a bigger project than they thought. Apparently there's some issues with the exterior walls on this floor and the one below us."

"I guess what are you gonna do, right?" the woman said.

"Just work around it, pretty much."

"What do you think," she said to Sarah.

Sarah shrugged, feeling the stirrings of inconvenience. "How far is it? Queen Anne, you said?"

He nodded. "Right on the hill. You can't miss it. It's in a home office—private practice."

The woman had her car keys in one hand and jingled them. "Might as well head over there." She looked at the card. "Should be easy to find."

The man smiled. "Great, I'll let Dr. Reynolds know. Sarah, how about you?"

"I know where it is," the woman said. "Think I've been by there." She looked at Sarah. "We could drive together if you want—you could follow me. I mean, up to you."

Sarah pondered, looking at the card, then at her watch that wasn't there. "Okay." She smiled at the woman. "I guess."

"I do the same thing," the man said.

"What's that."

"Forget my watch, but look for it all the time like it was there." He smiled. "It's a habit isn't it?"

"Don't want to be late—you know they'll charge you by the minute anyway," the woman said. The man vaguely shrugged his shoulders.

Sarah, looking at the card, said, "Doesn't even say 'shrink' on it."

The man picked up the phone. "Well, technically he's just a therapist. We refer psychiatry as needed. Yes, hello, can you let Dr. Levin know Sarah Easton is on the way? Yes, and Ruth Gaines for Dr. Reynolds. Yes. Thank you." He put down the phone and looked up: "Well, they are expecting both of you."

* * *

Before exiting the ramp, Sarah and the woman chatted briefly about where the location was, and who should follow who. Sarah noticed that the impatient look from the office seemed more relaxed and wide-eyed out here. The woman pulled out first, in a gray Lexus.

As Sarah drove, she again debated blowing off the appointment. She should've told the receptionist back there. He was new—she'd never seen him before. Kind of good-looking. Maybe a little too well-dressed for a guy answering the phones, but then again, the practice was small and spendy, and maybe that's just how male receptionists dress in a place like that. She could call him and have him call Levin, just tell him she couldn't make it after all, that something had come up. Or just drive off and don't show up? This led her back to the thoughts she'd had on the way here. She'd regret not going. She'd feel guilty. She'd wonder later why she hadn't gone.

Today would be her fifth (or sixth?) session. They were her father's idea.

It had started with insomnia, then memories, then nightmares about what had happened to Tracy. She'd sought help from her doctor. Her doctor suggested a therapist, and the therapist had mentioned Levin. Levin suggested on the first day that repressed feelings of guilt were the source of the problems. Tracy's climbing accident last year had come and gone. The funeral had provided a partial closure. But then the problems had only begun.

She went to the University of California in Berkeley and flew home every Thursday to see this acclaimed specialist. She typically flew between San Francisco and Seattle weekly anyway, but on these days it was for the sessions. There were many other things she could do with Thursday mornings, whether in the Bay Area or in Seattle, or anywhere. The horses she kept at the stable on Bainbridge. There were people out there who took care of them, but it was her self-appointed job to take care of Tracy's Appaloosa herself. Going out with Cheryl, Dawn or Becca. Sailing with Edwin and the gang. Hanging out with her friends from high school. Or maybe studying for exams.

She passed the Lexus at a stoplight once, but was overtaken again a few blocks later. Another crazy client or someone who just needs a therapist? They went up the hill in Queen Anne and navigated the curvy streets, and after a couple of turns, she started looking for the address among the gardens and Victorian houses. She hadn't been on the hill in ages and had forgotten how peaceful it was here, with the beautiful views overlooking downtown and Elliott Bay.

Another turn, and her nav showed she was close. The other woman was just pulling up to a white modern stucco house, parking along one side of the driveway, next to a black BMW. The street was narrow and winding. Being on a hill, a high stone terrace wall rose on one side of the street, with houses above. There appeared to be no room for street parking, so Sarah pulled into the driveway, behind the Lexus. It was quiet. She heard a car pass by slowly on a street nearby, but it was otherwise dreamily silent. The house had a steeply pitched roof with red clay tiles. Trees and shrubs in front, everything trimmed neatly and fragrant from the rain. The narrow yard was bordered by a high wooden fence and gate covered in vines. A large tree with wet green leaves loomed in front, and to the side she could see out across the main part of downtown.

Sarah got out of her car. "Well, that wasn't so bad," the woman said while looking at her makeup in a small hand mirror. Sarah locked her door and they approached the entrance, and the woman rang the bell. Within seconds, a thinnish man in his mid-thirties opened the front door and leaned out. "Hello," he said to the woman. "One of you must be Sarah?" He seemed to roll the R with a certain emphasis.

The woman pointed. "I think she's Sarah."

"Then you must be—Ruth?" They all shook hands. "I'm Dan, one of the associates in our clinic. Sorry about the mixup today. Hopefully this won't last long."

"It's no problem. We found it okay," Sarah said.

He ushered them in and closed the door behind them.

From the foyer, a wide living room with floor-to-ceiling windows overlooked downtown. The view was breathtaking, and the place was decorated nicely. To the left was a smaller room with a floor of what appeared to be tatami mats and soft white light. Next to that was a glimpse of kitchen, and a modern dining room with hardwood floors.

"Well, let's get you both settled in. It's just down this way." They followed him to the right, down a hallway, passing doors on either side and skylights overhead. He opened a door and led them across an unlit and unfinished room with exposed plywood and particle board, and then into a long and narrow room with pine walls and red tile floor. This, too, seemed partly unfinished, or at least undecorated.

"A bit rustic. We're redesigning in here. The biggest gripe around here's been a shortage of contractors. At least the good ones who do the job right." As he walked he talked, almost to himself. "They take their time getting the job done, but don't forget to bill you all along the way."

The room was simple, with a small wooden table and two wide leather chairs beneath a small window that would overlook downtown if she could see through it. But it was too high in the wall. Two overhead skylights filled the room with soft light. On the far end was a closed door. Another door with two tiny windows within it led outside, to the garden.

He motioned to the chairs. "So, we get a break from the construction twice a week, while we're seeing clients." He moved the table aside slightly for them to sit. "Have a seat. Coffee? Chai? We have juice and—"

"Actually, is there a bathroom I could use?" the woman asked.

"Sure, just back the way we came. Second door on the right. Can't miss it." When she had left, he said, "Sarah, anything I can get you?"

"I'm okay, thanks." Sarah sat down and took off her jacket.

"Okay, let me know if you change your mind." As he turned to leave, he bent down to examine an outlet in the wall. Then he traced with his hand along the floor.

He noticed Sarah watching him. "With the construction, they messed with the phone lines in here. Never know what they're going to do next. Supposed to be working now." He patted his pockets as if searching for something. "Let's check that out." Sarah watched as he looked around the room.

"Probably way over by the front door." He started to turn, but hesitated.

"Your phone?"

"Yeah."

"You just need to test if the phone works in here?"

Seeing her get her phone out, he waved his hands. "Oh no, that's fine. I can go get mine."

"Well it's not like you're going anywhere with it. Here."

"Great, be just a sec," he said, taking Sarah's phone. Seeing a locked screen, he showed her and gave it back. She unlocked it and handed it back to him.

"Mind if I try it from the other room? That's where the phone is."

She felt the wall go up, but she'd already given it to him. "Okay. I guess."

"Be right back." He left the long, narrow room and went into the unfinished room. She heard the door quietly close.

Sitting in the chair, Sarah was aware of a hint of nervousness. He had her phone. She hadn't realized he was going to close the door and walk away with it. She had people in her contact list, websites, messages, private stuff. What was she thinking? And she didn't know him and even if she did, why had she just given him her phone? Come to think of it, had he even said his name? Maybe he had and she didn't remember. And where did the woman go? Why wasn't she back yet?

Relax. You thought he'd call from here and then hand it back, simple as that. He didn't, but he's gonna check the line and then be right back. That's all there is to it. Besides, he works with Levin, he's part of the firm or the clinic or whatever it is, so it's not like he's a complete stranger, even if you've never met him. And the woman, who knows, maybe she wasn't feeling well.

She leaned back and looked around the room. She was sitting on the end that would overlook downtown, if the tiny window above her allowed a view. What a strange window. Why have a room like this with no view of downtown, just a tiny window high in the wall? Looking across to the far side of the long and narrow room, where it was darker, she wondered where the door led. The wooden walls were bare. With some art like she'd seen in the rest of the place, it would look a lot more finished in here. If this was going to be the waiting room, it would definitely need some final touches.

It seemed like several minutes had gone by. She had the urge to look at her watch. And now she didn't have her phone either. No way to tell the time. She got up and looked in her purse, as though to make sure her watch might not be in there.

She sat down again and looked around. She could feel her fingernails on her right hand digging into the her thumb, first one, then another, then another. Over and over again.

When a few minutes had turned into several more, she stood up and looked out the two narrow windows into the garden as she passed the door. She stepped up the two steps into the unfinished room. In this room, a large drapery or curtain hung where a window would be. She started to walk across the room. On the other side of that door was the room she'd entered, and first met the "associate" just minutes ago. The door was closed.

It was obviously a quiet house. She went to the door and wondered whether she should open it. She didn't want to appear that she was uncomfortable. Would opening the door and peering into the hallway be construed as impatience?

But, she told herself, she was impatient. It was probably starting to push 11:00. She'd be halfway through the session with Levin by now if they'd started on time, at the usual place. And yes, she was uncomfortable.

She reached for the knob. Turned it. Even with a slight twist her fears were confirmed: the door was locked. She tried to pull. She tried to push. It wouldn't open.

She shook it roughly in every conceivable way.

Nothing.

CHAPTER 2

*O*kay, *there's an answer for this.*
This room and the long narrow one are under construction. The rooms are unfinished. Things don't work right yet. But if he's just going to use the phone to check something, why is he taking so long? And why haven't I heard a phone ring somewhere? He said he wanted to test his line. So shouldn't a phone ring somewhere?

Well, because the house is big, idiot. And the phone maybe doesn't work still. That's why he was going to test it. But shouldn't he have finished testing it by now? She put her hands on her hips and looked around the darkish room. *Okay, discomfort, yes. Panic? No.*

She went back into the narrow room and sat in the chair. After fidgeting with her nails, she got up and looked outside again, at the garden. She could see little but greenery and the high wooden fence.

She looked at the knob of the door that led outside, hesitating. She could try it. She could just leave. What was she even worried about.

When she tried to turn it and it didn't work, she felt a wave of something like hysteria. She suppressed the feeling. Telling herself that either Levin, or the man, or maybe the woman, would be in shortly, she sat down in her chair.

But she soon got to her feet, walked to the other end of the room, and tried to open the small door in the wall. Expecting it to be locked, she was surprised to feel it swing open. Inside was a bathroom. Narrow, compact. A toilet, a shower, a sink set into a small counter. Same pine walls as outside. She noticed there was no mirror above the sink. It was simple and bare bones, not much larger than a closet.

Disappointed that she had not discovered something greater, she went back to her chair.

When she guessed that about half an hour had passed, she knew she was starting to panic. She got up, crossed the unfinished room, and again tried the door. This time, she pulled more forcefully, turning it both ways over and over again. Nothing happened.

She raised her hand to begin pounding on the door, but stopped. By now it was clear everything was wrong. The man had disappeared with her phone. The woman she'd arrived with had vanished. The doors were locked.

Sure, but don't doctors always take a long time? Aren't they always late? *No, fool, not when they cost a shitload of money for sessions, especially for someone like Levin. You start on time. They don't have backlogs of clients. They pick and choose. So what if there was some kind of emergency? Levin or she had a heart attack? Wouldn't I have heard voices, some noise?*

Okay, then. I'll wait five more minutes. That way, if the doctor's on his way, he can show up. If something happened to one of them, I'll hear about it.

She crossed the room and sat down in the chair again.

She stared at the ceiling, at one of the skylights.

When she thought five minutes had passed, she walked up the two steps, crossed the unfinished room, and again twisted and pulled the doorknob.

Then she started pounding on the door with her fist.

"Hello?"

"Hello? Is anybody out there?"

"Hello!"

When she stepped back and stared, waiting, and saw no movement, she no longer entertained any ideas that she was simply being delayed. It was just not possible.

She pounded on the unfinished room door again. On the way back, she walked to the drapery on the wall and pulled it down forcefully. It appeared that a window had been there but was now covered in plywood. She looked around the dimly lit room. It looked solid, no way in or out except the locked door on one side and the doorway into the narrow room on the other.

She walked into the narrow room and pulled the garden door. Pulled, twisted, pounded on the door, and yelled. She went into the bathroom and reached to close the door behind her out of habit. She stopped herself. Why close it? There was no one here. No one coming. She closed it anyway, almost feeling a sense of power in doing so, as though gaining a personal space by her own volition.

She sat down and rummaged through her purse. Was there anything in there she could use? A nail file. A small can of mace. Some makeup. Her wallet. Two things crossed her mind. If she saw the associate, she would spray the mace in his face, and use it all.

Also, at this point, who knew whether the BMW was still in the driveway, but surely anyone passing by could see her Audi out there. At least she had some connection with the outside world. Maybe someone would see it and get suspicious. Sure. As suspicious as she got when she looked at any random parked car.

She again went to the garden door and examined the two narrow vertical windows. If she broke them, what would she gain? She certainly couldn't fit through them. Maybe she could reach out and twist the knob somehow from the outside. God, what were the odds that she could open a door from the outside that couldn't be opened from the inside?

It occurred to her that if she broke that glass, the room might get cool if this went on and on. It was warm out now, but if it got dark the temperature would drop, and this room would—

She stopped herself. *If it gets dark? That's hours from now. No way is that possible.*

She sat down in the chair. Thinking about the house, what it had looked like driving up, she tried to place the general surroundings. Maybe someone could hear her scream if she broke the narrow windows to the garden. Who else was here? Where had the woman gone? She had only seen someone who called himself an associate. No name, or something generic. No sign of Levin. No sign of any other patients, or clients, or whatever they were. The man could have planned the whole thing alone. He and the male receptionist. This could be the man's house, for all she knew. Maybe the woman was in on it too somehow.

She bent down and touched the drapery. It was fairly thick. She could use it as a blanket. So if she broke the garden window, and it got cold, she could handle it. She dragged it into the narrow room and threw it in the chair. She walked to the unfinished room door, and repeated her routine. She pounded again and again. "Open the door, you asshole!"

She went to the garden door and tried it, vigorously, also kicking it several times. Several half shoe prints now marred the door halfway up, and this gave her some sense of pleasure. When she stopped to catch her breath, she searched the room for anything she might use to break the glass. Not finding anything, she went into the bathroom. Eyeing the lid of the tank, she leaned over the toilet and tested it. It was solid, and heavy. It would smash anything if she used it right. Using both hands, she lifted the lid and carried it into the unfinished room. Planning to use the lid on the door handle, she noticed an object on the floor, just inside the door. Distracted, she set down the lid. It was a plastic bag. She cautiously picked it up and peered inside. It was a sandwich and an apple and a bottle of mineral water.

She looked around the room, and again tried the door. It wouldn't budge. "Hey! Hello?" She waited but heard no sound.

The sandwich was the pre-packaged kind, perhaps from a convenience store. The apple had not been cleaned. A thin film of white could be seen on the red surface. She felt hunger, but also reluctant to eat. Who knew where this had come from? What if that guy had put something in it?

She couldn't be sure, but it seemed that the light had faded. How many hours had passed? More than one. Two? Three? It was now probably mid-afternoon at least. Maybe late afternoon. She used some of the water and an edge of her shirt to rub the apple. She put it down and vowed not to touch it again.

What if I had my phone? What if I'd said no when he'd asked, or said I didn't have a phone? He didn't even have to ask, really. I just offered it to him. And of course if he was planning to keep me here, he would have found a way to get it, one way or another. Anyone who took the time to board up a window would take the time to make sure to get the phone.

This caused her to worry from a new angle. About whether she was in danger. Whether it was a sexual thing.

She looked around at the walls in the unfinished room. They were mostly just unpainted sheetrock. Only a small section in the direction of the living room was finished. But it, too, was probably sheetrock underneath. Sheetrock could be broken. If there was nothing solid in the walls, she could break into the next room.

Standing next to the garden door, she held the toilet lid with both hands and pushed it firmly into one of the vertical windows. The glass broke effortlessly. Then she broke the other one. She could feel cool air rush in.

She listened, looking out into the garden. It was certainly getting darker. She could hear the sound of a passing car somewhere nearby, but with the tall fence and all the greenery, it might as well be miles away. Straining to get a better view, she could see enough of the door frame to see that it had been screwed shut from the outside.

She put the lid down, and put her face next to one of the open windows.

"Help!" She hollered as loud as she could.

She waited, and listened.

"HELP!"

"HELLO?"

"HELP!"

She stopped. Listened. Turned around, looked through the doorway into the unfinished room. Whoever was out there, the man, whoever he was, someone, had probably heard her. She walked quietly but rapidly across the floor and put her ear up against the door in the unfinished room. Still she heard no sounds. She went to the chair and sat down. She closed her eyes and tried to think. For a long time, she remained frozen in place, unable to process anything, worrying about what might happen as the day wore on.

When she opened her eyes, she could see the difference: it was nearly dark. The bathroom had a light, and it was on. There was no other apparent source of light in the narrow room. The unfinished room next door had no light whatsoever.

She wondered what he planned to do, why she had been kidnapped and how long he planned to keep her here. She tried to think of anyone who might be behind this—if not him. Was there some signal or hint that she missed or ignored? Was it someone she knew? And was there anyone in her daily life who would notice she was missing?

It was getting colder. She used the drapery as a blanket.

She could imagine several scenarios. She went to school at Berkeley, and she spent most of her time at her apartment in San Francisco. Brandon was there. He might have called her. They were planning on going sailing, but that was tomorrow afternoon, when she flew back. She was supposed to call him later tonight. So he would not get her call, and that could mean he'd wonder why. Or maybe not. He might just assume something had come up, or that she'd forgotten. In fact, since they sort of decided to see a bit less of each other, her not calling would mean absolutely nothing. There was Cheryl. They'd been talking about going out for breakfast Saturday morning before she flew back to Berkeley.

She also had an apartment here, in Seattle. No one would notice if she was physically there or not. Everything was through her phone. Her father's place, where she'd grown up, was here, but she didn't always go there when she came back. So Imelda or Juan and the new guy who did the gardens wouldn't have a reason to notice whether she was in or out. Besides she had only flown up for a couple days, for the appointment with Levin and to see some friends. Her father would be busy, maybe in New York or L.A. since he was in those two places half the days of the month. She'd seen him this morning briefly, but he'd gone off somewhere soon after.

But that was about it. She couldn't think of anyone who had any reason to suspect she was sitting in a narrow room, trapped inside a house in Queen Anne. So her thinking always came back to the associate. Who was he? Whose house was this? What did he want? Whoever he was, he was a freak. What else could it be? She was 23. So maybe he was a middle-aged pervert. But if it was something like that, why wait around like this? Why the sitting here, locked up with no word from him? She was rich. Maybe that was it. Kidnapping, holding her ransom for money. But he hadn't mentioned anything. He hadn't said anything. He hadn't shown up for hours.

Every time she would go through one of these thinking episodes, she would feel the urge to get up and try doorknobs again, or scream out the windows. When she stood up, she sometimes instinctively looked at her wrist, where her watch should be. But all she saw was the small cut she'd inflicted from a splinter of wood, and it occurred to her that she'd never lived without access to the time. She had never wanted to know the time as much as she did now, and had never imagined existing without access to a watch, a clock, a calendar, anything that told the time. She felt herself dwelling on how her life, people's lives, seemed to revolve around routines, habits, schedules. Talking to Brandon tomorrow night, calling Cheryl in the morning, having breakfast with her before catching the plane back to San Francisco.

All of it based on schedules from which she was now removed.

She wished she could talk to Brandon now. She would tell him everything she sometimes felt like she couldn't. She closed her eyes and thought of his hands, the way she liked to run her fingers across his palms.

Suddenly, she heard the brief sound of a door closing. Wrapped in the warm drapery, she looked up with a start. It was totally dark outside. Alert, she looked around the dark room. The light of the bathroom glowed starkly at the far end of the room. The doorway leading into the unfinished room loomed darkly as usual. Feeling tension, she listened for sounds from the unfinished room, where she thought the sound had come from. She was sure it had been a door. Had she dreamt it? Was the man in the room somewhere?

She got up slowly. She carefully edged toward the doorway. Peered into the unfinished room. Nothing was visible. Standing near the open doorway, she looked around in the darkness, considering her options. If he was in there, in the darkness, she could not see or hear him. But if no one was in there, why the sound? So the bastard must have come and gone in silence.

She looked back at the drapery lying in the chair. Its shape was just visible in the dim glow from the bathroom light. She could use it. If he was in the unfinished room, and he came her way, she could spread it on the floor, just below the doorway into the unfinished room. If he came in, she would yank it hard. He would lose his balance, fall down, and she'd have the upper hand, even if for a minute. She could use the toilet lid on him. She could picture his face, begging for mercy. She wouldn't give him any. Not anymore. Not now.

She resolved to do it. She knew that if he was in there, he could probably hear her every move. He could be standing there, waiting and watching.

As she spread out the drapery, she thought she saw something on the floor in the far end of the unfinished room, near the door. It was barely visible. Another bag? Was this how it was going to go? Meals laid out in a plastic bag every now and then while she remained locked up in the dark?

She waited, listening, looking. No one came. No more sounds. She could feel only cold permeating the air from the broken windows behind her. Slowly, tentatively, she stepped into the unfinished room. Trying to focus on the object ahead of her, she made her way through the gloom more by routine than by sight. By now she knew where to grope, where to step, the shape of the door handle when she reached the far end of the room. Reaching the door, she bent down and felt in the space in front of her. It was another plastic bag.

She brought it into the bathroom and set it on the counter. In the bag was another sandwich, and a cup with a tightly closed lid. The cup was hot. She slowly pried off the lid and lifted it to her nose. It smelled like tea. She tasted it. It was chai.

She sat down in the chair, momentarily ecstatic with this new discovery, and recalling the man's mention of the chai earlier. Her hunger had somehow subsided, even though she hadn't eaten anything all day, but she knew that even if she were hungry, she wouldn't eat anything he gave her. At least not for now.

But the chai was a stronger temptation. She started to drink. The warm liquid soothed her throat, and seemed to warm her all over. She drank a few sips before suddenly setting it down. She spat out the bit that was in her mouth, realizing it might contain something. She tasted nothing noticeable, but how stupid could she be, especially now. Of course, if they were going to poison her, the apple would have fit the stereotype better. She applauded herself for having the sense to stop when she had. She went into the bathroom and poured the chai down the drain.

But when she got back to the chair and sat down, she had to admit, it had been nice. The room was cooling rapidly, and the drink had not only been warm, it seemed to have had a calming effect. It had definitely taken the edge off. But she had to keep working. She had been thinking about the wood strip between the two broken windows of the garden door. With more effort, she might be able to break it. If she did, she might be able to squeeze out. She stood up.

Almost immediately her knees felt loose. She fell back in the chair.

Startled, she started to pull herself up. But something was wrong. She felt weak. Neck muscles barely able to support her head. Vision seemed strange. Not blurry, but when she turned her head, the image of the table, then the drapery followed and got mixed up with the image of the bathroom light. It was confusing, and frightening.

She blinked her eyes several times and shook her head before falling back into the chair. This time she could not get up.

Gradually, she saw herself reflected in a spoon, her head large, completely filling the narrow room. She felt her own lips say something, but it was just an opaque sound. Every detail of her lips, teeth, overwhelmingly large as she spoke. Protesting, demanding rights. Flying, seeing the white rabbit watching from outside the window with one eye, then none.

Floating past the window on her back, out the door.

CHAPTER 3

When Sarah opened her eyes, it took several seconds of blinking to get her bearings.

She had a mild headache.

She looked around, searching for anything familiar. She recognized nothing. She was on top of a green sleeping bag. In a room with wood walls. Brightly lit from a window on each end. Air was warm. A bit dry. The sweet smell of wood smoke. Two walls angled inward above her, meeting in the middle, forming a high ceiling where they joined. Everything made of wood. Wood beams. Wood planked walls.

She sat up. There was a small window on both the front and rear triangular walls. She could see thick wood pieces, like two-by-fours, over each, on the outside of the glass. The floor was wood planks, with rows of nail lines visible. A circular rug was spread out near the bed. There was a square hole in the floor. She could just see a wooden ladder leading downward.

She pictured she was on the attic level of a cabin of some kind. An A-frame.

A desk was situated oddly against one of the inward-slanted walls, near the window on that end. It was piled with junk. Next to her, a night stand near the bed had a candle and some dusty items on top of it. She opened the drawer. A deck of cards, box of matches, a fingernail clipper, some coins and bottle caps. One of her shoes was on the end of the bed. Another was on the floor. She checked herself, seeing that her clothes were on.

She got out of the bed. It was actually a narrow cot, just enough for the sleeping bag. She stepped carefully toward one of the windows. Looking outside, the first thing she noticed was the snow. How deep it was, how white and clean it was. There was a lot of it. Tall pines surrounded the small clearing below, and they were covered in snow. She could see the back end of a blue SUV. To the extreme left, she could barely get a glimpse of the back end of another car.

So she was in the woods somewhere. Everything was white outside. The snow looked deep. Her first assumption was that she was in the Cascades. Nowhere else near Seattle got snow like this. Nowhere else looked like this.

She tiptoed to the square and peered carefully down. She could hear no voices or sounds. Near the bottom of the wooden ladder, she could see a red-hued rug that covered part of the wooden floor. Stooping down to get a better look, she could see one end of a table with a bench on each side.

As she strained to see more, she saw a shadow cross the floor. She shrank back as a solidly built man walked slowly past the bottom of the ladder. He was wearing a mask over his face. She recognized it immediately: the mask from the *Halloween* movies. The man disappeared for a few seconds, then returned. This time, he looked up at her. The mask was menacing with the empty eyes staring at her, a slight twinkling and movement deep within the blackness. She knew it was impossible, but she was aware of a feeling of familiarity. He left.

After a few minutes of waiting, she heard only an occasional shuffling sound downstairs. No one came to the ladder, and several glances out her windows revealed nothing different. She became suddenly aware that she was hungry. Her throat was parched. She edged toward the square and looked down. She listened, and detecting no sounds, started to descend. When she'd climbed down a couple of rungs, she bent to get a better look.

The lower floor was one room, and it seemed smaller than she expected. In the front wall was the main door with a window looking out to the clearing. There were windows on both sides of the room, and all were obscured by white sheer curtains, allowing light but preventing a clear view outside. The back end of the room had two doors. One was closed and one was open, showing a bathroom. She assumed the other went to a bedroom. A small kitchen area ran along one side of the room, with a sink, small stove and fridge, and dishes drying in a rack on the counter. On the opposite wall was a sofa and a chair. A coffee table was in front of the sofa. Roughly in the center of the room was a dining table with a bench along either side. The table was covered in a red-and-white checkered cloth and had a chessboard, coffee cups, a bottle of wine, and a glass jar with cutlery sticking out of it. A burning wood stove stood closer to the wall where the sofa was.

As near as she could tell, the coast was clear. So the man must have left. But as she descended another rung, then another, she felt it before she saw it: a dog, quickly lunging in her direction. She climbed rapidly, nearly slipping. Reaching the top of the ladder, she scrambled through the square and turned to look. A Doberman, nearly black, and with a silver chain collar around its neck, was struggling to climb the ladder, with its front paws on the second rung. Sarah could feel her heart hammer. As she watched the dog give up, she noticed another Doberman come into view, curious. So there were two of them.

She heard a door open and the sounds of objects moving below. A woman's voice. The dogs turned and were gone. Then the sound of a man's voice. Then a third set of footsteps. Three people? A door closed—the front door. She went to the window and looked out. The two dogs were in the clearing, running around in the snow.

As she watched, a woman's voice spoke from below.

"Sarah? Don't worry about the dogs, they're outside now. Can you come down please?"

The voice sounded familiar, and for a minute Sarah could not make the connection. Her thoughts were all over the place, and she knew she was not organizing anything, was not thinking anything through the right way. She had to focus.

Then it hit her. This woman's voice: it was like the woman from Levin's office. But that made no sense.

She thought back to the office, to the house, the drive to the home office. If her voice was familiar, if she was the same person, the other client, then what if the man was the one from the office, the "associate" who'd disappeared with her phone? No, he was too large. The associate guy had been thinner. But there was something. She thought back, back, further, to the lobby. She thought that's where she'd first seen the woman, but even that was vague. When she entered the office—that was it. The receptionist. The bulky good-looking male receptionist. Was he the one in the Halloween mask? She wanted to avoid the conclusion. Had those two somehow worked together to deceive her and now she was...she'd taken the bait. Hook, line, and sinker. Even considering this possibility, she felt stupid, and vulnerable. She had been kidnapped, and they hadn't lain a finger on her. She'd driven right to them, to some strange house, and they never even touched her.

"Sarah? We just want to talk to you," the woman said. It had to be her, the woman client. She'd arrived to check in for her appointment, just like Sarah, and had been redirected to the house, then disappeared. Her voice was so matter-of-fact, the way she called up, like it was a routine, like Imelda calling her and Tracy to dinner as kids.

She didn't move, pondering her situation, thinking about the narrow room and the toilet lid and the chair. She looked toward the far window and wondered what would happen if she broke it, if she could force her way out, where she would go, how far she could get, what was out there.

"Tell her the dogs'll come back if she doesn't," a man's voice said. That voice too sounded somehow familiar.

She looked toward the square in the floor. "Who are you?" she said.

"Well, that's what we want to talk about," the woman said.

"Come on," the man in the Halloween mask said, irritation in his voice, "can you just come down? It'd be a lot easier that way."

"You're probably thirsty," the woman said. "And if you don't have to use the bathroom by now, you've gotta be some sort of uber child."

"Plus, I've got some chai for you." This was from the voice of another man, and now that she was focused on the connections, the voice was instantly recognizable. She couldn't believe it. It had to be the "associate" from the house. The chai reference was all it took to solidify the notion.

She approached the square. The woman was right, she did have to go. As she looked down, the woman and the two men were standing there, in their masks, staring up at her. The bulkier man in the Halloween mask. The other man was thinner. He wore one of a grimacing face—like a Japanese kabuki mask. The woman was wearing a horror mask, like the one in the *Scream* movies, with downward sad eyes and a long droopy mouth. The man with the Japanese grimace mask was taller and thinner than the others. Dressed in black, he had a silent presence that loomed above the others, and the fact that he remained silent, just staring, gave her the sense that he was the one in charge. His kabuki mask was of a grimacing character, a pantomime of unrest. He had some kind of bracelet on his right wrist, a chain with some kind of locket that he kept flicking in and out of his hand.

"Not until you tell me who you are."

"Oh come on," the Halloween mask said. "This is gonna take all day."

"All we want to do is talk to you," the woman said.

After a pause, she cautiously began to descend the ladder, keeping an eye out for the dogs before remembering they were outside. The three watched as Sarah looked around the room, and at them. The ladder descended more or less into the center of the lower level, next to the wood stove. A video camera was in the room, on a tripod near the table.

"Bathroom's in there if you need to use it," the woman said. She pointed to the door behind the ladder. Sarah thought the Scream mask made her look ridiculous, maybe too large or bulky for her face.

Sarah went into the bathroom and closed the door.

It was a claustrophobic pine room, purely utilitarian, with a broken light fixture in the ceiling and a naked bulb hanging by wires. A sink set within a narrow counter, mirror above it, cabinet below. On the counter was a plastic soap dish with a bar of soap that was dry and cracked on top, sitting amid a pasty muck of soap slime. Disposable razor next to it. A toilet. Shower stall, with a pink shower curtain, stained in several places near the bottom. Two bottles of shampoo, one that looked like a bargain brand, and the other from Aveda.

She looked at herself in the mirror. Five-five. Blonde hair was straight and ran a little past her shoulders. It looked disheveled, and she straightened it out. Her eyebrows were darker. Her nose was rounded at the tip, just like her father's. Her mouth was relaxed and normally her lips were just open enough to show the hint of two front teeth, just like her mother's. She'd always thought her face projected a confident, curious exterior, and people told her that her brown eyes were large, inquisitive. With her eyebrows furrowed, people told her she had a commanding gaze. But the doubting part of her, which often kicked in, had never thought her face was overly attractive, and needed the right finishing touches to fill in the weak spots. Right now, she seemed to see only its basic essence, nothing but nervous apprehension. Her eyes looked worried, tense, and uncertain.

She opened the bathroom door.

"I have some coffee ready, if you want some," the woman said.

"As you ponder that," the man in the Japanese grimace mask said, "we might as well get started. Time is of the essence." He spoke with a British accent, something Cockney mixed with something northern, if Sarah had to guess. Even when he talked, his voice seemed to carry authority. The bracelet chain flicked back and forth. His voice...of course. His build looked like him. He sounded like the man from the house, the associate or whatever he'd called himself, except she hadn't considered his accent then.

"I'd like some water," Sarah said.

No one moved.

"I said I have some coffee," the woman in the Scream mask said. "This isn't a special order situation."

"I said I want some water."

The woman looked toward the Brit, and his grimace mask nodded back at her. The woman went to the kitchen, poured some water from the sink, and handed it stiffly to Sarah.

"She's kinda hotter than I remember, hair all messed up like that," the Halloween-masked man said, apparently to anyone. "That morning after look."

"What the hell difference does it make to you," Sarah said angrily. "And where's my phone!"

The Halloween mask began to chuckle. "Sounds like you handed it right over. That's the word on the street."

"A little testy this morning," Scream said.

"Spunk. I like that. Blonde, pissed off, and hot," Halloween said.

"A bit rich for you I'd say. She pro—"

"Right, leave it out," the Brit said. "Why don't you have a seat, Sarah."

Sarah drained the glass of water and handed it back to the woman. "More water, client. You are the client from that day, aren't you?"

Clearly annoyed even through the Scream mask, the woman stared back at Sarah.

Sensing the annoyance, Sarah felt a rush of confidence. "Look at you. Why the masks now? Like I don't already know who you are!"

"Sarah," the Brit calmly interrupted with his grimacing face. "When you're done interrogating us, let us know, okay?"

"Well? I saw your faces yesterday, didn't I? You, the new receptionist? And you—an associate. Must be a psychiatrist. How long have you been in the practice, doctor? And you—" She looked at the woman. "How is your treatment plan going? Mine's great. Maybe we should compare notes sometime." The Scream mask stared blankly back at her, holding the glass in hand, seemingly unsure whether to respond or to fill the water again.

"That's enough water for now," The Brit said. "You done now, Sarah?"

Sarah felt herself losing the edge, the courage fading, all of these hidden eyes on her.

"Right," he continued. "Let's start out with the basics. By now I don't think it needs mentioning, but you've been kidnapped. We are your—well, your hosts, I guess you could say. Hopefully this is a temporary situation that'll end soon, just as long as you keep your cool and your father's interested in getting you back. Our objective's not to harm you, but simply to reach a financial arrangement. When that's done, you're back in your boyfriend's arms at Berkeley and going to Levin once a week."

Sarah simply looked in his direction. The grimacing face looked back, unmoving. She could feel the gaze from the other two.

"But, why do—"

"Why me, why me?" Halloween said, in a mocking voice.

"Why?" the Brit said. "Well, the why part's easy. Because your father can pay what we're asking. We keep you until the time comes, and that's it.

We use this video camera to show how unharmed you are, how you're in good hands, and you lay out the demands for him. We'll use a couple of props to help him get the message if we have to, but the essence, the basic message is purely financial."

"What makes you think he'll pay anything?"

"Maybe she's right," Halloween said. "A distant father, hoity toity servants and people to take care of her all the time, he probably doesn't even know her name."

"Hoity toity, sounds like your childhood," Scream said.

"Yeah, not on my wages," Halloween said. "Only enough for one fork per meal, not six."

Sarah glared at Halloween. "Has pay for receptionists gone down?"

He came toward her, with his hand raised, as though to backslap her.

The Brit held up his hand. The bracelet chain slid down his wrist. "Can you please not do that? Just sit down." Halloween did. "As for your question, Sarah, we think he'll pay because he's in the business of doing deals. Which is what this is."

"The business he's in is hotels. Not kidnapping."

"Well, should I just put the kettle on and we have an intellectual tiff over the nuances of that distinction? So he's in the hotel business. It doesn't really matter. He could sell rocks for all I care. Point is, he's the kind of guy who makes deals with people who already have millions, and makes millions in return. The business someone like him is in is, well, business. Sometimes you have to hold something hostage from the other side until a fair deal can get worked out. I think Dad knows all about that."

As if according to script, Halloween stood up. The handle of a gun could just be seen sticking out of his belt. Sarah hadn't noticed it until now.

The Brit nodded toward Halloween, seeing her notice the gun. "We don't want to have to get persuasive. But we can. As for whether he pays or not, Daddy's got a decent kidnapping/extortion policy. It's a fact we can't deny." He stretched. Though she couldn't be sure, he almost seemed to yawn, holding his fist over the mouth of his mask.

"Well, enough said about that. Anyway, we know a bit about you, such as yesterday was to be your latest appointment with Dr. Levin. Levin is supposed to be the best there is—therapist to the stars. He cost a 'shitload,' to use one of your phrases, but every shekel is worth it, even though you have to fly back from your studies at Berkeley once a week to see him. Of course, it—"

"One of my phrases?"

"Pardon?"

"So how long have you been spying on me?"

"Sarah, so many questions."

"Who are you?"

"There's the 'why' again," Halloween said, scratching his neck. He had a can of Mountain Dew in his hand.

"Well she's gotta ask," said Scream. "Wouldn't you?"

Sarah glared at Halloween. "I said 'who,' you idiot, not 'why.'" Halloween loomed toward her and flashed a look that was menacing even through the mask.

"Come on, that's kidnapping 101 stuff," the Brit said. "Obviously makes no difference who we are. Let's not get off track. Like I said, we are just your temporary caretakers. The first thing we need to do is make the video so your dad can see the danger you're in."

"The danger?" Sarah looked at the Brit. "Look at you. All of you. These masks. You're pathetic. It's like the horror con in San Diego. Is your accent even real? Do you work the phones at a front desk somewhere, is that your day job?"

Halloween shook his head. "Will she just shut up so we can get on with it. Fuck, I need overtime for this."

The Brit held up both hands. "Okay, just everyone please calm—"

Sarah interrupted: "Where's my phone, you bastard!"

"What's next, ask us to take our masks off?" Scream said.

The idea formed suddenly in her mind. It seemed to happen without her approval, and she seemed to go through the actions as though being led along. She was aware in the back of her mind of the gun in Halloween's belt, but she dismissed it. She stood up, leaned toward the woman, and reached for the Scream mask. The woman pulled back. In a blur, she saw Halloween move, and before she could avoid it she felt his hand on her face, a sharp blow that caused her to fall backward into the couch.

"Try that again," Halloween said.

"Don't be daft, Sarah," the Brit said calmly, with a flick of the bracelet. "Keep your head."

The three stared at her. Sarah felt her face with her hand.

"Like I said, we're not here to hurt you. You can use the pain as a reference point if it helps. So, can we all agree to just sit the hell down and stop these little outbursts?

"Right. I guess now seems like the perfect transition into the ground rules. They are simple. First, understand that you're in a remote cabin. If you're wondering where, the answer's pretty obvious if you look out the windows upstairs. You're in the bloody middle of nowhere. So the next time you think about something like you did just now, think also about where you are. If, say, you come on some notion of turning the tables on us and making a run for it, remind yourself you'd freeze to death if you got twenty feet in the snow out there, 'cuz that's how deep it is.

"You have your own room, so to speak, upstairs. Small, but good enough. The three of us are stuffed down here, so you have it pretty nice if you think about it. The loo's down here, so you'll have to let us know when you want to come down. If no one's down here for whatever reason, you'll have the company of the two canines to look after you. They aren't blood-hungry per se, but if you screw around with them, they'll respond in kind. Keep that in mind if you even think about trying the door."

Sarah could feel Halloween's eyes on her. Scream's arms were folded across her chest.

"We'll try the three square meals a day plan to start. Hopefully it won't go on for long. All you have to do is ask when you need something, if you get hungry or have to come down. Let's see, there's no phone here. No cell coverage even if you did have your phone, which you don't. There's just us and the woods. Any questions?"

"Are we in the Cascades?"

Halloween put his fist near his face. "Hey Siri, where am I?" He said sarcastically.

"We are here," the Brit said. "That is all. Guess we're all persona non grata."

"Very existential," Scream said.

"What happened to Levin?" Sarah said.

Halloween answered. "A mystery. I don't know. Anyone?" He looked at the others, then stared back at her.

"He's dead."

"Please. What do you take us for? He's fine. And in case you're wondering, he's not part of this. But it was interesting how easy it was to convince him and his staff about the building issues.

"Right," he continued. "Well, your father's been contacted. He should know the situation by now. We told him in our message that we'd get a video and our formal demands to him today. I was thinking we could do that now." He waited for Sarah to reply, and getting none, continued. "Great. You stay right there and make yourself comfortable." He went to a counter and handed her a sheet of paper.

Scream got up and checked the camera on the tripod.

The Brit said, "Pretty much word for word's probably easiest."

CHAPTER 4

"She's gonna have to move a bit, get more into the light," Scream said.

"Sarah?" the Brit said. He and Halloween were standing on the sidelines, behind the camera.

Sarah turned to face the camera as Scream moved the tripod a bit. She could feel the glow from the windows on her face. Curtains let light in but mostly obscured any view outside.

"Any time you're ready," the Brit said. "Let the lady know." The bracelet on his wrist flicked several times.

"The lady? Is that your name?"

Scream stared emptily back at her. "Shut up so we can get this done."

"You know," said the Brit, "the more of this sort of squabbling we have to sit through, the longer this is all gonna take. Does that make sense to you? Sarah, I don't want to put too fine a point on it, but you know, you're the one who's kidnapped here. I think it's in your best interest to do what you can to get out of here. Just my opinion of course."

Sarah stared glumly at the page and began to read.

"My—my name is Sarah Easton. I am the daughter of Mark Easton. Today is March 9. I am being held by someone named the Person, for the purpose of collecting a ransom from you, my father, Mark Easton—"

She stopped, looking up at the camera.

"Can you pause," the Brit whispered to Scream. "What's wrong, Sarah?"

"Nothing. I'm okay."

"Need a break already?"

"I'm okay."

"Right. When you're ready."

"I am being held in safety in a location of no significance. I will be held with no further communication until Person receives a response from you in the form of ten million U.S. dollars. The demands are very simple, and are laid out in detail for you in the manila folder you will find on top of the filing cabinet in your home office. In general, they are as follows: Person will release me when you provide the cash. The deadline for this exchange is seven days from today. This should allow you enough time to make the legal and financial arrangements, as specified in the document in your office. When Person receives evidence of the delivery, I will be released. During—" Sarah cleared her throat, looking at the camera and the three staring at her, then again at the paper.

"—during this time, my life depends on a successful conclusion to these demands. This means that if at any point you contact any entity of the law to attempt to manipulate the outcome of these demands, I will be harmed physically or psychologically. I hasten to add—"

Sarah slowly looked up.

The Brit nodded.

"I hasten to add that the second of these two possibilities could have a devastating impact on the rest of my life in several ways. With this recording you will find a bullet. This is a .44 Magnum shell similar to the type that could be used if, if you don't—" Sarah looked up again. The three faces stared back at her. Halloween cracked his knuckles impatiently.

"Um, if you don't follow these instructions carefully. This bullet is also your sole means of communication at this point. Here is the first step you must take. On top of the red cabinet in your office, beneath the stack of magazines, you will find the aforementioned manila folder. Read it carefully.

"Indicate your willingness to follow these instructions by placing this bullet, on end, on the inside sill of the middle window of the Starbucks on James and Yesler at 8:00 A.M. tomorrow morning. No earlier. No later.

"All through this process, it is going to be a strong temptation to involve law enforcement, perhaps to show them this recording, the manila folder and its contents. Or maybe the bullet? It would be simple enough to have them see if they can match some fingerprints, look for clues in the background behind me, find a way to trace the cash. These would be foolish moves, because there are several identical bullets that could find a way into my brain."

After a second or two of silence, Halloween began clapping, slowly, sarcastically.

The Brit gestured with one hand for him to stop. "Good work," he said. "That all work out?" he asked Scream. He turned to Halloween. "Get that ready. I wanna get this part wrapped up as soon as we can."

Halloween took the camera into the kitchen and began doing something with a laptop.

Sarah was staring into the notes in her hand, her mind blank. The Brit grabbed the paper from her. "I'll take that. Thanks." He looked at his watch. "Well, we might as well have a quick lunch. Nothing fancy, you understand. Here, have a seat." He motioned to a spot on one of the benches at the table with the checkered tablecloth. Then he went to the fridge. The bracelet chain rustled around on his wrist as he took things out.

Sarah went to the bench and sat down. She watched them each do little tasks, organizing things. Scream was taking down the tripod. Halloween was working on the laptop. The Brit took some plates and silverware from the drying rack along the window, by the sink. He set a plate in front of Sarah. Then he placed a bowl of potato salad and plate of cold cuts and a loaf of sliced bread in the center of the table. Then he stood there, looking around from behind the mask, as if trying to remember something. He went back to the fridge and took out a jar of olives.

"Do you like olives?" he said. Getting no answer, he said, "Help yourself. I love them." He took a bit of everything and put it on his own plate. "Do you want to eat here, or upstairs?"

"Up there."

"Sure. Take what you want. It's a bit informal now, like I said, but we'll do better tonight."

She took some of the food, held her plate with one hand, and climbed the ladder.

* * *

Sitting on the bed in her confine, she heard the sound of the front door closing below. She went to the window overlooking the clearing and looked out. As she did, she examined the makeshift bars on the outside of the window. Two-by-fours had been nailed over the frame, spaced about eight inches apart. Even if she broke the glass, she didn't see how she could get past those.

Through the two-by-fours she could see the three of them outside. As they walked, the woman tried to put on a hat, causing her Scream mask to partly fall off. The Brit noticed, and immediately looked up with his grimace mask, in Sarah's direction. The woman was careful not to show her face as she struggled to brush the snow off her mask and put it back on, but when she got it on they seemed to argue. Scream pointed to Halloween, who expressed himself with his hands, while the Brit pointed toward Sarah's window. Sarah shrank back.

She heard the sound of a car being started. She looked again and saw Halloween climb into the passenger seat of the SUV. The Brit was at the wheel. The vehicle rolled to the right, out of sight, and Scream was there, waving, as if bidding them farewell. She disappeared from sight, then came the sounds of the front door opening and closing, and the woman saying something, evidently to the dogs. She heard the sounds of water boiling in a kettle, a spoon stirring in a mug.

She crept carefully toward the square in the floor. The floor squeaked as she walked, and she assumed she could be heard. Now she could hear the soft sounds of classical music. She looked down through the square. The woman was in her Scream mask, sitting on the couch, reading a book. Her legs were curled underneath her. She did not appear to notice Sarah.

Sarah sat down on the cot. She felt restless and bored. She felt that something was looming on the horizon, as if something was marked on a calendar, ready to happen. But when she thought it through, there was absolutely nothing. All she could picture was the sitting here, waiting to hear about some result of the demand.

How long would it take to get things moving? Ten million dollars? That could take forever. How did you just obtain that kind of money without raising all kinds of red flags? If they knew about the house like they seemed to, why not just ask for the money he kept in the safe? It wouldn't be anywhere near ten million, but it would be instant, and it would be unmarked and no one would know about it.

There were noises downstairs, off and on, all afternoon. While the men were gone she heard the woman downstairs, doing things. The dogs occasionally whimpered, or groaned, or switched positions and made their collars tinkle. The music died, it was silent for awhile, then it switched to jazz. More tea was made.

Every time Sarah peeked through the square she expected to see her without her mask. But Scream was always there, with the angular downward eyes and long droopy mouth, staring at the book. For the first time all day, she began to wonder if she was wrong, that maybe the other client and the woman downstairs were different people.

If that was the case, was she wrong about the men as well?

She stopped the thoughts. She sensed that she was beginning to lose her composure. She had to stay on edge.

* * *

From the cot, she looked around the room. She fidgeted with her hands. She wished she had a watch.

As she sat, she became slowly aware of a discomfort. Watching as the ends of her nails dug into her finger tips, she knew she felt filthy. She felt herself trying to come up with reasons, a source, a cause of the filthy feeling. Her teeth. She cupped her hands and exhaled. She hadn't brushed her teeth since, since when? Yesterday? The day before? No, it would have been yesterday morning, before going to Levin's office.

Levin's office. That's how all of this had started. She'd thought about not even going. If she hadn't, she wouldn't be here. Or would she? If they knew as much about her and her life as they seemed to, they could've done something, something like this, at any point. They even knew about the staff at the house. They had somehow found a way to slip a document into Dad's office. She wondered how that had happened, and when. If they could do that, there would be little stopping them from kidnapping her, one way or another.

But she'd made it easy for them. She'd driven right into her own captivity.

It suddenly hit her. Dad was supposed to read the contents of the demand. They said they'd put it in his office, on a filing cabinet. But when she'd left yesterday morning, he'd been on his way out. If he was out of town, how was he supposed to get the demand? If he didn't, he wouldn't be able to put the bullet up in the coffee shop window. If he didn't do that, what would happen to her?

But he had mentioned that he had an appointment at home this evening. So wherever he was going today, he was also coming back. So he'd be able to get the demand and do the thing with the bullet. She wondered if he'd notice she was gone. How long would it take? The last time he'd seen her, she'd been on her way to the airport.

Levin. The shrink who took care of the rich and famous. That's how he'd introduced himself the first time. He'd said it was a joke he told all his new clients. *Clients.* He said nobody says *patients* in this business, that it was archaic and made everything sound so clinical. So she was a client. What good was it doing anyway? The first few sessions hadn't been about anything except introductions. And how long was she supposed to keep going? It seemed absurd, flying back from the Bay Area once a week just to see him, to talk to him. And talk about what? Just talk, Sarah. Talk about anything that comes to mind.

Oh, God.

She closed her eyes. The image came quickly. Tracy, falling from the edge of a rocky cliff. They'd said she'd been roped correctly. Had been wearing a helmet. How far had she fallen before she, before—God, there is no God, if there was a God how could that have happened. And why wasn't she able to think of this kind of stuff when she sat with Levin in that office with that weird Persian rug with the concentric circles, with him saying just talk? That's when she was supposed to think like this, and blurt it out in some stream-of-consciousness type meandering thing, wasn't she? Yet in that office she couldn't think of much but the way Tracy had fallen off the cliff and died.

No God? Shouldn't happen to Tracy? Well why shouldn't it happen to Tracy?

Because she was my sister, that's why! She suddenly forced her eyes open. The filth. Her teeth. She was wearing the same clothes. She wanted to wash her face properly, to take a shower. That was it, this feeling. Filth.

Her eyes went wide and she held the pillow tightly. *No. No, it's not that. They know everything about me. The people downstairs. I was tough down there. I was pretty good. But I had felt myself shaking, trying not to show it. This thing is real. It's really happening. The Halloween mask guy has a gun. Ten million.*

She stood up. She sat back down. Thoughts of Tracy. *Think of Brandon!* Brandon's hands. Brandon's voice, soft, in her ear. The way his hands felt on her skin, on her neck, moving down her back. Tracy, falling. The phone call had come on the way to the party. Her cell had gone off and Dad's number was in the display. She could have let it ring, gone to the party and listened to the message later. But Dad never called her when she was in San Francisco.

Sarah nearly laughed as a quick image of Tracy's misshapen haircut came and went. She'd been sixteen, Tracy fourteen. They'd each gotten a small tattoo and were trying to keep Dad from finding out, and Tracy suddenly deciding to go all the way and cut her hair herself with a clipper.

And her hair had been so long the last time Sarah had seen her. Like her own, except Tracy's had been browner, darker. A braid to keep it together. One of those stupid tabloids had taken a picture of her before and after and published them with a story about Tracy's party phase, the night clubs she went to, the money she spent, the people she hung out with.

Sarah slowly turned, to stare at the square in the floor. The square. The ladder leading below. For a long time, she stared at the square, and listened. She heard nothing but the occasional crackle of flames in the wood stove.

It's not the filth. This is actually happening. They haven't hurt me but it's real. I just read a ransom demand. I am being held by three people in the upstairs of a cabin somewhere. They somehow know everything about me and I have no privacy, and they may have done something to Levin and who knows who else. They are after money.

She felt anger taking over, and she welcomed it.

Restless, she walked to the desk. One of the legs was bent slightly, and it made the desk lean a bit to one corner. It was covered in junk. Faded newspapers, some corroded batteries. Wires and fuses, a couple of dusty books. Stacks of old news magazines. She picked up one of the newspapers. It was dated 1981, with some article about Ronald Reagan on the front page.

She crept quietly to the square in the floor and looked down. The woman was not on the couch. Sarah carefully put her head through the square and looked around. No woman, but one of the dogs, near the fireplace, raised its head. She whistled quietly. The dog approached, looking up at her with its ears alert. "Are you hungry?" She took a piece of ham out of her pocket that she'd hidden, ripped it in half, and threw it at the dog's feet. The dog eagerly ate the ham, wanting more. The other dog approached. She threw the remaining ham.

When they were both done, they looked up at her with soft eyes and a searching, tentative expression.

"Good dogs," she whispered.

Then she heard the toilet flush. The bathroom door opened. Sarah scrambled away from the square. She went to her bed and lay beneath the sleeping bag.

CHAPTER 5

The day slowly grew darker. The smells of cooking wafted up through the square. Daylight faded quickly after the sun left the tops of the trees. She guessed it was probably about five. But she knew it could be four, or six. The light had a bluish hue, a shade that hinted at a span of time, but nothing specific. Her room was getting darker, and there was apparently no light source. She looked around for a switch, a lamp, but found nothing. There was nothing on the ceiling or the walls that looked like a light of any kind. She did find a candle and a box of matches. She took one of the matches out. As she was about to light it, the British accent called up.

"Sarah?"

"What."

"Wondering if you'd do us the honor of joining us for dinner."

She didn't want to go down there. Eating lunch up here alone had been fine. She didn't want to be around any of them.

"Sarah?"

"I'm not hungry."

"Well, I've got something I think you might like."

"There's no light up here. It's dark."

"All the more reason to come down."

"I need light up here!"

"You've got light from the windows during the day. At night, well, that's quiet time, isn't it? Except now. Come on. There's one of your favorites down here."

She hated to admit it, but this did arouse her curiosity, if only to see what he was talking about. And she was hungry, despite what she'd said. The odds and ends she'd taken for lunch hadn't added up to much. And she was thirsty. She got up and cautiously peered through the square. She could see Halloween and Scream sitting in the living room side, he in the middle of the sofa, she in the chair. Their masks looked so rigid, watching her, waiting for her to come down. She began to climb down the ladder.

The table was full of food and dishes. Candles, two bottles of wine, a platter of something with a lid on it and a couple of side dishes.

The Brit picked up one of the bottles and sniffed it through his grimace mask. His bracelet chain rustled. "Where do you like?" He indicated the benches on either side of the table.

Sarah shrugged. So it was going to be this mock guest treatment every time.

"Well, how about here. Comrades?" The other two got up.

The Brit fiddled with a small speaker on the floor, then sat down. Soon the soft sounds of Stan Getz began. Halloween and Scream sat on the other side of the table.

The Brit said, "Sorry we didn't send you an invitation. I thought we'd updated the guest list, but I guess not." She wondered if he was a bit drunk. Scream laughed.

Over the soft samba sounds, Sarah looked at the platter. It was large fillets of what looked like a white fish of some kind, covered in a dark sauce with green onions and chilies in it. There was a plate of green beans. Strangely, there was also a bowl of macaroni and cheese. As she stared at all that was in front of her, she became aware that all three masks were more or less looking at her.

"Well," the Brit said, adjusting his grimace mask, "if you're waiting for us to say a prayer, we're gonna skip that just this once. Dig in." He reached for the wine. "Care for some?"

She wanted to keep a clear head and didn't feel like wine anyway, but it looked like he was going to pour for everyone, and she wanted to avoid irritating any of them. She vaguely shrugged and he poured a small amount in her glass. Then he filled his, then the others'. Halloween reached for the macaroni and cheese and looked closely at it, turning the bowl. Scream took some of the fish. Halloween got up, went into the fridge, and brought back a half-eaten sandwich.

Seeing this, the Brit said, "What."

"What kind is this?"

"I don't know, she made it."

Halloween pushed aside the bowl.

"What, your egg thing?"

"Yeah." Halloween took some fish. He seemed about to eat it, but didn't.

"Well where are the eggs in macaroni and cheese?"

"I don't know, don't noodles have eggs in them? Never mind."

"He's allergic to eggs," the Brit said to Sarah. "Makes him about the pickiest eater I've met since I was a little fucker on the other side of the pond. And there were some picky little fuckers there, I can tell you, knowing only English food. Pass the *haricots verts*."

Sarah took a bite of the fish. It tasted like sea bass, or grouper, and the sauce was based on soy, with hints of ginger and garlic. It was soft, flaky, absolutely delicious. She felt briefly exhilarated, and wanted to keep this feeling to herself.

The Brit lifted the lower part of his grimace mask, and pushed a fork beneath it. The fork came out empty. Sarah found herself staring at this bizarre scene until he turned to face her. "Not bad," he said. "If I say so myself."

After another awkward-through-the-mask sip of wine, he said, "So, I know you're probably thinking this is pretty odd, huh. Sitting here eating a fish dinner with a bunch of people who plucked you out of your former life and shoved you into this one? Well, if it helps, I can tell you we're not gonna eat like this every day. It's just that I think we kind of got off on the wrong foot this morning, know what I'm sayin'? You did a great job on the video by the way, good work. But the whole plan here is to keep you safe and in, you know, some state of comfort while Daddy makes up his mind, and I think that part of the message sort of got lost."

"Sorry about that, little one," Halloween said sarcastically. "I'm all shook up about the way I handled everything."

"Come on, Tony. Remember, new phase here? Let's—just let's everyone be nice. For awhile, anyway." As he stood up and walked toward where the laptop was, Sarah knew she'd heard it. Tony. So that was his name, this Halloween mask? "Anyway, just thought it'd be nice to have a dinner, talk a little, iron out some differences, that kind of thing."

As he talked, Sarah stole a glance at the others. Scream was trying to pull aside the lower part of her mask, tipping her glass. Sarah caught a glimpse of her mouth. Her lips were full, and for an instant, she felt like she had a sense of a personality behind that mask. The glass barely fit in the space she gave it, and she was clearly flustered. Tony was in the same situation in his Halloween mask, lifting the lower part, awkwardly pushing some of his sandwich in.

The grimace came back, holding a sheet of paper in one hand, and a small container in the other. "I hope you like the fish. I know it's one of your favorites."

He noticed her stare. "Oh come on, don't be surprised. I realize it's a bit unfair. But it's the nature of our relationship, you know. We have to know a bit more about you than you do about us. If there's one thing about capers like this, it's that everything can be so cliché. You know the story, we all do. Captor knows the victim's intimate secrets. There's a demand made for money. The captive's always rich, unless they plan to harm them somehow. Not our bag on this one. But think about it, how many times have you heard about it? Daughter of the rich man, the industry tycoon, the powerful government official, captured and held for ransom? And here we are, doing just that, living that very thing. In a way, it's nice to know you belong, you fit into a group of others just like you, you know?"

Not waiting for a response, he sat down and took a one-hitter out of his pocket and stuck it into the small container. He slid the bottom of his mask aside just enough to put the little pipe in his mouth. He lit it and inhaled, then offered it to Sarah. She shook her head. He gave it to Tony. Tony lifted his Halloween mask, took some, then gave it to the woman.

"I don't smoke much," the Brit said. "But once in a while, you know."

"You don't have to justify it to me."

"Like you never smoked in your life," Tony said, looking at Sarah. "Anyway, to answer your question, I think this is damn good fish. A pretty fancy meal, don't you think?"

"Very nice," Scream said, blowing smoke out. The smell of marijuana was strong in the air.

"Well, don't you, little one?" Tony said.

"What?" Sarah said.

"Come on, you heard me."

"No, I didn't."

"I said, don't you think this is a fancy meal?"

"Sure, I guess."

"*Sure, I guess.* Yeah, whatever. Probably not fancy enough though, huh. Here we're missing the silver spoons and the half a dozen glasses and all that, right?"

Sarah stared at him. Tony. She knew it was the fake receptionist.

"Yeah. And you fly to Europe or wherever on a whim. Ride around in a limo, carrying some yippy dog under your arm, right?"

She knew replying was pointless but couldn't stop herself. "You must have been born and raised in this cabin."

The Halloween mask glared hard at her, and she could feel the piercing blue eyes beneath the mask.

The Brit pointed his fork at Tony. "I think she's got you, Tony. And I'm warning you," he said in a serious monotone, "a little cross examination is fine, but don't sit here and try to use her to fill in for your own inadequacies." But by the end of his line, he was suppressing laughter.

Tony bowed toward Sarah and said in mockingly serious tone, "You're right. I'm sorry. I offer my deepest apologies, and I vow to treat you as an equal in the days to come."

There was a silent pause before both men started laughing heavily.

The grimace picked up the bottle as his bracelet slid. "Well, *ça va!* Sorry Sarah, cheap shots at the aristocracy. More wine, more wine! You see, Tony's just opening up a bit. That doesn't happen much. You must have quite an effect on him."

Scream groaned suddenly, putting her fork down. Sarah saw a forkful of fish fall from beneath her mask onto her plate. She wiped behind her mask, then picked up her glass. "This sucks."

"Just take it slow," grimace said, now holding a sheet of paper he'd brought over. "So Sarah, here we all are, nice and cozy, opening up to each other. Tell us about yourself. Let's get to know each other a bit. You know, what you like to do, who you are, that sort of thing."

"Well, didn't you just say you knew more about me than I do about you?"

"He said that was the nature of the relationship," Tony said. "Very distinct difference."

"She has a point though. Come to think of it, we haven't done anything like formal introductions yet, have we. Okay, let's start again—and we gotta stop starting over like this. This could add days to our journey here. Anyway, I'm yours truly, you can call me Ian. This oaf here in the Halloween mask is, as you surmised, Tony. Tony Doe."

"A pleasure," Tony said, again doing a sort of bow in his Halloween mask toward Sarah.

"Tell her about the mask, Tony Doe."

"The mask?"

"What you told me. Even I didn't know. And I thought I was a movie buff."

"Oh. So in the original *Halloween* movie, this mask is of none other than William Shatner." He pointed with both hands at his mask. "You know, *Star Trek?*"

"Amazing," Ian said. "Never would've guessed. Doesn't look anything like him. Anyway, m'lady here in the Scream mask is Jane. Jane Doe."

The woman raised her glass. "Woo hoo."

Ian poured more wine. "How did they both happen to have the same last name? Doe. Must have been, like, fate or something."

"That's not all," Tony said. "We also both happen to live in Anytown, USA."

"123 Main Street," Jane said.

Tony laughed at that. "Two complete strangers, both signed up for this gig, and we both turn out to have the same last name. What are the odds?"

"Right," the Brit said, "well as for who we are, there really isn't much to say about me. I'm from the Isles, in case you haven't noticed. I'll be Ian for this gig. I like good food, and don't mind cooking it, especially when I'm in a remote cabin with a kidnapping victim and two Yanks who couldn't boil water without a recipe."

"Not true," Jane said. "Who made the macaroni and cheese?"

"Well, she's got me there, she makes a mean mac and cheese from the box. Let's see, I like football—that's soccer to you. I like pop culture, movies, despite the gaping hole about *Halloween* and William Shatner.

People say I'm a tough kind of fucker, but they don't know my soft side, the way I like cute pet videos. A total mug for those. Well, except for the time I killed a kitten in a microwave, but every ten-year-old boy has a moment of discovery like that, you know? But I think you'll see I'm the softy here, the nice guy, compared with, say, Tony here, nothing but brute force. A bicep. If only you could see his real face. I always thought he looked a bit like James Dean. Certainly more than William Shatner. Or would if he wore a pompadour. You ever have your hair done up in a pompadour, Tony?"

"Can't say I have."

Ian motioned with his hand toward Jane. "And then there's our friend, Jane, here. Jane, can you tell the group a little about yourself? I feel like we're really opening up here." He drained the rest of the wine into Sarah's glass.

"I don't want anymore," she said. Tony promptly reached for her glass, lifted the Halloween mask above his mouth, and downed it.

"Well, let's see," Jane said. "Not much to say, really. Just a plain and simple working woman, you know, working the fields, ironing, cleaning, raising several young children, hoping they turn out better than me. I guess that's about it."

Sarah could see Tony's shoulders shaking with silent laughter.

"Right," Ian said, also clearly amused. He turned to Sarah and said in a low tone, as if confiding in her, "Don't listen to her, I can't see her raising kids any more than I can see the bloody queen being a virgin. And now that Philip is gone, well—"

There was a stifled laugh from Jane, but Sarah's impression was that the laugh was forced.

"And I can add to that brief introduction," Ian continued. "She's a modern woman all the way through, gorgeous on the outside, mildly intellectual on the inside, annoyingly self-righteous at times, and with a mean streak waiting somewhere below the surface. The woman of every man's dreams one day, fine as long as you can hold her, but then let her go, and snap." Ian raised his hand, as if clenching a knife and stabbing repeatedly. "Honest to the point of recklessness."

"Self-centered in the extreme," Tony said immediately.

The men clinked glasses and laughed, but Sarah could almost see a downward cast to Jane's expression, even behind the mask.

"So," Ian said, "that leaves our friend Tony. Thanks for sharing, Jane, I knew it took a lot to do that. Tony, welcome to the group. Care to share a little about yourself?"

"Well, you know, I guess like Jane, not much to say, really. Just a plain and simple working man—never mind. No, I guess if anything, a good cigar. A good romp up in the hay loft with the farmer's daughter. A good steak. The good things in life."

"He fancies himself a gentleman of leisure," Ian said, "the type who feels comforted when a flight attendant pours him a drink. In some parallel universe, he's always fornicating, eating, smoking, living fast and dying young. Leading man, dark rebel. Breeding in captivity. He gets close to that fantasy from time to time, and then there it is, that egg allergy, always lands him on the go to jail square. Plus there's that temper. You should watch that, Sarah. Which brings us to you."

Sarah stared blankly.

"Well, you can't have a support group without everyone opening up a little. Tell us about yourself."

"Tell you what?"

"Whatever you like."

"But you already know who I am."

"Okay, you're what they call a hotel heiress—although with MeToo, even that term will probably have to be neutered at some point. A debutante. Your dad's empire stretches to every part of the world, keeping people snug at night, giving them a place to do their PowerPoint presentations, make deals, shaping the way a city looks on the telly when war breaks out and all the journalists have to stay in one place. You're a junior at Berkeley."

Ian looked at the sheet of paper on the table. The bracelet chain fell on top of the paper and he flicked it to the side with a quick snap of his wrist.

"Let's see. You have a horse. You've had one since you were little. You did some equestrian stuff for a while, but you wavered in and out of that as you grew up. But you still keep your horse, and of course Tracy's after she died, on a farm on Bainbridge where your dad has a few dozen acres. You have a family cabin in New Hampshire. Your father's from that area, though you haven't been back there much since Mom ran off with that guy from Virginia. Funny he turned out to have a cabin just down the road. You like sailing. You often do that with your boyfriend and a couple other friends. You play tennis. You go to Wimbledon. You like seafood. You drive an Audi, in Seattle anyway. An Acura in San Fran. You're thinking about law school. You have a bunch of girlfriends, and the aforementioned boyfriend named Brandon. You're famous enough to show up in tabloids now and then, but that was mostly as a side effect of Tracy's party phase. Other than that, you keep a fairly low profile."

He looked up. "Sound right?"

"So you got all that from following me around?"

"Well you can't just rush into a thing like this without knowing anything about your victim. It's not professional."

"Victim? I thought I was a guest."

"You're right. Sorry, our guest. Questions?"

"Yes."

"What."

"I was wondering, when we made the video, and I had to read all that stuff, it said that if he called the police, I could—"

"That you would get killed."

Sarah shrunk back a little at the stark mention of it. "So, but, what if someone already has?"

"Somebody, as in who?"

"Okay, I mean my dad. What if he decided to call the police?"

"Why would he?" Jane said. "You yourself told him not to."

"But I've been missing since yesterday. People might be wondering what happened."

"Like Brandon? Cheryl?"

"I don't know, anyone. It wouldn't have to be my dad. What if someone called the police?"

"Ah, I see where you're going," the Brit said. "Well, what makes you think they think you've gone missing?"

"Well, not getting back from my appointment, not returning any calls, not—"

"Not going home for lunch? Not seeing your dad? Not catching your flight? What? Dad shows up a couple times a week. I'm sure Vincente, or whatever the gardener's name is, and those two women who do the cooking and cleaning aren't gonna panic. I never was able to figure out if they're even legal, so I doubt they're going to make the call. Besides, did you call them when Brandon didn't show up last month for the concert? J.J. looked pretty peeved about it but you seemed to blow it off well enough. You didn't panic. You didn't think he'd gone missing."

Sarah looked at him, feeling suddenly terrified and exposed. "If you know about that, then—"

"We know plenty. Let's leave it at that."

"How long am I supposed to be here?"

"Until your dad gives us the money we've asked for."

"It could take days to get all that together. That much, do you have any idea?"

"Then there's your answer."

"Well you're wrong if you don't think anyone's gonna call the police."

"I guess it's possible. But then, what isn't?"

He stood up and stretched. "Don't worry Sarah. Someday your prince will come." He looked at his plate, then the plates of his companions. "You know, it's not practical, having to eat like this, these masks. I feel like I'm in a circus, or on a diet." He looked at Sarah. "You want to take a shower?"

The sudden shift caught her off guard. The idea of a shower changed her focus. "Yes," she said. Just as quickly, it occurred to her that they wanted her to take a shower, to get out of the way, so that they could take off their masks and eat. That nearly made her want to say no to the shower and linger.

"There's a towel somewhere, and everything you need should be in there already."

"What about clothes? Did it occur to you that I might need new ones?"

"Well as a matter of fact, yes it did. Put that one down to Jane, always thinking of the finer points like that." He went into the bedroom.

"I do what I can," Jane said.

Ian came back with a duffel bag. He set it down on one of the benches. Sarah looked inside, stunned to see some of her own clothes. "These are from my room."

"Yes."

"From one of my dressers."

"The maple one."

"But how? Who took them?"

He shrugged. "Must've been the Oracle at Delphi."

She could feel all eyes on her. Wanting to be alone, she took the bag and went into the bathroom. She locked the door and looked at every corner and crevice, as if expecting to find a camera, a peep hole between the pine boards of the wall, a pair of eyes in the mirror.

There was a knock. "Sarah?" Ian's voice.

"What?"

"Just one thing? Can you hand me that razor? By the sink?"

She found it and opened the door a crack to hand it to him, but as soon as she closed it, she wished she'd noticed the blade before. Why hadn't she thought to look around the bathroom better until now? She'd seen the razor but it hadn't occurred to her that she might want to hide it, to use it for something, maybe take the blades out and hide them somewhere, for an emergency. She found herself rapidly envisioning using the matches and candle upstairs to melt the blades out of their casing, then use them to cut her captors. Now that would never happen.

She showered, and as she dried herself, searched the room, hoping not to lose any more opportunities. In the simple cabinet below the sink was a can of bug spray and some mouse traps. There was a plunger and a toilet scrubber inside a little plastic bucket. Nothing of any apparent use.

She slowly opened the door, just enough to see out. Tony was sitting in the middle of the sofa, cracking walnuts with a pair of pliers. He had several nuts in one pile, and cracked shells in another. She couldn't see Jane. Ian was sitting at the table in the kitchen with his back to her, doing something on a laptop. The dogs were both lying near the front door. With no one watching, or distracted as they were, she wondered what the chances were of simply walking out the door. If the dogs weren't there, she didn't see how getting out would be a problem. After that would be the issue, since she knew nothing about the surroundings outside other than the clearing visible from her window. Any move might make the dogs panic. But she wondered. Maybe the hint Ian had dropped about the dogs being dangerous was just talk. They'd eaten the ham she'd thrown them earlier and had appeared grateful for it. Maybe they could be bribed somehow, distracted, if the right time came. If she had enough food, she could let them eat in one corner while she quickly made a dash for the outside world.

Jane's mask suddenly appeared in the narrow crack. "You about done?"

CHAPTER 6

J eff paused the Tesla near the San Francisco Coffee on Fillmore as they passed. "You guys want a foo foo drink or something? On me."

"On you?" Brandon was in the passenger seat, rolling a golf ball in his palm.

"Goodwill gesture, since I crushed you both."

"What do you think?" Brandon tossed the ball to Dave in the back. "Sound legit?"

"Dubious," Dave said. "Pretty sure you owe us anyway."

"You guys just gotta figure out that second hole. Gets you every time."

Dave handed the ball back to Brandon. "Christ, man, you actually do monogram your balls, don't you. Never even noticed."

"Guys like Brandon," Jeff said, shaking his head. "Guys who name their balls—they got issues, you know?"

"What can I say," Brandon said. "You gotta have balls big enough to label in the first place. Both of you could take a page from my book."

"So it's a book now?" Jeff said. "So yeah or nay on the caffeine? There's someone behind me."

"Hey—forget it. Plan B," Brandon said. "I got that Scotch."

"That Scotch."

"Yeah, that Scotch."

"As in, the Macallan?"

"The same."

"You been holdin' out on me?"

"Just came in last week. Haven't had time to hold out on anyone yet."

"Like you have to ask twice," Jeff said, skipping the coffee shop lot. "You in, Davy Jones?"

"Don't have to ask me twice either."

Jeff drove a few blocks to Brandon's building and found a parking spot. Brandon hoisted his clubs out of the back and they went through the main entrance and crossed the lobby. Metal cutout letters formed a sign near the elevator bank: The Pacific Heights. Brandon waved his phone near a panel, the door opened, and they got into the elevator.

"Monogrammed balls," Jeff said, shaking his head. "You got little towels and shit to go with 'em?"

"You're obsessed, dude. You gotta breathe deep, let it out slow."

"We've played what, a dozen, two dozen times?"

"Something like that."

"I never noticed the monogrammed balls."

The door opened to the third floor and they walked down a short hallway lined with dark red carpet. Occasional wall sconces gave a soft glow to the walnut-paneled walls.

"That's 'cuz they're new. Or newish. Sarah gave those to me a while back. Couldn't just say no." At his apartment door, Brandon waved his phone and they went in. "But if I did, I would've gotten the red letters instead of black."

"You kill me, man."

The living room was spacious and had a contemporary look with short Berber carpeting, walls textured in warm white tones, with wood paneling on one. The tall windows showed a view of neighboring buildings and partial rooftops as the streets angled down toward the bay.

"Have a seat, gents," Brandon said as he left the room with his clubs.

Jeff sank into one side of a leather couch and thumbed through one of the heavy art books on the coffee table. Dave examined the paintings on the walls.

"So what's the diagnosis, doc?" Jeff said, watching Dave. "Does the art pass muster?"

"Some nice pieces here, yeah," Dave said.

"Guess you'd dig it, being the artsy collector type."

"This one's good. Montclair. Signed, too."

"Colors are nice, I guess."

"Minimalist."

"Yeah, and looks like a big smudge of paint dragged across the canvas."

"Which, it is."

"So instead of stating the obvious, I should have just looked at it."

"Pretty much."

"And I was gonna make some smartass comment like my nephew could do a job like that."

"Hey as long as your nephew can find a market for it. I think some of this guy's stuff goes for like, six figures."

"Damn. Is there some rule that they're worth more if it's somebody no one ever heard of?"

"Trust me, there are plenty—"

"You're wasting your time, man," Brandon said. He had changed out of his golf attire and was buttoning his shirt in front of a framed mirror. "Don't think you're gonna get much traction with a guy who only understands fast cars and golf."

"Well I don't take culture lessons from a guy who monograms his balls, that's for sure," Jeff said.

Brandon slapped Jeff on the shoulder a couple of times. "I would expect nothing less." He opened a drawer and took out a case containing a dozen or so watches, removed the Breitling he'd been wearing at golf, and seemed about to choose another.

"Those got your name on it too?" Jeff said with heavy sarcasm.

"Matter of fact, this one does. Good call." Brandon took out a silver watch with gold tones. "Just initials, small, back of the bezel."

"You're serious aren't you."

"Ah, nothing earth-shattering, come on. Was a little something we bought in Geneva last year. We took the train up there when we were staying in Milan. Nothing says Geneva like a matching set of watches, right?"

"If you say so. I'd even drink to that if I had something in my hand," Jeff said.

"On that note." Brandon opened a door in the wood-paneled wall and removed a bottle and three glasses.

"There she is," Dave said. "Behold."

"You guys okay with neat?" Brandon poured and handed each a glass. "My take is, gotta go virgin on that first sip. Can't tarnish that with ice."

"Or water," Jeff said.

"Or anything," Dave said.

Brandon nodded. "There's protocols to maintain. Standards."

"To standards, then," Jeff said.

"Standards." They all clinked glasses.

Brandon sat on the other side of the sofa from Jeff and leaned back. "Oh that is nice."

"Yeah," Jeff said. "A little mean at first, then the backdraft hits you."

"Where'd you get it?"

"Edinburgh."

"When?"

"Couple months ago. Found this little place on some back street, about the size of a closet, but what they had was all top shelf stuff."

"You were in Scotland again?"

"Just a quick trip," Brandon said. "Had a few days so I squeezed it in. Love it there."

"Me too. Last time I was there I drove up to Aberdeen. Talk about rugged."

"I've heard. Maybe next time."

"You go there with Sarah?"

"Nah. Solo flyer. A friend from Italy wanted to show me a place."

"Nice, you buying or just window shopping?"

"Just lookin' for now. Maybe someday."

"You and her still doing that sailing thing each week?" Dave said.

"Yeah, most weeks. Don't know about tomorrow though. Can't seem to get ahold of her."

"She here or up in Seattle?" Jeff said.

"Seattle. Probably just takin' it easy for a few days."

CHAPTER 7

Upstairs, in her own space, the cot felt surprisingly comfortable. After the shower, she felt recharged, refreshed. She'd brushed her teeth. Hunger was gone, and though she was loathe to admit it, the food had been great.

But even as she sat there, she just as soon stood up, then sat down again.

Am I actually supposed to just curl up and go to sleep? Is this the routine I'm supposed to give into? They made a fancy meal, drank wine and smoked, joked about the kidnapping, then let me take a shower and send me upstairs to bed? Night after night, day after day. Was that how it happened with people like me? You get kidnapped, and then to let them think you're a model prisoner, you slowly give into them and allow some sort of routine to get established?

Thoughts began to pile up. It started with the bizarre conversation below, the way Ian or whatever his name was had introduced everyone, including making up a name for himself. Were any of the names real? That chain bracelet thing on his right wrist. Did he ever take that off? It rustled constantly. When he walked he flicked it in and out of his palm. When he picked something up it rose or fell and he dealt with it, always snapping it around, making that noise.

The note she'd read. The demand for money. Did they really expect the whole thing to happen without someone finding out somehow? All the stuff they knew about her. Ian had a whole list. He'd rattled off item after item, and they'd all been right on. How long had they been stalking her? How many times had they been in her living space, whether in San Francisco or Seattle, or her room at her father's house in Seattle? They'd stolen clothes from her dresser somehow. They knew about Brandon not making the concert. She wondered if they knew the reason. They had obviously known about the appointments with Levin.

Along the way, someone must have noticed something. Her car. Would her Audi still be sitting in the driveway of that house in Queen Anne? No way. They would have thought about that. And of course, they had her purse, with the keys. Brandon. Would he wonder what had happened? Would he notice? She wasn't sure. They were planning on sailing tomorrow, and she was supposed to have called him about that. So maybe if Brandon hadn't heard anything by now he would at least wonder, maybe start poking around. But not very likely.

In any case Cheryl would know by now. She'd have to. She'd be the first to suspect something was wrong. They were going to talk tonight, maybe go out. Definitely breakfast tomorrow morning. So if Cheryl didn't hear from her by tomorrow morning or afternoon at the latest, surely one of them, her or Brandon, would be in touch with each other.

Ian had a point though. Just because she didn't make the sailing event wouldn't mean much to Brandon, even though she never missed sailing. By itself, missing the phone call with Cheryl tonight or not making breakfast tomorrow might cause concern. But Brandon would probably assume she was still in Seattle. Cheryl would assume she'd gone back to San Francisco. They might talk to each other, but even if they did, they wouldn't have any reason to think she was missing. Not yet. Ian had it right. No one would suspect much of anything yet. She had a life that was in and out of everything, all the time. There was no schedule, no routine, except her classes at Berkeley. And recently, Levin's appointments on Thursdays in Seattle.

She wondered how long this might go on. They'd said seven days. If it was a day or a few days, she had to admit she was relatively comfortable. But what if it went on for ten days, or even just the whole seven? It could take that long for Dad to get that kind of money together. She assumed he'd have to contact people, lawyers, bankers. He'd have to somehow start getting cash together according to whatever instructions they'd provided. The longer she was here, the more likely it was that someone would notice she was totally missing, and call the police.

And then what? Would they really make good on what they'd said they'd do if someone called the cops?

She began to set her mind on the idea that even if there were the slightest chance of that happening, that she had to act first and find a way out of here. But where was she? How far away from a road? Ian had said it was in the middle of nowhere, but what did that mean?

Until this evening, everything had seemed a bit like minor occurrences, clues and hints indicating a picture of what was happening to her. It had seemed surreal, almost like a series of bumps in an otherwise normal day or two. Until dinner, and even until the shower, she'd felt somewhat detached, even cocky. She'd thought about reaching over to pull off one of their masks, trying to be defiant, not answering questions.

But as she dwelled increasingly on the situation, it all seemed very real, very tangible. She began to get bombarded with images of that long and narrow room, the toilet lid, the way they'd deceived her. The way she'd fallen backward into the chair after drinking the chai. The way the dogs had come at her. The image of the three masks down there, looking up at her through the square. Everything was in sharp focus. She felt overwhelmed by the crush of it all.

She tossed and turned as the evening wore on. At one point, as she felt herself fade away, she could hear faint moaning sounds from below. Hoping it would stop, she stared into the darkness of the room, at the faint glow from the square in the floor and the angled light it cast on the steep ceiling. She tried closing her eyes, to think of something else. She tried putting a pillow over her head. The moaning went on and on, with an occasional grunt from one of the men. When it was finally over, relentless snoring began.

She lay wide awake, feeling miserable. Frequently, she wanted to know the time, but had no way to tell.

She thought of Brandon. They had decided to slow down and see a bit less of each other after Christmas. The last time they'd talked, she'd been busy, in a hurry, and said she'd call back. She hadn't. Now she wished she had. She wished she could see him now.

She pictured him, maybe at his place, checking his phone, trying hers, maybe talking to one of their mutual friends, setting up the time for sailing tomorrow, but now wondering whether it was still on.

CHAPTER 8

The floor lamps were on low, and the room was mostly dark. He used two medium-sized monitors for his laptop, and the glow from the screens lit his face. He was organizing things in files, updating spreadsheets, making notes, and clicking through checklists.

He was tired, but he couldn't relax. He could feel the lingering effects of the Scotch from earlier, but his mind was full of dates and items, things to cross off and things to account for. He disliked this feeling of being ensnared by countless tasks undone, but it was a feeling he knew well. It seemed that lately the overthinking, the searching for the uncrossed Ts, the what-ifs, had become a permanent state. There was so much to do and sometimes the crush of it all seemed impossible.

He was nearly finished with a complex project for work. His paid internship at G25 Labs required his full capacity most days, and when he was not there he was ducking in and out of classrooms, conference rooms and staff offices for the graduate program at Berkeley. The complicated scenario displayed on his laptop screens was the part that took the rest of his time. He likened it to a story with a million moving parts involving dates, timelines, characters, and plots so thick he sometimes felt in danger of losing sight of the larger picture. There were so many variables and potentialities to consider.

Yet when he stepped back and let his mind roam, he knew today had gone well. He had accomplished a lot. He allowed himself a certain measure of satisfaction, sensing that seeds he'd sown for so long were now starting to show tender, green leaves. It wasn't always like this. There were days when doubt completely dominated and gave him no reprieve. But now —right now, here, in this moment—he felt it. G25 liked his work, which was hardly surprising. He had a technical frame of mind, and the code-based engineering scenarios he was assigned came naturally to him. He recognized he should spend more time with certain professors at Berkeley, the ones who were supposed to measure his progress and give him feedback. He spent a lot of time working his research projects online, doing what he could, but he knew there were many loose ends. Another thing to work on, another thing unfinished.

Looking at his watch, he began to log out of his networks. As he waited for the systems to shut down he poured some mineral water and looked out the window. The windows of the five-story apartment building across the street drew him in, and as he casually scanned them, he wondered which of the cast of characters would show up tonight.

When his phone rang, he checked the number. Seeing it was a Seattle area code, he allowed himself another reward: a tiny self-congratulation. He'd anticipated a call from one of Sarah's Seattle friends.

"Hello?"

"Hey, Brandon, it's Cheryl, in Seattle."

"Hi Cheryl."

"Hey, sorry for calling this late."

"No problem. What's up?"

"Well, you haven't talked to Sarah have you?" There was tension in her voice.

"No. Not for a bit now."

"Do you know if she's here, in Seattle I mean?"

"Far as I know she flew up there yesterday morning. I haven't talked to her. Phone's off or something."

"Do you know if she's at her place up here or her dad's?"

"Not sure."

There was a silence before Cheryl continued. "So, she went to her, the —"

"Her shrink?"

"Yeah."

"Yes."

"Hm. Maybe I should give her a call."

"You could," Brandon said, letting a second or two pass. "But I might as well tell you. I assume she's already told you, but we—well we sort of decided to slow things down a bit. Maybe it's a bit of that, and a bit just feeling stressed out from school and stuff."

"She mentioned that." Another pondering silence from Cheryl. "I just feel helpless, not being able to reach her, and if something's wrong, I can't do anything."

"Well, if it makes you feel any better, I'm in the same spot. I don't know, maybe she's just not answering her phone for a while."

"Sure, that really makes me feel better. Okay, well, I guess I'll just wait and see what happens."

"If I hear from her I'll tell her you called."

"I suppose. Okay. Thanks, Brandon."

"No problem."

When he hung up, he pictured Cheryl, and other friends of Sarah, calling each other, wondering what was going on, mystified by Sarah's absence. He wondered where Sarah was at this exact moment. He admitted a sense of irritation that he had no way of knowing. But he also knew it was completely out of his control.

He saw that a couple of the windows across the way had lit up. Though most were obscured by curtains or blinds, some allowed a view within, and in one he could see a man with thin, dark hair, bearded. One of the regulars, who usually only returned later in the evening. He appeared to be talking as he came and went from view. Brandon went to his bedroom, got his SLR camera with a long lens, and dimmed the living room lights all the way. Sure enough, the man was wearing earbuds. His facial expressions seemed serious enough that it could be a call about work, or something in his life concerning money, health, or family. He came and went from view, sometimes opening cupboards and drawers in the kitchen, putting things away. Brandon had never seen the man cook, so if these were groceries, they would be just simple staples. Given the late hour, and unless there was another person out of sight, the man would probably retreat from view, then the bedroom window would light up briefly, and the day would be done.

Scanning the other windows, he saw a shadow moving behind a translucent curtain on an upper floor, but there were few details to glean. He knew that the middle-aged woman who lived there normally kept a low profile. An open window further down showed a young couple on a sofa, watching a large screen. Based on the appearance of these nameless citizens and their various routines, the look and feel of their living spaces, the tone of their silent conversations, Brandon had surmised a whole assembly of nicknames, professions, relationship statuses, sexual preferences, income levels, hobbies, levels of education, potential medical conditions, and a plethora of other attributes. It was all just a side distraction, a little spin he did during these quiet moments when he looked out the window after a long day.

He didn't click any new photos, but as he turned off the camera, he noticed the display showed that the card was half full. He scrolled through the images, thinking back to when he'd taken them. Most of them were seemingly nondescript: buildings, doorways, cars. Some were even of documents. A bunch showed Sarah in different scenarios. He was pretty sure he'd uploaded these long ago and had forgotten to delete them from the card, but made a mental note to check in the morning.

CHAPTER 9

S arah woke to the sound of the front door being shut below. She lay in the warmth of the sleeping bag, letting her eyes adjust to the morning light and trying to get a sense of what time it might be. They were talking in low voices. She could hear the general sounds of dishes and cooking. The smell of coffee. There was a sound of metal clanking. At first she thought it was Ian's bracelet, but the sound was more metal to metal.

She got up and crossed the floor to the window overlooking the clearing. Same scene. The sun was out. The day was bright. She went to the square in the floor, peered down and listened. Tony was talking, but she couldn't make out what he was saying. As she stood on the edge of the square, she heard the door of the bathroom open and close. Jane appeared below. She wore no mask. Her hair was wet and a towel was in her hands. Their eyes met briefly before Jane turned quickly away. She was the woman client from day one. No further doubt. Sarah saw an attractive face, full lips, dark eyes, intelligent but with a suggestion of unrest. Jane moved out of sight, into the direction of the bedroom.

It had been brief, but the look in her eyes had been telling. She knew she'd been caught without her mask. But it was obvious that neither Tony nor Ian had noticed the slip. Jane was out of sight now, but a feeling lingered, as if some secret had been passed between them. Sarah wondered what to do now. She had to go to the bathroom. Jane, having been spotted unexpectedly, was obviously uncomfortable and was staying out of sight. Tony and Ian were in the kitchen area. Should she just go down there, or should she say something first?

She went to her bed and looked through her clothes, wanting to change. As she did, she heard Ian from near bottom of the ladder. "Good morning. Why don't you come down and get something to eat. Second full day of your new life." She heard him say "mask time," then the sounds of things rattling, dishes being sorted.

Dressed, and with awkward hesitation, she descended the ladder and began to enter the bathroom. Tony was standing over the table, thumbing through a newspaper and eating a bagel, shoving pieces of it beneath the lower part of his mask. A mug of coffee was nearby. Ian was doing something over the stove. He deftly kept the bracelet chain out of the way when he did things, but there was always that noise. A paper bag was on the table, and she could see two small containers of cream cheese next to it. The dogs were eating from metal bowls, and their collars were clanking up against the sides.

Inside the bathroom, she locked the door. She wanted to wash her face, but, contemplating the cracked filthy bar sitting in the dish of scum, used some of the Aveda shampoo instead.

She dried her face on the only towel she could find, what looked like an old dish towel, and a thought occurred to her. She'd missed the opportunity to keep the razor yesterday. She hadn't thought of it then, but if she had something like that, a tool, she might be able to use it for some future purpose. A way to cut things. She could hide it somehow. She could start a collection of odds and ends, things she might be able to use. She could try to get a knife from the kitchen, and hide it somewhere. If nothing else, she could use something as a weapon. But what? There was nothing in the shower with its filthy pink curtain but the shampoo and another bar of cheap soap. The toilet plunger and scrubber wouldn't be very useful. There were no toothbrushes, no bottles of this or that. She opened the door to the cabinet below the sink. She was shocked to see that the mouse traps and the bug spray were gone. With a flash of panic, she realized the only reason they would have removed them is because of what was on her mind right now, using them as potential tools. Or did they have a way to peek into the bathroom, watching her every move, and they'd noticed her looking the place over? She searched, looking at the pine boards, the smaller cracks in the wall, the ceiling, the lamp.

Finding nothing useful, and no holes in the walls, she tried to visualize the bathroom in relation to the rest of the place. The moldy shower stall itself was against an outside wall. This room was the only place where she could truly be alone, unwatched. With a few minutes now and then to herself, she could work on clawing her way out. She'd need a knife or tool of some kind. But how thick were the walls? And how do you carve your way through wood? It could take forever, and she'd be noticed. Why not just walk out the front door instead? No, the windows upstairs were her best bet. If she did it right, she could find a good moment, break the window, jump down. If she went out the back window, the snow would break her fall. Or, she could fashion a rope of some kind. The fall was not the problem; the problem would be getting through the pieces of wood that had been installed from the outside, like bars. They were solid two-by-fours and were spaced close enough together to make getting out impossible unless they were removed. So she'd have to find a way to cut them off, or break them, or get through them somehow.

A sudden knock on the door. "Sarah?" Ian's voice. "How's it goin' in there?"

She hastily closed the doors to the cabinet. Unlocked the door and opened it.

Ian was just outside the door in his grimace mask. "We have some food and coffee. Some bagels. Help yourself."

"Where did you get the bagels?"

"Where? I went all the way to New York City, can you believe that? The bagel mecca. Anyway, take what you want. Our decadent lifestyle's on hold 'til tonight."

Sarah looked for a coffee mug, but she couldn't find an empty one, and as she searched, she was aware that Tony was watching her through the Halloween mask. So he knew there wasn't a clean cup and he was just going to sit there and watch her. She refused to ask him, and did what she could to avoid even having him in her periphery. She took a plain bagel and spread cream cheese when Jane approached and set down a clean mug. "Morning," she said.

Sarah acknowledged Jane in her Scream mask. She could almost see Jane's eyes looking back at her, and if she read them right, they seemed to have a certain nervousness in them. Everyone seemed a bit on edge. Had the others found out that she'd spotted Jane without her mask? Did this mean that some new direction was forming?

"Do you take milk?" Jane asked. "We don't have any cream."

"I said I'm getting some later," Ian said.

"No, black's fine."

Ian continued: "Well, eat up. We've got another task to take care of and I'd like to get it out of the way as early as possible."

"Task?"

"When you're finished."

Sarah allowed the worried thoughts to enter her mind. For the next several minutes, everyone more or less sat around, waiting for her to finish. Once in a while, someone would slip their mask to the side and sip some coffee. She assumed they'd already eaten, having learned last night the difficulty in trying to eat in front of her with the masks on. No one spoke much. All of this did little for Sarah's appetite, and she set down her half-eaten bagel and waited.

Ian rubbed his hands together. "Well, it's been a busy day for yours truly so far. I've got some news. Not necessarily great. Long and short is that we need to make a new statement, refine our demand a bit."

Ian took the laptop and a large camera from beneath the counter, where the electronics seemed to be kept, and attached the camera. Angling the screen toward her, he said, "So, this is the coffee shop in question, the one you so eloquently referenced in your first demand." A photograph of a building displayed on the laptop. He flipped through several photos in rapid succession, showing increasingly detailed images.

"This is the interesting part. See the bullet there."

A close-up of one of the front windows showed a bullet standing on its base inside the window sill. Next to it was a handwritten note in large block letters, taped to the inside of the window. She was trying to make out what it said when Ian turned off the screen.

"What did it say?"

"'Call me.' I'd say he probably wants to make some nefarious demands of his own. Something along the lines of how he wants to see you in person, or talk to you before going any further with the transaction. Negotiate somehow? That'd be a safe bet."

"Well, then you have to talk to him. It might be important."

Ian laughed, and his manner seemed to change. "Not going to happen, Sarah. This is just the kind of thing they stick you with in the end. You know, no clues in a murder, the police getting nowhere. Except someone saw a white rental car or remembers a phone call, and years after the fact, some smartass subpoenas the internet company or they break into the cell phone, and they start digging around and bam, you're stuck in a Turkish prison."

Sarah was struck at how quickly Ian's normal calm demeanor was replaced by this frenzied description in his grimace mask. The tone in his voice had definitely lost its control. This event had not been planned or anticipated. And yet, it had been nothing more than a mention of a message.

"But," Sarah suggested, "don't we need to find out what he wants to say? I mean, what if it's about the money, that something's wrong?"

"No. In your demand you did not ask him to embellish. If you recall, all you asked him to do was comply with the demand. That, and indicate he got the message with the bullet. That he did. The other part is totally freeform. It falls outside the requirements."

"Well, what if he needs to tell you something important? Like the money, or he can't make the deadline or whatever."

"Then he'll bloody have to tell us a different way."

"How would he know that?"

"Because you're gonna bloody tell him."

"What?"

"Time to make another bloody video, Sarah, since you did so well on the first one."

Jane began laughing.

"What," Ian said flatly, looking at her.

"The 'bloody' thing. It's getting out of hand."

"That right?"

Tony nodded. "Seems like it's picked up a lot since yesterday."

"Not to say I don't like it," Jane said.

"No, it's great," Tony said.

"Blimey." Ian turned to Sarah. "I guess I didn't realize. Does it bother you, Sarah?"

Sarah simply glared at them. The three masks glared back at her.

* * *

Jane finished assembling the video camera and microphone. Ian was nearby, doing something with the laptop. Tony was in the bedroom.

There was no denying the tension in the air now. It had not been there yesterday, not like this. Now things were happening in a different way.

There was an element of guarded anticipation. Even the glint of their eyes behind the masks seemed different.

"Good to go," Jane said. The camera was on the tripod.

"Right. When you're ready, Sarah. Here's the script." He handed her a printout. "We're gonna do things a little different this time." He looked toward the bedroom, and her eyes followed, to see Tony emerging with his gun. He was wearing a pair of black leather gloves. With the Halloween mask it made him look even more sinister.

"Okay Sarah, take your place." Sarah walked to the spot Jane indicated with her hand.

"Okay everyone, ready? Let's do this."

Sarah looked at Tony, standing near the periphery but not in the shot. His mask stared back at her, unmoving. She looked at Ian. He nodded. She looked down at the notes in her hand and began.

"I'll keep this simple. Don't tempt fate, Daddy. Person will not, could not, make a phone call. He will not, in a tree. He will not, could not, with a bee. Don't try to trick him. Your clock is ticking by the hour, and we're now one day closer to our deadline. The more you try to stall, the—"

She felt sudden pain and stifled a small scream. Her hair was being pulled back. Wincing, she saw Tony's hand in front of her, holding an open revolver that had a single bullet partway inside the cylinder. With his thumb, he pushed the bullet in, closed the cylinder, and spun it, which created a rapid clicking sound as he pushed the barrel into her cheek. She felt herself pant but tried to stay focused. She had to look at the sheet from an angle since her hair was being pulled from behind.

She stammered: "Th-the more you stall, the more, the more you put my life at risk. The weapon you're seeing now is—I mean has—a very smooth trigger. The bullets it uses are very much like the one you so carefully manipulated this morning, and as I—"

She felt awkward, suddenly lightheaded, her voice flat and expressionless.

"—as I said before, a bullet like it—like it—can easily find a way into my brain. This is a .44 Magnum. Re—remember what Dirty Harry said. So, Daddy, get busy. Let's cut the small talk. You need to spend all the time you have getting the prize money ready."

Having reached the end of the script, she felt Tony release her hair. She pulled away and staggered toward the ladder. She hastily climbed up. In her personal space, she felt herself on the verge of whimpering. She fell into the cot and buried her head in the pillow. The back of her head hurt. Her heart was pounding.

When she finally rolled over, she could hear them doing things, putting things in order, getting stuff ready, cleaning up the gear. She was aware of real fear, the kind she could not ignore. She had the sense it could overpower everything in her consciousness. She felt a trembling feeling in her hands and legs. All the joking and sarcasm seemed so long ago.

After several minutes, she heard Tony say something, quietly.

"Not yet," Ian answered.

"Thought you would've finished by now."

"I'm getting there. Haven't exactly had a lot of free time for reading. Here, use this spoon instead."

"What is this, cherry?"

"I don't know. It's just red. Can you tell the difference?"

"I'd say pink."

"Well red, pink, I still say they taste the same. They should just call it red or pink because there is literally no difference."

"So you get to the part about the kite and electricity yet?"

"What?"

"The book you were tellin' me about."

"Oh. It's not even covered."

"Whatever."

"Serious."

"But that was one of his biggest things."

Their voices faded as they moved out of range. She could hear the sounds of shuffling, things being arranged.

Tony continued: "He was a Mason, right?"

"I don't know. Weren't they all Masons back then?"

Sarah heard the distinct snap of a briefcase or something similar. That and the chain of Ian's bracelet.

Ian let out a sneering laugh. "What, you thinkin' of becoming a Mason?"

"No, just wondered."

"Well you take it up with Jane. I gotta go. Be back whenever."

She heard the sound of the front door opening and closing, then the sound of a car starting outside. Within seconds, it faded away.

There was no sound to notify her, no advance warning. In the midst of the silence that followed the noise of the car, she listened for sounds of Tony and Jane below, and when she happened to look in the direction of the square, she nearly screamed when she saw the Halloween mask there. It appeared to be resting on the floor.

She stared, blank with nervous anticipation, ready to move if she had to. The mask with its blank, sad face, resting there on the floor, watching her in the cot. The slight twinkle of Tony's eyes could just be seen beneath. He put a small plastic bowl on the floor with a little spoon sticking out of it. Without a word, he was gone.

Too shaken to move, she remained in bed for several minutes, listening for sounds but hearing nothing. Only the slightest murmurings seemed to come from below, and they were faint, soft, and sporadic.

Finally, she got up, went to the edge of the square, and looked at the small bowl. It was a dish of pink ice cream.

CHAPTER 10

In the early morning Brandon was captivated by the grayish light. It gave a surreal effect to his bedroom, as though a grainy, cloudy mist had enveloped everything. The window showed no hint of sun yet, and the shadows in the room had an extra dark quality, as though reluctant to fade with the dawn. He felt groggy, somewhat out of it. Thoughts of Sarah mixed with thoughts of his schedule, then the forgotten images on the camera card from last night. He felt strangely detached, a kind of high. He thought about one of the times he'd followed Adam Liddy, on one of those Percocet days.

He recalled that day well. It had been the tenth or so time following him. Twenty milligrams and a strong coffee on an empty stomach. The combination had been just enough to feel the weight of the city drop away, allowing him an invisible feeling he sometimes craved. Streamlined, ghostly. He had floated across the streets of downtown San Francisco in a dreamlike state. People were coming and going in the cool air that morning. Commuters, tourists, workers, homeless, some waiting for the lights, some getting off buses and trains, scurrying to their offices, people unlocking doors and opening up shops, people waiting, standing, moving. The air was a turmoil of clanging sounds from trains, the beeping of service trucks, car horns, thousands of voices and conversations, the aromas of food, kitchens, laundries, diesel, grime, sweat, garbage, strains of coffee, grease, salt in the air.

He had floated through this volatile mixture like a mist, sometimes observing minor details, like the shiny surface of the tracks he walked over, the mark of a snuffed-out cigarette on a utility pole, the way a street sign pointed, a torn poster for a club's upcoming shows. He felt amused at the way snippets of conversation from a nearby person on their phone merged with the words of another not far away. With each sip, he would keep a casual eye on the man, not twenty feet in front of him, watching as he stopped at the usual lights, or turned as he waited for traffic to pass before crossing. The man had a coffee also, a Starbucks cup in his right hand. He'd had it since boarding BART in Oakland, and it would surely be close to empty by now. The man had been within Brandon's sight the entire time, from when the man left his apartment in Oakland. He'd followed the man to the bus stop, caught BART with him at the station, standing on the crowded train and holding the hand ring as they edged into the city.

He had repeated a similar routine dozens of times, and in various forms, with different men. Not always at the same time or place, and sometimes between other tasks or while running errands. Sometimes, the trip started in San Jose, or Berkeley, or even San Mateo or Richmond. Sometimes it was by car, or bus, or bike. He'd follow them from a safe distance, getting a sense of their routines, seeing how they went about their journeys, how well they stuck with a schedule, what distractions or side trips interfered with their daily lives. He'd follow behind, establishing the paths the man took, verifying the ins and outs of the man's commute, noting the man's stops. He'd round corners with the man, wait at stoplights, go into buildings with the man, stop for a bite, sit on a bench or on plaza steps near the man, waiting behind the glass of a coffee shop window, waiting and watching casually through a partition as the man got a haircut, spend hours sitting in a common area of the building where the man worked, as the clock ticked closer to the end of the workday. Sometimes he'd even sit briefly in a chair in the lobby of the man's workplace, dressed as a client. He'd wait, ghostlike, feeling invisible, and observe.

He would float through the thousands of nameless faces, picking up patterns, identifying routines, watching as the dots connecting these disparate lives started to form lines. Like the thirty-something man, who dressed in the accented brown jacket and dark pants most days, who would get off the bus near Front and Pine around the same time. Brandon would follow behind, keeping a reasonable distance, until he would enter a building and disappear up the elevator, off to work somewhere. Several times, Brandon rode up the elevator with him and others in the crowd, stopping at various floors, and following him and others as they got off and walked down the carpeted hallways to their offices. In some cases, he wished he could split, ghostlike, into two separate halves to observe people in multiple locations, like the pair who always got off the same train at the same spot on Market Street. He'd watch them kiss as they went separate ways in the morning, he carrying an umbrella and her a handbag. He knew the routes of a few who walked to their jobs, who showed up at predictable times, one from his place in the Panhandle, another from Chinatown.

Some days, he'd blend into the streets and avenues where long chains of homeless tents filled the sidewalks and abutted buildings as far as the eye could see. This blue tarp had replaced the worn green one; those shopping carts or old bicycles were in different places; the men who hung out at that corner had shifted to somewhere else; the trash and needles and human waste that littered the boulevards was cleared away today, to be replaced by more tomorrow. More than once, the conversation with his brother, about committing murder and hiding the body, occurred to him as he walked through this churning sea of human misery. If you were going to do it, here would be the place. Most of the people here were nameless, faceless, forgotten bodies with nowhere else to go. If anyone even noticed the act, it would be soon forgotten.

But it was hard to view the well-dressed office workers much differently. They didn't live under tarps or tents on the street, but how many of them lived with similar margins anyway? Getting by from one paycheck to another, many of them barely breaking even on their jobs because of all that went with living in the Bay Area: a decent place to live came with a high rent or mortgage; there were nice clothes to wear, transportation costs, maybe even a car. There were credit card and student loan payments. Groceries and entertainment added up in one of the most expensive metro areas in the world. How many of these busy professionals, running from one stop to the next, were a dollar away from becoming another statistic in the rows of tents and shopping carts within view of Market Street?

As he rounded a corner, he'd watched as the man set down his Starbucks cup on top of a garbage bin. The man had taken a call, spoken briefly, then pocketed his phone. He threw the cup into the bin, crossed the street, then entered the same building he did each weekday morning. Brandon followed him to the now-familiar elevator bank, keeping his usual distance. Brandon rode up in the same elevator, getting off on the seventh floor and walking down the hallway to an office, several paces behind. The man opened the office door and, noticing Brandon behind him, held it open. Brandon thanked him and followed him in. The man waved to the receptionist at the desk, who was on the phone. Behind her, on the wall, was a chrome sign with LKJ Architects printed in large black letters. The man went to a suite of labeled mail slots on the wall to one side of the front desk, took out some mail or documents from his slot, then badged into a door in the back of the lobby, and was gone. Brandon glanced at the name on the mail slot: Adam Liddy.

The receptionist had hung up her call. "Good morning, can I help you?"

"Hello, I had an appointment with Adam Liddy this week but need to reschedule it. Wondering if there's any chance of a spot today?"

"Adam Liddy? Let me check," she had said, scanning her screen. "And what is your name?"

"Well I'm not actually sure who set the appointment. Our firm's representing a trustee and we had some earlier discussions—one of us was going to reach out. I can find out who but maybe if we see if Adam has anything today, I could…"

"Sure," she'd said, scanning. "He has a two o'clock today, otherwise it would have to be—"

"Nothing earlier today?"

"No, sorry."

"He's totally booked until two?"

"It looks that way. I can take your name and have him call you."

"Sure," Brandon had told the receptionist. "Tell you what. Let me go back and check our schedule. I'll call you back. Thanks for your help."

He'd gone to Adam Liddy's apartment that day, for the first time, knowing he had a few undisturbed hours to get in.

Brandon blinked out of his dreamy recollection. The gray light was fading into the normal light of the day, and the grayish mist was receding. The dark shadows had retreated. He got out of bed, went into the bathroom and took a shower. It was going to be a busy day.

CHAPTER 11

An hour, maybe two, had passed. Sarah was on the cot, staring at the ceiling.

Thoughts returned to Brandon, and the way things might be right now had she chosen to call him back instead of blowing him off the other day. She had increasingly begun to think it unlikely that he would even notice she was missing, at least for now. She even felt guilt, and wondered what he'd say if she asked him how he'd truly felt, the way she hadn't called him back then, or later. Probably that he'd forgotten about it as well, no big deal, but the expression on his face would show a more complicated picture. The disappointment would be hidden by the tough exterior, but she'd see it in his eyes. It would show in the same way the discomfort showed when he was out of his element, surrounded by things that felt natural for her. Like the way he obviously didn't know how to act around the staff at her dad's house in Seattle, or even some of her friends when they did things together. It had always been part of what attracted her to him, that boyish uncertainty.

Now that she thought about it, now that they were taking it slower, she worried all the more. Maybe he wouldn't think anything, having heard nothing from her. So she'd miss the sailing thing today. Would he even notice? Slowing down had been his idea, so maybe he wasn't thinking about her at all, and just assuming that her silence and the missed sailing gig were because she was avoiding him, or that she just wasn't calling because she knew he wanted to avoid her.

She looked at the melted ice cream in the bowl on the floor. She hadn't touched it. She thought of it as a control thing. If she could refuse to eat things offered to her, she had some measure of control. Otherwise, there was nothing to do but wait up here. Wait until Ian got back with news. Wait until the money started flowing. Wait until the next big thing.

Occasionally, she could hear them talking in low voices. Things were mostly quiet below. She'd heard a clinking dog collar once. A groan another time. Jane and Tony would talk in hushed tones about something, and then everything would go silent again for awhile.

Now they were talking again. For minutes at a time, Sarah could hear the higher points of his voice or hers, but at no time did she get a complete picture of the topic. She heard Ian's name. Her name. Something about food. The word "olive." Sometimes, beneath the talking, she could hear things moving around, rustling, like sheets or covers on a bed. She felt as though she was listening to a recording of a secretly taped conversation, trying to transcribe something, listening over and over to the parts no one could understand, knowing that the incriminating evidence was somewhere on that tape, and the lawyers had to have it, the case depended on this evidence.

She knew they were talking from the bedroom. She hadn't seen inside the bedroom yet, and so didn't know what the sleeping arrangement was down there, but what she was hearing sounded a lot like they were both in bed. The sheets or covers rustled a bit, then they'd talk, or moan a bit, then things would go silent. Then it would all happen again.

She wondered if they were wearing their masks. She wondered how preoccupied they were.

Her mind began to spin. She began to form connections between things. She speculated on a series of situations, outcomes, all based on those two down there, occupied, busy, out of touch with the rest of the cabin and not concerned about it.

She got up and was about to kneel down and look over the edge of the square when the floor beneath her creaked. She'd noticed more than once that there seemed to be certain parts of the floor that made noise, and parts that didn't. Even yesterday, she'd noticed it but filed it somewhere unimportant and had forgotten about it. But now, as she thought about it, she knew these were the kinds of things that might make a difference.

The creaking sound must have been heard below as well, because Tony appeared. His mask was on, but his shirt was off. He looked up at her, and even beneath the mask she knew he was giving her some smug version of a smile. He walked into the kitchen area. Sarah could hear the sound of the fridge opening as he rummaged around.

Jane appeared next. She was in a robe, tying her dark hair in a ponytail, trying to keep her mask in place as she did. Sarah watched her as she strode from view and joined Tony. They dipped slightly out of sight but she could hear them preparing something, in hushed tones.

After some time Jane called out: "Sarah? We're having some lunch if you're hungry."

Cautiously, Sarah went down. Tony and Jane were sitting on one side of the main table. A variety of food was laid out. They were remarkably silent, saying nothing as they tried to eat through or around their masks. She made herself a sandwich and took some olives, then went to the chair near the sofa. She ate with her plate on her lap, trying not to face them but feeling their eyes on her.

There was a pile of walnuts and shells on the coffee table. With no conversation or music, an oppressive silence filled the room. The dogs were outside, so there was no clanking collar noise. The fire was burning low and made almost no sound. Every mouthful of food, every crunch, every swig of liquid seemed to echo around the room. It was irritating, grating on her mind and nerves. The discomfort made her appreciate her isolation upstairs. Somehow she pictured the slime in the soap dish and could not avoid matching it with unseen images of the food in their mouths.

They were slowly working through their food, moving their masks as needed, and she guessed that, like before, they'd probably eaten most of their lunch before she'd come down the ladder. Sitting here now was just a formality. They were immobile and silent.

Finally Jane got up. "Never did feed 'em," she said.

"Shit," Tony said.

"I'll take care of it."

Jane went to the front door and put on a coat hanging on a hook. As she did, Tony stood up, clearing the food from the table. Sarah watched him when he had his back turned, and as she did, something clicked in her mind. There were the requisite lunch items here and there. Bread, mayo, the same cold cuts from yesterday. The chess board she'd seen yesterday had been taken away, but the candles from last night were there. So was the glass jar with the cutlery sticking out of it.

Something was occurring to her. She wasn't sure what it was, but knowing the masks were busy, she felt herself scanning the table, the counter, the dishes, the whole kitchen area. The cabinets were rough, and curtains hung instead of doors in places. The gas or propane stove, the small fridge, the basic drab sink. Her gaze returned to the jar of cutlery. There was a small collection of forks and a couple of spoons. As soon as her eyes locked on it, she knew she'd noticed it before but that it just hadn't registered. In addition to the other stuff, there was also a steak knife in there, with a serrated edge on the blade and a wooden handle.

Tony went to the front door and looked out, seemingly immersed in thought. Sarah caught a small glimpse of the dogs running around, and Jane outside getting their food ready.

Her eyes returned to the jar. She'd let the razor get away without knowing what she might do with it. Not this time. The knife was there, in the jar, and her captors were busy. As with the razor blade fantasy she'd had, she knew that if she had something, even a small steak knife, she'd be better off than with nothing. She'd be prepared. She'd have a secret weapon, a mechanism of defense or a tool of escape. She focused on the knife, going through the logistics of obtaining it, and not making any mistakes.

She glanced at Tony again and again, expecting him to turn and ruin her chances. She knew every time she did that she was losing time. If it was going to happen, now was the time. She quickly stood up and took the first step toward the table. Another, then another, and she was halfway there. As she approached the table, she kept an eye on him, listening for Jane, starting to doubt, starting to wonder what she'd do if he turned now.

When she was at the edge of the table, scarcely breathing, she reached out. Her hands were trembling, and now that she was closer, she wondered how she could possibly get the knife out without rattling everything else. What if she stabbed—*no—get the knife now—all of it, just grab the whole jar and go.*

With her eyes moving between him and the jar and with her heart hammering, she reached out, delicately taking the jar in both hands just as Tony began to turn. She turned and retreated. Three steps, trying for casual, knowing he might notice something.

The ladder was another few steps away. Things felt surreal. She wondered if he'd turned, whether he was watching her now. Would he see the jar was missing? Of course he would. He'd notice it right away.

She was facing the ladder. It was a few steps away. She felt like going through a security gate, knowing it could go off anytime. And it suddenly occurred to her that even if she got the jar upstairs and got the knife out, she'd still have to bring it back down and put it back on the table, minus the knife—before they noticed the jar missing. That would be even harder. But it could wait.

When she was almost at the ladder, she heard his voice. "Hey." She'd known it could happen, could happen any time. Now it was.

She stopped. She stood with her back to him, feeling her heart pound, waiting for options to present themselves. She held the jar close to her chest. Maybe he was talking to Jane. No, Jane was outside. She reached toward the ladder.

"You," he said. There was no mistaking it.

She waited, holding her breath.

"Well? You done?"

"What?"

"You didn't finish your food. If you're gonna take it, eat it. I don't wanna have to get all this shit out again later if you get hungry."

"No. I'm okay. Think I'll go upstairs."

"What, food not good enough? Looking for some fancy truffle sauce or something?"

"No, I'm kinda tired, that's all."

"Well, how you gonna eat it up there if you don't bring it?"

"What?" Sarah felt her heart sink. Panic was setting in. "I'm not feeling well, I have to use the bathroom."

"What, is there a bathroom up there I didn't know about? Aren't you headed the wrong direction?"

"No. I was—there's the dish of ice cream up there and—" She felt all control slipping away. "I'll bring it down."

At the ladder, she looked up. She realized that she needed both hands to climb it. That would make it obvious. She eyed the bathroom door. She could go in there first. Hide the jar. Make it look like she was sick, then come out and go up. This was a mess.

Then from behind her: "What's wrong with your arms?"

"What?"

"You wouldn't be hiding something, would you?"

"No." She winced. It sounded so lame. She began to move toward the bathroom, knowing she had no other options.

If she shuffled sideways into the bathroom, it would be just as obvious as going up the ladder with one hand. But she had to do something. She rubbed her neck with her free hand in a meager attempt to appear natural, and stepped through the door into the bathroom. As she did, she heard Jane come in from outside.

Sarah closed the bathroom door and looked around wildly. The cabinet beneath the sink. It was the only place. She turned on the faucet, for white noise. Reached down, opened the cabinet.

She heard Jane's voice: "So what's she gonna do with that?"

"With what."

"That jar."

It happened quickly. There was a moment's silence as panic took over. The footsteps approached. She was unable to move, as if held down by millions of tiny hands. She hastily bent down, trying to get the knife out. Got an edge of the knife between two fingers. Began to pull it out. But it was shorter than the other items, and her hands were shaking, and the knife kept slipping.

The bathroom door swung inward heavily and hit her arms just as she got it nearly free. She watched in horror as the jar fell to the floor, breaking into pieces and spilling its contents with a commotion of silverware and shards of glass.

She stared emptily at the mess on the floor. Tony's boots were there, just on the edge of all the broken glass. The knife stood alone, inches from her hand. She could get it. The possibility of using it presented itself. Tony's foot, bleeding. Her with the knife, lunging toward him as he fell backward. Or she could use a jagged shard of glass. He would beg for mercy. She wouldn't care if she cut herself.

But she started whimpering. She waited for the wrath. She couldn't move, as though doing so might set things into motion. As they were, the inevitable punishment was on hold. Things were suspended. The tiny hands still had their grip.

"And what the hell were you planning to do with all this shit?"

She slowly stood up, eyes on the floor.

"Huh? I said, what were you planning to do with all this shit?"

Getting no response, he continued, slowly: "Fine, then repeat after me: 'I only wanted the knife.'"

She continued to stare at the floor. She felt herself starting to cry.

"Come on, say it: '*I only wanted the knife.*'"

"Tony," Jane said, "enough."

Tony bent down and picked up the knife. "Oh stop crying, Sarah. This is what you were after, wasn't it? Or did you want to practice bending spoons or something?" He turned, showed the knife to Jane, standing somewhere near the ladder. "Check this out. Little one thought she'd try to take a knife."

"But why?" Jane said in a baby voice. "To stab us?"

Sarah suddenly stalked past Tony. Jane stepped aside as she went for the ladder. She climbed it as fast as she could.

"That's right, get upstairs, high society!" Tony called after her.

Sarah ran to the cot and sank down, face in her pillow.

"And no more food, by the way! Remember the half-eaten sandwich down here, 'cuz the dogs are getting it. You just lost mess hall privileges."

CHAPTER 12

Around 1:00 P.M., the mail truck arrived at the apartment building. The carrier got out with a mail bag and entered the lobby. After about ten minutes he got back in the truck and drove to the next stop. Brandon put on a pair of latex gloves, locked his car and walked with a steady, deliberate pace, passing a young couple just leaving the building, and strode casually into the lobby. He took out the key he'd made for #232, just a resident picking up his mail. Within a few seconds he'd taken out Adam Liddy's new mail, put back the stuff he'd taken yesterday, and relocked the box. Out of habit, he always positioned himself so that his back was facing the security camera in the corner when he swapped the mail, even though he'd disabled the camera nearly two weeks ago. He could still see the frayed and severed wire near the ceiling as he opened the inner door. He first went to the parking garage in the basement, heading past the spot where Liddy kept his car, and noticing it was gone, went up to #232 and listened carefully before letting himself in.

He no longer needed to enter Adam Liddy's apartment very often. Not like this. Not like the early days, when he was still determining the best candidate for the job. In those first few weeks, he'd spent dozens of hours following the ten or so finalists, researching their lives, observing their routines, until settling on Liddy. In the first phase, it had been necessary to enter his apartment to obtain things, modify documents, place objects or rearrange details. During these visits he got a unique sense of the man and his personality, the parts that didn't show up online: documents, awards, clothing, keepsakes, journals, books, art, magazines, sloppy observations or memos on the desk or on the fridge, things in notebooks and sticky notes, the liquor he kept in the cabinet, the food in the kitchen, personal documents in his desk drawers, memories from childhood in his closet. It was these documents and memories that Brandon would gradually manipulate. In the beginning it was just a slightly faded letter, apparently printed on an old printer typical of those from Adam Liddy's youth, or a handwritten note from a staff or authority figure, stuck within a yearbook or a comment made in a work file, hinting at Adam's strange relationship with girls or women. Little offhand pieces of evidence that detectives would later focus on when they began to investigate the Sarah Easton case.

He went quickly to the desk where Liddy kept his laptop. He opened the drawer on top, the one that contained mostly odds and ends. He took out a small thumb drive from his pocket and placed it on top of the junk. It was nothing overly significant: just another small sampling of websites and news articles containing references to Sarah. There were a few photos, some copied from publicly available news sources, some taken with a telephoto lens.

While he was there, he went into the bedroom and looked in the storage boxes in the closet. Everything he'd placed during earlier visits was still intact, buried and apparently not discovered yet. Like the thumb drive he'd just placed, everything had its place. These little snippets looked like remnants of earnest online digging. The kind of digging, Brandon mused, that a middle-aged pervert might do. Also scattered here and there in Adam

Liddy's various archives were documents and papers and receipts and records, all hinting at his obsession with women, with celebrities, with Sarah.

He replaced all the boxes, corrected any evidence of his presence, took a last look around, and left. All the way back the camera images he'd noticed last night were on his mind. He cursed himself for the sloppiness. Even though he kept the camera locked up in a box hidden in his apartment, he knew the risk of leaving things like that anywhere. If anyone happened to find it—somehow, for some reason, someone just looking at the camera if he had it out—and somehow glanced at the images on that card, it would be nearly impossible to explain. How many times had Sarah herself been over and with him or even alone, in his study, near that storage cabinet, within inches of that locked box with the folded quilt on top hiding the lock.

When he got back he wasted no time. He went straight to the box, took out the camera, and went through the images in detail. Many of the shots were buildings and public places: locations Sarah frequented or places where she interacted with others. Some of them were taken from afar: Sarah in Seattle or in the Bay Area, getting into her car, Sarah leaving one of her apartments, Sarah at a bar, talking with someone, Sarah walking across a street. Some were of Sarah in a crowd, laughing with several friends. He remembered following her to that party at a club in Beverly Hills. It had been nearly impossible to get close enough for the shots with the security people everywhere.

Now that he'd looked at them, he deleted everything. He knew he'd already uploaded all of the images weeks ago and they were buried deep online. In fact, some had made their way onto the thumb drive he'd just dropped off at Adam Liddy's place. When he was done, he put the camera back in the box.

He quickly shuffled through the mail he'd picked up. One was a handwritten letter—probably Liddy's mother. Another was from the Oakland library. He was ecstatic at another piece: it was from the California DMV. He took it out and opened it. It was the replacement driver's license that he'd "applied" for on behalf of Liddy, who must have lost his at some point. It had taken at least two weeks longer than Brandon had estimated. Its arrival meant he no longer had to check Liddy's mail every day.

As he was about to place the mail into the box to review tomorrow, a larger, heavier piece slipped out. It was an overnight express letter. It was in a larger envelope but had been stuck within some junk mail of the same size. Now that he had it, he faced a dilemma: pieces like this had tracking numbers. If Liddy was paying attention or expecting the letter he would probably wonder why it wasn't in his mailbox. In the past, if Brandon had noticed express or priority envelopes like this he would leave them. With the tracking they were too risky to take, plus they were impossible to reseal after opening. Even if Liddy was not paying attention, the letter was a risk.

He checked the time. He wouldn't have a chance to go there until later. He put the mail into the box, then locked it up and replaced the quilt on top. He would have to deal with it as soon as he got back.

He powered up his laptop and logged into his VPNs, then burrowed his way into the mesh of folders where he kept his notes and files for the project. He updated the call log, adding notes about the call from Cheryl last night, comparing the actual outcome to the notes he'd predicted over the past several weeks. He knew that another call could come at anytime. In fact, he anticipated another of Sarah's friends would contact him today. Later in the afternoon he would go out to the pier for the weekly sailing gig that he and Sarah almost never missed, ready to deliver the line about not being able to reach Sarah. He would be ready for the probing questions and the furrowed brows and the sense of doubt.

CHAPTER 13

Sarah stared out the window. There was nothing from Tony and Jane. No moaning, no talking. Maybe they were in the bedroom, but it was quiet. She could hear the dogs move around occasionally.

Out there, the white snow and green pines formed a complete picture of winter. Unrelated thoughts occurred to her, ranging the whole spectrum from pretty to bizarre. She wondered what she would do if she had to go to the bathroom before Ian got back. No way could she call down to them, not now, anyway. Nor could she simply go down the ladder. The dogs would come. If she'd thought to bring some food up, she could try to bribe them like before, but she'd messed up trying to steal the knife and pissed Tony off in the process. She could ask Jane, but then Tony would hear it and make a sarcastic comment, or more likely explode in anger. So she'd be stuck up here, unable to go downstairs, and without a place to go up here.

She knew these types of thoughts were occurring to her more often, and it worried her. Was this how it started when you cracked up? Wasn't this only the second full day? Couldn't this go on for twice that, or ten times that long?

By now Brandon would know something was wrong. They'd been planning to go sailing today, and when she didn't show up for that, what would happen? She thought the time was set for two. If she knew what time it was, she would know one way or the other. God, why couldn't they have left her a watch, or given her a clock. She had to admit, she was getting pretty good at guessing the time based on the way the light looked. Or was she? She really had no way to verify her guesses, but her sense of the passage of time seemed to be getting more and more accurate, culminating in the darkening of the clearing out there.

So she didn't show for the sailing gig. What then. Did Brandon wait around for a while, then go anyway? She wasn't sure who else was supposed to go today, but of course Edwin would be there. Maybe Susan. A couple others. People came and went. But no matter what combination of friends she mentally put together on the boat, she realized that over the past few weeks of sailing, no matter who canceled or joined, Brandon and her were the two who had always made it. This sent her worrying in a new direction, bringing her back to Brandon again. People may know they had distanced themselves a bit from each other (more he from her, she knew), and yet he stuck out as the one who'd been the closest to her in a tangible way for any amount of time. But when she didn't show up at the pier today, what would he do? What would any of them do?

This morning she hadn't met Cheryl for breakfast. She hadn't called her last night. She hadn't called this morning. She hadn't called anyone nor answered her phone since Thursday morning. Now it was Saturday.

Before she could stop it, a new thought suddenly entered her mind. She imagined herself sitting up here for days, more days, day after day. She would get good at guessing what time it was based on the way the sun moved around, when it was sunny. But what if she forgot what day it was? It could happen. She could go along like she was now, knowing the day, guessing the time. And then one day she would not be sure. Maybe it would be Tuesday, and she wouldn't be sure if it in fact was already Wednesday. She wouldn't know. It would get worse, until she only knew vaguely that six weeks had gone by (or maybe seven?) and she'd be totally wrong, oblivious to any sense of the date. She knew she'd lose it then. She'd be out of control.

She went to the cot and got under the sleeping bag.

So, she hadn't answered her phone. People might've been, hopefully had been, trying to call her. No one could get in touch with her, and that might make people wonder. But then again, everyone might just assume she'd been out of touch for whatever reason. Maybe they'd think she got sidetracked, or changed her schedule. Or that she just hadn't called people back yet. But surely people would start to put things together, especially if someone tried her and could never get through, and no call back. They might let things wait for a while, just assume that she was busy. But Cheryl would worry, that much she knew. She always worried. So would Becca.

But what would anyone do after all the wondering and worrying? Even if Brandon or Cheryl or Susan or anyone else did suspect something was wrong, what could they do? Ian had said her father had been contacted. Would Brandon or Cheryl be in touch with him for some reason, and if so, would he try to hint something to them, even though no one was supposed to call the police? No calling the police, but what about contacting other people? Would Dad slip some clandestine message of urgency to Cheryl or Brandon if they tried the house phone? Come to think of it, as far as she knew no one even knew the house phone.

If someone tried the house phone, Burke would answer it. They would ask him if anyone had seen her since whenever, Thursday, more likely

Friday. He would have no reason to think anything was wrong. He just wouldn't know. As a matter of fact, he probably wouldn't say anything, until he knew who he was talking with. In any case, she was only there once a week on average, and even when school was not in session and she was at home more often she might not see him for days at a time because she was in and out all the time between San Francisco and Seattle.

Same with Dad. New York, London, Paris, L.A. No one would have any reason to suspect anything was wrong, based on physical or phone presence. To them, nothing would be different in the routine. The permanent people around the house, not just Burke but the rest of the staff, would probably not know one way or the other. Maybe they'd expect to see her Thursdays when she flew back home, but if they didn't see her, well, what of it. No one at home would probably know anything was different than usual.

So that left San Francisco, and Berkeley. Brandon would probably be suspicious, he'd think something was wrong, but he probably wouldn't be overly concerned yet, because they'd decided to keep some distance. And he definitely would not call Dad. Not unless he had to. She knew they didn't like each other, though they'd only met a couple of times.

Everything could take days to start happening. Someone would call the police eventually, for sure. But it could take days. All the little things in a daily and weekly and monthly routine happened with occasional clicks and bumps, and if something didn't happen the way it always had, it didn't automatically send off alarms.

And when the police got the call, what then? How would it play out? Surely Ian knew someone would ultimately call the police. They must have planned for that. Of course. She was in a cabin in the middle of nowhere. The cops would interview people. Ask questions. Check schedules. They'd talk to the last people she'd seen, or had been supposed to see. Like Levin. What had happened to him, anyway?

She shivered, thinking about how it had happened Thursday morning. She hadn't even technically been kidnapped, not at first. It's not like there had been a struggle. She'd driven there, with one of her captors! Ian had been there and faked a story, and she'd bought into it just like that. She wondered if the story ever made it to the press, how it would sound. The daughter of hotel mogul Mark Easton has been missing for x number of days. She was last seen driving to a doctor appointment. Only the location of the appointment was changed. She was instructed to drive to his home office, which she did willingly, with one of the suspects. She parked the car and walked right in, having never been there before. She didn't care, she just drove there and was never seen again. Matter of fact, she handed him her phone when he asked for it, which would have been her only means of escape. Word is, she was insured. Her dad's kidnapping and extortion policy was up to date and very generous.

Everything revolved around her phone. It was the point of contact to everyone. It would be full of messages by now. It would be ringing. And they had it.

CHAPTER 14

As Brandon pulled into the parking lot of the marina just after two, he found Pete and Edwin waiting, looking out toward the bay and chatting. The marina was full of people, busier than usual. The smell of salt water was strong in the cool air, carried toward shore on a light breeze, a perfect day for sailing. Brandon parked and put his sunglasses on top of his Land Rover.

The three shook hands and caught up with some small talk. Pete never talked much around Brandon. As with some of Sarah's friends, there seemed to be some sort of barrier to entry, and without Sarah's presence as a buffer, Brandon felt an intense desire to put in his moment, then leave. Edwin was the de facto leader, being the owner of the boat, and anyone who showed up sort of waited for hints from him. He assigned roles or let people fall into their preferred task. You go there, this guy keeps an eye on the jib, she'll watch these lines, you can try the wheel. It was always a revolving set of people who showed up for the trips around the bay. As they stood around waiting, Brandon told them he hadn't heard from Sarah.

"Oh" Edwin said. "So she's up in Seattle?"

"I think so, yeah," Brandon said. "So probably won't make it today. Not only that, but I have a meeting in an hour, so I won't be able to either."

"A meeting on Saturday?" Edwin said.

"No rest for the wicked."

"That's too bad."

"Wish I could—just bad timing."

"We can always catch you next time. We'll keep a martini for you."

"I'll count on that."

"So is Sarah doing okay?"

"Yeah, I think so. I think she's starting to really get somewhere, with—well not sure how much you know about it—"

"Oh yeah—I know she's had her ups and down with that." Edwin looked at his phone, an incoming call, which he declined. "Well that's too bad. I don't know if she's missed more than once or twice all the time we've been doing this," he said.

"I know," Brandon said.

"Speaking of, I called her last night. Her phone went right to voicemail."

"Yeah, who knows. Maybe wants some down time or something."

"A mental health break?"

"Maybe a break from all of us," Brandon said.

Edwin stared back at him, with the kind of look he figured many of her friends would have on their faces: *why would she say that to you, Brandon, instead of one of us?* "I suppose," Edwin shrugged. "Like I said, I've hardly seen her miss, but then again, I guess I don't know the last time I saw her not feeling well."

Brandon kept his contempt within but could hear himself replying in a dozen different ways. "Well, like I said, I gotta go."

Edwin seemed ready to say something, maybe some probing question, but there was a honk behind them, and he waved to an approaching car. A couple Brandon recognized vaguely came up, the girl holding a bottle of wine, and the guy coming up to talk with Pete and move in on Edwin's hand. Brandon took a couple steps back, which was all it took to eject himself from the circle, and leave. He got in his car, and as he drove away, saw them in his rearview mirror, talking, laughing, hugging, pecking each other on the cheek.

It was dubious whether Edwin had bought any of the story about Sarah. Brandon had known her friends would start to question her absence, not finding her in San Francisco, or Seattle, or anywhere. When the time was right, he'd call the police and report her missing. Until then he'd keep people waiting and wondering. And when the time was right, Adam Liddy would be on the receiving end of the suspicion. Once this was all over, there would be a broad investigation, cops talking to everyone Sarah knew, and the media making a big deal out of it for weeks. The tabloids would break records. Because it crossed state lines, the FBI would be involved. Because of her father, it would make international news. They would ask questions of people like Edwin, and Pete, and all the others in her circle. Throughout it, he would play the role of the naïve boyfriend, stunned at what had happened, shocked that it looked like the mastermind behind the whole thing was a nobody named Adam Liddy.

He entered the parking lot of a diner on Hearst Avenue and stopped the car. He and one of his work colleagues were meeting for a late lunch and he was still ten minutes early. There were times like this, when the enormity of the task before him seemed so daunting there was no way he could pull it off, even though the game was in the late stages and there was no stopping it. All the subtle planning and major moves had been made. Now it was just continuing this dual life, in perpetuity: an eternity of split personality that he had created and had to maintain.

During these times, he would sense an occasional ping of remorse. He tried not to view the project in emotional terms, but he knew he genuinely liked Sarah, if in an abstract way. He could put aside all the material aspects, her wealth, heritage, lifestyle, upbringing, and see who she was as a person. With all the layers of complexity removed, she was a somewhat vulnerable, highly curious, independent woman with an inner strength who had plans for her future, plans that didn't involve just sitting on her fortune. She was smart, witty, and energetic. He could see all that, just as anyone could. Yet he was undermining her trust to capitalize on her weaknesses and rob her blind. The objective part of him told him that the entire thing was only business. Sarah would be unharmed. Her father wouldn't personally lose any money since his insurance would pay for it, and even if he did, it was better than having something happen to his daughter. When the payment was made, Sarah would be released, Adam Liddy would be the main suspect, and Brandon would carry on quietly, cooperating with the investigation, keeping access to his newfound wealth at bay. Only later would he begin the layering and integration of the money. It would take several more months, years even, for the job to be complete. In fact, it would likely never be finished. He would always have to live a lie, even when he and Sarah were no longer together.

But he knew there was another part of him, one that didn't have easy answers to all the facts of the case. A non-rational part. It came up for air once in a while, to rise near the surface and linger. When it did, he wished he could just remove himself from the entire operation, like putting in notice from a job, and just embrace Sarah fully, and be the man he let her think he was. In a way, as with some past relationships, he nearly felt sorry for Sarah. A kind of pity, maybe, as though his role was more savior and protector than companion. These moments were brief and sporadic, but when they came, they tore at him. They made him feel things he didn't want to acknowledge, and they pulled at things he didn't want to feel. Lines got blurred. Who would he protect her from? Himself?

When he was about 16, he'd gone camping with his younger brother, who would have been about 12 or 13. Around the fire the first night they'd gotten into a deep conversation about murdering someone. The conversation had evolved out of one topic, then another. They'd pondered all the aspects: how to hide the evidence, how to create distractions, how to bury or hide a body. Neither of them saw it as real projection, just speculation, a plot line from movies or books. He sometimes recalled that conversation, but with the experience of more real crime behind him. How hard it might be to actually pull the trigger, or swing the bat, or stab or slice with the blade. He imagined that if he murdered someone, as the months went by, he'd be the type who might break character and start losing focus. Not a random, sudden killing or self defense, but a premeditated, planned, calculated murder. The panic in the eyes of the victim, the last struggles for air, pleas for mercy, or the cries of pain would eat at him long after the act. Those images would haunt him, creeping up when he least expected it, and shatter the lie. They would come up in dreams, or in a conversation with a relative, or a parent of the victim. All the methodical planning and preparation would fall to ruin. At a moment like that, he wondered, would it be easier to suddenly end the lie and turn himself in, instantly releasing himself from an eternity of guilt? Similarly during those moments of weakness he could see himself just wanting to end the scheming and just hold Sarah in his arms. It sounded so simple.

Too simple. Sarah would love the embrace. But for him it was just a role to play. Only Marcella had ever felt right in his arms.

He checked his watch. A few minutes still. He watched as a family of four crossed the parking lot and got into their car. The way the dad helped the young boy up into the back seat looked so natural, anyone could see the real love of a parent for a child. The parents were busy in conversation with each other, engaged. They looked happy. Well, Brandon mused, they weren't talking about murdering someone and planning how to hide a body. But then again, why not? Maybe in some twisted *Twilight Zone*-like reality, they were a family of killers, with the parents teaching the kids the ins and outs of how to do the job properly. Or maybe the parents were speaking in lies, disguising the actual content of their conversation, with the kids thinking it was just fun and games. A picture of a happy family as a guise, while all of them were psychopaths.

That's basically what his youth had been. A shiny veneer on the surface masking a variety of alternate facts beneath. He and his brother, mom and dad, living in a smallish house on a quiet block in Van Nuys, with normal neighbors, and a normal high school, and normal middle-class Valley life. Two parents, two kids. Mom and dad were standard-issue. Neither was an alcoholic or distant or abused their sons, nor overachievers, nor was there some household dynamic to explain why one son would grow up to be a plumber, and the other would move to San Francisco and try his hand at arranging the kidnapping of a wealthy hotel heiress. Someone looking back at their histories could see that both brothers had minor skirmishes with the law, but the only significant record would be the brief stint in juvenile detention for Brandon. It would otherwise be clear that both brothers had moved beyond the small operation they had stealing things and selling them to classmates, or the small drug operation they ran, even the stolen car thing they dabbled in for a period. It would be far more difficult to see that much of that work had in fact continued, but only by Brandon, and only because he realized after getting caught once, that to succeed at this line of work would require living a dual identity.

He opened the car door and stepped out. He searched for his sunglasses, and not finding them in their usual places, looked under the seat, around the dash, but to no avail. He thought back to when he last had them: at the marina. He must have left them on top of the car. They had cost a small fortune. Another of countless things he had to pay upward to reach a baseline level. His economic background made it impossible for him to view something like that—brand sunglasses, the watches, the Land Rover, a gift for Sarah—as anything less than a required step in the larger plan. Eventually, when this was all over, he would look at stuff like that as everyday objects, necessities at a level of cost and comfort that matched his lifestyle. Baseline stuff.

It wasn't the cost. He needed to focus. He stood, facing the car, and breathed deeply a couple of times, closing his eyes. He slowly brought himself back to his part in the storyline. Things that had been in place for months, and lying in quiet dormancy, were now being activated. So he'd lost the sunglasses. It happened. Maybe Edwin and company would find it odd that he'd told them he couldn't make the sailing gig because "something had come up," yet here he was having lunch with a colleague minutes later. So it went. Everything he did now was part of a plan.

Now he had to go play the role and rehash the variation of the story, about how he hadn't heard from Sarah for a couple of days. He put himself back into the storyline, until he felt part of it.

CHAPTER 15

Now she remembered. It had been gnawing at her for something like an hour, something that she imagined would be an hour. *Up to date and very generous.* For some reason she'd recalled the phrase, articulated it to herself briefly in her rambling thoughts after the knife incident below and Tony's menacing words. She'd asked Burke about the policy, having found out about it. She'd never known there was such a thing as a kidnapping/extortion policy.

But why did I ask Burke about it? What made me want to ask him? It hadn't been long after Tracy's funeral.

Unable to remember, or concentrate, she lay on the cot and stared at the ceiling. Her mind shifted again to the knife incident. If she'd taken the knife, and not been caught, she could have used it to start whittling away at the two-by-fours on the windows. If she weakened them, she might be able to break one or two of them and jump out.

She felt herself harboring a burning hatred for Tony. At least Ian seemed to have some sort of intelligence. He was a leader, and he didn't seem to care what the others said or did, as long as they followed his orders. She felt afraid of Ian, but at least he showed some restraint. She didn't feel that way with Tony. The receptionist routine in Levin's office with Jane, both of them acting well in their roles, he'd been nice, even convincing. Now every time she even thought of him, she cringed. The way he'd shown her the gun, pulled her hair, taunted her down in the bathroom. Taunting. Always the taunting. His resentment about wealth shown through every time he opened his mouth. And it worked. She feared him as much as she loathed him.

She rubbed her head where he had pulled her hair after making the second video. It still hurt.

So they deliver these videos somehow. Maybe they give them to Dad in person through someone, maybe Ian drops them off somewhere. Dad hears the part about failure to comply, about not calling the police. Of course he can pay, no doubt about that. The question is, will he just start getting the cash together? Or will he call the police first. Maybe he ponders a way to make a deal, try to negotiate somehow. Make it look like they're getting what they're asking for, but in fact working something out on the side, maybe with the cops, maybe not. He looks at the cards on the table, the way all the players hold their hands, their expressions, the way their eyes shift to the other players, the table, the cards, the chips. He finds a way to let Ian think he's getting something, but then he throws down his hand and takes it all. He evidently tried to communicate with Ian, indicated he wanted to talk to him. So he had something to say. But what? What if there was a complication, or he can't make the deadline, or something else crucial, and Ian's refusal to talk with him...

She stopped herself. A single thought formed in her mind: *if Dad can't get in touch with Ian, or Ian won't negotiate, which is the same thing, then I have to find a way out of here.*

She looked around the room. The desk. Night stand. Rug by the cot. Square in the floor. Her home away from home. The place where she was going to spend the hours and days, wondering whether her friends would call the police, slowly fading through inaction into a shell of her former self. Waiting, waiting, not knowing what was happening.

It's only the third day. This could go on for twice that long. Or ten times that long. Oh God, I told myself the same thing earlier. I'm starting to repeat myself. Is this how you lose it?

How far was this place from a road? It could be anywhere in the mountains. Ian said the snow was deep out there. What would her chances be even if she did break one of the windows and somehow got out through the bars? Ian probably exaggerated a bit about the cold, but all she had was a light leather jacket. Then there were the dogs. She'd have to do more than throw some stupid ham at them. But if she got past them, if she broke the window and got outside, she could try for the car or the SUV. Would it be unlocked? Would the key be in the ignition, just sitting there? If this place was deep in the woods somewhere, and guarded by dogs, they probably wouldn't expect anyone to steal it.

But what if the key's not in the car?

Then you'll run.

But where would I run? He said we're in the bloody middle of nowhere.

Then you have to use the car.

But what if the key—

She rolled over. The light was fading. Evening was coming.

Then she heard it. The sounds. The moaning. Softly at first, then gradually with more intensity, hues of sexual noise from below. The smell of marijuana drifted up once or twice. She tried to avoid the image, but kept picturing the two of them down there, on the bed, screwing.

No matter what, she still had to get outside first. That meant breaking through those bars. Or walking out the front door.

She nearly looked at her watch that wasn't there, but stopped herself. She didn't know the time. She never knew the time. She was becoming used to getting by without it, but it would be nice to look at a clock just once, just a quick peek, to see how close she was. She was getting better at noticing the way the shadows moved throughout the day as the sun crossed the sky. She'd never really thought about that before, the way time flowed, the way everything, all the shadows cast from everything, slowly changed throughout the day. Now she couldn't avoid thinking about it. It was all around her. She wondered about stealing a watch or clock, or at least a look at one tonight, when she went down for whatever evening meal they were going to conjure.

Judging from the light, she guessed it was probably around five or six. Maybe it was earlier. Maybe later. In any case, the light was like the light had been yesterday when they'd eaten. Then it had gotten dark. She'd noticed last night that once the sun completely set, it was total blackness out there. No lights of any kind, anywhere.

Tony began moaning. The bed began creaking vigorously. Jane's moaning continued.

Sarah felt intense irritation. She looked around the room, searching for a way to do something. She pondered the darkening details of her confine. If she really wanted to escape, she'd have to be resourceful. Not do anything rash, like the knife thing, hoping that Tony wouldn't turn or Jane wouldn't come in. She'd have to do better next time. And worse, now they would probably be on guard. If she'd been more careful, she'd be better able to try things.

She got up. Again, she noticed the way the floor creaked in certain areas and was silent in others. She noticed the way the rows of nails in the floor seemed to create the effect of long, narrow zones. She stepped in one area, then another, testing sections, seeing which made noise and which didn't, making her way to the window in front.

She studied the window sills, the thickness of the glass, which she could determine by seeing the edge where a piece of moulding had chipped away. She tried to get a sense of how strong the two-by-four bars on the window were. The things on the desk, in the drawer, and the wobbly leg. The matches, and how many were in the box.

Desk leg. Matches. The thought of setting fire to the place occurred to her. The image of flames had occurred to her once or twice, but now she entertained the idea in full. She looked at the desk leg on the table. Feeling excitement, her mind pondered lighting a fire using the old newspapers. The smoke would choke her in the short term, but she could break the windows on either end, and as the flames got higher, she could scream for help, and they'd come up. By then she'd have the desk leg off the table, having pried it loose. The first person who came up through the square to look would get the full impact in their head. Then the next, and so on.

Idiot. First, the sight of the first person being hit would keep the others from coming. Maybe, if they wanted me alive, they'd get me downstairs, and we'd all have to get out while the cabin burned down. Then things would really be agitated. I could take advantage of that to get out, run somewhere, anywhere.

But it's cold out there. I don't know where I am. And the dogs.

She felt the doubt creep in. She welcomed it, to stifle this urge to light the place on fire. Now, she had them believing she was just quietly sitting up here. That was her best weapon right now. She would wait. Further opportunity would arise. And the more she thought about it, the less she thought the fire idea would work. What if they didn't take it seriously soon enough, and the smoke filled the attic level before escaping out those small windows (assuming she was able to break them) and asphyxiated her?

When the moaning stopped, she soon heard them talking in low voices. She couldn't hear what they were saying, but an occasional laugh or a teasing denial stuck out, and she found herself recalling the times like that with Brandon, after, just lying there and talking. The best thing about Brandon was his hands. His hands were large, but they were so soft, gentle. She would tease him that he didn't have a working man's hands. Sometimes she would just hold one with both of hers and study it in the dark.

It was nearly dark outside. It was becoming hard to see. She went to the cot and lay down on top of the sleeping bag and covered herself with the blanket. She wondered what time Ian was coming back. She wasn't that hungry, but she felt restless. She wanted the break in routine: dinner. Something that captive people looked forward to.

She felt herself fading away. With the darkness came a slight drop in temperature in the room. It made the sleeping bag seem even warmer and inviting. But she wanted to stay awake. She felt herself begin to doze. She opened her eyes, and blinked. She had to stay awake. If she fell asleep now, she'd wake up in the middle of the night and be up for the rest of it, awake in the darkness, having to listen to the moaning down there.

She closed her eyes again, just to rest for a minute or two.

CHAPTER 16

Brandon went through Adam Liddy's mail from earlier. Two pieces had obvious value. Using a stovetop kettle onto which he'd fitted a narrow pipette to direct the flow of steam, he slowly worked open both letters in the usual manner. One was from the Oakland Public Library. Another, handwritten in cursive script, was from Liddy's mother. The library item was about overdue books, and he felt disappointed that he hadn't been able to make a better guess about the contents before opening it, but nonetheless the letter pointed out relevant facts about Liddy, and he never discounted these. Two outstanding architectural reference titles. No surprise. Liddy was an architect, a mid-level partner in a smaller firm.

The letter from his mother contained a photo. It showed some people standing in front of a 70s ranch-style house with brown wood siding, spaced comfortably apart from nearby houses, against a backdrop of rolling brown hills. Brandon recognized it immediately: Liddy's childhood home, outside Billings, Montana. The house was unremarkable, yet solid. He assumed the people were relatives. He read the handwritten letter carefully, memorizing the relevant contents, and forgetting the rest.

When his phone rang, he checked the number. He didn't recognize it, but the area code was Seattle again. He let it ring. It would most likely be one of Sarah's friends.

He folded the letter and pictures back into the envelope, did the same with the library letter, and used a thin glue stick to seal them.

He logged in to his system and reviewed his list of contacts, looking at the indicators he'd placed next to the names of people he knew would try to reach Sarah. He cross-referenced names with schedules. While he was at it, he checked the upcoming course schedule for his stuff at Berkeley. As usual, there were multiple things he had to synchronize, and as usual, he had the feeling he was leaving something out. Maybe many things. He was sure it had happened countless times since he'd embarked on this project. The camera card was just one example.

He checked himself. There was that word again: project. He always caught himself when that term popped into the fore, like an unwanted song that wouldn't go away. He preferred something like "design" or "model" which in his mind fit more in line with the way he looked at data flows, sequences, decisions, and obstacles.

Looking at the schedule for Berkeley, he knew he could make at least one of the classes. He would typically drop in and do some of the checkin work he'd need to get a sense of the assignment or prep for something. At this point most of the work he was doing there was project work. But it was all a formality. Above all else he had to show up and put in the effort.

He listened to the message. It was from Becca, one of Sarah's friends from Seattle. He let some time pass, getting up to get a snack. When he relaxed into his recliner, he dialed the number. Becca answered right away, which told him that she must've gotten his number from Cheryl or someone else and having left the message, was ready for any news about Sarah.

"Becca? This is Brandon. You just called?"

"Hi, I got your number from one of Sarah's friends, it's about Sarah."

"Sure."

"Well, I talked with Cheryl, do you know her? We're all friends. Anyway, I talked with her today and she said Sarah's not feeling too good or something?"

"Not sure. She's sort of AWOL."

"Yeah, I called her, and she's not answering, and was wondering if you knew anything."

"I haven't been able to get in touch either. I half think she might just need a day or two off. Maybe she shut her phone off."

There was a measurable pause. "For what, two days? What're those odds?"

Brandon kept his calm demeanor. "I know." He also paused, for effect. "Honestly, Becca, I think it's—well I think in a way this is actually good news, or it could be."

"What do you mean?"

"I mean, now that she's finally dealing with Tracy's death, you know, she's coming to terms with things she hadn't expected. I think you know she's been in therapy."

"Yes."

"So I think it's helping. Maybe she just needs some time."

There was a contemplative pause. "Okay. But she never shuts off her phone."

"What can I say? I agree with you. Could be her battery's dead and no charger, I don't know."

"But here's the part that worries me most," she said. "Cheryl told me Sarah's here in Seattle."

"She is."

"At her dad's house."

"That I don't know."

"Well, the thing is, when I called her number there, the guy who answers, you know, the guy who answers the phone there? He said he hadn't seen her since Thursday morning."

"You called that number?" Brandon felt the rapid flash of heat on his forehead. He had assumed no one would call her father's place, because no one knew the number. Sarah had told him that herself. He collected himself quickly, added a hint of confusion. "Hm, I guess when she called me I just assumed she was calling from there. Could be staying at a friend's place in Seattle."

Another pondering silence. So it was sinking in to Becca that she was not the first one to be called, and if Sarah in her sorry state was staying at a friend's house or somewhere else in Seattle, neither she nor Cheryl had been on the list.

"What number did she call from?" She said. So she was going to push it.

"Her cell."

Another silence. "Okay, just thought I'd check if you knew anything," Becca said finally.

"Yeah. Sorry. But like I told Cheryl, I'll let you know if I hear from her. I've got your number here now."

Before she hung up, Brandon quickly added, "Oh, Becca? Call me if you hear from her first, could you?"

When they'd hung up, Brandon swore. So she knew about the house phone in Seattle, her father's place, the house in which Sarah and Tracy had grown up. He knew for a fact Sarah had told him that no one knew the number. So she must have forgotten giving it out, or not realized that at least one of her friends had obtained it somehow. He knew it wasn't publicly listed, because he'd tried numerous ways to look it up, just in case. He knew the number, because Sarah had given it to him, but he had been under the impression that it was only used by the guy who answered it, Burke.

The handful of times he'd been there, he'd maybe seen Burke twice. Sarah had introduced him the first time as a bookkeeper or lawyer, and he was the one who answered any calls to the house phone. He breathed easier now that he saw the connection: The phone number for the house was almost always answered by Burke. Burke took care of the legal stuff for Sarah's father. Even Sarah wasn't sure exactly what he did. But any call to that number would go to Burke. Burke may or may not know if Sarah was in the house. He might not see her for days on end. The fact that he'd told Becca that he hadn't seen Sarah since Thursday meant nothing. It only meant that he hadn't seen her since Thursday. Like any other Thursday.

He entered the call into the log. Then he drove to Adam Liddy's apartment to quickly step into the lobby and return the mail.

CHAPTER 17

Sarah sat up. For seconds, she felt dazed. The room was dark. She could hear laughter and talking and music below. The smell of food, of garlic, onions, lemon, was strong in the air. An undercurrent of thyme, rosemary. A hint of something sweet. Under different circumstances, she thought, she might call this place cozy. Under the present, she was probably going to get a lecture on the knife incident from Ian as Tony and Jane stood smirking in their masks nearby.

She heard Tony's voice, saying something about slaves.

She slowly got out of bed. She'd fallen asleep. Exactly what she had not wanted to do. She wondered if they'd already eaten, if she'd missed out on that. She was hungry, and her mouth was dry.

"Well sure they used incline planes," Ian said, flicking the chain. "Problem is, you still need hundreds of people to get the blocks up those, thousands actually. Turning corners, rolling the blocks over logs. It would take generations of people. And the higher you get, the longer it takes."

The music was the same Stan Getz CD that had been on last night.

"I know that," Tony said, "my point is, it's only a theory. No one knows for sure."

"How else could they have done it?"

"Well how did they get the blocks from the quarry sites to the building areas?"

"Same deal. Slaves."

Jane said, "What I don't get is, for a society that spent as much time as they did thinking about immortality, they didn't leave anything behind telling how they built 'em."

"Which is exactly what I'm saying," Tony said.

"Okay," Ian said, "if aliens did it, then why did they only build them there?"

"There's pyramids in other parts of the world."

"Not like the Egyptian ones, come on. And if those things in Nazca are landing sites, why don't they have those in Egypt too?"

Jane said, "Well, it could be because they lost their funding halfway through."

"Yeah, funding. Would explain the different styles," Tony said. "I'll drink to that."

"You know what I think it was?" Ian said. "Poor nutrition. Why do you think aliens are so small? They never got any bigger than those pictures you always see, with the big heads and the black eyes and shit."

Sarah went to the square and peered down. She did a double take at what she saw.

No one was wearing a mask.

Tony was on the sofa, eating potato chips. Jane was in the chair closest to the kitchen. Ian was stirring something over the stove, tasting it with a wooden spoon.

"That raises the question, though," Tony said, "why the big heads?"

Sarah simply stared, kneeling at the edge of the square.

Ian said, "Well, the big heads are—"

His gaze met Sarah's. For an instant, they simply stared at each other. He had dark short hair, a lean face, two, three day's growth. His eyes were dark and piercing. The "associate" for sure. When something on the stove boiled over and hissed, he turned quickly and tended to the pan.

She saw Tony and Jane look up. Jane looked prettier than this morning, more complete. Her eyes were large, somehow more sensual and complete than the fake client persona she remembered. Tony was the same, perhaps a little leaner. It was hard to picture him as a receptionist anywhere.

"Well," Ian said, "come on down. Join the party."

She looked between their faces again, as if to verify what she was seeing. She looked away when she felt Tony's gaze linger on her and a wry smile began to form on his face. He was definitely the Tony from Levin's office. And the expression on his face definitely matched with what she'd often thought lurked beneath the mask.

"Yeah," Ian said, "we talked about the masks. Well, are you coming down or not?"

As Sarah began to descend, she saw the evidence of another full-scale meal. A couple of new baguettes were on the table. Several bottles of wine, two of them open. The table was set. And a large coffee mug now held the utensils, sitting in the middle of the table. She didn't see the steak knife.

"Um, mind if I use the bathroom?"

"Be our guest," Ian said. "In fact, we would be honored, your highness."

So it was going to be one of these conversations. Ian sure didn't sound like he was too concerned about the knife incident. Maybe they hadn't told him yet. Or maybe they wouldn't. When she was about to wash her hands with the shampoo, she noticed that the old bar of soap was gone. It had been replaced. There was a new bar of the same kind. She could not deny it, this small thing lifted her spirits.

When she emerged, Ian said, "Well, what do you think?"

Did he know she'd noticed the soap right away? He wanted feedback on it? "Sorry?"

"Oh come on, the new us. The maskless phase."

She looked between them. The way everyone was looking at her made her suddenly uncomfortable. Something about their real faces was unsettling. Suddenly they were so real, and she'd been so used to the way the masks always stared back at her. Now every word or gesture seemed to have a new depth. And the way Tony looked at her, with his steely blue eyes, the real Tony, was far more threatening than the Tony with the mask.

"Want some wine?" Jane asked.

"Ah. Here." Ian picked up a glass and handed it to her.

When she only sort of took the glass, he said, "What's wrong?"

"Nothing."

"Yes, it's the real us. Seeing is believing." Ian held up a bottle. "Like some red?"

She didn't answer before something again boiled over on the stove. Ian jumped to it. "Eating was a bitch in them, true. But it was something else. Something I was thinkin' about on the way back today. I just knew then, baby, our lives had changed."

Tony said, "Can't you just tell us the name of the movie?"

"You have to guess, like I said."

"I know what it is anyway," Jane said.

"Well, don't tell Sarah. She just woke up."

Sarah noticed Jane try to mouth something to her. Sarah had no idea what she was trying to express. She felt awkward, standing near the table, with the empty wine glass that both Ian and Jane had offered and neglected to fill. And now Jane was trying some silent communication.

Ian took a frying pan from one of the lower cupboards. "So I'm comin' back, and get off the main road down here, and I'm faced with puttin' that thing on again. That mask. Sweating, stifling hot, lookin' like a bloody idiot."

"I thought it was pretty good," Jane said.

"Ditto," Tony added.

"Wrong. It was hell. A good mask, especially the kind used when kidnapping people, should have a decent place to breathe out of. That didn't. That was the big fault of that mask. Or the biggest anyway. It had many. Anyway..."

As Sarah tuned Ian out, she noticed Tony watching her from the sofa. Very subtly, he patted the space next to him with his hand and gave her that smirk.

Sarah looked away. Now she felt tense and nervous. She knew it was obvious to everyone present. Tony kept staring at her. Ian was humming something. Jane appeared to want to be nice to her, but didn't seem to know what to do. Sarah contemplated going upstairs.

Almost as if he'd been able to read her mind, Ian, without looking up, said, "There's sullen master Po, on the couch, unable to reclaim his lost youth. Remember, Tony, new phase here? Be nice to our guest."

Jane, noticing Sarah's empty glass, lifted the bottle. "Oh no. Sorry, Sarah. Here, sit down here." She smiled as Sarah sat down, then poured.

"Jane, can you give me a hand?"

As soon as Jane had left, she felt Tony's gaze even more. Jane and Ian were in the kitchen, muttering back and forth over the thing on the stove. Sarah took a sip of her wine, trying to avoid Tony's gaze, and she casually gazed around the room. She wished Jane would come back; when she did, she would block Tony's gaze. His eyes were on her, off her, on her again, as he stretched out on the sofa. She turned away from him.

When the conversation paused and a silence seemed to fill the room, Sarah shifted her gaze toward the kitchen. Jane and Ian were standing there, kissing heavily. Ian had his arms around her waist, with one hand in a back pocket of her jeans.

Ian suddenly pulled away, seemingly distracted by one of the bottles. "Open up that Merlot," he said. "Is that what that is, Merlot?"

Sarah carefully eyed Tony. He had been watching the pair, now watching Jane open another bottle. She could see nothing peculiar in his expression: no obvious sign of anger or resentment. If anything, it was that wry smile, the smug smirk, resting there in one corner of his mouth. Maybe watching them pleased him. Maybe that was their arrangement at night, with Tony watching.

With Tony distracted and the other two busy in the kitchen, her eyes focused on the space beyond Tony. A calendar was hanging on the wall. And beneath it, on the floor, just off the edge of the sofa, was a small backpack. It was partially open, and she could see a bunch of papers—it looked like letters or mail—and a set of keys.

Ian laughed. "Check this out." He was wearing the Scream mask and had his hands in the air.

"Suits you, looks better than it did on me," Jane said, adjusting the mask to fit Ian better.

Sarah tried to get a closer look at the keys. Tony was still watching the two in the kitchen, wine glass in hand. If he was aware of Sarah, he didn't show it. He was clearly focused on them. In the backpack, she could see two keys and part of another. Two looked like they were keys to a door or padlock. The other one, what she could see of it, had the wider look of a car key.

"Very nice," Tony said, "hides your bad English teeth."

Ian then tore at the mask. "Get this thing off me. You can't even see out of these little eye holes. Anybody with eyes that small ought to be hunched over a microscope down in a basement, in a white lab coat. You got the cardamom opened up yet?"

"What do you mean, opened up." Jane said.

"All we have is whole seeds. I need them broken up."

"Jane didn't do her job," Tony drawled sarcastically from the sofa.

"When did I sign up for sous chef?"

"No way to treat a guest," Ian said. "Whole cardamom? We'll get bad reviews."

"Fine," Jane said. "Hand me that knife."

"Use this one. Flat blade works better."

Sarah got up slowly, keeping a careful eye on Tony and the two in the kitchen. Wine glass in hand, she slowly took two or three careful steps toward the far end of the sofa, looking at the calendar.

"Mm, interesting," Jane said. "Don't think I've ever had raw—"

"And what do you mean, bad English teeth, by the way?" Ian said. "Hell if you want to see bad teeth, you should've seen my uncle Eamon."

The calendar picture was of a meadow in spring. There was nothing else to be gleaned from it. It showed dust, and was the wrong month and the wrong year. Eyeing Tony, she carefully looked down at the pack. The key was a car key. No question about it.

Tony was facing away from her, looking toward the kitchen. Ian was bent over the stove. Jane was watching Ian cook.

"This all we have for garlic?" Ian said.

"You made the list," Jane said.

Knowing she had to do something now or lose her chance, Sarah acted quickly. She turned to face the kitchen. Used her left foot to drag the keys further out of the pack opening.

She panicked when Tony spoke. "You're puttin' tomatoes in that?"

"Yeah," Ian said. "Why."

The set of keys was under her left foot. She was frozen. Ian was looking in her direction now. He must have noticed her new position in the room.

"Just wondering," Tony said.

Ian's eyes were on her. She attempted to look toward the calendar again, feeling obvious, very aware that she was standing stiffly. There was no question he was looking at her, seeing that she'd moved from the chair, and was standing near the couch. The look in his eyes said all of that, and she expected him to ask her what she was doing. She knew she wouldn't know what to say, and began to think of a way out.

"Why, you have a tomato allergy, too?"

"No, just thought you were making scampi. The usual way."

"Cardamom in scampi? See, this is why I do the cooking."

When Ian turned back to his pan, Sarah kept her eyes on the calendar and edged the keys further out of the pack with her foot.

Then Tony shifted in the sofa. He sat up, rubbing his eyes. He turned toward her again.

Ian said something she could hardly hear over her nervousness, something about fusion cooking and scampi. She could not take her eyes off Tony, that look of surprise. And there was the wry grin forming, nostrils enlarging. He took his wine glass from the coffee table and while staring at her, reclined, putting his feet up. She averted her eyes, back toward the calendar. She tried to keep her left leg straight and natural. If he happened to look at the floor now, he would see what she was trying to do.

Staring at her, he said, "You make it up, master? You make the scampi next time?"

"Yes, grasshopper. Of course. Anything for grasshopper. Course, we'd need garlic for that, and I think we're out now."

"I'll add it to the list," Jane said.

Sarah moved her foot. She felt the keys dig into the floor.

Still staring at her, Tony spoke: "You like that calendar or what? You've been staring at it for five minutes."

Sarah felt suddenly helpless, wishing she could go back to the chair. If she moved now, the keys would be exposed and everyone would know. She said, "No I was just wondering if it looks like this place in summer. So, what kind of wine is this?"

Jane, looking at one, then another bottle, said, "Is that the Merlot?"

"I already asked and no one answered," Ian said.

Sarah quickly went for it.

She opened her fingers slightly, letting the glass fall out of her hand. The glass hit the floor and shattered. Wine spilled. She quickly bent down. She could see the reaction in her periphery. Tony getting up, Jane looking in her direction. She feigned surprise as she began to pick up the larger shards.

As fast as she could she took the keys from under her left foot and stuffed them inside her right shoe. They barely fit. The ring was large. She immediately began fingering the pieces of glass, as if to clean up.

"Christ, you clumsy ox!" Tony shouted, above her. "What is this, round two?"

A small amount of wine had spilled on his shoes. She looked up. He had his hand raised and nearly looked like he might hit her. He was poised there, ready, waiting, and she felt he might do it. She braced for it.

"Hey," Jane said, coming up behind him. "Relax." Tony went into the kitchen. Jane knelt down and began to help her.

"Sorry," Sarah said.

"It's okay, it's just a glass."

She could hear Tony and Ian talking. The sound of Tony wiping his shoes.

"Did you get cut?" Jane said.

"Just a little. Mind if I wash my hands?"

"Hey, what's this?"

Sarah looked to where Jane was pointing. At her ankle. She panicked. Jane knew. Just like she'd known about the jar today. She braced herself for what was to come. Jane would tell Tony, and he'd come over, and...

"What's it supposed to be? Looks like an elephant?"

"What?"

"Your tattoo." Jane was pointing at her ankle.

"Oh, my sister and I got these once. Matching tattoos. This one's a—"

"Hey, what is this, *Days of Our Lives*?" Tony said. He threw a towel from the kitchen into Sarah's face. "Clean up the damn mess you made."

They stood up and Sarah carefully walked toward the bathroom door. She heard Jane throw away the broken glass. Inside the bathroom, she turned on the light, locked the door, and breathed relief.

Putting her ear against the door, she listened. Jane was saying something about giving Sarah a break, trying for some compassion.

Tony cut in: "Come on, what movie was on your mind today?"

"Ah yeah," Ian said, "you remember that movie with Charlton Heston, where he was supposed to play a Mexican?"

Sarah turned on the water and let it run. Quickly she bent down and took the keys out of her shoe. She nervously scanned the bathroom for a place to hide them.

They would look in the cabinet. The shower was out of the question. She'd already looked for significant cracks in the walls. The ceiling was solid planks. The broken light fixture above was a possibility. But she didn't have time to think about it.

She turned off the water.

"Yeah I did," Tony was saying, "and I told you. Marlon Brando."

"Don't be daft. Everyone knows Brando was in it. No, the woman."

"Blanche DuBois."

Opened the cabinet door. She madly searched within for crevices, cracks, any place that might hide the keys. But anyone who looked in the cabinets would be able to find them if they looked. And they'd look in here if they suspected her. They'd already removed the mouse traps and the spray.

"See, the same thing happened last time. I'm not talking about the character. By that line of thinking the woman in *Rebecca* was Rebecca. Is that right?"

What would she do if she couldn't hide them. She'd have to go back out there and get upstairs somehow.

"Nice try. That was Joan Fontaine."

"So you're saying Joan Fontaine was Rebecca?" Jane said.

"See, now you're changing the subject again."

Sarah turned on the water again. She felt panic. The clock was ticking.

"I'm not changing any subject. You just don't know the answer."

She stared at the toilet.

"Well, if I said Rebecca, would you give me the point?"

A knock on the door.

She turned to look at the wood of the door, as if eyes might be looking back at her.

"Sarah?" Jane's voice said.

Sarah rapidly went for the toilet lid. Just as she touched the cool white ceramic lid, the door began to open. She lifted the lid of the tank just a bit and dropped the keys inside.

"You okay?" Jane was just stepping inside.

In an instant, Sarah lowered the lid, flushed the toilet and turned to face Jane. She said, "Just a little cut, nothing big."

Jane was staring at her. For a couple of long seconds, they just looked at each other, silently.

"Well, don't leave the water running," Jane said at last. "Food's almost ready."

Sarah dried her hands and followed Jane back into the main room.

Ian said, "You okay or what?"

"Yes. Sorry."

"So, are you done breaking glasses?"

Sarah nodded. She had the urge to say it, thought she might hold back, but said it anyway: "I heard you talking. Rebecca was dead before the movie began." Her own voice sounded flat and dull.

Everyone looked at her. A silence seemed to grow. After an eternity, Jane broke it, smiling. "Exactly what I was getting at. Joan Fontaine played the new wife. Rebecca was the first wife. She was never in the movie."

Ian, staring at Sarah, said, "Okay."

"See, you just can't handle girl power," Jane said, moving as if to put her arm around Sarah. Sarah edged away. Jane withdrew.

"Well," Ian said, "before you tried to change the subject on me, so ol' Chuck Heston was trying to play a Mexican, right? But all it was, was this lousy paint job with shoe polish or something on his face. Which is exactly what I felt like in that poxy mask. And if there's one thing I've never wanted, it's to look like a guy with shoe polish on his face. Especially a guy with shoe polish on his face who can't smoke a bloody fag because he can't get the bloody thing in his mouth. You know how pathetic that is?"

Tony laughed. "But what's the name of the movie? That's the question."

"I can't remember."

CHAPTER 18

He leaned back in his chair. It was just after nine. Not too late, but late enough so that when Burke or someone else answered, there would be hint of concern in the air. Tomorrow would be too late for the same effect. He had to make the call tonight, for the record, knowing that at this point every text, phone call, login, parking space, and transaction would be another potential piece of evidence to law enforcement.

He took a deep breath, let it out, then dialed the number for the house line at Sarah's home in Seattle. After numerous rings, a voice answered: "This is Burke."

"This is Brandon Harris. Can I talk to Mr. Easton please?"

There was a pause. "Is this about a meeting?"

"No."

"Who are you?"

"Brandon Harris."

"Who is Brandon Harris?"

"One of Sarah's friends. It's important. It's about Sarah."

Another long pause. "Hang on, please." Brandon imagined Burke going into the library, or an office, or calling Sarah's father on another line, and the father saying no calls tonight, I'm busy, and Burke saying, I think it's important, it's about Sarah. He felt mild surprise that Burke didn't seem to recognize his name.

After what seemed like several minutes, Burke came back and said, "Brandon?"

"Yes."

"I'll transfer you to Mr. Easton now."

After three rings, the deep and deliberate voice came on the line. "Hello?"

"Hello, this is Brandon Harris. Sorry to bother you this time of night." He paused, and was met with silence. "Um, I was just calling to see how Sarah's doing."

The silence continued. Brandon could almost feel the man plotting something to say. For an instant, Brandon felt a leveling of their positions: this man must have the instructions of the ransom note on his mind, but of course he would strive to project his authority, always in control, always in command, like he was used to. Brandon briefly felt a surge of power, even a trace of pity. Finally, Easton said, "Honestly, I haven't seen her for a while. You likely know more about her than I do."

Brandon felt the doubt creep in. He'd expected Easton to lie and tell him Sarah was there, that she was just resting, or something to make it look like business as usual. "No, I haven't seen her since she went up there on Thursday. She said she's not feeling well. Is she okay?"

"Well, it sounds like Sarah's already spoken to you. As I said, you seem to know more than I do, Brandon."

"But, it was last night she called me," Brandon said, feeling the doubt. The more he said, the more he could sense Easton contemplating, trying to reconcile things. Burke was probably listening, probably recording the call. Brandon had to remain confused, concerned, unaware of anything. He put a measure of worry, even hurt, into his voice. "Sorry, when she called, I guess I thought it had been from there." That felt better, but he still wondered what Easton's response to Becca had been earlier. What had he told her? The same thing? That he hadn't seen Sarah?

"Maybe you should try her on her cell, then," Easton said.

"Well, we've tried, I've tried. We can't get through."

"Believe me," Easton said, "if there's something wrong with Sarah, then I'd be worried too, but as far as I know, she's fine."

"Okay. Well, just thought I'd try. If you do see her, can you let her know I called?"

"I will, Brandon. Thanks for calling."

Brandon stood up and breathed relief. He could fake backstories, create timelines, invent characters and outwit nearly anyone, but talking with her father felt both surreal and—for lack of a better word: familiar. Perhaps it was because when he'd talked with him it had usually been about Sarah, and he could sense that he was manipulating actual bonds and connections, and that created a sense of guilt.

He'd felt that way since the first time. Sarah had invited Brandon and a couple of friends over for dinner to the house in Seattle. During dinner, they'd all been in awe of her father's great stories, about Africa, climbing K2, taking part in a balloon race, surviving a major storm while sailing in the Pacific, the hotels he'd bought on a tip from a legless war refugee in a Bangkok bar. Afterward, staff took away the dishes, the other friends left, Sarah went upstairs to do something, and Easton invited Brandon into an adjoining room with a big fireplace. They sat down and he offered a cigar. At the time, Brandon had wondered if this was intentional, a cliche wealthy mansion move just to see if Brandon would buy into it.

Conversation had begun pleasantly. Chit chat about college and life aspirations had led to questions about Brandon's family, his background. Brandon had been prepared. He'd stuck to his manufactured storyline. But things had become tense when Easton asked Brandon about his intentions with Sarah. He'd suggested to Brandon in thinly veiled terms that Sarah seemed to be going through a phase, a certain empty-headed attraction to opposites that rich girls have to go through, just like her near-decision to drop out of private school and go to public halfway through high school, all because of her desire to fit in with each and every one of her friends.

But there is something about background, he'd said to Brandon. Where you come from is who you are. Everyone in America is middle class, it's just a matter of where, and there are pitfalls with hanging out with someone entirely outside your league. Expectations are different, realities scramble things. Spring break doesn't mean some beach in Florida, it means Barbados or Côte d'Azur. Now, Sarah, she wants to do the right thing. Her heart's always been in the right place, but she's still a kid, in a way. She's stuck in a dichotomy of growing up with money, and yet hating wealth.

It was as if Brandon's created story about coming from an upper middle-class background was a simple charade, easily challenged and easily destroyed. Probing questions over Brandon's academic potential, future plans, and his past began to eat at his storylines, and Brandon, already deflated, found himself compensating, letting his insecurities show. *Who was your father again? What line of work was he in? Where did you say in*

L.A.? When the question had formed in the air that maybe Brandon would follow in his father's footsteps, "doing whatever it was he did" despite the part about going to Berkeley and his position at a well-regarded software startup, Brandon felt his temper flare. He knew it was because he'd worked hard to maintain the artificial history, yet her father was slowly closing in on working the actual humble details out of him.

But when Brandon had tried to recover his footing, glad the room was dark and hoping his nervousness wasn't visible in the firelight, he felt a sharp pang of bitterness, knowing full well that his resentment partly came down to his realization that inwardly, secretly, he admired this man. He was a complete contrast with his own father.

Easton seemed to sense the anger in Brandon, and in so many words told him to relax, that the reason he felt like he could put Brandon on the spot was because Brandon's relationship with his father sounded a lot like that with his own father. At that moment, something clicked. Before he'd had time to flesh it out, Sarah had come into the room. Suddenly Easton changed completely, throwing out something about the Mariners, as though he and Brandon had been talking sports or the weather the whole time.

Later that evening, alone, after hours had passed, Brandon had quietly smiled. Her father was obviously a man who was overcompensating. Rigid in his beliefs, staunchly defending a daughter he rarely saw. The convictions he judged on only a handshake could be quite mistaken, and it occurred to Brandon that he towed the tough protective father line only because that's what his station in life demanded. As if to compensate for not really knowing Sarah that well, when it all came down to it. As if to compensate for not having known Tracy that well either. And she'd died without him being able to rectify that. He was making up for Tracy by guarding Sarah, in his own distant, corporate way. It was an approach that one might have picked up reading a manual about raising a troubled rich girl: a list of items to be checked off every time a threatening male figure entered her life.

That first night had been far more valuable than he'd realized at the time. Her father measured Brandon up and down, and concluded he was invisible, a nobody, someone to be ignored and forgotten. Sarah was just going through a phase, lovestruck with someone outside her league, but it would pass. That night Brandon had learned the rigid personality traits of a man who was convinced he always had the upper hand.

When he had written the first draft of the ransom demand and the accompanying terms of the exchange to place in her father's office, he'd kept those rigid personality traits in mind. He'd given the demand note to Mike so that he could record Sarah reading it. That first visit had given him enough time to ascertain the layout and locations of rooms, where Sarah's personal effects were in her room, the staff that came and went, and which hallways and crannies they crawled in and out of, where desks and drawers and wardrobes were, where her father and Burke had their offices.

But he didn't like talking to the man. He was glad it was over. He knew there would be countless conversations with him in the future as the investigation began.

CHAPTER 19

It was gloomy outside. The skies were overcast, and the diminished light in her room was noticeable. There were sounds downstairs, things being moved around, raised voices.

When Sarah awoke the first thought on her mind was that no one last night had mentioned anything about the knife incident. No one had said anything about her attempt to take it. Had they mentioned it to Ian, and it just hadn't come up last night? It was possible. But unlikely. They'd been too happy, too drunk last night. Tony and Jane hadn't said anything to Ian. They'd screwed up while the boss had been gone. They'd been in charge of the prisoner, and had turned their backs and the prisoner had taken advantage of an opportunity. Naturally they'd have had no incentive to tell Ian. They'd been screwing, and probably wanted to keep things nice and quiet.

She heard Ian say something. And Jane answer: "I wish you wouldn't say that."

"It's just a joke, relax," Tony said.

"Well it makes you sound really crass. More than usual even."

Ian said, "Oh come on, we're just having a go at you."

"Well look at yourself. Wasn't your own mother a half wit? Isn't that what you told me your dad thought?"

Ian said, "Well I didn't think so. Dad was stern, that's all. He got stuff done." He flicked his bracelet several times.

"That's what I'm saying, it shows."

"What, you live in London for six months and you got my whole family history down?"

"You know," Tony said, "listening to you two sometimes, I wonder why you don't just go for it, knives and all. Just get it done with."

Ian said, "It could come to that. I think she's got cabin fever. She's moody and isolated. Away from all that she loves. Away from her impoverished Charles. The poor guy, irritated with his wife's sluttish antics, his sunburned back under the hot sun, toiling away on the pig farm they built together. Opens a can of instant karma and—"

Jane faced Tony. "You know he was scared of his daddy?"

"What."

"Yeah," Jane said. "Didn't like that he was a budding intellectual. Wanted him to be a rugby player, but he was too thin, too girlish, too smart. Wasn't it around age ten he found your hand-written book, your take on the history of England, with the queen in lingerie and something about—"

"Grand ambitions, woman. I found my path."

"Oh?"

"Yeah."

"So is this it? Your path?"

"Sure, I just don't need organic food and Indian ragas to get there."

There was a silence. Sarah listened intently.

Ian continued. "Yes, see how easily summed up you are? The perpetual college student who never finishes, the woman who never gets pregnant, the one who hates her own country, the one who wants to rewrite her own history. Live in the moment, forever, always in your twenties. Always wondering—"

"Um, hate to butt in here," Tony said, "but anyone seen my keys?"

"What keys," Ian said sternly.

"The key ring."

"I saw 'em yesterday."

"I know, so did I," Tony said. "They were in the pack."

"Well that's where you'd find them then."

"So you think that's the reason I'm asking? Or would it help to mention they're not in there?"

Sarah got out of bed, stepping on the silent zones of the floor. She went to the edge of the square but remained out of sight. She crouched down, listening. She could feel the electricity in the air.

"Well why do you need 'em?"

"I don't, I'm just saying, what if the aristocrat up there got ahold of them?"

There was a silence. Sarah wondered whether Jane had moved out of the room.

"You know," Ian said, "it sort of occurs to me."

There were hushed tones. Then whispering began, and soon an entire conversation came and went. She caught none of it. But as soon as it had ended, she heard the noises of objects being picked up, things moving across the floor, being lifted, overturned, put back.

She was nervous, but ecstatic. She had caused them to scurry around like ants down there, panicked that she might have the keys. But it was one thing to get the key. The question was, did it match a car out there. She'd seen the SUV come and go. That's what Ian used whenever he left. She thought she'd heard another car once or twice, but wasn't sure now. She was pretty sure there was another car, just out of sight, just out of her range of view from her window. And the curtains on the windows downstairs kept her from seeing it from below.

She wondered what the other two keys were for. Maybe an outbuilding of some kind. Maybe the front door of the cabin itself. Maybe that house in Seattle in Queen Anne.

Today was the fourth—third—no, fourth day of this.

Was it?

She was briefly mortified. Yes, it was the fourth day. The third full day. How long was it supposed to go on? Ian had made it sound like he wanted a quick resolution. But what was going on elsewhere? By now Brandon and Cheryl would have been in touch somehow. Hopefully they would have called each other and started something. The gears might be rolling.

She suddenly became aware of the silence. The furniture moving had stopped. The muffled conversation had stopped. No more whispering.

She stood up. The silence was now uncomfortable. Seconds passed.

"SARAH!" Tony's voice.

She felt herself jump backward. She watched the square, waiting.

Then, the sounds of his hands on the ladder. The shape of his head suddenly emerging. She watched as he stood there, a couple of rungs up the ladder, struck again at how his head appeared to be resting gently on the floor, with no body attached. The last time she'd seen this scene, he'd been Halloween.

The head on the floor moved, looking around, blue eyes scanning. He scanned the cot, the space under it, the desk, the table, all across the floor, the windows. When he was finished, his eyes settled on her, and the cot. He made sure to pass his eyes over her, up and down, before looking at her face again. When he did, he simply stared into her eyes. She stared back. Silent seconds passed, and with each one, she felt increasingly uncomfortable. Finally she had to turn away.

"Top of the morning to you," he said. "Wonder if you could come downstairs. A little business."

She didn't say anything, not knowing what to do. He was blocking the way if he wanted her to go downstairs. She didn't want to get close to him.

"Come on, little one, now," he said with a little more force. His head floated off the floor as he began to climb up through the square.

She got up hastily. Suddenly the dimensions of the room seemed to shrink, just her and him alone. It was the first time she'd truly felt helpless around any of them. This was different than before. The way he looked at her, his expression. It wasn't so much threatening as weird, a feeling that he could suddenly morph into something other than what he was. She felt herself retreat as he got closer, now standing at the edge of the square. She could see that smirk sitting there.

She edged past him. As she climbed down, she heard him laugh at her, and glanced back enough to see him on his hands and knees, beginning to search her space. Ian and Jane were at the bottom of the ladder. Ian had his arms crossed. The dogs were standing near the door, staring at her with curiosity as she descended. As though everyone, including the dogs, were about to accuse her.

"Your highness," Ian said. "Mind if I ask you a question?" His voice was excessively calm. He casually scratched the side of his nose. Jane leaned against the counter. A mug of coffee was nearby.

"You didn't happen to pull a little stunt last night, did you? Breaking that wine glass like that?" He flicked his chain. The locket in the middle, which she had never seen up close, appeared and disappeared.

"What?"

"Maybe use that to create a little distraction?"

She could hear Tony upstairs, turning things over, getting rough about it. She had known this would happen. She did her best to avoid looking directly into Ian's eyes.

"Sorry about the glass, it just—it dropped."

"And you got a little cut."

"A little. It's okay."

"A little cut, yes. And when it broke, you didn't, say, find something near all those little broken shards, did you?"

"What do you mean."

"So you haven't heard us down here for the last fifteen minutes?"

She shook her head. "No. I just got up."

"And I was just elected president."

Sarah looked at him blankly.

"Kind of surprising, considering I'm not even a citizen, and I can't even run. The honor was sort of bestowed upon me. Isn't that interesting?"

Discomfort mounting. "I heard you talking about keys and moving things around, but I don't know what keys you mean."

"You're the crafty and sly type, aren't you. In your own way."

"No, I'm just—"

"Just the basic model, entry-level? What, no added features? No upgrades, extra modules? You don't like to be considered intelligent? Maybe not Harvard like your dad wanted, but U.C. Berkeley's not bad." Ian stepped closer, stared at her purposefully, his face less than an inch from hers. "Do you have the keys? Yes or no will suffice."

"I'm sorry, I don't know what the keys even look like."

Ian sighed. He turned to Jane. "Right, go ahead."

Jane looked at her. "Sarah, you mind undressing? We can do it in the bathroom if you want."

"What?"

"I need to search you."

"Search me?"

Ian said, "Either that or you tell us right now where they are."

"Where what are?"

"Get in the bathroom."

She looked at Jane. Jane held the bathroom door open. Sarah reluctantly walked through. Jane followed her in, then closed the door.

Sarah said, "Why are we doing this?"

"Just take them off."

"But—"

"What, you think I like this? Come on. Let's get it over with."

Sarah turned away from Jane and began unbuttoning the top of her pajamas. When she was done, she let the top fall to the floor. She stood there, feeling tense. The air felt cold on her bare skin.

"Come on. Everything. Hurry up."

Sarah slowly slid everything else off, feeling awkward and uncomfortable. When Jane asked her to turn around, she did. Jane used her hands to explore every part of her, and did not hesitate to search the same place more than once. Her hands were soft, she noticed, trying to turn her mind away from the thought. She wondered how things might go if she had the razor, or the knife, something to somehow hold Jane hostage, then make demands on the other two. But how ludicrous. She, naked, with a tiny little razor, trying to use Jane as a hostage.

Would they even care what happened to Jane, anyway? After that little conversation earlier, it wasn't easy to say. In any case, so she used a razor or knife on Jane. What then? Sarah would stand there naked trying to make a demand, with a little razor at Jane's throat. They'd probably start laughing. There would be that wry smile from Tony. Then he'd lunge.

A sudden thought flashed in her mind. Where did Tony keep his gun? She hadn't seen it much, since they'd made the second video.

"Okay," Jane said, "get dressed."

Sarah reached down to get her clothes. She could hear the sounds of Tony overturning things upstairs. The floor squeaked heavily under his feet and things were crashing around.

Jane began to open the door. She turned and said in a low voice. "I hope you're not hiding them, I mean on you, you know."

"What?"

"Fine!" Jane hissed. Her expression suddenly changed, as if she'd just been hit. "You lying bitch." She left, nearly slamming the door.

Sarah reached up to lock the door. As she tried to slide the lock into place, she saw that the bolt had been removed. *God, they know everything*

I'm thinking. The regular latch was still in place, but the bolt was gone. She couldn't lock it anymore. She had no real privacy left.

She turned on the water and washed her hands. Letting the water run, she flushed the toilet. As the water was gurgling and the tank filling up, she carefully lifted the lid enough to see inside. There, in the murky water rising within the tank, was the ring of three keys she'd hidden last night.

After allowing herself a brief glance, she immediately replaced the lid, taking care to edge her fingers along both sides so it would slide into place without making any noise.

She turned off the faucet. Then she went straight for the ladder.

CHAPTER 20

In the early days of the project—the design—Brandon built a schematic to help him search for the perfect alibi host. It was during October, when the pieces of this complex model really started moving. He'd built most of the framework long before, fashioning it with parts and leftovers of various projects he'd created to streamline workflows with complex sets of variables.

When he viewed it on his two monitors, he could track the flow of information and progress across multiple dimensions including time, people, communications, and actions. It had several layers which could be laid on top of others, allowing for multiple outcomes to unfold per decision, or to model what-ifs based on input criteria.

The first broad action showed completed: create a bogus survey about daily commuting preferences. Advertise the survey in Craigslist. Make it appear to be from a local county transportation department in partnership with some local universities. Promise a gift card for honest responses. User information will not be used for anything, but is required for eligibility and to distribute the gift cards. After eliminating bogus or useless respondents, he had entered all 17 potentials into the design flow. They were all professionals who commuted to the Bay Area for work (by targeting commuters he was able follow them and monitor their schedules.)

Another completed action included the creation of two fake websites to make the survey and the study seem legitimate. He knew there was a chance of the ad or the fake sites being discovered by the mentioned universities or the county, but he assigned a small risk score to the possibility.

On another part of the schematic flow, for each candidate he input information gleaned from their LinkedIn or professional profiles. Another part received their social media details, and from that any work connections or their presence on their employers' websites, indicating their physical work locations. That allowed him to follow them, and for some, to discover where they lived. These starting points opened up a myriad of other spying opportunities, and he had a rich starting point since many of them openly showed their friends, family members, colleagues, educational history, workplaces, hobbies, relationships, interests and timelines on their social media pages. Each category of information went to its assigned spot on the workflow.

He input several factors for each candidate once he had established their routines and found a way to enter their homes, which he was able to do about half the time. If there were computers, tablets or phones he would attempt to break in using password guesses based on his review of their lives and social engineering nudges that he had started early on with each person based on information they had provided in the survey.

When the attributes that best suited an alibi host became evident and lines of the various candidates began to converge, he was able to isolate winners. He narrowed these qualities down to a perfect loner type. A single guy, unattached. An uncomplicated working stiff who shuffled mostly between home and day job. Someone without any obvious red flags, nothing flashy, an everyman who could blend into the background and not stand out. Someone with a routine, a professional who was busy, gone a lot, and lived alone. Social interactions minimal. Someone whose background could be cobbled together from college and high school records, whose hometowns, proms, weddings and life events would show up on some kind of radar. Someone with a mediocre financial situation, ideally with a decent amount of debt, someone who didn't pay attention to every single transaction, or monitor his credit. Someone without a major criminal record.

All of these lines and grids pointed to one final alibi host: Adam Liddy.

When he'd decided on Liddy, he adjusted the inputs of the model to shape someone who was not just a loner, but a loner with some hidden issues around women. These issues would be evidenced by an awkwardness around girls and women growing up, as shown in various shreds of evidence that would be found in the closet of his apartment, where he kept some of his childhood possessions and memories, or in a box in the garage of the home he grew up in in Idaho, or in his desk drawer right there in his apartment, in documents or thumb drives or on his computer. This awkwardness would show up in his professional life, as indicated in documents from his work history. He would have observations about women, collections of images, videos, porn, deep fakes, celebrity profiles. Evidence of his infatuation would be scattered across his entries in a private journal, notes and interactions on dark corners of the web, comments in online sexual fantasy forums and discussion groups. The suggestion of this discomfort could be seen through innuendo or documentation, at his various jobs over the years, as shown in certain documents to be found on his electronic devices or in his apartment someday, like the letter from a past employer's HR department documenting "unprofessional conduct" and a warning, or the note from another previous employer highlighting "discomfort with female authority figures" and a remediation plan. Along with these documents would be Adam's notes: the way he had kept these letters all these years for the day he would get back at them, the way he'd get even with these intrusive charlatans. Women would start treating him better. They would understand him eventually. The women who had so negatively affected his career and had ignored him or questioned his character would not be forgotten. He knew where some of them worked. He knew about their lives.

Part of this complex with women would show up in his fascination with celebrities, particularly the ones most in the limelight. These actresses, singers, influencers and socialites were always online and in the media. He would have a vast collection of saved images from websites, screenshots, photos he'd taken in public, along with histories and observations, various internet searches looking up where these women lived, the places in L.A. or the Bay Area, the beaches and hotels and restaurants and nightclubs where they hung out. He'd have notes about their schedules, the places they'd show up for arrivals or photo shoots or rehearsals, the conventions, signings, fundraising events, or casting trials.

Brandon had created every note, photo, collection, observation and internet search and had placed them amongst Liddy's physical and virtual spaces over time.

Much of his knowledge of Liddy had begun with the survey but rose exponentially when he'd been able to gain entry to his laptop. With some password-guessing, passive social engineering and using Liddy's Apple ID and keychain, Brandon obtained copies of his tax return, which gave his income, bank accounts, social security number, and asset information. He found his birth date in the contacts list; various websites such as Amazon contained his order histories; bookmarks and visited websites were visible in the browser history; this history included online banking, subscriptions, utilities and internet plans, places of interest, maps, things he'd searched for —a broad spotlight into his life.

From this trove of data, and the drawers of the desk, the books on the shelves, documents in the apartment, Brandon had nearly everything he needed from Adam Liddy. The only thing Adam Liddy himself was missing was a motive.

Then Brandon began the gradual process of manipulating histories and adjusting timelines. He slowly turned Adam Liddy, at least the one based on documents, photos, and other details, into someone with a more sinister character underlying the quiet exterior: someone with the motivation to commit a crime, someone smart enough to try to cover the evidence, but not smart enough to do it well. A man with a documented and twisted sense of discomfort around women, morphing over the years into an unhealthy obsession. A man who might put something together in the back of his mind one day, pondering, thinking about his debt, and the way it defines him as he approaches middle age. A man who, while browsing the web one day and seeing the pretty hotel heiress in the news again because of the relentless paparazzi, might have the flashing thought occur to him: what if he kidnapped her, literally just grabbed her off the street, out of the blue, and held her for ransom? Asked for millions of dollars for her safe return?

The research had taken weeks. Some of the work had been boring and monotonous, like the repetitive visits and stalkings during the daily grinds, following along with a careful eye on Liddy several rows ahead or half a block ahead in a crowd. There were endless mornings spent hanging out near Liddy's Oakland apartment in the morning, waiting for the man to come out and catch the bus to the BART station.

Some had been rewarding. He had driven to Billings to visit the childhood home. He'd taken his time, enjoying the drive and stopping at a couple of spots to check out brewpubs and to do some fly fishing. He had obtained a certain amount of information, under various guises, from Liddy's high school, and from the resort where he'd worked during his summers. He'd placed some of the incriminating documents and photos in Liddy's childhood home, that generic 70s rambler in a bland suburban cul-de-sac. Getting in had been easy enough, with the back door unlocked; during a midmorning rendezvous, he had quietly entered, placed a few samples amongst some of the boyhood nostalgia in the basement, and left.

Some had been thrilling, like the time on his way out of Liddy's apartment, assuming he still had an hour or more window, when the man himself showed up early, getting his mail in the lobby and coming home. They had passed each other quickly as Brandon was leaving, and though Brandon had looked down, for an instant they had locked eyes.

CHAPTER 21

Ian called up and announced that she could get something to eat if she wanted.

She was sitting on the floor, amongst the ruins of her confine. It was a disaster. She contemplated not answering Ian, but thought better of it. And she had to admit, she was hungry. She cautiously went down the ladder, not sure what she'd encounter. She hoped she could just get something and go back upstairs and be alone.

The room was tidy, though the furniture was slightly rearranged from this morning's rough search for the keys. The wine bottles from last night were neatly stacked by the front door. There were two bagels on the counter and two or three halves of buttered toast.

The atmosphere in the kitchen area was awkward and uncomfortable. Ian was doing something with a leather attaché case on the coffee table. She noticed that his bracelet was off. It was lying on the table. Before she could get a look at it, he picked it up and slid it on, rustling the chain.

"That's breakfast," he said flatly without looking at her. "Take it or leave it."

Tony was at the main table, eating cereal, toast, and drinking coffee. Jane was on the sofa, with her legs curled under her, reading a hardcover book. A little carton of milk was next to her coffee mug on the table.

Sarah took one of the bagels, which was hard, probably leftovers from yesterday. She drank some water, using one of the cups on the counter.

"Mind if I eat upstairs?" she asked.

"What are you waiting for?" Ian said.

Before she left, she took a slice of toast as well, then climbed the ladder, glad to be alone. After a few minutes, she heard the front door opening.

"What time you getting back?" Jane's voice said.

Ian said, "I don't know, depends how long this stuff takes. Probably by dark."

"Hey."

"Yeah?"

"Sorry about this morning. All that stuff."

"You're a nasty piece of work."

"Drive carefully." The door closed. The SUV started, and faded away.

Sarah looked around her room. It was complete mayhem. Tony had overturned her mattress. The sleeping bag and blanket were on the floor. The cot frame was on its side. The night stand was knocked over. The drawer had been removed and its contents dumped onto the floor. Everything was wiped off the desk, scattered across the floor in chaos and dust. Her clothes were tossed everywhere. Looking at this scene, she felt angry and violated. But there was something else. There was a certain measure of sadness. This was her room. Her living quarters. Her personal space. And it was in ruins. It had been totally gutted. She felt like she could cry when she pondered the work it would take to restore it to the way it had been. Dust had been kicked up everywhere, making her sneeze and her eyes water.

She started with the clothes, putting them back in the duffel bag. Putting the drawer back in the night stand and replacing the contents. Putting the cot back on its four legs, and the mattress, blanket and sleeping bag on top of it. As she put things away, the room began to look as it had. When she was done with the cot and night stand, she stood with her hands on her hips and stared at the array of junk from the desk.

First she moved the desk up against the wall. The one wobbly leg looked like it might cause the desk to tip over. She pictured putting all the old newspapers and magazines and fuses and wires back on top, just to have it all pitch onto the floor again when the leg gave way. She struggled to wedge it up against the wall, and as she did, noticed the way the wobbly leg was held by a couple of loose screws, pushed in from the top of the desk. It looked like it had been repaired at some point. She shook it, judging how much effort it would take to remove it. It would make a decent weapon if she did. But she couldn't risk doing anything stupid right now. She picked up the stuff from the floor in big armfuls and tossed it onto the desk.

When she was done, she sat on the cot and took a bite of the cold toast. She had the keys, hidden in the toilet. Now what? One of them was a car key, but what did it belong to? Not the SUV. Ian would've mentioned something when Tony brought it up. She knew there was probably another car outside, but who knew, it could be an old junker that wouldn't start. She'd only seen the tail end of it, and that wasn't enough to see what shape it was in or what model it was or how old it was. The key didn't look that old. In any case, they'd made a major fuss over the missing keys. That could be because the key was for the car outside. Or maybe they needed the other keys on the ring for something. A shed or outbuilding with something vital in it, a padlock.

She heard the bed downstairs creaking.

She put her hands over her ears. But she could still hear the sounds. It was like every other time. She detested the fact that she had to listen to them, unable to shut it out. She kept visualizing the two of them down there, and like every time, she felt a small sense of guilt, as though she was invading their space. She told herself the opposite was true, that they were invading hers. But when the sounds came, so did the images. She tried to put it out of her mind, to think about something mundane, going to a doctor appointment and sitting in the waiting room staring at the wall, at an eye chart or a picture of a muscle. But her mind always drifted toward the bed below.

She wished she had a door, some kind of covering, over the square. She pressed her hands tighter over her ears and felt herself begin to cry. She stopped herself, struggling to remain silent, and floated into a loose misery between crying and not crying.

Staring at the square, she suddenly realized she was wasting time. She had a chance to do something while they were distracted. All their time screwing down there was a missed opportunity. They were busy. She could get the desk leg off. She could use her leftover toast to bribe the dogs, maybe get into the bathroom and get the keys. Somehow she could get outside and try it on whatever car it fit.

But I don't even know if the key's for the car out there. I can't just go out there and if it doesn't work come back in. It's a one-way deal, success or failure.

I could try for another knife.

If nothing else, I could just get the keys and have them up here with me.

No. Look what happened earlier. Tony had turned over every object up here to find them. He hadn't. But if they'd been up here, and he'd found them, I'd be fucked now.

The creaking and moaning continued. She picked up the toast, and tiptoed toward the square using only the silent zones. The floor creaked once, and she stepped back, marking the spot in her mind. She was continually improving her knowledge of the silent zones. Fanning out from the square in rows, toward the windows on each end of the room, the nails in the floors marked the boundaries. The floor made the least noise near the square, and she carefully used this moderately quiet zone to approach the ladder.

The moaning stopped. They shifted around on the bed. Then it began again.

At the square she went down two rungs, then dipped her head down to look. She glanced around for the dogs but couldn't see them. They must be inside somewhere, she guessed somewhere by the door. She had the toast ready to toss. She went down another rung. The moaning stopped. She froze and waited. When it started again, she slowly lowered herself another. She was one from the floor. From there, she could go into the bathroom. As she was about to make the final push, she heard the tinkle of a dog collar. Her nerves suddenly on alert, she saw one of the dogs suddenly raising its head from behind the sofa, near the wood stove. So that's where it had been. She got the toast ready.

But the way the dog was looking at her, with a tentative expression, ears up, curious, it almost seemed happy. The other dog was out of sight, but if this one was in the main room, she assumed the other must be in the bedroom, or under the table. With hope, she tossed the toast in its direction. The dog's eyes followed as it flew quietly through the air and landed a few feet away. It bent down and ate it in two bites, licked its lips and continued to look at her. Its soft brown eyes and calm expression were hypnotic. She could see a certain eagerness, almost a playful look. As she stared, she noticed its gaze shift slightly to the side. Then the eyes darted back toward her. Then again to the side. This time, its ears also seemed to relax a little, then perk up again. Sarah felt herself smile. This dog was shy! The bloodthirsty persona Ian had tried to portray was fake. She could picture the dog rolling over if she approached, wanting her to scratch its belly. With a little snack in her hands and the right approach, she could get past this dog if she had to.

But her reverie ended when she realized that the creaking from the bedroom had stopped. She quickly pondered her options. They might just be shifting positions. They'd be at it again and she'd have another few minutes. She had a chance now to go back up the ladder, if she was quick. If they were finished, they would probably get up and do whatever needed to be done around the place before Ian got back.

But as she stared at the dog, she saw the gaze for what it was. It was not that it was shy. Its eyes were focused on something, but not her. It seemed to focus on the space behind her. Feeling optimism fade, she slowly turned.

Jane was there. Naked except for a towel she was holding in front of her midsection, she was standing in the bedroom doorway, looking directly at

Sarah. Sarah stood on the ladder, frozen, feeling the fear overtake her, knowing that Jane would call Tony from the bedroom. She started to close her eyes and wait for the inevitable.

But to her surprise, Jane put a finger to her lips and indicated the square above with an upward glance. Sarah took the hint and quickly scaled the ladder.

CHAPTER 22

Brandon had never really set out to target Sarah. In a way, she had simply fallen into the victim role, just as Tracy had fallen out of it. His efforts with Tracy had abruptly ended after her climbing accident, and it was only later, after the funeral, after the condolences, after some time, that he gained a wide enough perspective to see some of the mistakes he'd made.

The women he'd researched before Tracy ranged from movie stars and corporate executives to B-list wannabes. Even a couple of lottery winners. All were wealthy. Some were famous. Others were known only in their social or professional circles. With each level of fame and status came a different level of accessibility.

Early on, Tracy had felt unique. He had heard about her in the way most people knew about Tracy. At the time, she was 21. She'd been a fixture in the rags and in the social circles of the coastal celebrity culture since high school. There were appearances at L.A. nightclubs, when the cameras would catch her and her celebrity companions; the inflammatory tweets; a couple of much-publicized arrests; the drunken escapades in Italy; the affair with the much-older tennis star; the reality show she was in occasionally. For a while, she had her own video channel. She had hundreds of thousands of followers on social media.

Her world intersected with the world of cameras and glitz, but as a hotel magnate's daughter instead of a bonafide star, she was just outside the main celebrity fray. Yet it was obvious she was surrounded by the same hangers-on, enablers and yes-men. He saw a solitary figure somewhere within that cadre, someone surrounded by hundreds but with few apparent friends. He had spotted that vulnerability and used it as a beginning. At first it was mild flattery on social media. Then manufactured accounts of being at the same parties and conjured evidence of the same circles of friends. Then offering to help her when she needed away from watching eyes, offering his time for anything she needed. At first it was connections to people, things or drugs, but later it was conversation. He greased the latter connection by mentioning how he'd grown up around an equestrian lifestyle, the horses his family owned on Bainbridge, the races he'd done, the nickname he had for his favorite Arabian. He had known full well that most of Tracy's riding days were behind her due to lack of interest and the rigors of her relatively empty lifestyle, but by appealing to her professed love of animals and using the equine connection, he'd been able to reach a side of her that she'd obviously learned to hide from nearly everyone else. From there he'd adapted to her moods one session at a time.

In so many ways, she was a lot easier than Sarah. Tracy had been—how else to put it—simple. Sarah was more probing and inquisitive, and he couldn't just slip facts to her and hope they'd stick. He would have to follow through. Sarah would ponder the implications. Why did that happen? Whose name is that on the invitation? When did they arrive? What are the reasons for this or that? She needed integrated logic to build up a confirmation. He had to keep up. Even though he was good at ad libbing, with her he always had to have facts at the ready.

And though he thought he had gotten to know Tracy fairly well, he soon realized with Sarah that none of that mattered. The little nuggets he'd gleaned from his time with Tracy were not transferable. Sure, they were sisters. They'd grown up together and had many of the same experiences. They had some common interests. They had a father who was gone a lot when they were little, and was distant even when he had been there. The mother had exited the picture at some point with another man. There were familiar servants and staff, and private schools, and limousines, and the place in New Hampshire, the summers in Long Island, and all the "ultra wealthy" gambits in life. But they were completely different personalities. Sarah was much more cautious. The thinker of the two. Didn't care much for the limelight. Went to college and actually studied. Had some vision of a career. But the misfortunes in her life—Tracy's death, the absent father, the absent mother, the lack of a hearth—had left a void. Perhaps it was the same void Tracy had, but while Tracy had filled that need with parties and escapism, Sarah filled it with questions, seeking connections, wanting no loose ends.

With Tracy out of the picture, he had a clean slate to improve his backstory, keeping the parts that worked, removing the parts that didn't. At the funeral, Sarah had only vaguely recognized him. It had taken another introduction for her to even recognize his name. Brand new. Brand new Brandon.

Once he got a sight on Sarah's situation, he found a comfortable zone, and once again meticulously edged his way in. Early on he saw some of the gaps he'd overlooked with Tracy. For one thing, he hadn't even thought of using someone for hire to assist in the kidnapping.

Another was the personal angle. It had been clear early on that Sarah was not involved with anyone. He had presented himself as a sympathetic understander should she ever want to talk. He could identify with her pain, he'd said, because his younger brother died when he was younger. They'd exchanged numbers, and texted now and then. They had lunch a couple times. They met on the waterfront once or twice. During one of those midday sessions, he asked Sarah if she'd like to see the Arabian that he kept on Bainbridge, that he had grown up around horses but hadn't had time for anything equestrian once he got into grad school and started his career in software development. Would she like to see it? An affirmative response that day meant quick lessons in riding and finding a place on Bainbridge with an Arabian. He approached the owner of a stable where suitable horses were kept and presented himself as an agent for an ad agency that wanted to shoot a commercial and needed some horses. Riding lessons and several questions got him up to speed on terminology and the layout of the stable. He had known about Tracy's Appaloosa on Bainbridge, and sure enough, upon hearing his suggestion, Sarah offered to show him her own horses and suggested combining both efforts.

"He likes you," he'd said after they'd walked around the grounds. They'd stopped by the fence where the chestnut brown Arabian had edged its nose toward Sarah. As she stroked the horses's neck with one hand and held a crop in the other, Brandon reached out to brush aside some strands of hair that had fallen over Sarah's eye in the breeze. His lips met hers.

It hadn't been particularly difficult after that to increase her attraction to him. He'd pretend to enjoy it, if that's what it took, and if it seemed to please her. He found those weak spots and gaps in her, the needs and longings and the what-ifs, and did what he could to satisfy them. He'd do things with her, or decline to, when the time was right. Agree with her, challenge her, hold a mirror to her. He would lead, or follow, as situations changed. He'd let her study his hands in the dark, the way she liked to. Or whatever else she liked to do or have done.

One thing he knew for sure, and it had been the case with Tracy just as it was now with Sarah. He had no hesitation framing it in the simplest possible terms: the plan had to work. On most days he projected an image and to the maximum extent possible, lived it completely. But sometimes, during quiet moments alone, or when he was immersed in the economics of the project—the design—he could see the stark reality that lay beneath the illusion. Even if he forgot it momentarily, all it took was a look around his apartment to lay it bare. He lived in a high-end unit, in a high-end building, in a pricy part of an expensive city. It was one part of a larger impression that he had carefully manicured. He subscribed to an attire service and kept a few tailored suits in his closet. His tennis racket, golf clubs, and downhill skis were top of the line. He kept a newer Land Rover in the parking garage below. He spent plenty on travel, often with Sarah, or common friends.

The monthly bills for the apartment, the car, entertainment, clothing subscriptions, the rotating art pieces, travel, eating out—the whole lifestyle that went with hanging out with an income bracket that he'd attached himself to—far exceeded anything he made, or was worth. He interacted with people from work or school and the fellow students with whom he'd formed various levels of friendship, and with those relationships came rounds of golf, weekends in Aspen or Vale, getaways to the Caribbean or Europe, and of course the weekly sailing gigs with Sarah and her friends, the high-priced nightclubs, the discreet restaurants where the movers and shakers and entertainers dined. There were expensive membership fees and club dues. To most of his acquaintances, these were baseline costs, part of a lifestyle that went with a certain station in life, a long-term income and position in society. For them, it was all casually transactional. Incidental expenses like these were as much a non-issue for them as buying junk food or video games or weed had been for him as a teen growing up middle class in Van Nuys. Something you didn't have to think much about, or save up for.

It was all part of an investment. The people he hung out with had all grown up with a certain level of luxury, whether it was cars, houses, trips or obsessions. They lived it and were living it and would pass it onto whatever offspring they produced. They were mostly in the upper echelons of whatever bracket they adhered to, for tax purposes—mostly "reluctant ultra wealthy" as Sarah described herself and her friends. They lived their lives with a set of basic expectations. Although every single one of them would insist they were middle class, changes in the economy were not an issue; their long-term financial goals were similar to that of their parents: graduation from a good university with a nice degree, and placement in a good firm or appointments on boards were a given; a certain ownership of second homes, real estate, investments and the accoutrements that went along with these were standard issue.

But Brandon had bought his way in, on credit. Most of what he paid for —the trips, the rent, the car, the expensive bar tabs—were on borrowed cash or creative financing. He skimmed a fair amount from the accounts and identities of people he tracked online or in person, and he moved funds between different accounts, but always in the back of his mind were the figures with a lot of zeroes behind them. It was a lifestyle he had not grown up with or come into, so he had acquired it and made it a baseline, to fit within some radius of the top one percent.

The rest he filled in with what came naturally to him: persuasive conversation, greasing of wheels, social manipulation. At its essence, it was a kind of sales technique, to let the customer sell to themselves by letting them hear what they want to hear. The ability to combine conversation, charm, and wit in this way to open doors, establish connections, and ease transactions was a skill he had honed carefully over the years, and it was an algorithm he was constantly improving.

In this sense, the project was easy. The people he had to interact with, convince of something, transfer risk to, or just be there as alibi material, were so easily spun it was almost effortless. Like faking the inability to reach Sarah in front of Jeff and Dave, or to all the others. There were easy parts. Sometimes, when he reflected in this way, he saw the project—the design—as challenging and rewarding, almost like an abstract task to compartmentalize and resolve. All the months of planning and preparation, of making ad-hoc adjustments and pivoting quickly when necessary, especially after Tracy, was a project management case study. Thoroughly fulfilling in the way that finishing a game of chess was for the dedicated strategists of the world. But at the deepest part of it, it wasn't a project so much as a life commitment, one to which he was completely dedicated, day and night, round the clock, in waking and dreaming.

But at the end of any reflection session like this, he wound up looking at the mental picture of the receipts, the invoices, the bills for the lifestyle he'd purchased, and he knew it was no game. Everything was coming due, and everything rode on how well the day of the exchange went. There were transactions with a lot of zeroes around every corner. It was an investment. Hundreds of thousands, for ten million. The end result had to pay off. There was no other way. He'd put everything on the line for it. The exchange had to work out exactly as he envisioned.

CHAPTER 23

Sarah lay on the cot, staring at the ceiling. She'd been looking at the walls, the ceiling, the floors, the windows. She was unsure how much time had passed since Jane had spotted her. She hadn't heard any noise downstairs for a long time, except for one of the dogs occasionally shifting. Tony and Jane had been silent since their midday romp. She felt bored. She could feel her fingernails digging into the ends of her fingers, and she was aware that her nails had grown and were beginning to get uncomfortable. She knew about the fingernail clipper on the night stand, but it had black grime and rust on it and she didn't want to use it.

As she fidgeted, she looked at the details of her simple room. There was something about the patterns in the wood, the way the rows of nails formed lines across all surfaces.

The window was a sliding window that had been nailed shut. It couldn't be opened unless the nails were removed. The nails holding it shut appeared shiny, less tarnished than the surrounding nails, so she assumed they must be new. She could feel a slight coolness around the edges of the frame. She wondered how cold it was outside.

Walking to the desk, she again heard the floor beneath her creak in certain places. Treading the same area, she noticed a line where the floor seemed to dip ever so slightly when stepped on. There was a place by the square, and a place between the cot and the desk that were like this. The firmer places did not have any give, and made no sound. The strongest places appeared to follow lines across the floor, and she guessed joists would be below these lines. They followed the rows of nails in the floor, from one side of the room to the other, spaced evenly.

Finding her way along the strong parts of the floor, she crept silently to the desk. She felt as if she was practicing, rehearsing.

The desk was a mess. Everything was still covered in dust, having been tossed around. When Tony had scattered the items this morning, he'd probably been the first person to touch most of the junk in decades. She looked at one of the newspapers. The yellowing, brittle paper started to crumble as she thumbed through it, and as it fell apart she again wondered about the possibility of creating panic by lighting the paper on fire. She had matches. She could do it. But as before when she'd pondered the fire idea, she started to shoot holes in it. She was the one who was upstairs. Smoke rose. The smoke would hit her and not the others. If for some reason they didn't let her get out through the square, she'd die, suffocating in a fire of her own making.

What about using it to start a fire outside. If she got out of here somehow, and had to run through the wintry cold out there, she'd have a way to get a fire going. Or she could set this place on fire before she fled. She began to crumple it, as though to go through the actions of starting a fire. Then she imagined the snow, the cold, the being in the middle of bloody nowhere.

An article caught her eye. Something about an assassination attempt against the Pope. The article about Ronald Reagan. If nothing else, she could pass the time reading old news.

She crept carefully to the other window, enhancing her mental map of the silent zones. This window looked out the back side of the house, and from here, nothing could be seen except snow-covered pines. The snow looked deep on the ground and lay heavily on the branches and boughs. It was pure white, and as she'd often thought, would look pretty and serene if she were in a different situation.

This window, too, had newer nails holding everything shut. She looked at the frame, the way it had obviously and recently been modified to keep her from getting out. But this one also had two-by-fours as bars over the outside.

She glanced at the desk and again wondered about using the desk leg as a weapon. She pictured using it to swing with all she had into Tony's face. What if she killed him by accident? The tables turned, she in handcuffs, on trial for murdering one of her kidnappers. She wondered how a jury of her peers would decide that one. The leg could be used to break the window. If she broke it, she could at least get a better view of her surroundings. Then she might get an idea of her location. She knew the sun rose in the east and moved west. The window overlooking the driveway faced west, because the sun set over the trees there. From that, she knew north and south.

But what of it? What good did it do to know which way you faced if you had no idea where you were? She had no idea where she was, how far away from anything. But if she was in the Cascades, as she suspected, she could be an hour or more east of Seattle. The problem was, she could be anywhere in the Cascades, any distance from a main road or town. If nothing else, if she had a coat, a way to stay warm, some food, she could keep going in one direction, using the sun. Maybe she'd hit a road. That could lead to a larger one, or to a town. She might see a passing car or truck. She could flag someone down, get help, call the police. The place must not be that far from civilization. After all, Ian had brought fresh bagels in yesterday morning. They maintained some kind of shopping list, if last night was any indication. They ran errands. Ian went to town to take care of the ransom business.

Key. She had a car key. She had to find out what it belonged to. That was the only thing that made sense. She couldn't rough it out there any more than she could figure out what her father, or Brandon, or any of her friends were thinking or doing right now.

If she could somehow just get a better glimpse of what the place looked like in front. She went to the other window, practicing her silent footsteps, now familiar with the good and bad places. Now that she'd done it a few times, she knew she had to take a wide step as she passed the cot, then move to the right to follow the firm area. The wood even looked a little different in these parts.

From the window, she looked out at the driveway and tried to visualize how things were positioned. Directly in front, all she could see were snow and pines. The driveway was more or less just a clearing, a place where there were no pines. There were tracks here and there, footprints. The road out of the driveway curved off to the right. That's the direction she'd seen the SUV come and go. The garage or shed, or whatever it was, must be on the left side, out of sight, past that other parked car she could only see the tail end of. She'd seen the three of them walk in that direction the other day, when Jane had not had her mask on.

The light was beginning to fade. In the middle of the day, when the sun was out, the snow was stark white and the trees cast dark shadows on it, creating a criss-cross look of black and white, with bluish hues. But today the sky had been cloudy all day. Now that evening was approaching, everything was beginning to look muddled. Shadows were indistinct. The woods were starting to look dark blue, and cold. It was harder to define shapes. Darkness was on its way. When she'd seen it get dark before, she'd noticed the subtle changes. The way the sun landed on top of the pines, and sank through them. As it set, the harsh arrows of light shot through little holes in the boughs here and there, until the foliage became too dense and the light died out. Then only a lingering glow remained in the sky until that too faded to black.

As she stared out at the encroaching darkness, she heard a tapping sound behind her. The room was dark except for the glow from the square, and she could see Jane's head there. The first thing Sarah thought of was the rough interrogation she'd received this morning, after the key incident. Then she recalled how naked Jane had let her off the hook after catching her at the bottom of the ladder earlier.

"Hey. Brought you some tea. Want some?"

Sarah watched as Jane carefully placed a mug on the floor at the top of the ladder. "Mind if I come up?"

"Sure, it's your cabin," Sarah said.

Jane went down and came back with another cup. So she'd already had the tea ready, before asking. This made Sarah wonder how Jane would have responded if she'd said no, you can't come up. Jane climbed through the square and sat down near it, legs crossed. "Here you go."

Sarah approached and took the mug. She held it to her nose and smelled it.

"Don't worry, there's nothing in it. I know it doesn't mean much, but sorry for snapping at you this morning. You didn't deserve that." Sarah's immediate thought was that Jane was trying to be be nice. She felt like saying she didn't deserve to be kidnapped.

"Anyway, just wanted to say, sorry if you're uncomfortable. Hopefully it'll be over soon. And I wanted to apologize for this morning, the way he was—I was."

Sarah shrugged. "The tea's good."

"It's Darjeeling."

"Then again, the chai was good the other night, when—"

Jane nodded. "I know." She stared into her mug. She appeared tired. She seemed contemplative.

"Thanks for, you know, earlier," Sarah said.

"Huh?"

"When I went down the ladder?"

"Ah. Where were you headed?"

"I don't know." It almost sounded like the truth. Sarah lowered her voice. "If Tony had found me he would've—"

"He's a bit temperamental. Don't worry about him."

"Don't worry about him?"

Jane looked into her tea, then glanced around the room. "It gets dark up here when the sun goes down, doesn't it? I thought we had a candle for you."

"There is. I haven't used it yet." Sarah got up and located the candle. She was going to open the box of matches, but Jane said, "Here." She took a lighter out of her pocket, then melted some wax and stood the candle on end on the back of a playing card.

The flickering light gave a soft amber glow to the room. The wood of the floor and walls seemed to turn softer. Taking a sip of her tea, Jane turned, to look through the square. Sarah was momentarily struck by the casual way she turned. She wondered what was going through Jane's mind as she looked down there. Some latent sense of sisterhood, guilt, who knew. But she was aware of Jane's beauty. Her hair and skin, lit in the soft light of the candle, were, in a way, sensual. Her lips, parted slightly. The thought caught her off guard, and she recalled without wanting to the way Jane's hands had felt on her skin this morning. She wondered what kind of person Jane would be under different circumstances, if their roles were different. Looking at her in the light of the candle, she suddenly saw the image of her earlier, totally nude, the curves of her body. Then down there with Tony, on the bed, the moaning, the creaking, the talking in low voices. Her hair was tied back, but it was loose, and Sarah noticed the way strands of it lay across her smooth neck, across her lips. She knew her eyes were dwelling, lingering on this woman's features.

Sarah looked away when she felt Jane's eyes approach her. Looking into her tea, Sarah was aware of some guilty discomfort, as though she had crossed into some zone. She felt relief when Jane spoke.

"So, I never did find out, what is that?" Jane pointed to Sarah's ankle.

Sarah looked at her tattoo. "It's a Hindu god, Ganesha."

"I thought so. You said you and your sister got matching. Did she have the same one?"

"No, she got Shiva. We got them at the same time, but we wanted different ones. I got Ganesha, she got Shiva."

"The sun, right?"

"Yeah. You've heard of it?"

"A little. I took a class on world mythology once. I seem to remember something about Ganesha too, but it was a long time ago. Do you think there's anything to it?"

"To what?"

"Stories like that."

"I don't know. I mean, they're just stories."

"I suppose. But if mythology usually represents something, it must have some meaning, right?"

"I guess."

"So what does Ganesha represent?"

"Supposed to mean intelligence. Dedication to a task. Actually, I just liked the design at the time. Not sure I really thought that much about it."

Jane raised her brows. "I can see that in you. I mean you look intelligent. It fits you."

"How did you work that out, from the stuff you stole from my room?"

"No, I'm serious. Besides, I don't know about the stuff they took from you. I'm just saying that based on the way you look. Your eyes, they have a strong sense of purpose, if that makes any sense. I mean, you don't look like I thought you would."

"What did you think I'd look like?"

"I don't know. Well, more like your sister, I guess."

"How do you know what she looked like?"

"Well you know, I mean come on. She was in the news all the time. There was that reality show. When she—I'm sorry. I shouldn't have brought her up."

"I'm fine," Sarah said coldly. She looked into the candle flame. "It was a long time ago. Seems like a long time ago."

"A year ago. If it's worth anything, I know something about how you feel. My sister died when I was younger. Car accident. I was in shock for a long time."

"If you're just telling me that for sympathy, please don't."

"I wouldn't make something like that up."

"So why are you doing this then?"

"Doing what?"

"Well is this some pity trip, is that it? You know the reason I was on my way to my shrink when you—"

"No. Not at all." Jane appeared hurt.

Sarah felt she had something else to say, but looked back into the flame.

"No, it's not," Jane said, "I just want to know more about you, that's all."

"Well, why?"

"I just felt bad for earlier." Jane drank some of her tea. "If you don't want to talk." Jane moved, as if to go down the ladder.

Sarah reached out to touch Jane's arm. "No, stay."

"You sure?"

"Sorry. I guess you get used to being alone."

"Sure."

"Sorry to hear about your sister. That was nice of you to say."

Jane smiled. "Well, enough about sisters, huh? Let's talk about your boyfriend. Are you close to him? What's his name again?"

"You mean you don't know?" Sarah was mystified.

"I forget."

"Isn't that one of those kidnapping 101 things, like Ian said?"

Jane shrugged. "Guess I must've spaced it out."

"I figured you'd know since you broke into my room and stole all my stuff before you kidnapped me."

"I had nothing to do with that."

"Well, Ian mentioned it the first night I was here. Don't you remember that, when he laid out the ground rules?"

Jane seemed perplexed, trying to recall. "No. Guess I don't."

"Brandon."

"That's right, come to think of it. That's a nice name. What's he like?"

Sarah shrugged, wondering if Jane was just playing dumb. "He's sort of, like, one part brain, and one part GQ poster boy."

"GQ poster boy?"

"Yeah, I mean he's in graduate school and he works at a software startup and—I'm not even sure exactly what he does there—but the other side of him is all sports. Like, he's into weird stuff, like powder skiing—you know, off the main routes, where they go up in a helicopter. Scuba, more adventure type stuff."

"Good places around here for that. You ever snowboard?"

"Sometimes, yeah. You?"

"Not that great at it but it's fun. So what else about him?"

"Well, he's good with people, though you wouldn't know it at first because he has sort of a hard exterior shell. He says he can size someone up just by looking at them, then tell them things they want to hear."

"You think it's true?"

"Sort of. I've seen him do it. A party trick he does sometimes."

"So, does he tell you what you want to hear?"

"No way, he couldn't if he tried."

"How's that?"

"I'd know when he's faking stuff."

"I thought he was good at selling people what they want to hear?"

"But I know that's what he does, so I'd see right through it."

"So you have some sort of feminine intuition."

"I guess. You get a connection with someone, you can see past that kind of thing."

"You know all his secrets," Jane said.

"Or all his alibis."

Jane smiled and looked away. "So, how did you meet him?"

It took Sarah a moment to reflect. She felt aware that she knew the answer, in an unspoken way. It was there, ready to come out of her mouth, but now that it was this close, she realized she'd never said it before, to herself, or anyone. She hesitated, then finally spoke.

"I met him at my sister's funeral."

Now that she'd said it, she knew she didn't want to answer any more questions. In fact, she wanted to turn the questions toward Jane, to get her to reveal more about her relationship with Ian and Tony, how she got involved in this, why she was here. She knew Jane could be manipulated, that it was probably the best weapon she had. She should be asking Jane the questions.

But as she eyed Jane's measured response to what she'd said, and tried to think of things to say or ask, her thoughts kept returning to Brandon and the way they'd met. Her mind turned to fog and she felt emotions taking over. Something was occurring to her that she'd never considered. Before she could restrain herself she blurted it out. "I know it probably sounds to you like I'm in love with him. I don't know if I can say that. I know I'm at risk for liking him more than he likes me." *There, I said it.* She stared into the flame.

Though she could feel Jane's eyes in her periphery, she felt her mind going over something, connecting dots she'd never tried to connect. "He gave me a watch last summer, like from a matching set. One for him and one for me," she said, as her mind drifted. "We—we were in Switzerland."

After a silence, Jane said, "Sounds nice." She looked at Sarah's wrists. "Sounds serious. I mean if you're at the watch level. That's way up there. Even if you were, you know, having doubts."

Sarah continued to stare into the flame. She felt both wrists, as if searching for the watch. She could feel her eyes widen. "Not long after that, he said he wanted to take it slower." Sarah let her eyes drift to Jane's and saw the concern reflected in her gaze.

"Ouch."

"I mean, it's not like he was thinking of someone else. Nothing like that." But Sarah felt that she was suddenly admitting or stating facts that she had never acknowledged. Now she was telling Jane, one of her kidnappers. Someone she didn't know at all. Someone she wanted to hate. She felt her mind stretch, going back, searching, scanning. She knew she'd never seen Brandon wear the other watch.

They both sat there in silence, looking into the candle flame as it wavered slightly. Sarah felt suddenly empty, and had no words to express this sudden rush of thoughts.

The uncomfortable reverie was suddenly broken by Tony's voice. "Hey!" he hissed from below.

Sarah, stunned, looked down through the square. It was mostly dark. Tony must have been sleeping or sitting in the dark while they'd been talking up here.

"I suppose I better go," Jane said quietly.

Sarah collected her thoughts. In the candlelight, she could see the change in Jane's expression. Instead of the girlfriend confidante, it had been replaced with the Jane from downstairs. Her first thought was that Tony wanted his dinner, something like that.

But as Jane began to go through the square, Tony, now near the bottom of the ladder, whispered intensely: "Get the fuck back up there!"

Jane, confused, froze in a half-crouched position. "What the?"

"Shh!"

Suddenly a section of coiled rope flew through the square from below, hit the floor and started sliding down. Jane grabbed it. "What's this for?"

"For her."

"Why?"

"There's someone coming," Tony hissed.

"What?"

"There's someone coming down the road. I need you to shut up. And make sure the rich kid doesn't try any of her tricky shit. Use the rope."

CHAPTER 24

With each passing hour, it seemed that sand in a vast invisible hourglass was tumbling downward. The disappearing sand was creating a kind of moving sinkhole, which could swallow him whole if he missed a step or prolonged a decision. His schematic diagram highlighted all the variables. There were fewer of them now that events were coalescing around an endgame. But they were still there. And there were still so many things to do.

With latex gloves, he lifted the assembled rifle and looked through the scope at the paintings on the wall, then aimed it out the window into the apartments across the way. He adjusted the focus several times before finding a good balance, watching as any of the familiar denizens showed up. He set the gun down, then lifted it again, feeling the heft and balance. He held it in both hands in front of him and pondered the multiple pieces. It was black, metal, lightweight, easy to store, and it could be broken down into components.

With the scope and stock adjusted the way he wanted them, he used a chamois cloth to polish every surface of the weapon. Then he did it again. When the metal was polished, he carefully removed the metal stock and turned it over in his hands. When it was detached, Brandon thought it looked something like a specialty tool, something industrial. Unlike traditional solid wooden stocks, this was metal, minimal, and contained mostly just an outline of the classic stock shape. He had fashioned a special holder for this stock out of foam pieces and wood, sort of a brace that could hold the stock between each end, so as not to touch much of the surface. He dropped the stock into a plastic bag, then put the bag and the special holder and a small remote camera into a backpack and drove to Adam Liddy's apartment.

As was his custom most times he went to deal with Liddy's business, he parked a block away and walked the rest of the way. Going around to the back of the building, he let himself in the back door, then went down to the parking garage level. The garage was fairly run-down, being in an older apartment building: aging concrete floors, low ceilings with pipes and wires, and dim fluorescent lighting. A background smell of gas and exhaust hung in the air. About four cars lined each side. Short wooden semi-walls between the car spaces gave each occupant a sort of personal garage space, with storage lockers, cabinets against the walls, and a bench where some residents had tools or non-valuable loose items sitting out. Each space had a number on the floor, indicating the resident apartment.

Brandon knew there was a single security camera down here, near the garage entrance, pointing toward the parked cars, but he'd cut the cable along the ceiling last week when planning this move. Just like the camera in the front lobby, it fed to a dated monitoring system that was meant to record constantly until space ran out. Given the apparent age of the unit, he estimated that after about two day's worth of footage, the system would record over itself, over and over. Useful for reviewing events that occurred over a two-day window but useless if it didn't record at all.

Adam Liddy's garage space was relatively neat, if dark and dingy. His car was an older Honda Accord with a couple of dents and scratches, and seemed to be a sort of brownish color. Brandon tried a couple of the cabinets. They were locked. An older tire was propped up against the dividing wall, next to the workbench, on top of which was a funnel, a container of carwash detergent and a rag.

He removed the camera from the pack and switched it on. The camera housing displayed a red light when it was recording but he had eliminated that with a piece of tape. Positioning it to capture a view of the front of Liddy's car, he hid the camera within a crevice of one of the cabinet doors. He took the rifle stock out and used the rag to remove it from the bag and place it gently on the hood of the Accord. Then he shook the Accord roughly a few times until the alarm activated. He quickly headed toward the apartment entrance door and went up the stairs to the second floor. At the door to #232 he knocked.

"Hey buddy, your car's going off down there," he said, then went quickly down the stairs to the lobby and left through the front.

CHAPTER 25

Sarah's thoughts turned instantly to the driveway. Someone was coming. Tony clearly was not ready for this. And he clearly hadn't had time to tie her up himself, telling Jane to do it. Yet Jane was more preoccupied with glancing downstairs and at the the tea dripping down the ladder. She knew Jane wouldn't use the rope.

The candle was burning. Downstairs was mostly dark, with the only light coming from the burning wood stove in flickering amber hues. So from outside, would this person be able to see the light through the window? The rope being flung from below had knocked over Jane's mug and spilled the small amount of tea that had been in it. It was dripping over the edge of the square and down the ladder. Jane was looking around for something to wipe it up with, but kept her finger on her lips and seemed paralyzed by indecision.

Sarah's mind was full. She had to get the attention of this stranger. What was this person doing here? Were they approaching on foot, or had Tony heard or seen a car? She listened but could not hear the sound of an engine. Tony was totally silent, down there in the dark, and she guessed he was probably hoping the person would see a dark cabin and go away. That made her want to turn on every light in the place, to break the window, to scream out through broken glass. Would someone looking at the cabin from outside in the dark see the light from the upstairs window, one single candle?

One of the dogs growled. She could hear Tony whispering and trying to silence it. Then one of them barked. Jane was looking down through the square. An occasional amber flicker from the fire hit her face. She was clearly trying to keep her distance, to avoid being seen from below, curious about the stranger but wanting to remain hidden.

When the knocking started on the door, both dogs began barking wildly. She could hear the sounds of Tony corralling them into the bedroom, where they continued to bark. It was a long while before he opened the front door. Then the murmur of a man's voice: "...to bother you like this—" his voice faded out "—could give me a pull out of..."

Tony's voice. "What happened?"

Sarah wondered what the response would be if she yelled now, while the man could hear.

"Think I took the turn too fast. Didn't seem like the snow was that deep and there were plenty of tire tracks. Anyway, got stuck in the ditch just before the fork down there, where your road splits off. It's not too far in but just enough so I can't get over the hump. Like I said, the snow's a lot deeper than I thought."

"Yeah it's a sharp turn."

The barking continued.

"Think you'd be able to give me a pull? I've got a tow rope."

"Well, I wish I could, problem is my car's dead. How far down the road are you?"

"Or if you have a phone I could use."

"Hang on." There were a couple of loud knocks near the bedroom door and Tony giving some command. The dogs stopped barking.

"No phone service. Sorry," he said.

"Hm. Well, leaves me kinda stuck. If you know what I mean." The man chuckled. So did Tony, in a forced way.

Sarah eyed Jane. She could see the tension on her face.

"Yeah, well, damn, sorry I can't do more for you."

"Oh well." After a silence the man said, "So, do you live here alone?"

"Ah, no, it's not my place. A friend owns it."

"Oh."

"Anyway, wish I could give you a pull, but like I said my car's DOA."

"I could take a look at it if you want. I'm pretty handy. Maybe we could get it going. I just need to—"

"No. It's the transmission. No chance. Thanks though."

"Okay," the man said. "Well, just for kicks, mind if I come in, just for a minute or two? Warm my hands? Guess I'll have to come up with a plan B. It's cold out here."

No initial response from Tony, and she wondered if he'd actually say no. But soon came the sounds of the man coming in, kicking the snow off his boots and the door closing heavily.

"Can't believe something like this happens just a few minutes from a road. You ever try to flag someone down on a road with no cars?"

"Can't say I have."

"Well, this is a cozy place. Always wondered what it looked like on the inside."

No response from Tony.

"So how do you get around, with your dead car and all?"

"Like I said, a friend of mine owns the place."

"And he's got a car, I take it?"

"Right."

"Guess that would explain all the tire tracks."

"Tire tracks?"

"On the road." The man laughed purposefully. Tony did the same.

"Say, you're not one of Peterson's nephews, are you?"

A quiet moment followed, and Sarah tried to imagine the searching expression on Tony's face. Now, she thought, would be an ideal time to try something. She eyed Jane's motionless expression, staring intently at the floor, at the dripping tea, as if able to see through to the scene below. She felt the urge to do something.

"You must know Peterson. Or maybe you haven't met him, if your friend bought this place from him."

The moment was slipping away. Sarah looked toward the zones in the floor, the noisy parts that she'd memorized earlier. If she caught the man's attention somehow, she could at least plant some doubt. Maybe he'd feel uneasy enough to call someone when he got to a phone. But what would Jane do? She had been apologetic, even kind, tonight. But Sarah had little doubt that if she tried to pull something, the reaction would be swift and severe. Jane wouldn't save her from Tony this time.

"Oh, sure," Tony said. "You caught me off guard there. I guess everyone knows someone named Peterson. No, I'm just a family friend. Why?"

"I don't know, just thought maybe. My son's place is on the other end of the fork. He's overseas and I come up to check on it now and then. I've known Peterson for years and he has a couple of nephews that come up."

"Okay."

"Hunting or fishing, mostly."

"Sure."

"So you just taking time off from the city?"

"Yeah, something like that."

"Live in Seattle, or?"

This was met with silence, and the man continued: "Funny we've never met. I always seem to run into someone on these back roads." More silence. "You're kind of the quiet type, aren't you?"

"Never thought about it."

"Hey, what kind of dogs you have? You got more than one?"

"They're good-sized dogs."

"Oh. Not good around strangers?"

Slow footsteps and movement approached. Jane sat frozen, and Sarah could see the legs of the man pass by, toward the wood stove.

"Oh, this feels good. Hands were getting cold out there. Didn't really plan on goin' on a walk tonight, know what I mean?"

"Yeah."

"You know it's around ten miles to my son's place from here? Hm, a ladder, that makes sense."

No response from Tony. Jane was shrinking into the darkness.

"Saves space, you know? Way better than stairs in these small places. So, what's up there?" The man approached the ladder. Jane ducked her head back quickly. Sarah felt herself wanting to lunge at the lit candle, to protect it.

"Hey, I was wondering. I saw what looks like two-by-fours across the window upstairs? What's that for?"

A silence, and then Tony said, "They were there already. So, is it that cold out there?"

"Understatement. Matter of fact, it's a hell of a lot colder than they said it was gonna be. You hear about that storm movin' in the next couple days?"

"No."

"Yeah. Big one. So they say."

"Hm, no haven't heard anything."

"Then again, don't they always say that? Big storm. Record this or that."

Tony remained silent.

"But who's 'they' anyway, right?"

"What?"

"Just kidding. Seeing if you're listening."

"So," Tony said, "your hands getting warmer now?"

"Getting better, thanks. So, what did you say was upstairs?"

"I didn't."

"Bedroom? Got a lamp or something going, looks like. Oh, a candle, maybe."

"Sure, we sleep up there. I mean I do. My friend sleeps in the bedroom down here."

"Hey, this ain't the '50s. You don't have to explain anything to me."

"I didn't mean that."

"Okay."

More silence passed.

"Hm. Got some water leakage or something, looks like." After a short silence, the man said, "Smells like tea."

Sarah stared at Jane's ceramic face.

"So, how are your hands?" Tony said.

The response from the man was measurably slow. "Ah, yes. They do feel better. You really haven't heard anything about the storm?"

"No."

"Well, suppose I'll have to think up some sort of plan B on the way out of here. Hey, like I said, it's only ten miles."

"So you did."

"Well," the man said, "much obliged." The sound of the door opening. "Oh, you said a friend of yours owns this?"

"Yeah."

"So did Peterson sell, after his wife passed on?"

After a short silence, Tony said, "Yeah."

"Who's your friend? Might be nice to know him."

Sarah knew she could wait no longer. She could hardly contain herself. The man was leaving. It sounded like he was standing in the door, ready to leave. This was it. She looked around, at Jane, at the window, through the square.

"John."

She could scream. She had to do something.

"John? He have a last name?"

She eyed Jane's mug. It was on its side. It was within reach.

"John Doe."

There was a silence, and Sarah could picture the expression on the man's face. "Well. I'll probably meet him sooner or later, I suppose, this John Doe. So, didn't get yours."

Sarah nudged the mug toward the square. The noise was enough to get Jane's attention, and she reached out to try to grab it. Without allowing herself further delay, Sarah quickly pushed the cup over the edge. Jane reached for it desperately but it fell through her fingers. She flashed an instant piercing gaze toward Sarah while the cup crashed onto the floor below.

The dogs started barking again.

"Sounds like there's someone else up there." There was no mistaking the careful suspicion in the man's voice.

"My son, not feeling well."

"You've got a son up there, too? How many more you hiding in here?" The man chuckled.

"Yep, just us."

"Well, poor thing. You got any—"

"Look, I wish I could help you," Tony said deliberately.

"Well. I can take a hint. Wish me luck."

"Okay. Good luck."

The door began to close below, and Sarah was panicking. She debated quickly, even as Jane stared at her. Now was it. Tony would probably do something to her. Or he'd tell Ian. Or, or—

"Help!" She screamed. Her voice sounded so meek.

"Shit," Jane screeched, reaching for Sarah's mouth.

"Hey, I said use a rope on her!" Tony's voice from below.

Louder this time. "HELP!" The man was walking away. She was losing her chance.

Sarah scrambled to her feet. She had to get to the window. Jane called down to Tony: "He gone yet?" As Sarah edged way, Jane reached for her ankles, causing her to fall. "Hey. Tony!" Jane cried.

"Yeah. He's not coming back."

"Goddamit!" Jane yelled, fumbling with Sarah's ankles. Sarah kicked away and ran toward the window and began pounding on it.

"What the fuck is going on up there?" Tony was coming toward the ladder. Jane was on her feet now.

"HELP!" Sarah cried, pounding on the window. Looking out she could see nothing in the darkness. "HELP!"

"Sarah!" Jane pulled at her from behind.

She could hear Tony's voice somewhere behind her, getting nearer. She continued pounding and yelling. Sensing his presence, she braced for it, starting to crouch. Before she could cover her face Tony struck her with a swift blow. His open hand hit her left temple and she fell against the wall and to the floor. She quickly began pushing herself away, expecting him to follow, but he turned and left.

"Jesus fucking Christ!" he seethed as he went down the ladder.

"Sarah, you okay?" She could see Jane in her periphery, approaching. Through the pain, Sarah held a hand to her face. She could feel pain in her eye.

"Let me see."

"Get away from me! Just go away!"

Jane turned quickly, took the rope and went down without anything further. Sarah could hear both of them talking in low tones, with one voice or another rising occasionally. She could hear the dogs crossing the floor to the front door and being let out. She felt her heart sink. She had lost her chance. She'd been afraid of the consequences, and had only made some paltry attempt with the mug. She'd screamed too late. She had failed to get the man's attention and she'd been hit. If she'd simply gone down the ladder, she'd at least have the man's attention, and as long as he was there, Tony wouldn't have been able to hurt her, unless he dealt with them both. She'd let the chance slip because she was scared of Tony. It hadn't made any difference. She felt around her left temple and eye. The pain seemed to be fading but it was still intense.

She stood up and looked outside, searching the darkness for any sign of the man. It was too dark to see anything and in the modest light from the cabin all she could see was the raging snow. That poor man. He'd said it was ten miles to his son's place.

CHAPTER 26

Adam Liddy was in the living room of his apartment, sitting on the sofa. Stacks of notebooks and papers lay in loose piles around him. He was writing in a notebook and occasionally sketching on a tablet. He had the TV on low as he worked. He was in his late 30s, somewhat stocky but not overweight, and had thinning sandy hair. He had a weary sort of appearance, or as his ex had told him on more than one occasion, "A 70s smart guy look, like Colombo." His pronounced cheekbones created a sort of hollowness in the cheeks, and dark eyes surrounded by some shadowy dimensions gave him an intellectual flair.

The research he was doing for a client's construction project had been sucking him dry lately, but he was nearly finished. He was nearly ready to consolidate all his notes and give them to his drafter to start the schematic drawings. He still needed to coordinate with the engineers and verify a few requirements with the city's planning department, but he was getting close.

Now that he had the updated property inspection in hand, he could probably wrap most of this project up tonight. He still wondered where it had been all that time, or if he just hadn't noticed it. The tracking number showed it had been delivered Saturday morning—no signature required—but he'd checked his mail and it hadn't been there. Then later in the evening after looking everywhere, he'd gone to double check, and there it was. So had he just not seen it the first time? Or had it been placed in someone else's box accidentally and realizing it was not theirs they called the post office? If not, how else had it wound up back in his box if it hadn't been there before? Either way, he had it now, but it ate at him the way things ate at him in general.

He stood up and stretched. He opened the fridge, and finding nothing appealing, pondered ordering some Chinese delivery. He went to the junk drawer in the desk and poked around until finding a menu, and as he thumbed through it he heard a few knocks on the door.

"Hey buddy, your car's going off down there," a male voice said.

Liddy adjusted his shirt and unlocked the door and opened it. Nobody was there, but sure enough, he could hear a car alarm downstairs. Must have been a neighbor who'd been in the garage and noticed his spot number. He got his keys, locked the door and went down to check it out.

CHAPTER 27

J ane called up: "Sarah, you need to use the bathroom or anything?"
Sarah heard her but saw no point in responding. She lay on her bed, her mind blank.

After a few seconds, Jane appeared in the square. In a fairly quiet voice, she said, "I think if you have to use the bathroom, now would be a good time." She had a rag with her and started wiping the leftovers of the spilled tea.

Her tone gave Sarah the sense that something was in the air. After what had just happened she spent no further time thinking about it and went to the square. "I do need to use it."

"Sure. Hey, let me see your face."

Sarah looked at Jane, who examined her closely. She reached out to touch her left temple. "It's swollen. Does it hurt still?"

"It's just numb now."

"I'll see if we have any ice." Jane descended. "Oh, can you bring that other mug."

As she cautiously went down the ladder, Sarah could feel Tony's menacing glare from the kitchen area where he stood watching her with curiosity, arms folded across his chest. She handed the mug to Jane.

"I mean, there's nothing but ice in every direction," Tony said. "I can get some snow. Maybe we have a plastic bag or something."

"Thanks," Jane said, then bent down to pick up the remnants of the broken mug.

Tony opened several drawers and found a bag containing some plastic cutlery, dumped them into the drawer, then crossed the room and looked out the front door, peering out into the darkness. As he started to put on his boots, Sarah noticed on the counter a box of crackers and a brick of cheese with a small knife sticking out of it. He must have been snacking on it before the stranger came.

Seeing the opportunity, she glanced between Jane, Tony, and the knife. She knew she was starting to overthink, to imagine the outcomes. As Jane started to rise, she took two wide steps to the counter, reached for the knife and quickly slid it into the front of her pants. She stepped back quickly while pulling her shirt over the handle. Then she went into the bathroom and pulled the door as tight as she could.

"Where'd she go?" Tony said.

"In there. Here, I'll keep it in the fridge."

"She okay, or what."

Jane's voice went low and Sarah could only hear whispering.

Sarah took out the knife. It was a small paring knife, fairly sharp, blade about four inches long. She turned on the water in the sink, then softly ran her fingers along the edges of the toilet lid. Dropping the knife in, she carefully lowered it. She used the toilet, then flushed it. Listening for new sounds outside, and hearing only the vague whispers, she washed her hands. So now she had a knife and a car key. This lifted her mood considerably.

"So we gonna wait 'til he gets back?" Tony said, in a normal volume.

"For what?"

"Dinner."

"I don't know."

"Thought he said he'd be back by now."

"Yeah but look at it out there."

She dried her hands and looked at her face in the mirror for the first time. To her shock, the area around her left eye appeared reddish and bruised. Like Jane had said, it was swollen. The eye itself looked puffy and was partly shut. As she felt it with her hand, she nearly felt like weeping. She wondered how much worse it would get.

Tony's voice suddenly sounded irritated. "Hey, you see that knife that was here?"

Sarah listened with trepidation.

"What knife," Jane said.

"I'm seriously in no mood to go through this shit again."

"I don't know what knife you're talking about."

"The knife that was right here."

"Just get another one."

"The point is, she was right there a minute ago."

"So was I. I would've—" Jane's voice went lower.

"Oh, come on. She can hear everything we're saying anyway." His voice rose: "Right Sarah?"

"Come on, enough tonight. Just let it go."

"Let it go? Last I checked, she's the prisoner. Remember the roles? Or did we all come here to play house for a few days."

"Well if she took it I would've seen it."

Then she heard the sounds of drawers being opened rapidly. "Where the hell are things in this dump, anyway? That old coot must've ate with paper plates and—" She heard the sound of him smashing something into the plastic cutlery he'd emptied a few minutes ago.

"Calm down. Have a glass of wine."

"Oh, that's another thing. We're nearly out."

"I think he's getting some."

"The last stuff Mike bought all tastes the same to me."

"Shh!" Jane hissed.

"What? Oh." Then his voice went quiet, and they started whispering again.

Mike. So Mike was Ian. Sarah was sure she'd heard him say it.

"Speaking of," he said in a normal voice, "how long's she been in there?"

Sarah got ready. She wanted to make it to the ladder quickly.

"Hey Sarah?" Jane's voice said.

"Yeah?" she said into the door.

"Almost done?"

"Uh. Just a minute."

"How about now?" Tony said, loudly. Then to Jane: "I don't like her being in there like that. Who knows what the fuck she's doing."

"Sarah?" Jane said.

She opened the door. Jane was standing nearby, with a wine bottle in one hand and an empty glass in the other. Tony was near the fire with his back to her, adding wood and stirring it with a poker.

"We're having some wine," Jane said, "if you want some."

"What?" Tony said incredulously.

Jane glanced at him. "Oh come on, a little wine. She had some last time."

"Yeah and look what happened to the glass. Besides if we're running low, why are you giving it all to her? This ain't the Ritz."

While looking at Sarah, she said: "It's just a way of saying sorry, for up there. Here, have a glass." She poured. Sarah took the glass, her eyes watching Jane's face. Jane's eyes seemed relaxed, calm. She was suddenly in one of her good moods. Sarah wondered again if she was high, whether the swings were biological or medicinal. But what would have kicked in so fast, after the incident upstairs? Or was it something from earlier just taking effect?

"Um," Sarah said, "I was wondering if I could take another shower."

"Sure. Don't see why not."

"Okay."

"Oh, we have some snow. For your eye."

"Okay. I'll get it after."

Tony sat down on the sofa and began cracking walnuts with the pliers. Jane came close to Sarah and said quietly, "I was going to mention it yesterday, but I have some good soap. Yardley's." Sarah noticed the expression on Jane's face. There was a hint of playfulness, a rebellious look in the eye, as if she was really going the extra mile behind Tony's back, risking great things. "You shouldn't have to use that stuff Mike brought."

Sarah saw the happy drain from Jane's face and regret take over. "I mean Ian." The playfulness was gone. Jane was again on Tony's side.

"Jane." Sarah said.

For an instant, they simply stood there, looking around each other. Tony's nut cracking continued in the background, and Sarah could hear him laughing quietly to himself. She suddenly felt an urge to appeal to Jane's softer side to help her get away from the cabin, to reach for the playful part again. She whispered, "I won't say anything. Promise. I didn't hear anything."

Jane turned away suddenly. "I'll get the soap for you." Now there was anger in her voice.

"You don't have to."

Jane ignored her and went into the bedroom. Tony was busy with the nuts, forming piles. She looked for the dogs. One of them was lying near the couch. The other was in the kitchen. She couldn't tell them apart, and wondered whether this would be a problem when it came time to bribe them. Which one had she given the food to? Had it been the same dog both times? Did they have the same personality?

Jane made no eye contact when she returned. She held out a towel and bar of soap with a glum face while looking in Tony's direction. Sarah took both and went into the bathroom. As she closed the door, she heard Tony say, "Happy family."

"Whatever," Jane murmured absently.

"And I wouldn't let her keep that wine glass in there. Never know what she could try."

Sarah downed the wine and opened the door. Jane's hand was waiting. She closed the door, angry at herself for not thinking to keep it. She could have broken it and used it for something, for anything. Maybe to stick into Tony's throat.

She went into the shower and waited for the hot water to start flowing. Like last time, it took a while to come, and she knew it wouldn't last long. Still, she took her time, reveling in the hot water and the being away from her captors, until the water started to turn cool.

As she dried herself she heard the sound of an approaching car. For a brief instant, she went through a couple of quick scenarios in which the man, suspicious, had called the police, or was returning to ask more questions. But she knew it would more likely be Ian, returning from his business, wherever he went. Mike. *Mike* returning.

She dressed and combed her hair and slightly nudged the door open to take a look. He was just coming in, stomping his feet in the doorway. Snow was falling heavily, and the dogs darted through the open door. Before she pulled the bathroom door closed again, she noticed the way Ian came in and took off his jacket. There was something about the way he looked at the others, the expression on his face, that made Sarah immediately uncomfortable. She felt an urge to withdraw. She noticed the glances on the faces and could feel the heaviness in the air. She caught a few exchanges of whisper-like conversation, and she knew something was wrong. A dozen possibilities occurred to her, all bad. Dad was not paying. They needed to keep her longer. They'd decided to kill her. Dad had called the police.

Then she heard Ian's voice, louder now. "Bloody hell it's snowing. Huge storm. It's all over the radio. I could barely get in here."

"Beautiful, though," Jane said.

"Looks like happy hour started, uh?"

The sound of pouring. "Ah, a Cabernet tonight. How unique. We almost done with that case yet? I'm getting sick of this stuff."

"Getting there."

"Well I got a couple new ones anyway. Okay, listen," Ian said, then lowered his voice again.

Nervous, Sarah strained to listen but could not make out what anyone was saying. She positioned herself carefully, putting her ear on the door, even daring to push the door open just a little. What little she heard only fueled her fears that it was about her. Once, then again, Jane said something that sounded like "she" or "Sarah" and Ian said something that seemed to acknowledge that. When the whispering was done, a short silence followed.

"Well Tony, that's what makes you so Irish," Ian said, in a normal tone.

"What the hell does that have to do with it?"

"What, you'd make a perfect Irishman. Don't you think, lassie?"

Jane murmured, "I guess. I mean, not sure where that came from."

"You know Ireland's rich as hell nowadays?"

Getting no response, he continued. "Yeah. You know, you always think of the poor Irish, right? Potato famine, that dancing they do with the fiddles, generations brought up in poverty, holding together against the English with Guinness and shared Celtic misery?"

"You stop at an Irish pub on the way back or what," Tony said.

"Well, it's all changed now. They're bloody rich. Thing is, they don't know how to handle it. Like any country that's come a long way, they don't know how to deal with it, all the money and the stuff that goes with it. Foreign investment. Film production. Manufacturing. They're up against the crime and debauchery that goes with a full-fledged capitalistic system stuck inside the mire of a Catholic conservatism that's out of sync with reality." He paused. "Ah, this is nice, once you get that second or third sip.

I thought I was getting sick of the reds, but, lo, no longer. This one's actually good. What's this again?"

"Same old," Jane said.

"Weird. Not bad for same old." The bracelet slid down his wrist and he snapped it back.

"Okay. Well, thanks for that, Father Knowledge," Tony said. "Anyone Irish here?"

"You," Ian said.

"Yeah what does this have to do with anything?" Jane said. "After what you just told us about—" Her voice dropped off.

"Nothing. Just another in my series of mini lectures. I thought Tony'd be interested at least."

"Yeah, I'm fascinated."

"So there you go. A little intellectual stimulation on a Sunday night. Who knows, maybe one of you could write a paper based on my lectures, get a degree in something? Maybe publish a book."

From near the front door, Tony's voice said, "Holy shit it's really coming down now, check this out."

"The road in here was crap. Turn on the light," Ian said.

After a few seconds, Sarah heard Jane scream. "Oh God!"

"What the—" Ian said.

Footsteps rushing toward the front door. The door opening. Sarah pressed the bathroom door open carefully, enough to look toward the door. The outside light was on, and she could see snow falling in large, heavy flakes, stark white against the darkness beyond. One of the dogs was out there, to the right of the door, pacing nervously around the SUV. Jane was looking out as Tony and Ian were bent over something in the snow. The other dog came into view, and it seemed agitated, different than usual. It nearly seemed to look toward Tony for an answer, then back to the spot in the snow. Enough snow had fallen for Tony and Ian to make deep tracks where they stepped. They rolled something over. At first it looked like a bag of something, a pile of clothing. But a hand flapped into view. Her first thought was that it was frozen. Maybe they'd found a body buried in the snow. But the hand moved. It started clutching at Tony's feet.

She saw Jane gasp, and felt herself do the same. There was someone there, lying in the snow. Tony and Ian were talking, their mouths moving in silence. The dogs were circling. Ian pointed toward one side of the clearing, where the road led. They both looked in that direction and seemed to discuss something. Now that she could see better, Sarah perceived blood on the face of one of the dogs. And there was blood on the hand in the snow.

Together, they lifted the person between them, more or less standing him on his feet. Her first thought was that he must be the guy who was here before. Maybe he'd started out, found the storm too tough, and turned around. And when he got back, the dogs attacked him before he made it to the door. She shivered. The man's head wobbled loosely as they dragged him across the visible part of the clearing. His legs dragged along, making two strong tracks in the snow. When they passed near where she assumed the other car was parked, they disappeared from her view.

Jane turned, clearly distraught. Sarah withdrew into the bathroom and pulled the door shut quietly, again wishing she could lock it. She considered going upstairs, where she'd be safe. She'd have to do it now, before the men came back in. But before she could act, she heard the front door open. Heavy footsteps, kicking snow off shoes. Door closing.

Ian said something. Some whispering. It went on between them as Sarah felt increasingly rattled. She pressed her ear to the door to listen. She sat down on the seat of the toilet. She looked at the lid behind her. She felt a sudden desire to lift it, take out her knife and keys, and run out of the bathroom screaming, slashing at anything or anyone in her way. For a brief moment a certain conviction seemed to sweep over her, and she felt that she could kill or wound or do anything if she had to, even to the dogs. The feeling came on strong and she imagined several rapid-fire scenarios in which she emerged victorious.

But just as quickly, the feeling receded, and fear began to trickle back in. Little by little, she saw the details as they stood. She didn't have a chance against three of them. She didn't know the situation with the car and the key she had. She only had a small knife. Not to mention the dogs. She had been completely mistaken in even thinking about trusting or bribing them. They were killers.

The only good thing she could come up with was that the man had said they were only minutes from a road. It definitely went against Ian's claim that they were in the middle of nowhere. Then again, it could be any road. A road in the middle of nowhere.

Sarah jumped when she heard Ian yell from the kitchen. All she caught was the "bloody hell" part and the sound of a glass shattering against something.

It was soon followed by a reaction from Tony: "—was I supposed to know?"

"You got that bloody right. How could you perceive that, I wonder? You perfect creation of stupidity!" Ian was yelling.

"Don't try your master and servant bullshit on me today. I'm in no mood."

"*You're* in no mood? You fucking Irish loser. You don't even want to know about the day I've had. So did you just let him in? Did you offer him any wine? A comfortable chair?"

"Oh come on. Like I said, it could've been anybody. I didn't see—"

"I don't care who he was!"

"Well then what are you bitchin' about?" Tony's voice was defensive. "It was some old codger with a stuck car."

"Some old codger who's now dead!"

Jane began to say something but was cut off instantly. "Christ! You two run a circle of perfect bloody ineptitude. If you lot wanted to package it and sell it you couldn't do it better if you tried!"

"Why are you doing this?"

Ian answered in a soft, deliberate mocking American accent, a lousy version of Southern. "Do you know, darling, how pathetic that sounds?"

"I liked it better when you were talking about how rich the Irish are."

"That made things a lot easier for you, didn't it?" Back to British. "You like easy things, don't you? Easy to please, easy to lead, easy to lay."

"Shut up."

Ian's voice was furious. "Shut up? Sitting around here screwing all day, getting stoned, so lazy you decide to add a dead body to the mix."

Sarah could hear someone, she assumed Jane, stalking into the bedroom. Slamming the door. The bathroom door shook and Sarah had to hold it to keep it from swinging open further.

"Yes, run! Hide!"

"Hey, relax," Tony said. "We'll deal with it."

"You! I'd keep your mouth shut, you bloody ass!"

There were steps just outside the bathroom door. Ian's voice shouted into the bedroom. "Hide! Why don't you go if you can't take the pressure! You don't want to talk to me? Try talking to your husband! You signed up for this gig, darling! Bonnie and Clyde all the way, right, you bloody cow?"

Sarah could hear Jane crying in the bedroom. And she could hear the bracelet getting flicked around on his wrist.

"What a laugh," Ian said. Now he was back in the kitchen. "You lot. And you, you poxy cockwomble, you let someone like that ask all those questions. What did you think, he was just gonna walk away and that was it, never mention the cabin and the strange new happy family to anyone?"

"Doubt he's gonna talk much now."

"Do you know what a FUCKING job it is to deal with bodies! You start with a gig like this, all above the board, purely white collar, nobody gets hurt—and then this shit! And in the middle of winter, in the middle of wherever the *fuck* we are. And who the fuck knows how many people knew that guy was COMING DOWN THIS ROAD!"

The front door opened and slammed shut. From the bedroom Jane's crying. From the sofa Tony muttering over the walnuts. Sarah didn't know what to do. She was stuck in the bathroom. She held her breath with a hammering heart, listening carefully near the door. Ian must have gone out.

She tentatively pushed on the door, enough to see out. First glance around the room revealed Ian, standing outside the door, smoking a cigarette. She'd never seen any of them smoke anything but weed until now. Tony was sitting in the middle of the couch, leaning forward over the walnuts. The dogs were in the kitchen, by the front door.

She eased out and made for the ladder. She silently and quickly climbed up.

CHAPTER 28

Just as the early morning sun hit the walls of the apartment across the street, Brandon logged into his encrypted system. He was finishing a croissant. Next to a mug of coffee on the edge of his desk was a picture of he and Sarah together at a hotel in Iceland. She was smiling. He had been caught at the wrong moment, with his eyes just off to the side. The person Sarah had asked to snap the photo had offered to take it again, but Sarah had said it was perfect, that she'd liked the abstraction. It would let them remember the moment better than a "normal" photo would. It was bordered perfectly by the dark teak frame Sarah had given him for his birthday—well, what he'd told her was his birthday. It would be clear to anyone looking at the photo that they were a couple, that there were feelings in that shot. He knew that Sarah hadn't posed like she was in the photo, with her arms holding him from the side. He'd photoshopped and repositioned her arm using parts from another photo, to make it look that way. If he had any doubts about whether his handiwork seemed authentic, all it had taken was the visit from Sarah with the frame. A birthday gift. He'd watched her put the photo in the frame herself, then start recalling the place and time and smells of Reykjavik, and the warm waters of the hot springs they'd visited. She hadn't noticed the change at all. The fake photo had, then and there, become legitimate.

The folder named Starbucks contained several entries, each marked with a specific date and time. Each was a brief message, just a few words. Entry #1 had read "CALL ME" and #2 was "Discuss." Today's was Entry #3: "READ ME OR 911." This one also had some additional notes to go with it.

Two weeks ago, when Brandon had stayed with Sarah at her Seattle apartment, he'd gone to get coffees for them one morning at the Starbucks on James and Yesler. Before arriving he'd stopped at a quiet place to put on a pair of glasses, baseball cap and a temporary goatee. While waiting for the coffees, he'd pulled aside one of the baristas he'd noticed on previous visits and mentioned a surprise he was planning for his dad's birthday. Could she help? It would be a heartwarming gift for a man who had just turned 60, and had beaten cancer. The job was very simple, but it had to be clandestine and punctual. All she had to do was place messages in the same window sill on certain days, as specified. There were three messages and one gag prop—a fake bullet, because his dad was also a former Seattle cop. Yes, the messages seemed random and pointless, but it would make sense to his dad when he saw them. It would be worth a $50 tip now and another $50 afterward.

Brandon checked the time. Soon, the barista should be placing #3 in the window.

While the first two notes were meant to be read from outside and then forgotten, #3 contained a detailed message, sealed in a birthday envelope. It was meant to be picked up and read. Written to appear to be from Sarah's father, it made some counter-demands: that he'd used a private investigator to find some details about her potential captors; that they could settle this away from the public eye but for a substantially smaller amount than the original demand; that he called their bluff and didn't believe they'd harm Sarah; that this smaller amount would be delivered at an abandoned gas station outside Seattle at 3:00 P.M. Wednesday; that if her captors didn't like these terms he could go to the police with what he had.

Brandon took the chance that these nudges and hints would be enough to cause Mike to believe the suggestion that the police may be involved somehow, and that Sarah's father was demanding a new amount, time, and location for the exchange. He took the chance with the barista following through as well. He'd thought about installing a camera nearby or hiring an anonymous person to check on whether the signs were being placed in the window, but these were risks, and like all other risks in the project—the design—he entered them into his schematic and assigned a score to manage them properly, knowing risks could never be eliminated entirely.

When Mike read the contents for #3, it should introduce a certain amount of pandemonium into the hostage scenario and establish the exchange details: the gas station at 3:00 P.M. Wednesday.

Brandon turned his attention to Doc1. He would need to make a couple of final adjustments to it, then it was ready for delivery. In a way it was the *pièce de résistance* of the whole effort: brief, to the point, and contained all the basic facts of the exchange. It described details that only someone familiar with the Sarah situation would be privy to, yet it was written in a haphazard way that gave it a certain spontaneity. He called it Doc1 for no other reason than that the nondescript name it defaulted to when he'd started creating it seemed fitting for such a grand finale. During a moment of calm here or there he liked to allow himself time to embrace the simple things, when so much of the project—the design—was such a complex of moving parts.

When discovered and interpreted the way he hoped, the details on Doc1 would cement Liddy's role as the perpetrator and establish his knowledge of the entire operation, concluding with trying to collect a ransom payout. Doc1 had specifics on it that would tie him to the crime: the location of the exchange, timelines, steps taken, specific buzzwords and of course the whole concept of releasing Sarah for cash. The cops would start to connect it with the other evidence found in Liddy's apartment, online, and even at his childhood home in Billings if they took it that far. It would be the beginning of a complicated investigation into the motives and planning of a man who masqueraded as a simple architect by day but who hid a darker side of himself after hours.

He would bring Doc1 to Liddy's place today. Today was the final day of dealing with Liddy's apartment. When he was sure Liddy had left for work, he would enter the apartment, place Doc1 in a good spot within the apartment, and go to the garage to pick up the camera he'd left and find out the status of the gun stock left on Liddy's car hood. While he was there he would place a few additional items: a photo album showing a stalker pursuing his prey. Pictures that showed Sarah had been followed, observed, and tracked for months. As always, he'd stripped the metadata from the images and made some visual tweaks to some. There were unfinished letters to Sarah, written in Liddy's style, timelines, notes, secret fantasies, sexual scenarios, even a series of situations in which the imaginary couple went on a cruise together and had sex in clandestine places, always coming close to getting caught. Brandon had spent hours composing the notes and letters, always taking great care to go over the copies of Liddy's actual correspondence to check for stylistic points, common errors he might make, and so on.

Presumably Liddy would leave for work at just after seven. Brandon would have to wait until after eight to be safe. He still had time. As he waited, he let his mind wander. How had Mike done it exactly. Alone, or with help? Was it a slow manipulation, or a quick grab somewhere in public? Whatever Mike's real name was, he had asked for Sarah's schedule and whereabouts and routines, and had said nothing of the act itself. They had not met in person, nor did either know what the other looked like. They kept most details from each other, out of caution. He had no idea where Mike was keeping Sarah or how he'd delivered the demand video.

No more than Mike had any idea that Brandon was dealing him out. When Mike read the details of Entry #3, he would see that Sarah's father had evidently made some demands of his own; the amount, location and time of the exchange had just been dictated to him.

The plan was that no one would be hurt. The entire thing was a cash transaction. But he would be prepared. He was ready. The concept of killing someone had only entered Brandon's mind once, and it was long ago, in a conversation with his younger brother. That conversation had remained with him and he'd taken the essence of that notion, distilled it down to a task, and removed all the accompanying inhibitions and stigma. If it came to that, where was the guilt if he was removing a threat? He would be killing Sarah's captor, someone who had violated her right to freedom. Hadn't he vowed to himself to protect her? The shot—hopefully only one—would be calculated, clean, and precise. He'd practiced on and off for weeks. Adam Liddy's fingerprints would be all over the gun stock. The gun would be found at the abandoned gas station, somewhere near Mike's body if it came to that. It would be enough to cause confusion: was Adam Liddy behind the trigger? Had Liddy sent someone else?

He acknowledged the risk that Mike might send someone else to show up at the exchange—maybe several—or otherwise try to disrupt the steps laid out in Entry #3 for his own benefit. He assigned a score to that possibility and shelved it. He felt confident that when the money was presented, Mike would be the one to step forward and collect it, reduced amount or not. Mike would expose himself at that moment.

Beyond the exchange, beyond the investigation, he would play the boyfriend role with Sarah and be available while the questioning began, gradually putting more and more distance between them. He would eventually disassociate himself entirely from her life and fade away. He'd already set the first stage by suggesting that he and Sarah see a bit less of each other.

CHAPTER 29

S he welcomed the morning light. No sunshine, but a soft white glow, and she would take what she could get. From the warmth of her sleeping bag, she looked toward both windows. She could see that it was snowing heavily, even more so than last night. She noticed the sound of a car moving back and forth outside. She got up, placing her feet only on the silent zones, and listened for sounds. Classical music was playing from a small speaker below, probably the CD player.

She hadn't slept well. Last night she'd lain in the darkness simply staring toward the ceiling for an hour or two before fading off. She'd had a bad dream of some kind but couldn't remember any of it, only waking from it. She'd fallen back asleep with the images of the man outside and the dogs and the big argument and Ian's bracelet and the way Tony had cracked the walnuts at the end. She'd faded for a while, then woken again with the idea that maybe she would never get out of here because of whatever bad news Ian had obviously brought home with him last night. Then there was Jane crying, and Ian smoking outside the door. She'd had the distinct image of being in some kind of heavy danger. Of dying, even. This last thought had stuck with her and kept her from sleeping until she tried to empty her mind of everything. That had worked until a new round of snoring began from below.

Then she'd recalled something that had been on her mind ever since the conversation with Jane last night, before the stranger. She knew it was something specific but had been unable to recall. Finally it had come to her: the thing about the kidnapping/extortion policy. She even remembered the time Brandon had asked about it. It was last year, maybe in late fall? They'd been talking, going back and forth with playful, teasing things, and he'd asked her whether she was covered on a kidnapping/extortion policy. At the time, she'd seen it as a question that someone might ask someone like her, but in a joking way. She hadn't even heard of such a policy, and when Brandon said she should ask Burke about it sometime, she did. She found out what it was, and that yes, she was covered. She was pretty sure she never followed up with Brandon, and she forgot about it. She never thought about the matter again.

Until yesterday. It had kept her awake for what seemed like hours, wondering why Brandon would ask, even out of strange curiosity. And it had actually crossed her mind: could such a policy be used if the police were not involved, if there was no police report? She'd felt guilty, aware that she was tacitly questioning Brandon's motives, even if only to exclude him, but the instructions had been clear: no police. One swirling thought had led to another, to things she didn't want to picture. *I met him at my sister's funeral*. She'd never seen nor met him before Tracy died.

She paced silently to the front window and looked out. With the snow the sky was bright and it took her eyes a second to adjust. The SUV had a plow on the front and was clearing the driveway, pushing the snow up against the already high walls of snow surrounding all sides except the road out. Tony was driving, sometimes leaning his elbow out the open driver window. He had a cigar out one side of his mouth. Both dogs were running around, chasing each other. Their dark coats were speckled with snow. She looked toward the spot where the man had been found last night. It was completely smooth, not a hint of blood or anything else.

She crept to the square and peered down. Jane was sitting in the chair by the stove, reading a book and drinking something from a mug. She couldn't see Ian anywhere. *Mike.*

She waited, listening, for a few seconds. "Hello," she said. She half expected Jane to show some badge of mayhem from last night, after all the lights went out and the punishment really began. Or at least to look puffy from all the crying. But when Jane looked up, she appeared energetic. No puffiness, no long face. "Morning," she said. Her voice sounded oddly cheerful. "Want some coffee?"

"Okay. Sure."

"I was going to make some breakfast too. Anything you want?"

"Doesn't matter, anything's fine."

"Well we don't have the best selection. I'll get a cup. So, how about some toast anyway?" When Sarah descended, Jane handed her a mug, then looked in the fridge.

Near the base of the ladder, Sarah looked around, trying to see outside. As usual, the curtains on all the windows blocked a clear view of outside. And usually the dogs or the men would have prevented her from considering going to look in any case. But she could do it now. Edging away from the kitchen, she started making her way toward the front.

Jane seemed to notice her, probably realizing she'd changed positions, but just as soon went back to the loaf of bread in front of her, evidently unconcerned. Sarah noticed that the bread was a solid loaf that Jane had to slice. So it must have come from a bakery. Someone must have gone into town. Or had Ian brought it back last night?

When she got to the front door, she parted the curtain and looked out the window. It was a whole new world. Instantly, things she'd not seen before came into view. She could better get a partial view of the shed toward the left. And there was that car. It didn't look that old. No way the transmission could be out. It was piled high with the new snow. Ian was just beyond it, near the open doors of the shed, doing something. She recalled the man and wondered what they'd done with him. She knew she'd seen his hand move. Had they killed him? Or was he still alive somehow, out there in the shed? It didn't look like the kind of place that would have heat. It looked dark, dirty, a place for tools and things.

"You like just butter?" Jane said.

"Yeah. That's fine. Thanks."

"Any jam, anything?"

"No, that's okay."

"Would you mind getting away from the door?"

Sarah took one more look and backed away.

"I know you want to look out there, but if either one of them sees you doing that, well." Jane sat down on the chair by the stove and set a plate of toast on the coffee table. "Have a seat, let's have some breakfast before they come back in."

Sarah sat on the couch, surprised by Jane's upbeat attitude. It was as though the gloomy whispering and stares last night, the huge argument, the stranger, were all in the distant past.

Tentatively, she said, "So, are you okay?"

Jane smiled. "Yeah. You?"

"I guess."

"You know, I used to have an uncle who liked mustard on his toast," Jane said, studying the piece of toast in Sarah's hand. "Yeah, every morning. But it had to be Dijon. He hated yellow mustard. I do too. Seems like a weak excuse for mustard, you know."

Sarah nodded vaguely. She glanced at the book Jane had been reading, face down on the coffee table: *Great Expectations*.

"So you have an uncle who liked mustard, and you have or had a husband. What else do—"

"No, we can't talk about me."

"Oh."

"I just mentioned the mustard thing to make small talk. Not about me."

"Okay."

"Okay."

"Looks like you like Dickens?" Sarah said, trying again.

Jane glanced at the book. "Yeah. One of my favorites. Don't know how many times I've read it. Ian got me into it."

Sarah sort of smiled. "So what else do you like to read?"

Jane said, "You want to borrow it? I'm done. I was just going through it again. A dozen, I bet."

"A dozen?"

"How many times I've read it. Guessing of course. Hey, you know what? There's a bunch of books and stuff out in the shed. We can get you some if you want. I meant to ask you anyway." Jane handed her the book.

Sarah noticed the expression on her face, like she'd just done a good deed and was expecting a pat on the back, some kind of recognition. Once again, going the extra mile behind Ian's back.

"Thanks."

"Sure," Jane said. Now Sarah noticed in her eyes that searching expression, as though she was trying to guess Sarah's thoughts.

"I don't think anyone knew how long this would last," she said. "This whole thing. They always said it could be days or weeks. So it's kind of hard to plan for everything, you know. And I know you're kidnapped, and there was no excuse for the way we—" She looked down, into her coffee. Sarah caught a glimpse of something—sorrow, perhaps—sweep briefly over Jane's expression, and just as quickly disappear. "I guess what I'm saying is, we can at least try to make you comfortable, you know?"

Immediately, Sarah returned to the images of last night, the expression on Ian's face when he'd come in and they whispered something back and forth, then the way he'd let Jane have it.

"What do you mean, 'they' said."

"I'm sorry, did you want milk in your coffee? I didn't even ask. We don't have any cream."

"It's fine."

"I like it black too."

"No you don't."

Jane looked back at her as if stung.

"I've seen you put milk in your coffee. "You always say 'we don't have any cream' and then you put milk in."

"What does it matter what I put in it?"

"Never mind about the coffee. Anyway, you just said 'they' said."

"They?"

"A minute ago. You said 'they said it could be days or weeks' or something like that."

An exasperated look came over Jane's face. "You know, the people who set this whole thing up."

"No I don't know. How would I know?"

"I thought I might've mentioned it."

"Well you didn't. So you mean, it's not just you guys?"

"Well, no. We're just the ones who are doing this part, in charge of you."

Sarah felt herself becoming alarmed. "Well who else is it?"

Jane looked at her as though she'd just been accused of something. "I mean, even if I knew I couldn't just sit here and tell you."

"Well how many people are there?"

"I don't know. I don't even know who they are."

"Are you kidding? How can you not know?"

"Why should I? It's not part of what we're doing. Besides, only Ian knows. He said it's best that we know as little as possible about certain things, this being one of them I guess."

"Like the fact that his name's Mike?"

Jane glanced sharply at Sarah. "His name's Ian."

"But his name's Mike, right?"

"His name's Ian."

"Oh. I see."

Jane looked into the coffee table, then suddenly smiled. "So, did you grow up in Seattle? Well I guess obviously you did."

Sarah stared at Jane. "Are you two, you know? I mean, how does Tony fit in with—"

"I bet you've traveled around the world a dozen times."

"Things didn't look so good last night, the way Ian was—"

"Shut up!"

Sarah recoiled.

Jane slowly said, "Sorry. Just wanted to know you better is all."

"Well I don't know why. What, are we supposed to sit here like we just had a manicure or something?"

"Kind of feels like that, doesn't it?"

"No. Is it supposed to?"

"Doesn't sound that bad, actually. I bet you know all the good places."

"I hate manicures," Sarah said sharply.

"Oh."

"Are you shocked? Disappointed?"

"Hey, you're not eating your toast."

"What happened to that guy last night?"

Jane looked back at her and her eyes neither flinched nor gave anything away, yet in the air between them hung a sort of mutual understanding. If Sarah had been able to read her mind she would not have understood better. The image of Tony cracking the nuts came back to her.

"I think I'm gonna be sick."

"Sarah."

She quickly ran to the kitchen area and leaned over the sink. Sarah did feel ill suddenly, but foremost on her mind was a way to get at her knife, any knife, some tools, the keys in the toilet, a method, anything, to get out of here. She could do something now. It was only Jane. The men were outside. Knives and things had to be nearby, in these drawers. She saw Jane appear behind her, always someone there to keep her from the red zone, a minder. She tried to heave, but nothing came.

"You okay?"

"No I'm not okay!"

"I'm sorry, Sarah, for all this."

"Don't be. Let's just skip the manicure for now."

"Okay, let's skip the manicure. Look, I know you're wondering what went on last night. All that talking down here, the whispering? Well, he didn't want me to tell you, but what the hell, you know his name, right?"

Sarah acknowledged her, waiting.

"He was in town yesterday. Doing the business part of the thing, you know, this thing? And he got some bad news. Turns out your dad figures he'll try to do things his own way."

"His own way?"

"Yeah. And you have to promise you don't tell him any of this, okay?"

"Is that some kind of joke? Like I'm just gonna get Ian's attention and say, 'Hey, guess what Jane told me?'"

"Ian thinks maybe someone got the police involved."

Sarah felt herself turn cold.

"We don't know who, doesn't matter, really. But somebody might have."

"My dad?"

"I don't know, like I just said."

"Why did he say that?"

"I don't know. I just thought you should know about it. Because things are gonna be a little different now."

"What do you mean, different?"

"Tighter controls, something like that."

"Tighter controls, what does that mean?"

"I don't know anything. We'll find out from Ian later."

Sarah suddenly remembered the bullet. "But the video we made. I asked you, I asked Ian what if he called the cops? And in the demand, it said if someone called the cops, that I would—"

"I know."

"But some of my friends might be worried by now. One of them could have—"

"Look, I never should've mentioned it. I thought you might as well—"

Loud footsteps suddenly stomped on the landing outside the front door. The door opened and Tony came in. He looked around, then focused on the two of them standing in the kitchen. Sarah avoided eye contact.

Jane said, "She isn't feeling well."

"Oh. Well, we're gonna go now. Shouldn't take too long."

"Okay."

When Tony had closed the door Sarah said, "Mind if I get some water?"

"Sure." Jane filled a glass from the tap.

The door opened again and Tony leaned in. "I would keep her upstairs. She could try anything. Need some help?"

"It's okay."

"It's not okay. She could take you if she had to."

"Okay, she'll go back upstairs. Just let her have some water first."

"Well, see you later. The dogs'll be outside." He winked at Sarah. "Bye, little one." He closed the door.

When the door closed Sarah looked at him walking away. "I hate him."

Jane smiled at her. "He's okay. Here, let's sit back down. You didn't have any of your toast. You want something else instead?"

"Don't you remember what he made me say? With him and that—that Magnum or whatever it was, that gun in my face? That stuff about the bullet?"

Jane took her time responding, and this only made Sarah worry more. When she finally did, her voice was measurably distant. "If you're asking me what happens now, I don't know, it's not our decision."

"Was he serious? That I could be killed?"

"Come on, Sarah, no one's talking about dying."

"What about that guy last night?"

Jane looked toward the stove. "Fire might need some wood."

"Where are Tony and Mike going?"

"Ian."

"Where are they off to? To dump his body?"

"Sarah, you're getting ahead of yourself."

"Well tell me, then. Why would they need to keep me alive? If you get the cash, that's the end of story, right? You get what you wanted, you don't need me anymore. How could you let me go?"

"Because that's how it's set up."

"But I know what you look like."

Jane creased her brows.

"Well, doesn't that make you wonder? The first couple days, you were wearing those masks. Then you stopped. Didn't you think I might remember your faces? Don't you think the cops are going to ask what you guys looked like?"

"Look, I'm not comfortable the way this is going."

"*You're* not comfortable!?"

"It was obviously a mistake, I never should have mentioned it." Jane forced a fake smile. "You want the deal? Maybe it's like this. Maybe they need you alive for the first few days, just to make the demands, to show you're okay. If they get the money, maybe they don't need you alive anymore. Once they get the money, who knows. Anyway, I don't know either way."

Sarah felt lightheaded. She let her gaze wander toward the doorway. Near the door, she noticed a fairly heavy jacket hanging on a hook. She had noticed it before but didn't know who it belonged to. Beneath it was a pair of boots. Her mind started to connect the dots. Key in toilet. Coat and boots at door. Car outside. She even thought about asking Jane about the car, whether the transmission was really shot. She thought better of it.

"I'm going to the bathroom now. Or do I need to ask you first."

Jane nodded in the direction of the bathroom. "Be my guest."

When she entered the bathroom and pulled the door shut, she looked in the mirror and was horrified to see that her left eye was black and blue. The lid itself was dark. It was swollen halfway shut. The side of her face just by the eye was bruised and purple. She felt the area with her fingers. It was tender, though not as painful as last night. Jane hadn't said a thing the entire time they'd been talking! She had certainly been able to see it. It was obviously worse than it had been last night. Jane had said she had some snow for her eye last night. That had been forgotten. It was too late now.

Feeling anxious, she sat on the toilet with the lid down. She considered getting her knife and keys. She could keep them near her, so she didn't have to go to the bathroom to get them. If she had them with her, she could make a run for it when the timing was right. And right now, with only Jane in the house, was not a bad time. The problem was, the dogs were outside.

And the doubting part of her reminded her that she'd been lucky yesterday morning when Tony had looked upstairs, everywhere, but not found the keys. If they'd been up there and he'd found them, she didn't want to imagine the retribution. And afterward, when Jane had searched her here in the bathroom, they'd only been inches away from Jane's groping hands. No, the keys had to stay where they were. They were safe.

What if she somehow got Jane to ask the dogs inside? They were usually pretty tame when they were around one of them. She could start talking to Jane again, get her distracted, maybe somehow get her and the dogs away from the door, just enough to get some time and run for the car. Jane might try to chase her, but she'd be fast. Plus, hadn't Tony just said she could take Jane? She'd never even thought about it. But she began to see futility: all Jane had to do was let the dogs run after her. The same thing that had happened to that stranger. In fact, hadn't it been Jane who'd let them out?

She pushed the door open quietly.

Out there, on the sofa, Jane had picked up her book and had her legs curled under her. Her coffee was in one hand. She truly looked like she could have just finished a manicure. The dutiful housewife, waiting for the roast to finish in the oven. Waiting for her man to come back home. Except

Jane had two men, and a husband to boot. Yet she had none. Sarah felt a surge of pity. The woman sitting there was surrounded by men, yet she seemed completely alone. She was a soul in search of something in her life that she hadn't yet found. Noticing Sarah, she looked up from her reading.

"Um, I think I'll go upstairs for a while. Thanks for the coffee."

Jane smiled. "Sure. Let me know if you need anything. Don't forget your book."

Sarah took the book and climbed the ladder. As she sat down on the cot, she heard the sounds of the door opening downstairs. The dogs came in. So Jane was not on her side yet. She had let the dogs in to do their job as guards.

She lay with the sleeping bag draped over her, staring at her usual spot on the ceiling. She tried to keep her eyes open. Every time she closed her eyes, even to blink, she thought about what might happen to her. What was the thing about "tighter controls" supposed to mean? She admitted that even knowing bad news would be better than not knowing at all. All she had now was open and wild speculation. She ruled out good news completely.

She had no reason to believe they would let her go, money or no money. She'd seen their faces. On this she blamed them. They'd started with the masks, then abandoned them. And she knew their personalities, to a point. They'd talked about themselves. She felt she knew Jane better than she wanted to. They didn't hide things, like their weird threesome thing, or Tony's allergies. Ian was a Brit. She couldn't imagine that locket was only on for this gig. If there was a police lineup at some point, she could pick them out without hesitation. Surely they knew that. Surely Ian knew that and was going along with that knowledge. So what could it mean, other than she would never be in a position to identify them, because she'd be dead? Once they got their money, the deal would be done.

And now the cops had been called. Was that for real, or was it manufactured tension to keep her paranoid and controllable through fear? She felt at odds, disagreeing with herself. She had a rush of hope that Ian probably was feeling fear now, that the cops might be aware of the situation. The cabin was remote, but that guy yesterday might have been a detective of some kind and somehow found the place based on some clues, or maybe just by accident. So maybe there was an urgency in Ian's mind now.

Or he indeed was a random stranger, but the cops were involved anyway.

Either way, when they got their cash, they had no reason to let her go. They'd have to remove the threat. Cops or no cops. She could not get the idea out of her head, no matter how she tried to lay it out.

Despite her worry, she felt sleepy. She was used to doing things, to activity. She was usually on the move. These few days, not getting any exercise, not getting outside at all, made her restless. Yet she was easily able to slip off into sleep at times, whether she wanted to or not. Boredom and worry were taxing her, and for an instant, she felt a hint of panic, that even if she didn't meet a harsh demise like the stranger last night, that this thing could go on forever and she would slowly wither away, fading, fading, until she was deflated, depressed and decrepit, with all the life sucked out of her. They'd find her years, decades from now, long since dead, with cobwebs all over her skeleton, just like the junk on the desk.

She had to work to keep her eyes open. She knew she was tired because she hadn't slept much last night, but it was the boredom and the worry that were really doing it. And the not knowing what lay ahead. The innuendo and suggestions. The whispering downstairs. The only things she was privy to concerned food or sex or trivial things. The rest was secret. She was hostage to whispered conversations. She knew ideas and conclusions were being traded back and forth on a daily basis because she could always hear the vagaries just beneath her, yet she could never hear the details.

She knew she had to stay awake. If she fell asleep now, she might be up all night tonight as well, listening to them screw and snore down there. She picked up *Great Expectations* and began to read.

Fatigue soon overcame her. She tried to fight it but felt herself losing.

CHAPTER 30

Traffic was heavy in the morning rush hour into the city. As Adam Liddy inched along he tried to go through the mental notes for his presentation. He had decided to drive today since he might have to visit the building site after the meeting. But at this pace, he thought he may have been better off taking BART like usual. It would be full and he'd have to stand with the weight of the book bag slicing into his shoulder but at least he'd be making progress. Not only that, driving meant parking and parking cost a fortune.

The little details were eating at him, just as they always did before a presentation, and he wondered how many things he'd missed. He still had time to make certain changes to the notes but there were many things he had no control over at this point. Had he remembered all the documents? Was everything signed? Were the diagrams the most recent versions? He would need to make copies of some of them when he got to the office. He'd have to get Anders to approve the change order for the builders later.

He sipped some of his coffee as he watched the taillights go on and off in front of him, endlessly. He mused at the irony of nearly being able to see his office building from where he was, knowing he wouldn't reach it for another half hour or more. A childhood wish for jet packs and flying cars remained unfulfilled. It was high time. Weirder things were happening. Drones were commonplace. Why not bridge the gap and put them to work ferrying people across the bay? But then of course the skies would be cluttered with drones and flying taxis. People would be inching along in the sky instead of down here.

This thing with the overnight delivery and the strange gap still distracted him. He still couldn't see how it had wound up back in his mailbox—unless the post office had come back. That must have been it. They had another delivery at his building, and while they were there they fixed it. Or maybe whoever had received it in error had called them and they came out and corrected it. It didn't seem that likely, but who knew.

And the car alarm—what the hell was that about? He'd gone down there to find a triangular piece of metal on his hood. It must have fallen or somehow wound up on his car, but he had found no scratches or dents. Nor was there any object within range that it may have fallen from. His car was fine. He saw no sign of entry. Nothing was missing in his stall that he could tell. It had occurred to him that maybe it was a lever or crank for one of the ventilation shafts, but it didn't seem to match anything he saw, and the size wasn't right. So he put it on his workbench. Maybe if it belonged to somebody they would come back and get it. If it was still there when he went back home tonight, he would bring it to the landlord.

Then he remembered it. An entire folder of contract modifications that he'd removed from the main binder. The contractors needed them for this project. He'd taken them out this morning to get the codes off them and had forgotten to put them back. He slammed his fist on the wheel. He looked at his watch. There was no way around it. He'd have to go back.

CHAPTER 31

Sarah was jolted out of sleep by a pounding sound. It was repetitious, loud, metallic, with a dull heaviness to it. Panic and confusion swept over her.

She sat up instantly. It was darker now in her confine. Much darker. The rear window was gone. She stared, confused. It was black there. Had she fallen asleep that long? Was it night? No, couldn't be. The front window was light, but it was fading, flickering, even. Tony and Ian were just outside it. Now she saw. The sound was from a hammer.

They must be standing on a ladder or something, nailing boards over the window. Ian was holding a board, and Tony was hammering the nails. She stood and stared in stunned amazement. The window was narrowing even as she watched. The wood was filling it in from left to right, board by board, and with it went the light. From the light that remained, she judged that a couple of hours had passed since she'd started reading, and she cursed herself for having fallen asleep.

Was this what Jane meant by tighter controls? Boarding up the windows? She could feel a new claustrophobia as she searched for the candle. In the diminishing light she found it and held it in her hands, turning it over and over. It was shorter now, since she and Jane had used it last night. Suddenly she felt grateful for it. What before had been another piece in a collection of junk now had purpose.

When they'd finished checking the measurements, Tony nailed the last board into place, and the room went almost entirely dark. The only light came from the square. Small amounts of light leaked through the boards here and there. She went to the front window and tried to look through a crack. She could see a narrow slice of the clearing, but it was just a teasing sample now.

Hearing a noise near the square, she turned to see Tony's head come through, with a piece of wood in his hand. He lay it across the width of the opening, then disappeared, talking with Ian below. Then more sawing and hammering. Within minutes, the light from the square was reduced to a faint glow. Then, with a final blow from the hammer, it was cut totally. The entire room was plunged in darkness except for harsh needles of light that slipped through tiny gaps here and there, useless, cruel slivers of light. With horror, she wondered if they were sealing her up in here alive. Was that the plan? Was that how they planned to get rid of her when they got their cash? Not by killing her, but just letting her die?

The light waxed and waned as the boards were measured and cut. As they progressed it became clear that they were building a makeshift trap door. They were testing it. Partially entering the square to check their work. Opening and closing it. Putting the final touches on it.

So they were going to lock her in here. In darkness.

She had to plan. She had to get out. She felt suddenly energized.

She knew she couldn't wait any longer. Jane had only mentioned the tighter control thing today, and now here she was, walled in up here. She couldn't wait around to find out what was going on with the cops, or Dad, or Brandon, or anyone. She had no news whatsoever of the outside world.

In fact, all she knew of the outside world was that there was a major storm, and that snow was falling. If she waited for the outside world to save her, she might lose her one chance to get away. She still had the chance. She had to plan.

This must be because of the close call with the man last night. She wondered if somehow the man last night had heard about her? If he was just a regular guy, with a stuck car, in the middle of a storm, and this thing had leaked to the press, he might've heard something in the news. If it had made it to the media, she guessed—hoped—it would be big news. Dad was good at staying out of the public eye except when he had to, but the tabloids found a way to sneak into their lives. A new deal, Dad's younger girlfriend, Tracy's death. It had been Tracy who'd made those sleaze mags happy a few times, before she'd gotten a little wiser around them. She'd been caught more than once, always at the worst times. And if something like this made it to the press, they'd be all over it.

She wondered how things would play out if the man had been a cop. She could see things moving in a certain direction, such as the cop not reporting back. That would mean more cops would come. They'd interview people. It would be in the news. This area would be searched. But even as she plotted out what might happen next, and after that, and after that, she found herself doubting. Of course they wouldn't send one guy, alone, walking down a road late at night in the middle of a storm, to approach a remote house. Even if he'd parked somewhere and walked down the road it would be pretty hard to hide a cop car. But on top of that, the man had mentioned his son overseas, and the son's cabin down the road, and he'd mentioned a

Peterson, like he knew the people who'd lived in this cabin before. He hadn't sounded like a cop.

She sat down on the cot and nearly felt like weeping. She dragged out the duffel bag with her clothes. The whole thing was hopeless. Even as she tried to think of ways to get out, to start some sort of plan, she began to see all the odds against her. Jane had let her know someone else was involved. So they were doing this on behalf of or with someone. Someone else, probably working in society, who was making sure the police didn't get involved, who was pulling strings on the other end, maybe arranging the cash payment somehow. Jane had said she didn't even know who they were.

The thought came on suddenly, like a bright spark. As she groped through the duffel bag it hit her that when she'd asked about clothes the first day, Ian had told her they'd thought of that. He'd even mentioned the exact dresser: the maple one. Getting in to her father's house was not easy. Not just a knock on the door or opening a window. There was a security gate outside and there were alarm systems. There were many faces in the house at any time but all of them were familiar. She couldn't imagine any of these three had actually gotten into the house, and her room, under some guise. The only person she could picture who'd been in her room was Brandon. She acknowledged the spark, rejected it, and moved on. She was starting to grasp at any connections she could conjure. She had to remain focused.

If money was all they were after, and they got it, they only put themselves at further risk by keeping her alive. So she was back to that again. They would kill her. Just like they'd killed the man out there.

The nails in the floor. The zones. She couldn't see them in the dark. But she knew roughly where they were. With the candle, she could see well enough. Maybe when her eyes adjusted to the dark, she could get by on the light from the spaces between the boards in the windows. Or she could light one match, then another, over and over. There were plenty of them in the box.

There were quiet areas and creaky areas of the floor. She could use both to her advantage. Use the noise to distract them, make them think she was busy doing something, pacing back and forth in nervous anticipation. *That's what they'd like, to have me nervous. They got that. I don't have to make it up. I'm scared as hell now.*

Calm down.

Think. Focus. So I use the silence. I get downstairs. Down the ladder. I somehow get past them, maybe when they're busy screwing or arguing, when the dogs are just far enough away. I go for the jacket, open the—

She recalled the image of the blood on the dog's mouth last night.

I'd have to save some food ahead of time, to bribe them. It's the chance I'll have to take. With the knife, I could keep them at bay if it comes to that. I could make it to the door.

I'd have to get the keys. Maybe I should get the keys up here after all, keep them with me. I could hide them somewhere. If for a short time, I could hide them behind the desk. Maybe under the rug. The edge of the rug is close to the square, and that would mean easy access if I was halfway down the ladder. I'd need them near me in case a chance came up suddenly, if the planets aligned in just the right way.

But what if they come up here and step on the keys near the square, or find them wherever they are? My chances of doing anything would be ruined.

And who was she kidding? All the escape plans were based on the square being open. Now it was fitted with a trapdoor. She was locked in. It was dark. She had nothing but some matches and a candle.

She got to her feet instantly, overcome by the sudden need to get to the matches. She groped her way across the floor, got to the night stand and felt for the box. She opened it, took out a match, and lit it. She nearly had to squint in the sudden flare of brightness as the sulfury smell hit her nose. The pulsing circle of light that surrounded her right hand was so warm and welcome she almost felt like crying. When the match nearly burned down, she lit another, then found the candle and lit it. When it was going, the warm glow made the place look much different. It brought out the color of the wood all around her. It also made the shadows look even darker off in the corners, where the light didn't reach.

As she watched the small flame, she realized that conversation from below was muffled. Maybe this was intentional: to keep her in the dark, literally. But now, she realized, she had an advantage. Her mind began to see things she'd overlooked until now. So she had no light and no solid view of the world outside, but now she had total privacy. As long as the hatch was closed she could use the silent zones and do something: work on the windows, come up with a plan, anything, in her own space, without them figuring it out. She bet they hadn't thought of that. And there were plenty of matches, so if the candle ran out, at least she could light them when needed.

If another stranger showed up outside, she could light all the matches in the box, do it next to the cracks in the windows, so they would see the flare. If it was dark outside, it would cause attention. Someone would have to notice them. It might be just enough. But if this occurred to her, she assumed it could occur to them as well. So it would be only a matter of time before they took the matches away. They would know she had the matches because Jane would tell them, and about the candle, too. Ian would say it's a risk, so Tony, go up there and get them. And while you're at it, take anything else she might be able to use.

So she had to hide the matches. She looked around, caught by a sudden feeling of time running out. On her hands and knees, she held the candle and crawled to where the angled wall and the floor met. A two-inch strip of pine molding ran the length of the floor along the base. Between each board forming the floor ran a narrow groove, about the width of a coin. Because these grooves ran the length of each plank, a small pocket was created just behind the molding strip, where it covered the groove. Into one of these narrow pockets she pushed a match. She tried to pull it out. She couldn't do it with her fingers alone, but using a bottle cap, she was able to edge it out.

One after another, she worked her way along the floor, pushing matches into the pockets. Some of the pockets were too large or too small, which she skipped, moving on to the next one, until she'd gone to the other end of the room. In each case, she pushed the match in red tip first, sliding it in so that just enough of the blank end showed above the molding. Within ten minutes she'd hidden half the matches in this way.

She noticed that even in that time the candle had become a bit shorter. Her mind immediately focused on timelines again. If only ten minutes shrunk the candle by this much, she would be in darkness before long. She propped it up on the floor and sat down next to the square. The hatch was in place and very little light leaked in around the edges. She could hear nothing below except the faint and blurred sounds of walking and soft conversation. Even with her ear on the floor close to the edge of the square, sounds were muffled. She began to dwell on the silence, and at how she could almost hear her own breathing and the rustling of her clothes. She felt uncomfortable, alone, and she knew this was how it was going to be from now on. It seemed only minutes ago she'd considered using her new privacy to her advantage and now she was feeling isolated by it. She'd wished just yesterday that she had a hatch or door in the square, so she didn't have to listen to them down there, on the bed. Now she had a hatch. She wished she didn't.

Feeling herself cave in to this feeling of solitude she gradually became aware of something else. She could feel a chill in the air. Not a draft per se, but as soon as she recognized it, she knew she'd felt it for a while. She knew what it was. The temperature was dropping. The hatch was preventing heat from rising. All the heat up here had come up through the square. Now it was blocked off, and the chill was only going to get worse.

Fear combined with unease. Unease merged with dim thoughts of the future. A childhood fear of the dark, the space under the bed, being trapped with no way out. She could feel her breath changing a bit, and she knew she was slipping toward total panic. She watched the candle flame.

I have to blow it out. If I burn the whole candle now, I'm going to be in total darkness. I could ask for another one. They'd have to give me another one. But they might not. I have to ration this one.

As she leaned down to blow it out, her gaze shifted toward the desk. She was drawn to something there but could not tell what. The light situation changed everything, made stuff look different. Instead of light coming into the room from three directions, now a lone candle flame from floor level illuminated objects from below, making vibrating amber shadows as the flame flickered in the drafts, making things take on different shapes, distorted sizes. The desk, as always, was leaning, with the one leg half broken, into the wall. There was something but she could not put her finger on it.

She blew out the candle, and as the wick smell rose into the air a noise came from the square. The latch slid open from below. A rapidly expanding crack of light flooded in as the door opened upward and Tony's head appeared. Watching his head rise, it occurred to her that he was in a vulnerable position. She could kick him, or hit him with something. She could jump on the half-open door and send him crashing down to the floor below. She could break his arm, snapping bones like matchsticks.

"How's it going up here? Cozy?"

Sarah stood near the cot and remained silent.

"What's that smell?" He was searching, looking around. His eyes landed on the candle. The wick was still smoldering.

"That's one thing that's gotta go." He pulled himself up through the square. Then he turned and looked through the opening. "Come on up," he said. Sarah watched as Ian came up carrying a flashlight.

"Well, your highness," Ian said as he looked around the room. "A little dark but hope you understand why we have to do it."

Tony began rummaging through the objects on the night stand, knocking things over. Sarah watched as he picked up the candle and suddenly winced in pain from dripping wax. It fell from his hands. He took the box of matches and turned it in his hands. "How long have these been up here?"

Ian was shining the flashlight around the room. "They've been here the whole time. She obviously hasn't burned the place down yet." He turned to Sarah. "But now that you have the idea in your head, well, you know."

"Why the boards on the windows?" She felt the desperation in her voice.

Ian turned to Tony and flicked his wrist, rustling his bracelet. "Get those matches. Smells like crap up here as it is."

Tony was looking around, under the cot, at the desk. He picked up a few things and put them in his pocket.

"So, about those keys," Ian said. "You still have 'em?"

"What?"

"Come on, things like that don't just magically disappear, not when you have a curious prisoner in the house who likes to take things. Where the hell are they?"

"I already told you, I don't know what you're talking about. Jane already searched me, don't you remember, and Tony already, you already looked up here."

"Right. Well, here's the fine print, Sarah. If you want to go downstairs, for the bathroom, you knock. You need water or whatever, you knock. We'll bring you food and water three times a day. You're gonna have to stay up here until we're finished with this project."

"But why?"

"I hope it'll be over soon."

"Well what's going on? Have you heard from my dad?"

Without replying, Ian went down. "Tony, search wherever you have to. They've gotta be up there somewhere. And see if you can find that knife you were talking about too."

She stepped back and watched in quiet desperation as Tony began overturning things. Looking in all the crevices, throwing back the rug, pushing stuff off the table, looking under her mattress, rifling through everything in her duffel bag, throwing all the clothes out. As he worked, Sarah glanced toward the desk leg. If she had it with her now, she would sneak up behind Tony and use her full force on the back of his head.

Tony went to the hatch and started to go down.

As he pulled the hatch shut, Sarah said, "It's cold up here."

"Oh," Tony said. "Almost forgot." He set the flashlight on the floor. "In case you need it." Then he closed the hatch.

"I said it's cold up here!"

Darkness enveloped the room. She heard the sounds of the latch sliding shut below.

CHAPTER 32

Brandon drove to Adam Liddy's apartment after 8:30. By now Liddy would be most likely on BART or even downtown. Brandon thought about all those times he'd followed him on that commute: waiting for a bus to the BART station, or driving there and searching for a parking spot, waiting for the packed trains, holding a hand rail as the train slogged through the morning rush with an eye on Liddy several rows ahead.

He went around to the back of the building, as he sometimes did, and took out his key. At the back door he saw a notice that resident keys would soon be changed, and to call the building management company for an appointment to get a replacement. Brandon read it once more carefully as he began to race through the scenarios. This was no small development. It meant that someone felt that the current security picture in the building was insufficient. It could have been management, a resident, or some other factor. It could have been Adam Liddy noticing the overnight mail delay; maybe the knocking on his door after the car alarm; someone may have noticed the security camera cables. Or it could be pure coincidence. Getting the keys in the first place had taken multiple tries using distractions and subterfuges, and he was glad he wouldn't have to go through that again.

As he entered he looked up at the ceiling, behind the security camera, and saw to his horror that the cable had been repaired. Black tape covered the spot where he'd cut and frayed the cable to make it look like an accidental tear. If the cable in the front lobby had also been noticed it would be clear to anyone that neither cut had been accidental. This must be the reason for the new key announcement. He wiped his mouth and focused as he put on latex gloves. From where he was standing he was in a blind spot for the camera, but as soon as he walked onto the garage floor he would be recorded. Estimating the outcomes of several options, he cracked the back door and reached out to tear down the key announcement taped to the outside wall. He dragged a five-gallon bucket of resurfacer to a spot on the floor beneath the camera, then reached up and used the notice sheet and tape to cover it. It was one of several bad options. He was glad today would be his final visit. He wouldn't need access to Liddy's world after this.

He went through the garage to Liddy's stall. His car was gone, so he must have driven to the station today. He was happy to see the metal gun stock sitting on top of the narrow workbench. In several scenarios he imagined the stock would have wound up in a dumpster somewhere, or in the hands of someone else, foiling this end of the plan. That's why he'd placed the camera, to track that possibility. He took out the special holder he'd built for the stock, and taking care to touch it as little as possible, gently placed each end of the holder on either side of the stock. Once secured in place, the stock was suspended within the contraption, held in place by only the two ends. A brace held them together. Liddy's fingerprints on the main part of the stock would remain in place if he was careful. He eased the assembly into a plastic bag, then into his pack. Before he left he took the small camera from the nook he'd placed it in yesterday.

On the far side of the floor he opened the inner door and went up the stairs to the second floor. At #232 he listened briefly, as he always did, before letting himself in. Liddy's place was messier than usual, with documents on the couch in piles and books on the floor. Stacks of handwritten notes lay on his desk. The top drawer—the one that contained the junk—was partially open. Brandon poked around, noticing the thumb drive he'd placed. He took Doc1 out of his pack, liking how it was partly crumpled and bent from being in the bottom, and tucked it into the drawer, letting the folded piece of paper rest on top of the other junk. He left the drawer open, as it had been.

He went to the closet in the bedroom, removed the photo albums and the small stack of materials written in Liddy's style, and tucked them into nooks between boxes and books, back in the recesses of this man's life.

When he left the apartment he went back down the stairs to the garage level. As he opened the inner door to the garage, he stopped and listened. He could hear the sound of the main wide door on the opposite side of the floor either opening or closing: someone driving either in or out. He waited several seconds, debating his best option, ready to move depending on what he heard. He felt certain that going out the front was not an option, assuming the camera cable in the lobby had been noticed and repaired like the rear one had. If someone was driving in, they would have parked by now and would soon open this door to go to their apartment. If it was someone leaving, the garage door had already closed, and they were gone.

Listening and waiting, hearing no further sound, he determined the safest option was to open the door, cross the garage and leave through the back door. It seemed nearly certain that someone had left and he'd find the garage empty. He would have to take the chance that he was wrong, and deal with it when it happened. He turned the handle and went through.

When he'd rounded the corner of the first stall, he looked toward Liddy's stall and was stunned to see his brown Accord there. Just as he was about to turn and go toward the lobby in spite of his misgivings, the driver door opened and Liddy himself got out, hastily fumbling with his keys and heading in Brandon's direction. With Liddy only five paces in front of him Brandon saw no choice but to walk past him; turning now would look contrived and obvious. He looked downward and walked steadily forward, sorting through the keys he was holding to make it appear he was preoccupied. He was shocked to see that he was still wearing the latex gloves. As soon as he passed Liddy, he closed his eyes and fumed.

He went straight for the back door on the far end, tearing the gloves off and balancing his pack, taking care with the gun stock. His mind raced. Had Liddy noticed the gloves? Had Liddy seen his face? Had he noticed the stock was missing from the workbench in his stall? Why the hell was Liddy home now! So many other thoughts: the torn remnants of the replacement keys notice on the outside wall. Liddy would have seen a man with latex gloves and a backpack holding a set of keys. He would have no way of knowing the keys belonged to his very apartment, and that man had just been there, but it would strike anyone as odd.

CHAPTER 33

Sarah swung the beam of the flashlight around the room, again noticing how the shadows looked different. The light was white, more sterile than the light from the candle. But she liked being able to place it somewhere and not have to worry about wax melting or having it burn out completely. Plus only a small bit of the candle remained. Tony had burned himself on the melting wax.

She still had the matches she'd hidden behind the molding. She could get them out anytime and use them one by one if she had to.

She sat down on the cot. She could definitely feel the cold increasing. How did they expect any heat to rise up here with the square sealed off? Had Ian thought about it? Did he care? Tony had ignored her on the way down the ladder, so obviously not. She pulled the sleeping bag over her and stretched out. Within seconds, she felt warm, and she knew that if it was cold enough now to need a sleeping bag, it would only get colder at night.

She switched off the flashlight and walked across the silent zones to the front window. Straining to look out through one of the narrow cracks, she could see that snow was still falling. She wished she could go out in it. She hadn't been in real snow since she'd last gone snowboarding. She felt bored, unable to sense what was going on below or outside. She thought Ian had just said they'd be bringing up food three times a day. So they expected her to stay up here, in darkness, with only a flashlight, all day long, and all night, just waiting for those meal and bathroom breaks. Maybe a caged animal was a better parallel than the solitary confinement one. Pacing back and forth in a zoo.

She shivered.

She could read to pass the time. She was about thirty pages into *Great Expectations*. How long would the batteries in the flashlight last? What if they ran out while she was reading, if she fell asleep like she had before? The flashlight would be on, aimed at a spot on the wall for hours, slowly draining, getting dimmer, until she'd wake up, blinking in the darkness in the middle of the night. She'd grope around for the light and only when she tried to flick the switch would she realize it was already on. That it had been on all night and was dead.

She turned on the flashlight and set it on the night stand, adjusting it so that the beam lit up a small area near the head of the cot. She got herself comfortable beneath the sleeping bag and the blanket. She began to read. Or try to read. She saw the words. Black on white paper. Reading the words but not absorbing the story. Her mind wandering. Thinking. Imagining. Distracted.

And then it happened. It was only a small flicker. But it was there. The beam softened a bit, then came back before flickering again. She threw down the book and grabbed for the flashlight. She slapped it against one hand. The beam came back. She waited for it to happen again, but it didn't.

As she reached for the fallen book she again noticed the desk in the far corner with its one wobbly leg. She held the flashlight to get a good look at it. Again, she noticed how it looked from the bottom. Now that the light was shining directly at it, she saw how the bad leg almost looked like it had been broken off at some point, then reattached. Or maybe it had never fallen off but was just not connected very well.

She bent down in front of the desk, and with the the flashlight balanced nearby, lifted one end of the desk and tried the bad leg. The leg shook easily. It was held in place by a couple of loose screws driven in from the top. The desk was heavier than she'd thought, and she had difficulty holding it with one hand. She tried again, this time pulling the leg to one side. The screws seemed to loosen a bit and she could hear a vague splintering sound. She lowered the desk, then lifted it once again and twisted the leg as far as she could. It made a brief, sharp, crackling sound, and as dust fell out from the screw holes, she knew she could get it loose with a few more attempts. Around the base of the leg she could see dust and wood chips that had fallen out. She'd have to hide those, just in case. She relaxed now, feeling suddenly warm and energized.

The light began to flicker again.

She shook it, feeling that a deadline was imminent. The batteries would not last much longer. She had to work fast. She had to get this job done and move on to whatever was next.

What is next? Sleeping? What else is there to do if I don't have any light? It's daytime outside but dark in here, and when it gets dark out there it will still be dark in here. Dark all the time.

She stood up and lifted the desk again. This time she twisted it from side to side, using the edge of the desk as a lever of sorts. A screw was still attached, but as she pulled on the leg, it slowly came free. She set it on the floor, then carefully pushed the edge of the desk closer to the wall so it could stay there, propped up without falling over.

She felt giddy as she leaned down on her hands and knees and scraped up the dust and chips that had fallen to the floor. She put them under a magazine on top of the desk, then she picked up the leg. It was solid. It felt substantial. It was thicker and heavier at one end than the other, and it felt good in her hands. She raised the leg over her head, and swung downward, at an imaginary target. She swiped it heavily from side to side, like a baseball bat. Each time she swung, it made a whooshing sound and she imagined the sound and fury it would make when it hit its target.

The murmur of low voices below was unclear. She didn't care. She had a new tool in her arsenal. She smiled. She nearly felt like laughing out loud. The dogs, if it came to it, would have this to deal with if they got in her way. Forget trying to bribe them with food. Those days were over. She swung it again. If Tony noticed her when she was getting away, she'd have the knife and this. Thwack! She'd slam it into the side of his head and then hit him again before he hit the ground. She swung upward. Ian would get it from below.

The metallic sound of the latch being opened shook her. She was standing there with the desk leg in her hands, totally exposed. She felt suspended, frozen, unable to move or think, knowing only that she was about to get caught.

CHAPTER 34

Liddy opened the door to his apartment and immediately set his eyes on the mess on the sofa. He could see the stack of modifications from the door, just beneath a manila folder. Now that he saw the folder it was an insult that he had missed them. But he'd been in a hurry. He'd been running out of time. Now he would have to go all the way back downtown. At least rush hour should have subsided a bit.

Noticing a blinking on his phone, it looked like he'd missed a call at some point. Normally he'd wait or ignore it but he had a couple calls out. He set the modifications folder on the floor by the door so he wouldn't forget it, then sat down and dialed in. It was someone from the building management office returning his call from last night. He was impressed.

The same receptionist who'd left the voicemail answered.

"Hi, this is Adam Liddy calling back. Looks like I just missed your call."

"Hello, yes. How can I help you."

"Well like I said, it's about the mailboxes."

"Some of your message got cut off. So, normally we don't handle any issues with the mail. What was your question?"

"My question was, does anyone except the post office have keys to our mailboxes?"

"I'm sorry, Mr. Liddy, can you tell me what property you're referring to?"

"Almeda Street. What would it matter, anyway?"

"Well, some locations have a separate key for the interior and exterior doors."

"Okay, but in general."

"In general, the postal service would have a key for the exterior, and for the mailboxes themselves."

"And so would the resident, obviously. Anyone else?"

"The landlord would have a set of keys."

"Including for the mailbox?"

"Yes."

"Okay, so three people would have a key."

The receptionist seemed to pause. "Is there any particular reason you're checking about the mailbox key? If you need a replacement, we can—"

"Actually I think it might be related to the security camera thing."

"So, we're taking steps to improve the camera situation—and thanks again for bringing it to our attention. We did send out notifications that we're replacing all resident keys, and—"

"I get that, and I appreciate it. Glad you're taking it seriously. This is the mailboxes, though. I was waiting for a letter that was delivered on Saturday —at whatever time they drop it off. But I didn't get that letter until later. It wasn't there when I first got my other mail."

"Have you called the post office?"

"Yes. Of course."

"As I said, we don't handle anything related—"

"This is not related to the post office. I already called them and there's nothing they can do. They said it may have accidentally wound up in someone else's mailbox."

"But it was eventually delivered, right?"

"Yeah, but if only the postal people and the landlord have a key besides me, how did it wind up in my box later? They already said they only deliver once per day. They didn't come back later."

"Have you checked with the landlord—Don Evans? He would be the only one with the other key."

"Yes. It wasn't him."

Now the receptionist was silent, as he'd expected.

"What I can do is have one of our team contact you. They may want to ask a few more questions."

When the call was over, he let out a sigh. Clueless. All they knew how to do was tow the customer service line, pretending their crappy building had any redeeming qualities whatsoever. He was surprised they hadn't asked about rent. Severed camera cables downstairs? He hadn't even bothered to ask about getting footage of the lobby. He was the one who'd noticed the torn cable, meaning the security cameras were just useless objects. And he doubted their line about maybe the maintenance crew had torn them. Anything to head off a lawsuit. Stolen or missing mail? Some weird thing dropping from the ceiling in the garage? Why didn't maintenance do anything about that? In fact, he reminded himself to get that piece of metal and show it to them. At least they were doing the right thing by changing all the locks once they heard about the camera cable thing. He wondered if they'd filed a police report like they'd said they would.

Before leaving, he sat down at his desk and logged in to his computer. He would email a photo of the modifications to his colleague just in case he was late. As he waited for his laptop to come alive, he opened the top drawer of his desk to get his sunglasses. While he was flicking the junk around, he came across a folded piece of paper. Curious, he opened it. At first he thought it must be something obscure that had wound up in the drawer by accident: a packing slip or some leftover printout that he'd saved for scratch paper.

But turning it around and trying to make sense of the weird notes, it seemed intentional, if completely haphazard and random. Something about a "Sarah" and a location outside Seattle, lines connecting what he could only assume were players in a quest or geocache game or something similar. Some numbers and a date were written in one part. Some circles and arrows pointed toward the Sarah name, with a couple other names.

Aside from the bizarre nature of the page, he tried to figure out how it had wound up in his drawer. He didn't recognize it from anywhere. The junk drawer had a bit of everything, including papers, but he'd never seen anything like this. He scrolled through in his mind, recalling anyone who'd been over, anyone who might have written some notes like that. He even wondered if his ex had somehow put it there when she was over. He'd have to look into it later. He had to get back downtown.

CHAPTER 35

S arah switched off the flashlight. Jane's head appeared in the light of the square, looking around, straining to see in the darkness. Sarah quickly wedged the leg back under the table, adjusting it to appear a little off center. She bookmarked the realization that anyone coming up here had a couple seconds of blindness as their eyes adjusted.

"Oh there you are," Jane said. "Can't see anything up here. I thought they gave you a flashlight?"

"They did, but I'm trying to ration the batteries."

Jane hoisted the object through the square. In the light, Sarah could see that it was another blanket. "Here. I brought this up. Ian said you thought it was cold up here. I have your lunch, too. Hang on."

When she came back up, she tried to get through the square while awkwardly holding a tray in one hand. The tray nearly fell over once, and Jane, obviously flustered, looked up to Sarah. The expression on her face made Sarah feel sorry for her, and she knelt down and took the tray. Jane disappeared again.

On the tray was a plastic bowl with some kind of rice, a banana, and a sandwich. When Jane reappeared, she had a bottle of water.

"Go ahead," Jane said. "It's not much, but it's not bad."

Sarah tried the sandwich. She opened the water and drank.

"Wow, it is a little chilly up here," Jane said.

"Because they blocked the square off. All the heat came up through there."

There was something gruff from Ian below. Jane looked downward. "Okay," she said grudgingly. She looked at Sarah. "I have to go. I'll come up for the dishes in a bit."

"Okay."

"Just knock, one of us'll come up."

As Jane began to descend, Sarah knew the light coming through the square was going to disappear and she'd be back to the flashlight. She glanced at the bowl of rice and banana, the tray, the way it looked. There was something that had stirred in her mind, something about the tray, but she couldn't place it. Jane was nearly down the ladder and there wasn't much time. The rice. No. The tray. No. There was a plastic spoon there, and a paper napkin. She glanced at Jane's disappearing head.

She quickly reached out, took the spoon and slid it under the sleeping bag.

"Jane," she said.

"Yeah?"

"Um, can I get a fork?"

"Can you use the spoon?"

"Spoon?" Sarah made as if searching for it. "I guess I don't see it."

"There isn't one? I thought I put one on there."

"Unless it dropped somewhere."

Sarah watched Jane's head reappear above the square and her eyes begin searching the floor and the cot. "Hm. Weird. I'll get you one. Be right back."

When Jane was gone Sarah went to the cot and switched on the flashlight. She took the spoon from under the sleeping bag and used the silent zones to move across the floor to the desk. There, she put the spoon under the same magazine she'd used to hide the wood chips.

She slid back to the cot and aimed the beam into the rice. She could see steam rising from the bowl. It looked like some kind of pilaf or fried rice and she wondered whether Ian had made it. She could see bits of what looked like ginger, small chunks of tuna, and there it was. The yellowish part. It had caught her eye before but now she saw what it was. Egg.

"Here you go," Jane said from behind her. Sarah turned. Jane was holding a spoon. "You're right, spoon's better for something like rice."

"Yeah."

"Well, knock when you're done."

"Oh, Jane?"

"Yeah?'

"I know I'll need to use the bathroom soon. I can wait until after eating."

"Sure, no problem."

Jane went down the ladder, lowering the hatch. As it closed, Sarah got a brief look at the latch they'd installed. It was a bolt mechanism that when closed, would slide into a fitting probably just beneath the square, out of her sight. Simple. Functional. And impossible to open or break from above.

She turned back to the tray on the cot. She picked up the sandwich and finished it. It was peanut butter. She drank some of the water, had some of the banana. She carefully lifted the bowl of rice and rotated it in her hand, holding it in the circle of light. One by one, she took out the tiny bits of egg and put them in a pile. She dug through the bowl half a dozen times, eating the rice, saving the egg. When she was done, she had about a tablespoon, maybe a little more.

She wrapped the egg loosely in the paper napkin and put it in her pocket. She waited a few minutes, then knocked on the hatch. The dogs began barking. After a few seconds the latch could be heard opening. Jane appeared.

"I'm done."

"Okay."

"And don't forget about the bathroom."

"Can you bring the tray down with you?"

Sarah took the tray and went through the square. She awkwardly held the tray with one hand and began to work the ladder. She nearly slipped and fell after two steps, finding it almost impossible to get down with one hand. She wondered how she'd planned to climb the ladder before, holding the cutlery jar in one hand. The first knife attempt seemed so long ago. Jane took the tray and brought it to the kitchen.

"Can I get some more water, too?"

Sarah looked around. It was so warm down here, with the fire going. The light outside was fading but it was light nonetheless. Sarah wanted to stand where she was and just absorb it. Ian and Tony were sitting at the table, eating. Ian was looking at a newspaper. Sarah strained to see something in it, a headline or mention of recent events, but noticed instead the pile of eggs to the side of Tony's rice. They were all eating this rice thing, and Tony had obviously picked the eggs out of his. She was so transfixed on this that she didn't notice him looking at the tray she'd just given to Jane.

"So, where's the napkin, Sarah?" he said.

Sarah, momentarily speechless, looked at the tray. Did he know she'd hidden the spoon? Ian looked up from his paper.

"What?" she said.

"The napkin. There was a napkin on there."

Ian said, "Why don't you go up there and look for it, then, hero? You're learning from Jane, recycling everything, using organic products, that's good."

"This isn't about recycling."

"It's about a napkin," Ian said. "Me thinks we have bigger fish to fry."

Tony stared at Ian. Ian stared back.

Jane was rinsing the dishes at the sink. As Tony and Ian finished their glancing exchange and went back to eating, Sarah searched for something among the food items in front of Tony, something she could somehow slip egg into. Nothing seemed like it would work, and even if there was something, she couldn't think how she could somehow get the egg into it, and make it seem like it wasn't there. And how did he react if he did eat eggs anyway?

She went into the bathroom and closed the door. Her eyes went toward the toilet tank. She wished she would have brought the spoon. She could have hidden that in there as well. She didn't know what she'd do with a plastic spoon, in fact probably nothing, but it would be just one more thing in her arsenal, another thing she'd acquired under their noses.

She heard a sudden shuffling noise outside. Tony and Ian exchanged some words. They were not at the table anymore. From what she could hear, Tony was just outside the bathroom door. Ian sounded like he was in the kitchen.

"You're paranoid," Ian said.

"We'll see." Tony's voice was close.

She could hear the clanking of dishes in the kitchen. She tried to picture Jane there, standing over the sink, by now sort of estranged in one way or another from Tony and Ian.

"What's this, then?" Tony again. He sounded like he was near the ladder. Had he actually gone up there to find the napkin? She felt the wad of egg in her right front pocket. When she got up there she would have to empty out the egg and make the napkin reappear somehow.

"Son of a bitch, you were right," Ian said, now closer to the ladder.

A sudden shrill sound came from the kitchen, followed by a clanking near the sink. Tumbling around, coming to a stop. After a few seconds, Tony's voice said, "This is the kind of shit I'm talking about."

Jane, softly, almost begging, said, "There's no way I—"

"Leave it out," Ian said.

Sarah again felt trapped in the bathroom while a battle was about to rage outside. With each passing second, and with no further words or symptoms of argument out there, she knew the wrath was going to come her way in short order. They must have found something. Jane was getting some of the blame, but sooner or later, the focus would come Sarah's way. If one of them had gone up there she hadn't heard footsteps above. Did they know about the silent zones also?

Something. Something about the things up there, in that cold room. Desk. Night stand. The cot. The square.

What if she blocked off the trap door with the furniture? The desk was far heavier than she'd imagined. The hatch opened upward. What if they weren't able to open it? What if it wouldn't swing up? Blocking it would give her time. Time to do something. Time to break one of the windows before they could get up there and stop her. She would have total privacy, maybe for a few minutes. She had to plan. She had to get up there. She wanted to go back to her cold room. She opened the door.

She felt more than saw Tony to her left. The others were not in sight. Before she had time to react his hand was around her waist. He pulled her hair back from behind with the other. She screamed with the sudden pain.

"Do you see that?" Tony said forcefully.

Wincing with pain, she saw where he was pointing. The plastic spoon she'd hidden was out on the counter, on display, along with the wood chips from the desk leg job.

"And where's the napkin?"

"Hey!" Ian came from the bedroom. He pulled at Tony's hands, trying to pry him loose. Tony's arm tore away from her waist, but he kept a grip on her hair. Sarah tried to twist away, holding her hair to stop it from being pulled out at the roots.

"You see what she got?"

"Get off her!" Ian yelled, swinging hard at Tony. Tony's grip on her hair instantly loosened. She pulled away, falling to the floor and quickly pushing herself away with both feet toward the ladder. She saw Tony protecting his face. Ian swung again, missing his face but hitting him in the neck. Jane started screaming. One of the dogs started growling.

Sarah reached for the ladder and began to climb. She saw in the periphery Tony reeling, holding his neck with both hands, clearly in pain, staggering into the wall. He fell and reeled toward Ian. Sarah pushed on the hatch above her and went through the square in time to hear a sharp cracking sound followed by breaking glass. Someone fell to the floor. Ian called out in pain, yelling something guttural.

Panting, Sarah closed the hatch. In the darkness, she groped for the flashlight. She found it by the night stand, switched it on and aimed it toward the desk leg. She debated keeping the leg near her, just in case.

But now they were going back and forth about something in lower tones. She caught none of it. She wondered where Jane was now. Probably in the bedroom, cowering.

The scuffle below motivated her more than ever to get away. And Tony's reaction confirmed her contention that any objects, whether keys, knife or plastic spoon, were best kept in the toilet than up here. Tony would find anything.

She took the napkin with the egg from her pocket and searched for a place to put it. As she approached the rear window she nearly jumped at the sound of the latch sliding shut. She was sealed in. She put the napkin on the sill of the rear window. A slight draft lingered, and a faint stream of cold air seemed to come around the edge of the window and fall straight down. She judged that to be the coldest place in the room. The egg would probably keep there until she could think of something to slip it into so Tony would eat it. She would find a way. She couldn't wait to see how he'd react, with his egg allergy.

This thought morphed into another, and she started to plan. She would hold off for now on covering the square with heavy objects. That would be during the final stage, since it would make it obvious she was up to something. At first she would work on the windows. The first task would be the boards they'd installed today. With the table leg, she bet they could be forced open. They were attached with nails, not screws, and from the outside, so she assumed it was possible to push them out. The two-by-fours were the problem. They seemed solid. She'd have to hit them pretty hard, and that would make noise. So when it came time to do that, she'd have to make sure she'd sealed the square off.

And that depended on the car key working.

And the dogs being inside.

And…

CHAPTER 36

Turning to both sides as he looked in the mirror, Brandon adjusted the wig once more. It was a shorter-length hairpiece of sandy color, and it was starting to look the part. He had shaved his own hair down to ensure none of his own color showed through. Using a small sharp scissors he trimmed the sides in a few places, working the sideburns, and parted the hair like Adam Liddy did. He trimmed some of the strands, to thin it out slightly. He pulled the wig tighter and pressed it closer to his scalp.

He took out the swatch of paint mixtures he'd created: a few whites, grays, some drops of brown and black acrylic, mixed into a few different shades and diluted with a bit of gesso for a matte finish. Using several cotton balls, he applied light layers to the sides of the wig, just enough to create the impression of approaching gray. He used a flat brush to apply thin streaks of it along the sides in random places. When he put some on too heavily, he wiped it to blend it in before trying again.

He opened a box and took out a tray of makeup. Using a container of different brushes, blenders and sponges, he applied contours to his cheekbones, shading slightly underneath and highlighting a bit on the tops. He drew thin age lines between his nose and mouth, and on his forehead, then blended them out, leaving small darker areas in random places along the lines. He shaded outward from the lines with varying degrees of color.

He applied darker shades beneath his eyes, blending in the colors to appear natural. Then he applied fine detail with a sharp pencil to create the effect of baggy eyes and fine skin wrinkles.

He was wearing two loose tees under his button-down blue work shirt, which made him appear bulkier. When he held up Adam Liddy's license and compared the photo to his image in the mirror, he was impressed. It may take some further lighting adjustments and finessing of little things, but he had to admit, he looked fifteen years older and fifteen pounds heavier.

Brandon stepped into the living room and looked at his phone. It was time to make the call. He sat down and thought through all the scenarios. When he'd anticipated as many possibilities as he could, he called the San Francisco police non-emergency number. He pressed the number for the missing persons area.

A woman answered. "Special Victims Unit."

"Yes, I was wondering—someone I know is missing and wondering how I should report that?"

"Do you know if this person is in danger of any kind?"

"I don't think so. It's just like she disappeared and no one can get ahold of her."

"When was the last time you heard from her?"

"I think Thursday?"

"And how do you know her: is she a friend? Associate?"

"My girlfriend."

"What makes you think she's missing?"

"She hasn't answered her phone."

"Is there anyone else you know of who might've been in touch or heard from her?"

"Yes, people we both know, our friends. No one's able to get through. And there's little things. Like, I found a note with a name on it, some Adam Liddy. I don't know who it is but I feel like I've seen this name before. And she's missed a couple events we were supposed to go to. Things like that."

"Okay, I'll need to get those names and other information from you. Can I start with your name?"

The call took about twenty minutes, and Brandon was given a case number and a contact. When he was done, he took a last look around the apartment. Finding nothing out of place, he set down the phone on the kitchen counter. It would have to remain here. He put on a ball cap, then went down the hall to the elevator, trying to keep the camera from getting much of his face. At the street level he looked for a taxi. Actual taxis were getting harder to find but after circling the block once and heading toward a nearby hotel, he hailed one. He told the driver to bring him to Hertz.

When he arrived he went inside and got into the queue marked with red stanchions. The place was moderately crowded, with half a dozen customers in front of him. He was almost exactly on time for his reservation, even with the taxi delay. After a few minutes of shuffling he was called to the counter.

"Good evening, do you have a reservation?"

"Yes, 7:30 P.M."

"Okay, do you have your driver's license?"

Brandon placed the Adam Liddy license on the counter.

"Thank you Mr. Liddy, one moment while I look up your reservation. Three days, is that right? A midsize SUV?"

"That's right."

"And what credit card would you like to use?"

"Same one I reserved with," Brandon said, setting a Visa card down.

The agent ran the card, entered some stuff from the license and spent several minutes going through things on a screen. Brandon stood patiently, looking more or less at the counter or at the agent. At length, the man handed back the license and the card, and placed the printout of the rental agreement for him to sign.

When Brandon left the Hertz lot, he drove to the shipyards at Hunters Point. He had driven his car there earlier and parked it in one of the abandoned garages secured with an easily breakable padlock. Now that it was dark, the vibe in the area was definitely more menacing. Rundown brick and wooden buildings with peeling paint, broken windows, graffiti, tires and car parts were surrounded with chain link fencing. As he got closer and knew where he was going he turned off the headlights. An occasional dim streetlamp or lights from parked cars lit the shadows here and there. When at the garage he eased in carefully, avoiding broken glass and metal parts, and opened the partially dilapidated garage door.

He parked the rented jeep next to his and transferred the stuff he'd packed for the trip. It took only a few minutes to hoist over a couple of duffel bags with some clothes, the rifle parts, some tools. Then he locked his car and backed out with the rental. When he'd shut the garage door and hung the padlock in its place on the rusted fence, in the evening glow it looked like the scene hadn't been touched for years.

As he left the shipyards he headed toward the East Bay, then made his way onto Highway 5 heading north. He adjusted the seat and got comfortable. Seattle was at least thirteen hours away.

CHAPTER 37

When Sarah opened her eyes she was instantly awake. She spent several seconds wondering if it was the next day yet, or still the middle of the night. She'd had strange ideas swirl around in her semi-waking state of perpetual darkness, and only now that she was alert could she see it for what it was. She was as much disturbed by the idea itself as by the notion that she was, once again, allowing something about Brandon to bother her. She felt guilty and tried to rationalize it by admitting that maybe she was just starting to confuse stressful ideas with actual memories. Being kidnapped and held for ransom would do that to anyone. Yet the idea kept coming back to her. When she'd given him the picture frame for his birthday neither of them had a photo printed out. When she'd found one and gone back to his place next time, he had one ready. It was of them in Iceland. They remembered the time and place and started talking about the sights and sounds and the smells of Reykjavik. But even as she fit the picture into the frame and they talked that day, she'd known something seemed off. She hadn't said anything because it was such a small thing, like confusing a teacher from childhood, or getting the year of a memory wrong. More of an annoyance than an error. Had she become confused or had she just forgotten holding him from the side like that?

She slowly eased herself out of bed. The floor felt cold on her feet, and the air was far colder than it had been when she'd fallen asleep. It might have been an hour ago, or maybe several.

She groped for the flashlight and turned it on, put on her jacket and moved across the floor to the front window. A modest amount of light came through the tiny cracks, barely enough to see what looked like early morning. She was relieved. The thought of waiting for the day to begin, stuck in some sort of suspended limbo between night and day, terrified her.

She listened for sounds below. Nothing significant for now. Their relationships seemed to be fraying. What would happen if the three of them just broke down? Their fighting and quarreling got to the boiling point, and one day Tony killed Ian, or vice versa, or Jane got wounded, or someone had to leave quickly, go to a hospital or something. Sarah would be stuck up here, trapped, forgotten. No food, no water, the days going by. For that matter, what if she feigned some injury or illness herself? They'd have to deal with it. Something beyond a black eye. The hint of an idea formed in her mind, slowly taking shape from a simple premise: she was held captive by three people at odds with each other. Tony and Ian kept Jane at bay. Ian criticized Tony. Jane disliked one, or both of them. She could stir this combustible mixture and light it up, use it to assist in her escape. Pros and cons came and went. Scenarios unfolded. She could use their corrupt dynamic against them. She set the thought aside, vowing to revisit it.

She went to the rear window and angled the light toward the sill, looking at the egg and napkin she'd hidden last night. Something about the napkin looked different. Her first impression was that it had somehow unfolded during the night. But when she looked closer, she was stunned to see not only the napkin misshapen, but the egg completely gone. She picked it up, holding it between two fingers. Parts of it were shredded. There were tiny holes here and there. She felt dazed. There wasn't a single speck of egg anywhere.

She shone the light around the room. Along the base of the floor. Up and down the steep walls. Under her cot. She looked at her feet and felt a discomfort. She hadn't heard a thing during the night. And if there were mice up here, eating something only inches from her, she felt she would have heard it. Especially now that the square was sealed off and she could almost hear her own breathing. As the beam moved along where the rear wall met the floor, she saw little bits of paper scattered in random places, mixed with little black specks. It *had* been mice.

Where did they get in? Where did they go? She wondered what the place really looked like in the darkness, after the light was switched off, those things scurrying all over, moving silently, always unseen. Surely they moved around in the kitchen, eating whatever they could find. Did the dogs notice them? How many were there? Had they been on her bed, while she slept? She felt her skin crawl.

She saw no obvious holes or places where they could come or go. The window was fairly tightly sealed, even with the tiny draft. And she doubted they would go outside unless they had to. Not when there were things to eat inside, where it was warm.

Finally, she noticed something. On the right side of the frame was a small hole, an irregular circle, between the edge of the frame and the paneling. It looked like it had been a knot in the paneling, and had fallen out at some point. It was only about half an inch wide. If they got through here, they could come and go easily. They could climb walls. If they lived within the walls, they could probably get anywhere in the house. Similar exit holes were probably everywhere in the walls of this cabin.

As she studied the wood around the window she noticed the way it was set within the frame. Like the front window, the glass was held within the frame by narrow strips of molding running along all edges, inside and out. Running her finger along the strips she could see that it had dried and cracked in places. New nails had been driven in to keep it in place, as with the other window. But unlike the other window, these strips were narrower, more frail, and clearly older.

Why hadn't she noticed this before? With the knife, she could pry them loose. She could pull the glass free and start working on a way to remove the boards over the window. She could work on it as she was able, when they were busy downstairs. When she was not working on it, she could put the glass back in and replace the molding strips. No one below would know. She could work on it until it was ready. Then she could get her things from the toilet, block the square, and make her move.

They were only going to bring her food three times a day, Ian had said. Even if they wanted to surprise her and come up at random times before she had a chance to hide her work, the latch made a noise that would warn her of their approach. Their eyes had to adjust to the darkness. If she had the flashlight off as the latch was being opened, someone coming up here would see nothing but darkness for a few seconds. She would have a narrow window, hiding in the shadows, but she'd have to be quick. She could use the desk leg, swinging it down hard.

She had a car key. She had a knife. She had matches. She could distract them, somehow manipulate them, turn them against each other. With the rising tension in the cabin it was not inconceivable. The knife and stretches of silent labor would open the window. Or the desk leg would smash it open, and it would smash the outer boards. She had options.

As far as she knew, no one suspected she had any plan. They all thought she was up here, meekly awaiting her fate, waiting for news. Tony and Jane had both come up here like lambs in the valley, not knowing how close they were to major personal catastrophe. It hadn't occurred to them. A lot of things didn't occur to them.

She switched off the flashlight. She felt optimism.

Breakfast came eventually. Just like she'd imagined, first the latch opened. Then the crack of light appeared. In the space of seconds, Sarah went through the motions of everything she'd just envisioned, and it played out beautifully. Ian's head was the model this time. And now it had a big imaginary dent in it as his mortally wounded body fell down the ladder. Blood spraying all over. This time there was no drama, no words. He had placed her breakfast on the floor without saying a thing. His bracelet flicked once as he closed the hatch and was gone. The darkness returned, but from the glimpse of outside light she got, she estimated the time to be around eight. The meal, under the glare of the flashlight, consisted of an orange, a mug of black coffee, a bottle of water, and a peanut butter sandwich on white bread. She was pretty sure the water was the same bottle from yesterday, refilled. She saw no spoon or napkin today.

When she'd eaten, she knocked on the trap door and Jane let her down to use the bathroom. When she was there she took the knife out of the toilet. In her confine, she balanced the flashlight and went to the rear window to begin her work, starting with the right side, closest to the mouse hole, and working toward the left along the bottom strip. When she had to pound on something, she used her pillow to muffle the sound.

After a few minutes, she found the molding relatively easy to remove, as long as she inserted the blade all the way in, as close to each nail as possible. More than once the blade nearly felt like it could break, and she cracked the molding in a couple of places. Fortunately the cracks were lengthwise, so when she tried to lay it back in place, the crack was barely noticeable. That was essential. They must not find out about her work. She worked methodically, pushing the blade in carefully, lifting, working the wood up, then moving on.

She had no idea how long the project was taking. She found herself looking at her watch that wasn't there, even after all the days of knowing she didn't have it. She estimated it took twenty to forty minutes, maybe an hour, to remove the first half of the molding. It seemed to take much longer than she'd planned, and her fingers were feeling the pain. She broke two fingernails. She wished she'd used even the rusty clipper on them.

She was alert for sounds as she worked. She had a system in mind, in the event she heard the latch sound. She'd have scant seconds to move the night stand back into place. If the visit was a quick trip, such as to deliver food or tell her something, she thought it was safe to leave the strips off. But if they called her down, that meant someone could come up and search. In that case, she'd need time enough to replace the strips. That would be the riskiest situation, and she knew she didn't have a solution for that yet.

Even as she went through these scenarios, she was thrown off by a knock on the trap door, then the metallic scraping sound of the latch. The crack of light appeared. The hatch began to open upward. Jane's arm was there, pushing up.

Sarah jumped into motion. She flicked off the flashlight and set it on the floor. Grabbed the night stand. In two giant steps placed it back near the cot. The pillow fell to the floor.

Jane's head appeared, looking, turning in her direction.

She grabbed the detached molding strips and stuffed them under her sleeping bag along with the knife. They could be noticed if Jane approached the cot but it was all she had time for.

"Oh, there you are. Okay if I come up?"

"Um, sure."

"What are you doing?" Jane was climbing through the square. There was something in her hand.

"Oh, just stretching."

"In the dark?"

"Don't really need light for it, and I don't want to waste the batteries."

"Speak of the devil." She handed Sarah two large batteries. She reached for the flashlight on the floor and turned it on. "These seem okay still," she said as she swung the beam around.

As Sarah set the batteries on her sleeping bag, she noticed a strip of molding sticking out from beneath.

"By the way, Ian doesn't know," Jane said, nodding toward the batteries, "so, you know."

"Sure. Don't worry about that."

Jane moved toward the cot. "Hey, your pillow's on the floor."

Sarah stepped toward the cot, hoping to block Jane from sitting on it. "Oh. I was using it to stretch."

"Yoga?"

"Nah, just stretching."

"I can teach you some moves if you like."

"Okay, maybe later. Are you pretty good?"

"I don't know about good. Just feels good." Jane had apparently noticed the napkin shreds on the floor. The beam was trained on them. "What happened there. Irritated at the napkin?"

"It's—I think there's mice up here."

"Mice?"

"Yeah. I saw one under here." Sarah bent to point beneath the cot, hoping to distract Jane's gaze while keeping her free hand on top of the molding strip.

"Just one?" Jane said as she swung the beam around. There was a look of humor on Jane's face, as though she'd just been told a joke.

"That's all I saw."

"Well one thing sure about a country place is mice. Goes with the territory."

"But there could be dozens of them."

"I'll see if we can get some traps. I know there were some downstairs."

"Those things could be all over the place."

"I'll get a couple traps."

Sarah sat down on the cot, taking care to avoid the molding and hoping to block Jane's view. To her eyes the signs of her work were obvious everywhere she looked. The missing molding from the window, the strips loosely hidden under her sleeping bag, the knife, the desk leg. The night stand drawer was just open and the small pile of removed nails was in there, in plain view. Even the tips of the hidden rows of matches along the floor. Jane could see any of it if she started to look.

She could not let her work come to an end like this. She went back to her earlier thinking. She barely had a plan but knew she had to try.

"Jane?"

"Yeah."

"I have to talk to you."

"What is it?" Jane began to sit on the cot. Sarah moved to better block any view of the molding.

"I—I know you can't do much. And I have to stay up here, and I get that. But I was stretching because, I have some sort of a pain."

"What, like cramps?"

"No. It's different. It's a pain. I think something's wrong."

"Where?"

"It's, like, right here." She indicated somewhere on her stomach. "It started a couple days ago."

Jane felt the spot. She seemed mesmerized and troubled. "And it's so chilly up here."

"Last night it was so bad I almost knocked. But I just knew how they'd react."

"Sorry about him."

"It's not your fault."

"He's awful. Whatever you think about him, you're right."

"I thought you said he was okay."

"Maybe I did, but not anymore, not after what he did. You want the truth, the thought of him right now makes me sick. I know I shouldn't tell you but Ian's out right now and it's just me and him and his dogs down there, and I needed a break. And part of me..." Her voice trailed off.

"Yes?"

"Well let's just say I wish this would end, this whole thing. I mean, don't think I'm using you as stress relief, 'cuz I'm not."

"Of course not."

"I'm sorry, we were talking about your pain. How bad is it?"

Sarah wondered how far she could take it with her. "I mean, it comes and goes. What if it's something serious?"

Jane seemed to ponder the outcomes. "Well, let me know if it gets any worse. I have some herbal tinctures that are good for joint pain. Might work for this."

"I think it'll be okay for now. I could use some water though."

"Sure."

"I've been feeling dehydrated. I don't think I'm getting enough."

"I agree. I'm sorry. I'll get it right now." She got up and went to the square. "Be right back."

When Jane had left, Sarah went into action quickly. The trap door remained open, and she took advantage of the light. She took the nails from the drawer and the molding from under her sleeping bag and began putting them into place.

Herbal tinctures? Jane wanted out just as bad as she did. What if she'd told her she thought this imaginary pain was appendicitis or a kidney stone.

Would Jane do the right thing and take charge, or would she roll over and let the men handle it? Ian, anyway. Sounded like Tony had hit a nerve.

When the molding was more or less reassembled, she sat on the cot and looked around. She saw nothing that would give her away, unless someone did a close inspection. Even the strips that were cracked looked, from a distance, like they had before she'd taken them off.

She began to wonder where Ian had gone. More business in town, with the person or people he was working with? She hadn't even heard the SUV start, and she wondered if that was because the windows were boarded up, or because she'd been distracted.

She could hear Tony muttering about something. His voice approached the ladder. Sarah retreated from the hatch as his hand appeared. The hatch swung shut. The latch slid home.

This meant she probably had more time until Jane came back with the water, if Tony didn't find out about it and stop her. She switched on the light. She got the knife ready. She picked up the night stand and put it by the window. She got the pillow. Then she went to the window and resumed her work.

CHAPTER 38

Liddy remained on hold with the Oakland Police Department. It had been close to a half hour. The phone was resting on top of his desk and the same muzak had repeated several times already. As he waited he continued to scan through the collections he'd found on the folders in his computer. A series of photos of a young woman —he'd found out her name was Sarah Easton from the name of some of the files—in different scenes. Some of the photos showed her walking down a street. One showed her picking up a coffee from a takeout window. In another she was driving a different car, backing in to a parking space. Some showed her through windows. In some she was alone, in some she was with other people. Some of the images were scans or photos of documents, such as a receipt from a gas station, or a boarding pass. One was a screenshot of what looked like a recent glance at her calendar, showing dates of events and appointments.

He'd had to look her up. Once he'd started digging around online he recognized her as the sister of the Easton girl who'd been in the media a lot a couple years ago. At first he wondered how long the images had been there, and how they'd got there. It could be the same situation with the paper he'd found in his drawer: one of his friends playing a joke, or his ex had somehow copied something over when borrowing his laptop. But who else could have been in his computer? And why would they copy photos of Sarah Easton over?

After hours of searching and pondering, he'd even wondered if he himself had done it. He'd had some nights when he'd worked late, and been drinking. He got off on tangents. He ended up down rabbit holes searching for things and wound up elsewhere, whether news, entertainment, something in a shopping cart. But he knew nothing about Sarah Easton.

It was only after something clicked that he made the connection between this Sarah and the Sarah on the piece of paper with the bizarre notes he'd found in his junk drawer. That's when it had occurred to him that it wasn't an accident or a prank.

The hold music stopped finally. "This is Detective Yamada."

Liddy leaned closer to the speaker. "Yes, this is Adam Liddy. I'm calling again about—well I guess, an entry."

"A break-in?"

"Yes. I think someone might have been in my apartment. But they—"

"Okay, do you have a case number?"

"Well no, whoever I talked to said I had to go online for a report."

"Correct, that's what we do with property theft."

"But that's the thing. I don't think it's theft. That's why I was hoping I could talk to a live person, because since then I've found out more. I think —I think someone broke into my apartment, and got into my computer."

"So someone broke in, but didn't take anything?"

"Yeah. I think they—I don't know, copied stuff over or something. There's stuff on my laptop I don't recognize. There's also this piece of paper with some weird notes on it. It was in my desk drawer. It's about this

—well she's sort of famous I guess, or must be. I'd never heard of her until I looked her up. Anyway, there's all these photos and scans and stuff on my laptop, and I—"

"Let me stop you for a minute. So is your computer missing, or is it not?"

"No, it's here. I just think someone installed or copied stuff onto it. There's these pictures that aren't mine. That's what I'm saying. I didn't copy or paste them or anything. I've never even seen them. They're just here."

There was a measurable pause. Starting to feel frustration, Liddy examined the paper in one hand. "And there's this piece of paper I found, like someone printed out something with a bunch of codes or details on it. It's some kind of notes, mentioning this same Sarah Easton. That's why I looked up her name. The photos on my laptop are of her too."

"So, to get all this straight, you've got some photos of someone named Sarah on your laptop, and a piece of paper with notes about her."

"Yeah, a piece of paper in my drawer."

"Printed out, you think."

"Yes."

"Okay."

Liddy felt irritation. "Look, I know how it sounds. The point is, I don't know her. I've never met her. Like I said, I had to look her up."

"And who is it?"

"Sarah Easton. I think she's one of the Eastons. You know, the Easton chain? The hotel?"

There was a longer pause. "And why do you think someone would break in to copy photos of this Sarah onto your computer?"

"I don't know."

After another pause, Yamada spoke slowly. "Tell you what. I can give you a case number, and we can have someone get in touch with you."

"I get this isn't capital murder. I promise I'm not trying to be a dick, but what does it take to actually get you guys to take stuff like this seriously?"

"Mr. Liddy, I appreciate your frustration. Look at what you're saying. You said yourself nothing's missing. You mentioned some photos of a famous person. How do I know you didn't take them yourself? That you didn't print out this mysterious note? That you saved all these pictures and don't remember it? And I'm guessing you also want us to deal with the homicides and the carjackings and all the other big-city stuff Oakland has to offer?"

"Okay I get how this sounds. Let's just assume it's nothing. But there's something else. I had a letter disappear the other day, then show up later. The landlord's the only other person with a key and he said it wasn't him. There's a security camera in the lobby that would shed some light on it but lo and behold, the cable was 'mysteriously' cut."

"Did you notify the landlord?"

"Yes, and the rental office."

"Did they call it in?"

"They said they did."

"I'll see if I can look it up. Hang on. Let me get some notes from you."

CHAPTER 39

Sarah guessed it was around noon when she removed the glass from the window. With the molding removed, she inserted the knife between the glass and the frame, pulled gently in several places, and eased the glass out. With the window removed cold air crept in but at least the boards they'd attached kept the snow out. They also hid her work from being noticed from the outside, should they go around the back and look up at the window.

She carefully set the glass on the floor and leaned it against the wall. The new boards were nailed in place from the outside, on top of the two-by-fours. It was actually a pretty good job. The boards filling the spaces were nearly perfectly cut. They must have two ladders since they had both been up there outside the windows. Both front and back windows were high enough they couldn't reach them from the ground.

With the heel of her hand she pushed firmly on one of the new boards. There was almost no give. On the two-by-fours there was none at all, as she'd expected. She looked toward the hatch. If she was going to work, she had to risk being caught. If the latch slid open now, she would not have enough time to put the window back together, let alone hide the desk leg. In fact, no matter what she did, she was sitting in the danger zone. If the latch opened, she would have to hide the glass on top of or under the cot, and hope they wouldn't look closely at the window. The molding and nails she'd have to leave. It would be obvious to anyone. The colder air would give it away if the other clues didn't.

She knew she was ignoring the danger, yet she felt compelled to work in spite of the risk. She had a plan. She was going to get out of here. There would be no waiting around for fate to swallow her up, or for them to take her to another place for hiding, or to make more ransom demands. Or to kill her. She was not going to let that happen.

She went silently to the desk, removed the leg and crept back to the window. Holding it level with the floor, heavy end toward the window, she pulled it back several inches, then rammed it softly into one of the new boards. She winced as the leg hit the wood, and sure enough, it made more noise than she wanted. But she'd felt a slight give. She waited. Held her breath. Listened. Then tried again. This time, she hit the wood a little harder. There was a sharp crackling sound near the bottom. The board hadn't moved much, but it was a start. Before she removed it further, she realized she'd need a way to keep the board from falling. If it fell to the ground, she would have no way to hide her work from inside or outside.

She sat down on the cot and thought about the boards, how she could hide them. She hadn't been on her bed for ten seconds when she heard two knocks. This time she sprang into action without delay, racing to place the glass within the frame. She set the loose molding strips on the sill, sat on the bed and hoped for the best.

"Hey," Jane said. "Sorry it took so long."

"That's okay."

She handed Sarah a bottle of water. "You must think I'm an idiot, huh?"

"What?"

"Doing this. Sitting here in a cabin with those two down there, and someone we kidnapped up here." It didn't seem Jane was looking for a response.

Jane sat down on the floor near the square. "I was gonna put something together later. Hopefully not a peanut butter sandwich. I would totally love a good pizza. Not that we haven't eaten well, sometimes, anyway, but I mean something like that, comfort food, you know." Jane noticed *Great Expectations* and picked it up. "Ah, looks like you've started. You like it?"

"Yeah, it's great."

"How far along are you?"

"About thirty pages."

Jane turned it over in her hands. "I bet I've read this twenty times."

"I thought you said a dozen."

"Oh, rounding up I guess." Jane looked at the back of the book. She ran her fingers over a spot where Sarah had used it as a hammer. "What happened here?"

"What?"

"Looks like it was used to pound something."

"Oh. Sorry. There was a nail sticking out of the floor. I stubbed my toe on it. You probably heard me pounding it."

Jane shook her head. "That's okay, no big deal. Not exactly an heirloom." She set the book down.

Sarah wanted to seize the moment. "So, speaking of which, yesterday you said Ian got you into Dickens."

"Yeah."

"So, does he read a lot?"

"Not really."

"So you're the reader of the two."

"Sort of," Jane said, "I do like to read."

"Like what else."

"Like, ever read any Russian literature?"

"I don't think so."

"Really? Dostoevsky? Tolstoy?"

"Not that I remember."

"It's great stuff. The Russian writers were so existential. There's always such an element of doom in the background, as if something bad is either on the way or is there, all around, but, it's like, the way the characters interact just makes you want to live in the midst of all that sadness anyway. I don't know how much sense that makes. *Oblomov* is one of my favorites. Ever heard of it?"

"No."

"It was written by Goncharov."

"What's it about?"

"Well, on the surface, it's about a nobleman with no conviction, who pretty much spends all his time in bed thinking about times when he was a kid. But really it was sort of a shot at the aristocracy in mid-nineteenth-century Russia. The czars had outgrown their purpose long ago, and the whole system was just sort of crawling along at the expense of... well, look what happened fifty, seventy years later."

"Sounds like something Ian would say."

"I think he mentioned it to me."

"So, is that sort of a metaphor for our situation here?"

"How so?"

"Well, you know, here we are, you're holding me for ransom. Is this sort of a way to create equilibrium somehow? Stealing from the aristocracy?"

Jane shrugged. "I never thought of it that way. I guess you could make that case." Then she looked down and silence followed.

"So, you and Ian—you're together?"

Jane looked into a darkened corner and vaguely smiled. "It's—I guess it's complicated."

"I mean, you didn't exactly speak highly of Tony just a bit ago."

"Weird isn't it," Jane said. "Sitting here talking with you about Russian literature. And existentialism."

"For sure. It's just, I was curious. Not my business, I know, but—"

"Yeah," Jane said, "we squabble a bit. Cabin fever."

"No that's not what I—I mean, how did you—how did you get into this thing then? Seems like Ian's the boss and Tony follows him, and you…"

"Yes?"

"Well, you—"

"I just sleep with them?"

"No, I wasn't going to say that."

"Sorry. Go ahead."

"It just seems like you're intelligent, you read Dickens, Russian literature, you know good wine, you even know about Indian mythology. I don't see how someone like that fits into a thing like this."

"I've always liked the woods, what can I say?"

"Me too," Sarah said, hoping to keep Jane going. "This cabin would be the perfect place to hang out with friends. I bet there's places to go sledding around here. Have you ever been horseback riding? The trails are great around here, I mean in the mountains."

At this Jane's eyes perked up as though she wanted to add something. But she just as soon looked at the floor. "I've never been horseback riding. And I don't think I've been in a sled since I was a kid. Probably wouldn't even be able to pull it off now."

"Well there's nothing to it. All you have to do is sit in a sled and go down the hill. Just try not to wipe out. And of course you have to climb back up."

Jane smiled, but Sarah could see it was forced. "It sounds fun. I used to be that way. I liked to try stuff, do new things, I had interests." She looked at Sarah. "What does that have to do with Russian literature?"

"Nothing. We're just talking about ourselves. And you do have interests. I can see you've got a lot more going on than this thing. That's why I just wondered where you came from, what your life was like before—"

"Well I didn't mean to suggest I don't have a life. I'm just saying, it seems a little foggy around the edges sometimes, you know what I mean?"

"Sure."

"Anyway, there was a guy. Some kind of special I guess. You'd probably like him. Man of mystery."

"Oh. What was his name?"

"Mister I'm-in-the-past. The kind of name you'd hear in a country song, maybe."

"I don't think I know any country songs."

"Well, let's see. I lived in Boise for a while a few years ago. I had a job in this bar. More of a truck stop, really. I was planning on going in and putting in my notice 'cuz I hated that job, the truckers who came in, and the people I worked for. Freddie was his name, and he was okay some days, but other days, I could've killed him. It was a low point in my life.

"So I'd just had an argument with my husband—we had this farm, it was mostly his—about money or something. There were always more bills and we kept having to sell off inventory to make ends meet. I don't even remember what started it, but anyway, it was morning, and we argued and I drove into town, and when I got to the bar, I saw that one of the windows was broken near the door. I didn't have the keys to the place, and no one seemed to be around, so I opened the door through the broken window and went in.

"At first I only planned to write a note saying I quit. But since I always got paid in cash, I realized they probably wouldn't pay me my last check since I didn't give any notice, so I opened the safe and took out about the amount of my usual check. Yeah, I had the safe combo, but I swear I didn't take any more than that, and there wasn't that much more in there anyway. So, just as I was writing the note, the back room door opens and two guys come out, that's Mike and Tony—I mean Ian and Tony—and Ian has a shotgun, and I thought I was dead. At the same time from the other side, Freddie, he was the manager, pulls up in his truck. He could see me through the broken window but not Ian or Tony, and when he started to come in, I tried to warn him about them, but he walks in, and they slip back into the office, and Freddie starts blaming me for the window right off the bat, which wasn't a surprise. By now he sees me with the money in my hand, and the safe door open, and the broken window, and it all just escalates like that, and that's when Mike comes out and, before I even know what to do, we all three are in a car, with the money from the safe and just on the road, and...."

Sarah listened for more, but realized Jane had probably said it all. In fact, she almost seemed to be leaning toward the square, as if now that she'd said her piece, it was time to leave.

"So, you left your husband, and you, all three of you—"

"Well I went to London with Mike for a while. We spent a few months in a small flat in Hampstead. I went back to school for a while and he did little odd jobs, mostly shady stuff and construction. Being in the U.K. was great at first, but it got dull pretty fast. The sky was always gray, and, London's great as long as you have money to spend, which we didn't."

"But you were going to school? What were you studying?"

"Long story. Maybe some other time."

"So, you decided to come back here, after London, to do this?"

"That's not why we came back. This came up later."

"And at some point Tony got involved?"

"It's all good. Maybe another time."

Sarah faced Jane directly. "You aren't like them, I can tell. There's a part of you that doesn't want to be here. More than a part of you. You're above this."

Jane looked back at Sarah. "Maybe I'll write a book about it, like Mike said."

Sarah felt so close to have Jane pull away now. "Jane, help me. Help me get out of here. We can both go. If you—"

Jane laughed and looked toward the square. Then her face turned serious, followed by a morose sadness that faded within seconds. "You're sweet, Sarah," she said. "I hope this ends soon. This whole thing."

Sarah felt unable to continue her plea, unable to respond. She felt betrayed. She felt an urge to push Jane down through the square. And now Jane was standing up, getting ready to go back down to her men.

"Jane."

"Yes, Sarah?"

"What did Mike—"

"Ian," Jane said coldly.

"What did Ian really tell you the other night? When you all got quiet and started whispering?"

"I already told you."

"What, just that maybe someone called the cops?"

"Yep."

"No. You were scared. I could tell. You had a look on your face. You guys whispered for an hour down there."

Jane simply stared back at Sarah. This made the earlier fears return. They'd subsided amidst the giddiness of her window project. Now they were back in full.

"Your dad's trying to pay less than Ian's asking. And he's trying to change the demand terms."

CHAPTER 40

Sometime in the morning Brandon pulled the jeep into the outer edge of a strip mall parking lot south of Portland. He'd stopped a few times along the way to get gas, food or coffee, but having come this far without any actual rest he decided now was the time. He got out and walked around a bit to stretch his legs and do some exercises. Businesses in the mall were opening up. Employees were parking their cars. Delivery trucks were coming and going.

In the car he reclined the seat and leaned back. It was noticeably chilly outside, but he kept the window open and let the cool air enter the car. He had made good time and was in no hurry, but he felt restless. Stopping halfway felt like leaving things unresolved, and he preferred to keep going while he had the energy. Not only did he have a lot to do when he got to Seattle, but it sounded like the snowstorm in the Cascades was lingering and making the roads chaotic. That would mean slow traffic if he got stuck in it and maybe even tire chain checkpoints if he picked a bad route. All of that could add hours. He set an alarm for two hours and closed his eyes.

He felt tired enough to sleep, but with all the moving parts churning through his mind, it took a while to fade away. Tomorrow at 3:00 P.M. would come up fast. It was the day when all the things he'd set into motion either came to fruition or fell to ruin. It was pass or fail, no middle ground. Tomorrow, he would be as much a victim as Adam Liddy. They'd both be suspects, at first anyway. Liddy would be a suspect for a few days or weeks, until the focus turned to Brandon. Or maybe that would happen sooner. They would grill everyone in Sarah's circle. The interrogations would go on for weeks, prodding and poking and questions about everything. They'd look into timelines and whereabouts. He'd have to show receipts and documents, prove he was here or there on this date or with so and so at a certain time.

Was he in San Francisco on Wednesday at 3:00 P.M.? He would be able to show he was. His car was in the garage. He was in his apartment the whole time.

But as the investigation went on, there would be only one answer to this and all of the questions they would ask. Who would have the motive to pull a job like this? Who would spin an elaborate scheme like this? Who would kidnap a wealthy woman and demand payment? Who had a resentment against rich women, even women of any kind? Who harbored some secret disdain for a certain type of celebrity? Who had documented issues around women? Who had photos and notes about Sarah all over his apartment?

He woke to a sharp tapping sound on his window. Momentarily dazed, he looked around to more cars in the parking lot. Then he noticed the shape of the officer outside. He sat up. A cop in a blue uniform was outside the window.

"Morning," the officer said, leaning in toward the opening at the top of the window.

Brandon saw the dark blue car nearby with Oregon State Trooper on the side. "Morning," he said.

"What's goin' on?"

"Pardon?"

"Just passed by and saw you zoned out at the wheel."

"Ah, just takin' a little snooze."

"Can you roll down your window a bit? Kind of hard to hear you."

"Um—I think I'll have to start the car first."

"That's fine."

Brandon started the engine and rolled down the window. "Just resting."

"Gotcha. You got your license and registration?"

"It's a rental, so—"

"Glove box would be my guess."

Brandon opened it and handed the officer the papers he found along with the Liddy license.

"Must be traveling?"

"Yeah. Long drive."

"Where you headed?"

"Seattle."

The officer looked between the license and Brandon's face. "Oh, what's goin' on up there?"

"Buddy's wedding."

"That's nice. I heard there's some kind of rough weather up there."

"Yeah, it's all over the radio."

"You all rested up? Okay to drive?"

"Yeah. No problem."

"Okay. Drive carefully. Enjoy that wedding." He handed the license back to Brandon.

As the officer left, Brandon put the license back in his pocket, somewhat surprised at how well the impromptu emergency had gone. He hadn't even flinched once. No hesitation. Business as usual. He looked at himself in the rearview. Even though the makeup had smudged a bit here and there, it had obviously done its job. During the drive, he'd kept his Liddy appearance on all the way, knowing something like this could happen at any time. Even in the cool air, the wig felt hot and uncomfortable. He pondered taking it off when he got on the road, but thought better of it. He was Adam Liddy. He had a wedding to get to.

He pulled out of the parking lot and made his way north.

CHAPTER 41

When lunch came, Sarah had the impression it was just stuff cobbled together from things they'd found: an overripe banana, a container of pudding, a plastic bowl of spaghetti with no sauce. That it would have been forgotten, that Jane probably had remembered it only while turning a page in a book or filing her nails. It came in a paper bag this time. It seemed that the food was getting more basic. Gone were the nights of dinners with wine and laughter. There was hardly even weed or screwing below, or if there was she couldn't hear it. Now it was long silent periods, cold darkness, and leftovers.

After lunch, she used her bathroom break to return the knife to the toilet tank. She felt instant relief when she replaced the lid. She was done with it now, and no one had found it. It was safe back in its place. By now, most of the molding was familiar to her. She knew which pieces went where, how they fit, and how to remove them without the knife.

She worked on the window on and off, feeling a mixture of emotions. If it was true that her father had made some sort of counteroffer or demand of his own, or the police were involved somehow, nothing could be worse. Jane had said things, in one of her generous moods. *Maybe they need to keep you alive the first few days.* Did that mean after the first few days— like, now—that was no longer true? She'd said something about Dad "doing things his own way," which may or may not have something to do with the police. Even allowing for grandiosity in the demand letter, they had no reason to keep her alive now. They already had one dead body to deal with. Why not one more?

Jane hadn't elaborated beyond little hints and tidbits. That could mean she was intentionally keeping vague whatever she knew. But more likely was that she knew hardly anything. Would Ian even tell her the finer points of matters like this? He probably gave Tony updates, but Jane? She was probably in the dark as much as Sarah was. How many times had Jane apologized to her?

And how much of what she said carried any weight anyway? It almost seemed like Jane wanted to befriend her, was reaching out to her. Some sort of escape from a mental captivity that may seem as real to her as Sarah's actual captivity. *Hope you don't think I'm using you,* she'd said. That story about jumping in the back of Ian and Tony's car at the truck stop where she worked? Took off running one day from her job, her husband, her marriage, whatever demons were chasing her. *Bonnie and Clyde all the way.* Going from a truck stop in Oregon, to a flat in London, to a kidnapping in Washington. Oh yeah, that. She showed up at her waitress job to take her last paycheck from the safe before the boss got there: she somehow had the combo for the safe but not the keys to the building the safe was in? Sarah wondered if any of the rest of her story was true. Whether anything she said was true. The poor woman. Sarah felt both pity and disgust at the same time. She knew she couldn't trust anything Jane said.

The friction between the three of them seemed to be increasing. One day it was all going to explode. Ian had always been the one in charge. That had been clear since day one in the masks. Tony had always come across as the tough one, but he was certainly a subordinate. Jane was the chorus in this tragedy, just there as some sort of foil between Ian and Tony. Just as Jane had started seeking refuge in conversation with the prisoner, Tony and Ian's cozy status seemed to be wearing thin. She'd heard the mild put-downs from the beginning, the occasional argument, but the actual fight last night was unlike anything yet. Tony's handling of the stranger, and of herself, seemed to have been the turning point.

She allowed herself to imagine the final day, the exchange going just as they'd planned, and her being released. It could happen. But she knew it was just as possible that with this new wrinkle in the plans, she could wind up dead. If her father tried to finagle an arrangement they didn't like, all they had to do was bring her out to that shed where the stranger had wound up. She began to visualize how it might go if it came to that, but stopped herself.

She had to stay positive. She had to get out of here before that outcome was possible.

She had a good feeling, the way it had gone telling Jane she had some kind of pain. By now surely she had built on Jane's resentment against one or both of the men. She could expand on it. She knew she had to act before allowing the ideas to fade, before letting the doubting part of her take over.

She went to the square. Looking at the hatch, she hesitated with her fist above the wood. *No, do it.* She knocked. A minute later, getting no answer, she knocked again.

The latch slid open, the door swung upward, and Tony appeared. A questioning look was on his face, his eyebrows raised. She felt delight seeing a big black and blue bruise on one side of his neck.

"Um," Sarah said tentatively, "is Ian still out?"

"Yeah, why?"

"Well, I just wanted to ask you, I mean, when he wasn't around."

"Ask me what?"

"Well, is it something that can spread? Is it contagious?"

"Say what?"

"So he was lying."

"You gonna tell me what the fuck you're talkin' about?"

"When he brought breakfast up this morning, he told me that if—I'm sorry, this is just what he said."

"Said what."

"That if you brought food up, I shouldn't eat it."

"Since when do I bring food up?"

"I know, he just said if you did."

"Okay, so what did he say. Shouldn't eat it because what."

"He said you have something that can be spread anytime there's moisture, or water. Like the rice the other day, that steam, it could have been in there. I just wanted to ask you about it first."

"What the hell, moisture? What the fuck are you on?"

"He said you tell people you have an egg allergy, but it's actually some kind of virus. Like HIV."

Tony stood in stunned silence until he half laughed. "Like HIV?"

"Yeah, that's what he said."

"I don't even know what the hell kind of story that's supposed to be."

"I know there's nothing to it. I mean, you don't get most viruses that way. I just don't know why he'd say that."

"Bigger question is why are you telling me?"

"Because he said it was your turn to bring me dinner tonight."

"My turn to bring you dinner?"

"That's just what he said. Anyway, after what he said, I just wanted to avoid a weird situation. And, well, obviously I don't want to catch anything."

When Tony only stared back at her blankly, she said, "You won't tell him I told you, will you? Please don't. I knew I shouldn't have mentioned anything, but it's my own safety I—"

"The fuck." Tony pulled the hatch shut briskly and slid the latch.

Within seconds, she heard the muffled voices begin. She strained to listen, but she could make nothing out of the conversation. She allowed herself a quiet smile.

CHAPTER 42

Mere coincidence: that was essentially what the Oakland detective had implied. The car alarm was probably because of the metal part falling onto the hood of his car. Maybe it landed just right so as not to cause a scratch. The overnight letter could have somehow been in his box the whole time and he hadn't noticed it at first, maybe tucked up against the side. The severed camera cable may have been from the cleaning or maintenance crew, just as the management company had suggested. Something with a long handle or a hook on it, maybe. Regardless, the part hadn't dented his car. He had eventually gotten the overnight letter. Nothing was missing from his apartment.

Liddy could understand Oakland P.D.—or any law enforcement—not taking it seriously. He'd started to doubt his own initial concerns. Maybe the photos of this Sarah Easton had no meaning whatsoever. Just simple byproducts of using the internet. Maybe he himself had downloaded and then forgotten about them, even inadvertently. The detective had asked him whether he knew her personally. If not, maybe he had come across something in the news or somewhere while searching for something else. Liddy had begun to tune out as Yamada paid lip service by saying all he had to do was look in his temporary internet and download folders and he'd find hundreds of photos and files he didn't recognize, of people, places and things. It was all a normal part of internet traffic.

He had even begun to see it from their point of view. No apparent crime had been committed. There was nothing missing from his apartment. He hadn't been hurt or threatened. He couldn't think of anyone with a motive. Liddy himself had admitted that his ex had borrowed his laptop, and that he wondered whether his friends had played a prank.

He had to admit, Yamada had been very nice the way he'd essentially told him he was imagining things, that he was basically wasting everyone's time. He'd politely suggested possibilities (which he had obviously been reading from a list, or bullet points) about storing information locally or on the cloud, software updates that didn't install completely, virus or malware possibilities, and contacting his provider. He'd even brought it full circle by pointing to an online identity theft checklist and recommending that Liddy keep an eye on his credit report. Even if it was identity theft, there was little the police could do. He could file a report with Oakland but most likely the damage would occur in multiple jurisdictions and probably in other states. Most of the financial big players would sooner write off the loss than spend time and money on an investigation.

The only time Yamada seemed to take him seriously was when he mentioned the overnight letter time slip and the severed camera cable in the lobby. Yamada had taken Liddy's information and would see if he could find the report. It might be a few weeks if there was anything solid. He'd given Liddy a case number.

Liddy had written down the case number and had been ready to accept it as coincidence and wait it out. But the email from his bank changed his mind. A couple hours after the call he got a form email from his bank asking whether he would like to add his new credit card to his online banking. He knew for sure he hadn't applied for a new card. So it was either a mistake or some kind of bank promotion.

When he called the bank, he found out that he had apparently not only applied for a new card and it had been approved, but now that he'd begun using the card, it would be easier to manage his spending by adding it to his online banking. When he was told he'd used it at a car rental agency and at several convenience stores between the Bay Area and Portland, he nearly hung up in disbelief. He mentioned that he'd spoken with the police just today about a possible theft in his apartment, and that the potential of identity theft had come up. The agent told him they could put a stop on the card and file a fraud/identity theft claim, but they would need a police report.

After he called Oakland P.D. back and waited to leave a voicemail with the same detective he'd spoken to, he went through his computer once again. He was now feeling not only irritated but nervous. He'd nearly rejected the identity theft idea since it seemed unlikely but now it seemed to be happening.

One thing the detective had mentioned earlier stuck in his mind: other than the recent oddities, could he think of any conversation, person, or event in his recent routine that stuck out, that didn't seem right? The overnight mail thing was obvious. The severed cable appeared intentional. His car alarm going off—

He stood up and looked around for his keys. He felt an instinctual need to keep them close now. With a feeling of urgency he stepped out of his apartment, checked twice to make sure he'd locked the door, and went quickly downstairs. At his parking stall he looked for any sign of the fallen metal object he'd seen. It was gone from where he'd left it on the workbench after finding it. He looked all around the stall, under the bench, under his car, in the shelves, but could find no sign of it.

He again checked the surface of his car hood. There truly were no new scratches or dents that he could identify. On the ceiling, a ventilation or utility pipe ran the width of his stall, but he could see nothing like that piece of metal, nor anything it might have detached and fallen from. He walked around the rest of the garage, making his way toward the back, checking the ceiling ducts and valves. A main artery ran the length of the room along the ceiling, ending at the back, above the main car garage door.

As his gaze ran to the end of the duct, he saw the cable for the security camera. He noticed a section of tape where a repair had been made. So both the front and rear cameras had been cut? He was not surprised. If someone had cut one, they would probably cut both, for the same reason. But he had to do a double take when he saw the camera itself. A folded piece of paper was covering the lens. It looked to have been taped on roughly and clumsily, but it was definitely holding the paper in place. He pulled out his phone and took a photo. He would have to call the management company again, and the police. Something was definitely going on, and whoever had covered up the camera had done it after the repairs had been made to the cable.

As he circled back and approached the door to go back upstairs, something began to occur to him. At first it was just a vague flicker of memory. Being stuck in traffic. Turning around to go back home. Driving back to get the forgotten documents. Pulling into the garage. He'd noticed a torn sign outside on the wall. It had been nothing but fragments and a couple pieces of tape. Opening his car. Walking quickly while getting his apartment key. Mind occupied, thinking of the project and the documents.

Then he remembered. He'd passed a man, somewhere around the spot he was in now: near the inner garage door. He'd looked up to acknowledge him as they passed. No one he recognized, but then, he didn't know everyone in the building. The man had been looking down, also in a hurry. They'd passed. That had been it. Liddy had gone quickly upstairs and thought nothing more of it.

He opened the door and walked upstairs, trying to recall that face. There was something about that face, that man. He had been fumbling with a set of keys—but there had been something about his hands. Yes, his hands. He had been wearing gloves. White or off-white latex gloves. Almost automatically Liddy began to form connections between the incidents in the building and in his apartment, and seeing a strange man wearing latex gloves. In the parking garage, where not only his car alarm had gone off, but the camera cable had been cut.

But there was something else. It wasn't just the gloves. Nor was it this man's proximity to other incidents nearby. When it came, Liddy felt suddenly lightheaded.

It wasn't just recalling a face he'd seen recently. It was deeper: he knew he'd seen that face not just in the garage, but maybe more than once. Something about it was familiar. Now that he reflected, it didn't seem even that long ago. Maybe weeks, maybe a couple months at most. He nearly rejected the idea that he was thinking of the same person, the same face. It was the kind of familiarity one could recognize in someone who stands in the same line, or shows up at a routine stop. Had he seen that man downtown, or on his way to or from downtown?

As he tried to piece together any connection, his mental scope widened. If he'd ridden on BART with him, it was maybe not a stretch. Once or twice, it was possible. Maybe there was a similar work routine, their work places were nearby, or their schedules were similar and he just hadn't noticed. No. It was something else. It was more than a random face on the street or the train. Something about the office. A client, or visitor. That was it. He hadn't given it any thought at the time, but now he recalled what had been an everyday event: he had held the door open for that man when they'd both walked into his office one day. As he'd gone into work one morning, that man had followed him in—a client he assumed—and he'd held the door, as one does. But how could it be? In the expanse of the Bay Area, how was it possible to see the same guy in his basement garage that he'd held the door for in downtown San Francisco?

With these new concerns, Liddy called the detective's number.

CHAPTER 43

S arah looked out through a tiny crack in boards covering the window for a while, then went back to the cot. As she sat down, she felt the sharp nudge of something. She pulled back the blanket it was under, and saw that she'd forgotten a piece of molding. With a sudden urgency, she crossed to the rear window and began to put it back into place.

But while she was there, with the flashlight pointing upward, something caught her eye. In the small mouse hole to the right of the window she noticed something yellowish within the confines of the hole. Looking closer, she saw that there was something stuffed in there. She used a piece of molding, pushed it into the hole, and carefully twisted it around, trying to hook the object. After two tries she pulled out what appeared to be a piece of insulation, several inches long.

Now that she'd removed the insulation, she was aware of something else about the hole. More so when the beam of the flashlight moved away from it. It was like a glow. She switched the flashlight off and looked closer. Yes, there was a faint light coming from within. She got close and looked in. The light seemed to be coming from below. There must be some kind of opening in the wall, to the bedroom beneath her. One of the mouse exits maybe. Another loosened knot in the pine, probably.

She put her ear up against the hole. She could hear voices. Sounds were muted, but she guessed Jane was saying something from outside the closed bedroom door. She heard the occasional clink and shuffle of things moving around. Jane and Tony must be in the main room and their voices drifting upward through the hole.

She leaned back and looked at the faint glow coming from the hole. This was incredible. She had a way around the permanence of the hatch, a new way to hear what was going on below. She'd have something to listen to tonight, when Ian got back.

She stuffed the insulation back, then sat on the cot, turned off the light, and remained under the covers, thinking, planning, plotting, riding a wave of mild euphoria. Some hint of a plan was taking shape. She had many options, not the least of which involved the car key, desk leg, window, knife, and now the listening hole. But to put it all together, to make it rhyme, depended on so many variables.

By now Tony hopefully had the impression that Ian had said something about him behind his back, something about a contagious virus. It was debatable whether he believed the part about the virus. The question was, did he believe the part about Ian saying it. No doubt Tony had by now mentioned it to Jane. Jane would say no, it's the first she'd heard of it, and she wouldn't know why Ian would say something like that. Sarah imagined the internal thoughts: *But if it is true, why didn't you tell me before we made the sleeping arrangements?* Doubt would be planted in Tony's mind, and he'd start thinking, wondering what Ian was up to. At the same time, Jane would begin to wonder about what Tony had said, maybe putting together this and the thing she'd heard about Sarah feeling ill, having some sort of pain in her stomach. Maybe there was a connection? Was there something going around in this small space? Maybe they'd discount the whole thing, see it as a weak attempt from a desperate prisoner. But maybe enough of it would sink in to cause some resentment and suspicion. They had plenty of that already. They were wallowing in it. Now there would be more. It was just a matter of channeling it in the right direction.

Meanwhile, she was working on the window. With a little more effort she'd have the outer, newer boards loose and believed she could find a way to prop them in place to avoid suspicion. She'd done it with the molding and the glass, and it had worked. The two-by-fours were another issue, but she had vowed to think about those only when she needed to. She would have to choose a time when they were making noise below, preferably when they started arguing. That could happen tonight.

Then, on one of her bathroom trips, she'd get the key and knife. She'd come back upstairs, put on her jacket, and get ready the things she might need out there. All of the matches for sure. She'd extract the window and the loose boards. By then she would have removed the two-by-fours. She'd get the desk leg ready.

Then she'd create a distraction. She'd get Ian's attention. When he came, she'd say that earlier she'd overheard Tony say he planned to take Ian's bracelet, that he thought he might be able to sell it or something. That Tony wanted to do it because of what Ian had said about the virus behind his back, and for hitting him on his neck. Maybe she'd throw something about Jane in there too, just to stir things up.

Again, maybe Ian would buy it, maybe not. In fact in his case, he would probably be a lot more skeptical. He'd need time to mull it over. But there would be the hint of resentment and mistrust. They'd probably be civil at first, pretending not to be affected by the prisoner's new round of lies, but that seed of doubt would be there. Maybe they'd argue. Maybe they'd start fighting.

Then she'd move the desk over the square, to block anyone coming up. Then she'd jump out the back window and hope like hell the key was for the car out there. If it wasn't, then she probably had no chance. She would be caught. Even if she weren't caught, if she were not able to use the car, how far could she get with only her light jacket on? It was snowing hard and had been since Sunday. She'd freeze. Ian had told her as much on day one.

The key had to be for the car out there. It was the only way.

As she went through the motions of her escape plan, she heard the sound of an approaching car. Ian was back.

She went to the square and put her ear on the wood of the hatch. Within a minute she could hear the muffled sound of the door closing below. The sounds of conversation. The tinkle and rattle of objects. Expecting to hear the hints of some type of confrontational language, she was surprised when things sort of quieted down. She pictured them sitting down there like a stoic family, everyone reading books or watching a movie with rapt attention.

She went to the listening hole and removed the insulation.

Voices were indistinct, but she could hear Ian. He was saying something about times and places and things to do. Her first assumption was that they were talking about the upcoming exchange. How was that supposed to work? Were they going to go into Seattle and just pick it up? Were they going to bring her and leave her somewhere, pick up the package, and disappear, like in TV shows? Or were they doing it through whomever they worked for, this other party out there somewhere?

After a momentary lull, she heard Jane's voice. There was some back and forth. Then she heard one of the men say her name. After another lull, Ian called her name, followed by a noise at the bottom of the hatch. She noticed how his voice came up partly through the hole and partly through the hatch. Two more knocks on the hatch and she heard the sliding of the latch. She quickly replaced the insulation and went to the cot and sat down. The hatch opened upward. Light filled the room and she nearly had to squint to focus on Ian.

"Hello, love," he said. He appeared mildly intoxicated. His eyes and face seemed to hold an excess of artificial joy. "Wondering if you're hungry yet."

She was. She wondered how it was going to start. Would he accuse her instantly, come right out with it and ask her about the virus lie? Or would he ask her down, and sit her in front of Tony, then question her with one of his sarcastic interrogations?

"Well?"

"Yes. I guess I am."

"So am I. Come down to the bathroom first, do that thing, then you can have the little surprise I brought for you." He put a mouse trap on the floor. His bracelet chain rustled across his wrist. There was a piece of cheese in the trap. "Cheese works best, and it's so bloody traditional. Hope you're happy."

So Jane had told him about the mouse traps. What else had she told him? Were all those trips up here, all the small talk, just a way to get info and bring it back to Ian?

"Just kidding. That's not the present. Anyway, come downstairs first. We need you up here so we can do some business in private later."

He waited, in his mildly drunken state. Then he moved, slowly receding down the ladder. She waited until he was gone, then followed. Tony was busy in the kitchen area with something. Jane was just sitting down on the couch. Sarah went into the bathroom. While there she began to entertain new strands of worry. There was something in the air. If they wanted to do business, why not just do it where they were, when she'd been upstairs? Why call her down just to have her go back up? She wished she'd known what their conversation had been about just now.

When she opened the door, Ian and Tony were standing there, watching her as she approached the ladder.

"Hold off," Tony said, grabbing her arm.

"What is this?" she said, trying to free herself. As she started to make for the ladder Ian grabbed her other arm and felt all over her, patting, pressing. Checking in pockets. Groping along her legs. Tony checked her socks.

"What—what are you looking for?"

"Nothing. Here you go." He handed her a small tray of sushi, a napkin and a pair of wooden chopsticks in a paper wrapper.

Seeing the way she simply stared at the sushi, he said, "Don't worry, it's been kept cool all the way. And there's nothing in it."

She took it and went up the ladder, feeling distressed and queasy. When she'd cleared the square, Ian said from below: "You know, I've been noticing you lately, Sarah."

Here it was.

"The way you've been watching us. It's funny, actually—or no, better yet, so cliché. Just like this whole kidnapping and ransom thing. The way things like this always work out, you know what I mean?"

She listened.

"The way the captors always seem to start fighting and bickering among themselves. They start arguing, there are power issues, they start killing each other. It's all the infighting and power struggles that do them in in the end. In the midst of that, sooner or later the prisoner finds a way to take advantage of this and starts thinking, hey, these people are distracted, they're busy. Hm, maybe I can use that to get away somehow. And it would just be so damn obvious!"

Sarah could feel the panic. Did Ian know something? Was it more than the lie about Tony and the virus? Had Jane told him about the fake pain in her stomach? Did he know about the window, or the hole? Maybe when she'd shone the light into it they'd somehow noticed it in the bedroom, when the lights were off.

"Sarah, you listening to me?"

"Yeah."

"Any feedback?"

"What do you mean?"

"Are you starting to think along these lines? About escaping, stuff like that?"

"No."

"Oh, well thank the lord. I feel comforted now. Just wanted to verify."

Ian knew something, and he wasn't going to say what. "I'm locked up here."

"Right? Anyway, you've probably heard by now, since Jane seems so friendly with you lately, that your daddy's decided to give us some spending money."

She waited.

"So if I were you, if you've been working on things, escape plans or whatever—and don't tell me you haven't—after all you have the keys, don't you?"

Sarah shuddered.

"Come on, might as well just fess up. We'll call a spade a spade."

"I don't know what keys you're talking about. I already told you. Tony searched up here!"

"Okay darling. If you have some grand scheme, just know that we're wrapping this thing up very soon. We'll take you to the spot, tit for tat, and the deal's done. Our contract done. So no sense trying some cocky scheme just to get yourself killed when you could've been set free the next day. Does that make sense?"

"Yes."

"Thank you, your excellency. Care for any wine?"

"No thanks."

"Enjoy your sushi. I know it's not much. You can eat all you want when you get out of here. Oh, I have some tea for you. I hear you guys've been drinking a fair amount of it. That's just so damn English. I'm proud of you. What's next I wonder, cricket and real football?"

He appeared with a mug of tea and set it down near the edge of the square. When he descended she heard him say, from closer to the bedroom. "I think the dogs are ready to eat now."

No one responded.

Ian, louder, said, "Hello? I think it's your turn."

"Me?" Jane said.

"They're hungry. Tony's tied up with something, and I've got these details for tomorrow."

"They ate late today. I doubt they'd eat anything."

"Jane?" Ian said with deliberate slowness. "I said, can you please take care of the dogs?"

There was a noticeable silence. Then Jane said, "Okay," but Sarah heard it as a question.

"Crack on."

There were some sounds near the front, then the main door opening and closing. Ian's head soon appeared in the square. "Enjoy." The hatch closed and the latch slid shut.

Sarah groped around for the flashlight, switched it on and aimed the beam at the sushi. On the surface, this nearly passed for a nice gesture. There were about eight pieces, mostly smoked salmon, shrimp, and rolls with tuna and avocado in it. She wondered what had made him decide to get sushi, other than the obvious reason. They'd found out from spying on her, or through some other means, that she liked it.

She also wondered where the sushi had come from. He'd been gone a long time today. And why had he come home half drunk? Was it elation that his requirements were being satisfied, that the exchange was set for tomorrow?

Then something hit her. She stood up. It occurred to her that Jane had more or less been sent outside just now. As Jane had said, the dogs had already been fed earlier, and it was almost always Tony who tended to them. Ian had told Jane that Tony was tied up with something, and that he himself had details to take care of. There was something going on. And now it was very quiet downstairs.

She went to the listening hole, using the silent zones on the floor. She used the splinter of molding to pull out the insulation, then switched off the flashlight. The faint light from below glowed within the knot hole, and she pressed her ear up against it and listened.

She heard their voices fairly clearly. Ian and Tony were talking in hushed tones.

"—that way. And here's that place," Ian was saying.

"Not a great road in this weather," Tony said.

"What'd I tell you about control."

"Well it is what it is, I guess."

"And as far as that other thing, what, you goin' soft on me? Like I said, we already crossed that line a couple days ago."

"If you say so."

"I do say so. She has no reason to think that way. Besides, it's just to make it easier for you."

"So, guessing you still want me to do it," Tony said.

"Of course. That's not my angle. Never has been."

"So tomorrow at 3:00, you sure?"

"Yeah," Ian said, "but we should get there earlier. Who knows what they're playin' at. We need to check it out first."

"Sure."

"And I was thinking, you should use zip ties this time. Rope is great, but look what happened the other day, all that screaming and kicking."

"Wasn't that bad."

"No, but you get my point."

"So, question is, what about you know who."

"What about her?"

"Still not gonna tell her?"

"Tell her what?"

"Okay. But if she starts asking shit, you're on your own."

"No, that's where you're wrong, Tony. We're in this together."

Sarah leaned back from the hole. Her hands were shaking and it was difficult to put the insulation back in.

She staggered in the darkness back to the cot and tumbled into it. In the pitch black gloom, she looked around her confine, in the direction of the windows, the hatch, the desk leg. She saw nothing.

Soon, she heard the vague sounds of Jane coming back in.

CHAPTER 44

The afternoon sky was gray and the air was cool when Brandon pulled to the side of the narrow two-lane to check his directions. Without his phone he had to use a map, and the one he had apparently didn't show some of the smaller roads. He checked with someone at a gas station to get his bearings, and then recognized the turns from his earlier visit. The landscape, even twenty miles northwest of the Seattle area, looked rugged, remote, and gave Brandon the sense of leaving civilization behind and entering a wild domain with each passing mile. Tall pines rose on both sides, and during occasional gaps in the wall of green, the view opened up to reveal mist-covered peaks, waterfalls, and rocky cliffs.

The motel was located between two small towns, down a winding dirt road and nestled within thick greenery. It was a relic from the past, a classic one-story with a main office on one end and a row of half a dozen rooms with patterned curtains in the windows and a pink metal door in each unit. The exterior was made of logs, painted brown. A sign on top of the office roof showed an angler pulling in a large brook trout. Beneath it was a sign in large red letters: "The Brook Inn." Most of the vehicles in the parking lot were pickups or RVs, some with trailers carrying boats.

After checking in at the office, he brought in his travel bag and set it on the bed. The small room had been updated at some point but still had plywood paneling on one wall, a reddish carpet, and a brown patterned bedspread. Above the older TV on top of the dresser was a map of the area, showing little illustrations of fishermen casting or whipping fly lines in and out of rapids.

He went into the bathroom and looked in the mirror. To his surprise, the makeup still looked convincing. Then again, he'd taken care not to rub or touch his face any more than necessary. He took off the wig, then ran a finger along some of the heavier parts, beneath one eye, amazed at how well it held even now. He rubbed off most of it with remover, then took a shower.

After the shower he drove about ten miles west, following the narrow two-lane to the next town and stopping to get something to eat. It was no more than a collection of buildings, a couple of bars and a cafe, but when he'd come here months ago it was the only place in the area that he'd found a storage locker to rent on behalf of Adam Liddy. The facility was sandwiched between a lumber yard and a small cement factory, and the unit he'd been assigned was on the back end. He drove around and opened up the locker door. Even though the locker was the smallest size available, the inside still looked mostly empty. He was glad: it only took him five minutes to load all of it into the car and close it up.

With the locker emptied he headed to the gravel pit he'd found on the earlier trip, about three miles away. The pit was on the far end of a logging road well off the main road. As he made his way up the narrow gravel road he felt aware of the ticking clock. The rise in elevation seemed to mirror a heightened sense of expectation, and when the thick walls of trees offered a wider glimpse of the surrounding terrain, he could see the mountain walls and the looming whiteness in the sky above them. The entire range above a certain height seemed to be covered in vast clouds as the sky shifted from gray to white.

When he reached the pit, he drove past the broken chain barrier and into the center of the gravel expanse. He shut off the engine and breathed in deeply several times, taking in the fresh aroma of firs and the tinge of damp coolness in the air. There were no sounds except the cries of hawks perched on trees on one end. The pit appeared to have been used in recent months but the tire tracks he found appeared to have been eroded by rains and the elements. No one came here, and if they did, it was not very often.

Of the things he'd brought from the storage locker, he left most in the jeep. They were for what came after the exchange: some clothing, including cold weather gear, different kinds of boxed and canned food, a tent and camping gear, rope, tools, and a hodgepodge of survival necessities. Much of it was contingency equipment, preparation for the outcome no matter which way the exchange ended.

Spreading a jacket on the hood of the car, he began to lay out the things he'd need at the gas station. A standard .243 rifle, the same caliber as the one he'd brought from San Francisco, except with the more common wooden stock. Two handguns, a 9 mm and a .380. Boxes of shells for the guns. A couple of hunting knives. Tools. He knew the layout of the gas station and where he planned to position himself, but he had no idea how many people he'd have to deal with.

He opened a box with the metal gun stock he'd brought from home. Putting on latex gloves he assembled the rifle, then carefully removed the stock from the homemade brace and attached it. The stock had been protected ever since he'd picked it up in Liddy's garage. He attached the scope and adjusted it to the settings he'd measured the other night. He looked the assembled rifle over and double checked to ensure all parts were tight. Then he attached an adjustable bipod to the barrel.

He loaded it and squeezed the trigger to test the accuracy of the scope. After several test shots and a couple of minor changes, he felt it was as accurate as possible up to an approximate twenty-yard range. The pine cones he used in the quarry as targets broke apart or exploded, sending up little clouds of debris.

CHAPTER 45

S arah was glad that she'd trusted her instincts all along. She'd been right. They were planning to kill her when they got the cash. Ian must have made the decision around the time they'd stopped wearing their masks.

The notion of being killed seemed like an abstract thought, a dream sequence, a surreal concept somewhere in the future with nothing tangible associated with it. She was aware it was not a serious consideration in her mind, that she wasn't attaching enough meaning to it. She was telling herself it was true, that that's what they had in mind for her, but she just couldn't fully visualize the idea that a day from now, she could be dead.

Dead. There. Using that word helped. That had meaning.

So they planned to drug her somehow, then tie her up. She wondered how they'd do it, how they actually planned to do the job itself, after she was tied up. It must be the drug itself, something lethal. Something in the food they gave her. Or maybe they'd do it after she'd passed out. Or they'd leave her to die somehow. She put the thoughts out of her mind.

She had not touched the sushi or the tea, convinced that one or both would have something in them, after hearing Ian and Tony. She'd hidden the sushi in the drawer of the night stand, and planned to dump the tea out the window when she'd opened it. They would see the empty sushi tray and mug and think she'd been a good prisoner, had eaten her dinner. Even if there wasn't anything in the tea tonight, tomorrow morning there would be for sure.

Sarah knew she had to start now. She had until tomorrow morning, one night until it got light and things went into motion. She would have to work on the window tonight, risking detection as they slept or screwed down there. There was no other way. Hopefully, she'd be able to get everything loose tonight, ready, everything in place. Then she had to get the key in the toilet. Everything she did depended on the car key. She hated the finality of the thought, but it was true.

She wondered about making her move during the night, under cover of darkness. It would mean getting the keys now, before it gets too late. She could work on the window, and be gone before morning, when they came looking for her.

Without hesitating or allowing her doubts to take over, she knocked on the hatch. Voices mumbled things, but no one came. She knocked again. Then Ian's voice, muffled and yelling: "What?"

"I need to go to the bathroom!"

"No."

She had not expected this. "But I'm sick!"

"I already told you, we have business!"

"Please!"

She waited. A minute, then another, went by with no response. But she could hear them saying something to each other, and Jane's voice.

Without the keys, she had no hope of doing anything except running blindly out there. Down the road. In the snow. Into the night. With the dogs chasing after her.

Maybe the key is not for the car.

Stop saying that. Stop thinking that.

Now was the time. Before they got quiet for the night. They were down there, talking in low voices, probably planning, making preparations. Maybe they were packing up. She assumed Ian and Tony were keeping Jane in the dark, and she wondered how they were dancing around the reality of tomorrow morning. What had they told her? Most likely, nothing. Come tomorrow, it wouldn't matter. It would all be over. Jane would assume the captive had been let free and the ransom obtained, and she could go back to that farm and her husband if she wanted, or continue on with Ian or Tony. Or both of them. Sarah knew it was too late to continue trying to play them against each other. There was no more time for that kind of intricacy. She had to get the keys and make a move.

The latch slid open. She flinched. So they were going to let her down. The hatch swung open slowly. Light filled the room. Ian's bracelet came into view. He put down a stock pot. Then he shut the hatch and slid the latch closed. The room went dark.

She aimed the beam inside the pot. There was a roll of toilet paper, and two pink pills, still in their shrink wrap. Antacids. She was supposed to use that? No more toilet access? If she was sick she'd have to sit on this pot and take a couple of Tums?

She heard the front door open. Soon after, the sounds of a car, the SUV, moving around repeatedly in the driveway. She went to the front window to take a look. The front light was on, and through a narrow crack she could barely see Tony, plowing the driveway, going back and forth. She was amazed at the snow. It just wouldn't stop. She hoped this wouldn't give her second thoughts when she started to think about how deep it was, or whether the roads would be clear. Everything illuminated in the faint light from the cabin was covered in deep white. The boughs on the trees all around were weighted down with thick layers of perfect snow, white on green. She estimated that nearly a foot had fallen in all, probably half of it since Tony had plowed the driveway last time.

No, no amount of snow would change her mind.

She would have to come up with an alternate plan. So she was not going to be able to get the keys tonight. She'd have to get them in the morning. They'd have to feed her in the morning. Surely they'd let her down then. Morning seemed so far away. But yet it gave her enough time to work the window. She had no time to waste.

First, she went to the window and carefully took everything apart. The molding, nails, and glass all came off easily. The first rush of cold air came in, surprising her with its power. It made working around the window an urgent experience, and she got the sense that if she was going to work with the window open all night, the room was going to get extremely cold. She went to get the desk leg and brought it over near the window.

She wrapped a blanket around the end of the leg, to minimize noise, held it back about a foot, and thrust it into one of the planks. It made a dull thud, not much noise at all, which pleased her. On the other hand, it nullified the impact of the leg because the blanket absorbed most of the impact. If she wanted to make real progress she'd have to hit harder, and without the blanket, and that would make noise. But since they were busy downstairs, talking, moving around, she took her chance and swung again, without the blanket this time. She let the leg hit on the lower part of the plank. The splintering sound encouraged her, and without thinking about noise or stopping to listen, she swung again. The plank loosened on the bottom, exposing the nails. She inserted the small end of the leg into the opening, used it as a lever, and pulled. The board pried loose, hung by the top nails.

There was no question about it. The room was getting very cold.

She stopped to listen for sounds below. If they found out what she was doing, Tony would be the first to come up. But what of it? She swore she'd hit anyone who came up before she'd let them stop her. Tony, with his wry smile. His head would be at just the right spot on the floor, like it had been the other day when he'd come up looking for the keys. Just resting there, on the floor, like a golf ball on a tee. This time, if she felt like it, she could send him back down the ladder in a coma.

She rammed the leg into the plank and let it fall outward, no longer caring about covering her tracks. She moved to the next one, swinging hard, listening every few swings for sounds from below.

With two planks removed, she had freed the space between two of the two-by-fours. It was not enough to get through, but now she was starting to see a way through. The window was looking more like an opening instead of a barrier.

She stopped to listen, putting her ear on the square, then over the listening hole. So far, she got no indication they were aware of what she was doing. She credited their quality work on the hatch for this. They were obviously busy doing whatever needed to be done for tomorrow. How do you hide what you did when you kidnapped someone? Did they plan to get the money and just disappear? After they'd killed her, where were they planning to hide her body? The same place as that poor man's body from the other night? How would they cover their tracks? DNA sampling could find them out from hairs, fingerprints, forensic evidence of all kinds. It would be all over everything. Or maybe they had no criminal record, nothing to match against. Or was the person or people they worked for going to cover everything up somehow?

Maybe they'd burn the whole place down.

As she worked on the next plank, she wondered what they planned to do with the money. What would they do with ten million dollars? It could certainly help someone disappear. But it also would leave clues all over the place. It would raise eyebrows. The cops would surely be able to track it through the financial system. Or were they getting clean cash? Unmarked and untraceable somehow?

She was allowing herself to get distracted. She had to focus. She'd known it was going to get cold, but this was a lingering, gnawing, distracting tug at everything she did. Her fingers were starting to feel numb, and she knew at this rate she'd have a hard time gripping things when push came to shove. But she had a feeling of being unable to go back now. She knew she couldn't start to doubt. She had to push forward.

As she tried prying the two-by-fours with the leg, using it as a lever, the beam from the flashlight started to waver. She stared in dismay as the light flickered, then went off completely. It came back again, but worried, she shook it. It stayed on.

The two-by-fours did not budge. She heard no cracking or splintering sounds and felt no give. She tried swinging, first holding the heavy end of the leg back about a foot, then swinging into it. Nothing happened, but it made plenty of noise. Way too much for comfort. This time she stopped her work to listen. She took the insulation out of the hole and put her ear up against the opening. If they had heard her, nothing gave them away.

She sat on the cot and stared at the two-by-fours. Doubt began to creep in. The two-by-fours weren't budging. They had obviously planned well when they'd put them in. What if she couldn't get them off? She had to face it. It could happen.

Her ears were cold. Her fingers were numb, and as she'd feared, it was now getting difficult to hold things. As she was sitting on the cot warming her hands by blowing into them with her breath, the light flickered again. It came back, but then began to fade, slowly, even as she watched it. She got up and shook it, tapped it in her palm. It went out. She shook and shook, but nothing would revive it. She switched it off, waited for a while, then switched it on again. Nothing happened.

She began to cry. In a matter of minutes, everything was going wrong. The two-by-fours. The cold. Now the light. She groped in the darkness near the cot, and finding a blanket, wrapped herself in it and wondered how she was going to make this work. She admitted, her earlier optimism had carried her through, had even allowed her to more or less ignore the conversation about tomorrow morning she'd heard below. She'd treated the death thing as an abstract concept but now she was feeling it creep toward her.

This is how it happens. First one thing goes wrong. Then another. And finally you are in a position where no amount of thinking or effort will save you. You die.

Feeling anxiety and helplessness mount, she felt around in the darkness for one of the matches she'd hidden behind the molding.

On her hands and knees, she groped her way to the part of the wall where she'd hidden the matches and felt for the molding. Feeling the slight bump of a match head, she eased one out with her fingernail and struck it, then quickly looked around for the candle. Tony had dropped it and there had been only a small section left at that point, but it was something. When she found it she stood it on end, wrapped herself in both blankets and the sleeping bag and pondered her situation. She had no flashlight. The candle was about an inch long and might last a half hour if she was lucky. The room was freezing. She could see her breath. So far she'd not been able to get the two-by-fours off, and she knew she might not be able to. She wrapped herself tighter.

She visualized the layout of the cabin, the clearing in front, the buildings and what she knew of the road. Obviously there was the SUV. There was the other car, the one she hoped the keys were for. There was some kind of shed to the left. The road seemed to go off to the right. All she knew past that was there were turns or forks and it eventually got to a highway.

Yesterday, after the conversation with Jane, the jacket and boots by the door had caught her eye. She'd had the general idea of stealing them, using them if she escaped. She wondered if they would be there when she needed them. It didn't matter. She was going to get out no matter what.

Feeling a new surge of motivation, she went to the desk, picked up a handful of fuses, coins and small objects. She brought them back to her place on the floor near the candle and laid them out. She placed *Great Expectations* on the floor. That was the cabin. A match became the front door. In front of it she placed the smaller fuses from the desk. These were the desk leg, the jacket and boots downstairs. Three batteries for Ian, Tony and Jane, in one corner, the bedroom. Two pennies for the dogs, in another corner. A bottle cap on the back wall. That was the bathroom, the epicenter, the backbone of the whole thing. That's where the keys were, in the toilet tank.

In the morning, she would knock to go to the bathroom. She would insist on using it, start yelling if she had to. She would get the keys and the knife and hide them on her, in her socks. Then she'd come back upstairs and get the leg ready. She would place the car key into the sleeve of her left arm for easy access. She'd have the knife in her sock. She'd put on what she could wear to keep her warm.

She would wait until the people, dogs, and circumstances were just right. Maybe it would occur just after breakfast, if there was one. Maybe before they left for the exchange. Maybe during a moment when Ian and Tony went outside to look in the shed, to see if everything was right to tie her and kill her. Or maybe while one or more of them were in the bedroom. At some point tomorrow, one or two of them were going to be busy doing something while the other would be on a sort of unspecified watch. When the right moment came, she'd get downstairs, past them, swinging or slashing at any person or dog in her way, grab the jacket by the door if she could, and get out to the car.

She ran through a multitude of scenarios. They all began with her knocking or waiting for them to let her down. She would get the keys. Either she would come back up here and wait until it was the right time to jump out the window, or she would find a way to get out the front door.

There were many variables that could affect her success. The location of her captors. Their movement, the way they'd run after her. The keys dropping in the snow. The inability to get the desk leg in time. The desk leg or knife ending up in someone else's hands and being used against her. Or her not being allowed downstairs at all.

All the main potential problems were summed up by the keys. They were vital.

If she got out there, and the keys were not for that car, she would have only two options. Stop in her tracks, which would probably make the most sense for long-term survival, or run down the road, which would be futile at best since they could send the dogs or simply drive the SUV to find her. Or Tony could just shoot her. She thought as far as running to the fork that the stranger had described, then turning toward the highway. If she got to the highway, there may be people driving by. Maybe someone would stop.

The little voice spoke, and the second-guessing began. Now that she thought of it, how would she know which way to go if she got to the fork, regardless of whether she drove or ran there? Would she be able to hear the sounds of traffic? In the snowstorm what if there was no traffic? Would she have time to listen, assuming they were chasing her? She could get there and get caught while trying to decide which way to go.

She felt hope wax and wane but knew one thing for certain. Without the car, she really wouldn't have a chance. That was the reality.

Everything began with the visit to the bathroom.

Everything revolved around getting the keys.

She felt warm now. Even relaxed. Even sleepy.

CHAPTER 46

A s the evening went on, Adam Liddy continued to find more Sarah Easton photos and documents in his computer and his cloud account. They seemed to be saved in batches or groups. Some of the photos had similar names and were saved in clusters of several, usually with similar dates. And the dates were all over the place. Some went back only a week or two, others months. There were folders containing photos, and folders containing screenshots and documents: paperwork, receipts, invoices, ticket stubs.

He had started to draw inferences between the batches of photos and documents and the content of the strange note from his drawer, but his attempts to find a purpose in either led nowhere. It occurred to him that if someone had planted the photos and documents on his computer and had placed the paper in his drawer, it was to create an impression that he knew or had something to do with Sarah Easton. But it seemed a stretch that someone would attempt that with him. He was an architect. He had no celebrity friends. He had no connection with Sarah Easton that he was aware of.

He considered other possibilities. That a celebrity photographer had uploaded photos to his own account and somehow a mixup had occurred. Similar logins. A hack. Liddy worried about that, especially now. He had changed his passwords today, but he knew it could happen. He'd had the thought more than once when examining the candid poses in some of the photos. It was like she was spied upon. Shots taken without her knowledge and from afar, as she went about her routines. Receipts and travel documents and even handwritten notes, in her writing, he assumed.

The strange note was cryptic. The arrows and lines and little sections of text had no apparent pattern. One arrow pointed to a section of apparent gibberish, like codes or long strings of characters and numbers, sections with no spaces punctuated by spaces and more sets of characters. The font size and style varied but was mostly small and difficult to read. Beneath a line of random letters and numbers, the name SARAH EASTON could be seen. A circular line pointed toward a section of strings of numbers, printed sideways. Within the sets of numbers were dollar signs.

As he tried to make sense of these patterns, he heard a knock on his door. His first thought was that it was a repeat of the car alarm thing the other night, some anonymous neighbor. This time he got up to take a look before they left. He felt nervous about this mystery person, but also angry. Before he got to the door, there was another knock. "Adam Liddy? Oakland Police. Can you open up please."

Liddy felt unease. He had been working with the Oakland P.D. He had expected a call back, but probably not this late. And certainly not a visit. And how did they get in the building? Did the landlord let them in? He assumed it was about his case. Maybe they'd found something.

He looked out the peephole and saw two officers standing there, in uniform. One was holding a badge up for him to see. He opened the door. The landlord was lurking nearby, watching from a distance.

"Adam Liddy?"

"Yes."

"My name is Officer Griggs. Oakland P.D."

"Detective Whitlock," the other one said, opening his wallet to show his badge.

"You guys work with—Yamada was his name I think?"

"We are placing you under arrest as part of an investigation into the abduction of Sarah Easton."

"What?"

"You have the right to remain silent," Griggs said as Whitlock brought out handcuffs.

"What are you doing? I'm the one who called you guys."

"If you do say anything, what you say can be used against you in a court of law."

"Are you being serious now? Someone came into my apartment. That's the whole point!"

"You have the right to consult with a lawyer and have that lawyer present during any questioning."

"You have this all wrong!"

"If you cannot afford a lawyer, one will be appointed for you if you so desire. If you choose to talk to the police officer, you have the right to stop the interview at any time."

CHAPTER 47

Sarah rubbed her eyes. At first she was in a waking fog, blinking but seeing nothing. She was aware of only darkness. Then she felt the cold. Panicked, she reached out and felt the space in front of her. She'd allowed herself to fall asleep. She groped around, feeling the cold fuses, the batteries, the book. And then the remnants of the candle, only a small piece of wick surrounded by a bit of wax.

She looked toward the direction of the open rear window. It had been open now for—how long had she been out? Two hours? Six? There was no hint of light out there. She had no idea what part of the night it was. She strained to listen, groping her way to the hatch. She could feel the indentations of the frame and the outline of the square. She put her ear on the cold wood. There was no sound from below. Even if she wanted to resume working on the wood now, she couldn't. They were asleep and they would hear the noise. She had no light, no way to see what she was doing. It was pitch black. She wouldn't be able to see where the silent zones were. She wouldn't be able to see the window. She couldn't even put the glass back in the window if she wanted to.

Sitting near the hatch and staring into the darkness, she pondered the space beneath her. Directly below, she knew, the ladder led nearly straight down. At the bottom and two steps away was the door to the bathroom. Once she started down the ladder, she'd be in there with the door closed in under three seconds. Toilet lid would come off, she'd adjust her clothes, lid would go on, toilet would flush, and she'd come out to do whatever they wanted her to do. Then she'd scan the situation, check out the locations of all the players. Based on that, she would either go back upstairs, or do something then and there.

She put a finger in one sock, then the other, to see if they would be tight enough along her calf to hold the knife securely. She planned to slip it into her left sock. She was right-handed and that would provide the quickest access to the blade. She went over the scenario in her mind again and again. Get the desk leg ready. Get downstairs. Get the knife and key. Get outside.

She waited, bundled in the covers. She was wide awake, staring at the window, waiting for the light. Waiting for the day to begin. She looked frequently toward the direction of the rear window, waiting for the faint reddish hue to fill a crack. That would signal the earliest part of the day. Then it would be a countdown until the light increased enough to see.

Slowly the downstairs came alive. The more noise she heard, the more she began to worry. Today was the day. She strained to listen, putting her ear on the hatch, but hearing only vague words. As she waited and wondered, she noticed the muted reddish hint of light. Day was beginning in the east and some meager amount of light was hitting the rear window. To her amazement, she could see snow falling in through the window. It had been coming in for hours, and now that the light was increasing, she could see that several inches had accumulated on the floor. She could see the parts of the window, lying neatly in a stack near the wall, and the burned out stubs of matches. The spent bit of candle. The fuses, batteries and objects on the book.

She began biting her nails. Her fingers were numb, but she bit and bit, worrying about the timing, worrying about outcomes, worrying about her resolve. She got up and brought the desk leg near her. It felt good to have it close by.

Things quieted down, then picked up again. Voices going back and forth, talking, the front door opening, the dogs going out. She closed her eyes and tried to breathe in and out slowly. She had to empty her mind. She tried to tell herself she'd already done the thinking part of it. Now it was time to act.

She crawled to the hatch and knocked forcefully. They would have to let her down. She would make them do it. She sat between the square and the rear window, hoping to hide their view. After a few seconds, the latch slid and Ian appeared. "Blimey, it's cold up here," he said.

"It gets cold up here at night," she said without emotion. "I need to use the bathroom. I can't use that pan."

Ian seemed to grin. "Sure. Why not." He stepped down.

Sarah closed the hatch and went down the ladder. She saw Tony standing near the front door with his jacket on, as if waiting, staring at her dully. Jane wasn't in sight, and she couldn't see the dogs. She went into the bathroom. Ian seemed to be in good spirits. She wondered whether he would send Tony up there to search through her things. If so, he'd notice the window right away. He wouldn't even have to go all the way up the ladder to see it. It didn't matter now. The ball was rolling. She would get the knife and key and start the day as she'd planned, regardless of what happened.

She had to act quickly. She used the toilet, flushed it, and while the water was running, began to open the lid on the tank. Even as she did, she began to feel power surge through her. Things were going into motion. Even as she began to worry about where the road led and how she'd get to wherever it went, she remained focused.

When she looked in the tank, her first thought was that she was just not seeing well because she was in a hurry. Because she knew the objects were in there. The water was murky, and they were well hidden. They'd been there the whole time. But she wasn't seeing them. She stuck her hand in and felt once, twice, three times, no longer caring if the knife cut her. It didn't.

There was no knife. She stared. Frantically, she groped every part of the tank. There was nothing there. No keys. No knife. The crush was immediate and overwhelming. She began to panic. She told herself just as quickly that she had to avoid letting them know. If she was going to panic, she had to do it later, in her own space. She felt again, everywhere in the tank water, with both hands.

No, no, no wait, please, maybe they're somewhere else? There's lots of moving parts in a tank. Maybe they—

"Sarah?" Ian's voice. "You okay?"

She felt confused. She would have to go out soon. She could get upstairs and get the leg. She'd have that. She'd come back down and start swinging at anyone. It was all she could do now.

"Sarah? You might as well come out."

She slowly opened the door. Ian was there.

"What's wrong? Looking for something?"

She stared down, at the floor, feeling empty.

"Not bad. Gotta hand it to you. You had us for a long time." She could see even from her gaze toward the floor that he was holding the keys and knife in his hand. His bracelet slid as he dangled them.

She felt a strong temptation to fall to the floor and start sobbing.

"But I got to thinking—it was that tattoo, actually, that did it. Your tattoo. Ganesha, right? The funny part is, I had the thought you might have dropped them in there when Tony kept going on about the keys, but I never checked. Not sure when you got the knife, but that was good too. It's a bloody pity you won't be able to use either one of these, after all that work. Took me a while to reason it out, to go through all the options, but then there it was, the one place you went right after that wine glass incident."

He put them down on the table. She looked up as he came closer. His face was void of expression. "Why don't you go back upstairs. Just stay there until we get things ready."

She did.

The latch slid closed.

She lost it once she was alone. Feeling the frigid air but not caring, she fell into the pile of blankets and sleeping bag. She found the pillow, pressed her face into it, and began to sob. She could feel the tears hot and wet in the pillow. For several minutes, she felt she could lose all control, screaming out loud endlessly. Everything was as black as it had been during the night.

CHAPTER 48

As Brandon progressed further east and the elevation rose, the weather turned and the roads gradually worsened. Within the space of a few miles, faint swirling patterns of snow blowing across the road turned to sizable drifts in places and the sky became entirely white. Snow started to fly past the windows and the scant number of cars slowed and followed defined tracks in the road as they headed into the storm.

He knew roughly where the gas station was from the previous trip, but it was several miles further down the twists and turns than he remembered. When he reached it around 9:00 A.M. he pulled into the clearing amidst raging snow so thick that he had to stay in the car to consider his next moves. The snow outside was deep enough that he would have to think about how to hide the jeep and the tracks it would make. Getting stuck in it was a possibility. On the other hand, the falling snow would quickly help cover his tracks.

The place was a small collection of partially dilapidated buildings with an old house in the back. On the right was the service shed, with barrels and old car parts to the side. It was a small white clapboard building with two old gas pumps in front and a garage door with broken windows. The two-story house, also in peeling white clapboard and with boarded up or broken windows, stood in the rear of the lot. Heavy snow weighed down on the sagging roof. A short set of stairs led up to the front door. To the left of the house was a small shed or garage. Saplings and larger trees grew along the walls, between the structures, and through the wood stairs.

There was a sign on a post but the letters were faded and obscured by accumulated snow.

In front, between the house and the road, was another shed, no more than a few feet wide, positioned about ten yards from both the house and the service garage. Brandon stepped out, covering his face from the blowing snow, and took out the bags containing the guns from the back of his car. He went to the small shed and pushed open the door. Some sort of engine and related pipes and machinery took most of the space. It must have been a generator or pump of some kind. Parts were strewn all over the dirt floor. The door had been partly open, probably for years, and the clutter inside was covered in snow in one corner.

He scraped some of the junk to one side with his foot. He propped a piece of old board on top of the engine as a place to sit, then freed the clutter from the door enough to close it most of the way. It would keep most of the snow out. The window on one side of the shed was intact and allowed a partial view of the road. An occasional car passed but he could tell drivers' eyes were focused on the road and not his car tucked between the buildings.

He removed the metal .243 rifle from its case with gloved hands and stood it on end in the corner of the shed. It would remain there, get discovered by law enforcement, and become part of the evidence against Adam Liddy. The prints on the gun stock would distract, cause confusion. The fact that they were only on the stock would make it appear that the gun had been wiped, but sloppily. The remaining prints, when they were traced to Adam Liddy, would act as a smokescreen. Assuming the Oakland P.D. was in some stage of an investigation into Sarah's disappearance by now, the discovery of the gun would raise questions: had Liddy been here, at the gas station? Or had he sent the rifle with someone else on his behalf while he remained in Oakland?

Brandon took out the other .243 with the wooden stock, and the two handguns, loaded everything, and placed them within easy reach. With the matters in the shed taken care of, he examined the terrain and obstacles around the lot to find a place to hide the car. He checked the snow depth and assumed it was enough to pose a potential problem, from getting stuck to creating ruts or tracks, all of which he would have to hide to disguise his presence. Before moving the jeep he took out the coffee he'd bought along the way, a blanket, and some snacks and put them in the shed. Then he put the jeep into four-wheel drive, steadied his foot, and aimed directly toward the spot between the house and the garage. When he reached the far end he turned sharply and let the jeep come to a stop behind the house. He stepped out and checked: the car was impossible to see without coming round the side of the house. He found a large piece of board and used it to loosely scoop snow into the wheel tracks, making his way back to the shed. Even as he did, the falling snow started covering up the marks and his footprints.

When he was done he stepped inside the shed and sat down on the board covering the old engine. He got as comfortable as he could. Now it was just a waiting game. The guns were loaded. They were in position. He was ready. He was prepared to wait for hours with a careful eye on any approaching car.

CHAPTER 49

Sarah knew she should spend her time doing whatever she could do to affect her escape, but she remained on the cot, motionless beneath her covers. Her eyes were closed, and she felt completely detached. On and off she vaguely visualized the window frame, the timbers, the molding, all the shapes and objects she'd come to know so well. But they were mere abstractions. She had no more will to do anything with them. She knew the two-by-fours weren't going to give. The trap door was sealed from below. Just as her captors had seemed to anticipate her thinking each step of the way by removing objects she might use, the revelation about the keys had been the death knell of her confidence. Not only had the doubting part of her taken over completely, but she was beginning to feel a certain comfort in simply waiting, preparing for whatever came next. In a way, there was a beautiful simplicity to it. She felt a complete loss of hope, but with it came a feeling of reluctant liberation: there was no possible action except to wait. She lay this way for what seemed like hours.

When she heard Jane's voice from beneath the square, she assumed it was the first step in whatever was supposed to happen today. She could hear the men outside, talking in the front. She had quick flashes of inspiration: about running when being led away; about something with their plans backfiring on them; about something being noticed or reported by a passing stranger at the last moment. But she knew it was fantasy. The conversation she'd overheard through the listening hole was still fresh in her mind. They had planned how today would go, and this knock was the first piece of it. It was starting.

But there was an urgency in Jane's voice. It was a whisper, and it seemed meant only for her. Sarah knew that voice well enough by now to know the highs and the lows. Jane had ranged from distant to compassionate over the last few days, but there was something different about her tone now.

"Sarah!" Again.

Sarah approached. "Yeah."

The latch slid and the trapdoor opened a few inches. Sarah saw Jane at the top of the ladder, crouched, nervous, looking around, as if to see if the men or dogs were around. She handed Sarah an iron poker from the fireplace. "Take this. Quick. You have five minutes at most to do whatever you can to get out. They're outside right now. I'm going to keep them busy if I can and get them inside. But this is it. When they start hearing the sounds—" Sarah heard the sound of the front door opening. Jane swung shut the hatch and was gone.

It took several seconds for Sarah to absorb what she had just heard. When she did, she felt the foggy malaise dissipate instantly. She stood up. She could hear their voices, indistinct conversation, but even though she heard no words, the heightened tension was unmistakable. Sharp rebuttals and protestations. She took the poker and went to the back window.

The snow on the floor was several inches deep closest to the window and she had to kick some aside to maintain her footing. She raised the poker and starting pushing at the remaining boards. With the weight of the poker, they began to fall away easily. As they twisted and tore away from the nails, more light began to pour into the room. Encouraged by her progress and unfazed by the snow, she started prying, using the window frame as a lever and working on the first two-by-four. When she heard the splintering sounds, her confidence surged. She was grateful for the poker but wishing she'd had it long ago. The desk leg probably would have broken by now.

As she worked, she wondered what had caused the change of heart. Had Jane felt so ostracized and isolated that something in her had just snapped? Was this an instant decision, something that just happened today? Or had she been slowly planning something all along? And what was Sarah supposed to do when she jumped out? What if Jane wasn't there, and Tony and Ian came running out? Where would the dogs be? She pictured herself jumping out and being alone in the clearing, with Jane trapped inside. Her mind went back to the scenarios she'd thought about time and again, things that Ian had said from day one. Nowhere to run. Freezing to death. In the bloody middle of nowhere. No keys. The wrong car.

And why was she trusting Jane? She'd told herself before that she couldn't, but those dynamics had been overturned. Something had changed.

When the first two-by-four gave way, the possibility of escape became real. Not only was the window letting in more light—and snow—but the gaps were getting wider. With the second one removed, she might be able to squeeze out. Definitely with the third one. Before swinging at the second beam, she paused. She knew full well that Ian and Tony could easily hear what she was doing. But if they could, they seemed busy with whatever they were doing down there. Their voices seemed to undulate and waver.

She heard objects being moved around hastily. Maybe something falling or being thrown. Jane's voice rose once, then again. Sarah continued to swing at the beams.

Suddenly a gunshot split the air from below, followed by yelling. The dogs barked. The front door crashed. Multiple footsteps struck the floor.

Sarah continued to swing. She could hear sounds in the front. Feeling her hope fade and wondering whether something had happened to Jane, she ran to the front window and looked out through one of the little cracks. With the snow she could barely see to the far side of the clearing. A car was backing up toward the front door, but from the left, not the right where the road led away from the cabin. It was a BMW, the same as the one she'd seen at Levin's place in Seattle. Had it been parked the whole time, just out of sight, near the shed, or within it? There was a layer of snow on top, but most had been brushed off.

The driver door opened. Jane stepped out, looked up toward Sarah's window, then quickly toward the front door. She instantly ducked, with her hands over her ears. A shot rang out from near the front door. Sarah saw an instant hole form in the trunk of the BMW. Jane ran around the other side of the car, scrambling toward a snowbank. Then Tony appeared, running in Jane's direction. He was holding a black pistol. It looked different than the one he'd shown before.

Small clouds of exhaust came from the BMW's tailpipe and hung in the cold air. The dogs were agitated, running back and forth and barking.

Behind her she heard the sudden sound of the latch sliding open. She turned to see the hatch beginning to rise.

She left the window quickly and raced to step on it before it rose further. Even as she stood on it she could feel the pushing from below. Ian began shouting. She swung downward with the poker toward his face. Trying to remain firmly on the hatch, she struggled to lean forward to grab one end of the cot. When she got a grip on it she dragged it toward her, then pulled the mattress off, throwing it and the sleeping bag hastily to the floor.

She heard another gunshot outside.

The pushing from below continued. She overturned the cot and let it crash down on its side next to her, just as Ian was able to lift the hatch a couple of inches. With the sudden weight the hatch slammed shut and Ian swore and cried out in pain. She worked to drag the desk and the nightstand over.

"Sarah! You fucking bitch!" The pounding was more forceful now. The hatch shook.

She went to the rear window, angled the poker, and swung into the third beam with everything she had. Once more, then again. As she worked she could hear the pounding behind her build to a crescendo, then suddenly cease. She turned to look. Ian must be planning something else.

She continued to swing at the third beam. The gap was nearly wide enough now. She dropped the poker and tried to pull herself into the frame as a tearing sound emanated from the hatch. She turned to see Ian using a piece of wood to jam up through the opening. The force of it was pushing the cot and other furniture aside. He was going to get through. As she struggled to climb into the frame she saw Ian's hand slide through, frantically trying to grab anything he could to move the cot. She ran to the hatch and swung downward onto Ian's hand, hoping to disable him, but he moved just in time. As soon as she turned the hatch swung open. Before she could get away, his hand found her ankle. She lost her balance on the snowy floor and fell backward. The poker slipped from her hand. She desperately reached for it but Ian shoved the hatch open wider, knocking aside the cot, and began to climb through. She kicked at him, pushing backward, but he had his head and both hands through.

She freed herself, ran to the window and pulled herself into the frame, feeling Ian right behind her. She hesitated briefly, looking down through the swirling snow, and jumped.

"Oi! Sarah—"

Up to her waist in snow. She first felt the stinging cold soak into every part of her. Then a a sharp pain in her left thigh. She cried out as she doubled over, tumbling into the snow. Disoriented from the fall and the pain, she heard shouting above and around her. She trudged through the snow to the left corner of the cabin. Falling repeatedly, she dragged herself along, daring once to feel her left thigh. Her hand came up red, and she felt a splinter of wood sticking out of her jeans. It felt deep and not something she could handle until she knew her situation better. She tried to ignore the pain, plunging forward and groping her way along the side of the cabin toward the front.

She ducked and paused at the front, feeling her body start to shake. With eyes on the front door she knew Ian would emerge at any moment. She could hear his voice inside. Tony and Jane were struggling not far from the front of the car, their voices a cacophony of painful cries and grunts. Tony was pulling her hair with one hand and punching her with the other as she repeatedly tried to choke him and scratch at his eyes. The dogs were biting at Jane's legs and bloody marks dotted her ankles as she screamed and kicked at them. Tony's gun was on the ground only steps away from the passenger door.

Just as she was about to run toward the car she saw Ian's shape leave the front door. She quickly ducked back as he looked both ways, searching wildly. He ran to the opposite corner, and she knew that when he didn't find her there he would come this way. She got down low, staggered into the clearing, and made her way to the rear of the BMW and to the passenger side. When she reached it she got on her hands and knees as the stench of exhaust washed over her. Ian was calling out to Tony. She could tell from his voice that he was crossing to the other corner now. He would see her. She dragged herself flat along the ground to the passenger door. Voices were just feet away and she could hear a dog approaching. She reached for the handle and pulled. It was locked.

"Hey!" Ian's voice, somewhere close.

She began crying and sank to the ground. As her face hit the snow she saw a dog in her periphery, heard the growling as it approached. The gun was a yard away to her right, and quickly weighing the pros and cons she dashed forward to grab it just as the dog tore at her right ankle. She quickly turned, pointed the gun in the dog's direction, and fired. The dog yelped and fell away. As she tried to stand Ian came near and kicked at her wrist, knocking the gun out of her hand. She lunged for his legs, toppling him over, and kicked herself toward the rear car door.

Fearing that she would reach the handle and it wouldn't open, she debated going for the gun again, but Ian was scrambling to his feet and he would easily get to it before she did. She pulled on the handle just as the other dog appeared behind her, growling. The door opened. She madly forced herself through and scrambled into the back seat and began to heave herself toward the driver's seat, but Ian was there. He had come around to the driver side and was reaching in through the door. She lunged forward anyway, into the driver seat, going for his forearm. She got it and bit it as hard as she could, again and again. He yelled and twisted away, grabbing her hair and pulling hard. She screamed in pain as he swung at her with his other fist, catching her right eye.

A sharp penetrating pain suddenly pierced her calf. The dog. She screamed in agony and tried to kick but felt a tugging as she slipped backward. Ian landed another blow on the side of her face. The dog pulled at her from behind. She kept kicking with her free leg as the splinter twisted in her thigh, finally landing a solid blow on the dog's head. She heard it howl but just as quickly felt the teeth again on her skin, sinking in deep, slipping, scraping past her ankle. She thought she heard Tony nearby, yelling something. She kicked and tried to bite Ian's arm again but she felt herself getting weak.

Then she felt the sharp impact of something on the back of her head. For an instant, her vision seemed to go dark. Time seemed to stop. The pain seared through her neck, down her back. She felt lightheaded. She blinked and shook her head. She felt snowflakes land on her face. She thought she heard a lullaby from somewhere.

Tony was trying to open the passenger door. She shook her head and kicked harder. This time she felt her foot catch the rear door frame. Pushed herself forward. Felt her hair being pulled back but ignored the pain as she reached for the shift lever with her shaking right hand and slid it into reverse. Just as Tony's hands gripped her ankles and she felt herself being pulled out the back, she reached for the gas with her left hand and pushed down hard.

The BMW instantly jolted into motion. Tony's voice uttered something. Inches away from her face she could see Ian stuck under the open driver door, being dragged backward with the motion of the car, still with his hand on her hair but with his grip fading fast. His forearm was full of blood.

She struggled vainly to see over the dash. Jane was running toward the passenger side. A sudden tearing sound mixed with a high-pitched scream to the left. Ian's jacket ripped, and she felt him break free as his hand let go of her hair. The open car door passed over him when he tried to wriggle free and she could see the sharp corner slice across his chest and stomach as he twisted and cried out in pain. She struggled to reach over and unlock the door for Jane but the car was still moving backward.

The car hit the cabin front wall and the engine instantly died. Jane got in and slammed the door shut. "Hurry!" Jane hollered, reaching over to turn the keys. She tried repeatedly.

Sarah pulled herself forward, struggling through the pain. Ian was on his feet. His shirt was torn off and he was bleeding heavily, but he stumbled toward them, half doubled over. Tony, approaching from the right, swung the gun toward the front of the car. Before Sarah could process what was happening she heard the sound. A small hole opened up in the window, just to the side of Jane, who ducked and let out a cry. Another shot, and the windshield in front of Sarah cracked.

Hearing herself scream, she pulled on the wheel to drag herself into the seat just as Jane got the car started. Sarah slapped the lever into drive and floored it. The tires spun briefly, then took. She felt as much as saw Ian to her left as she sped up and turned hard toward the road. Tony was on their right with the gun aimed at her. He struggled to get out of the way. A shot rang out, the front passenger window shattered, and the open back door struck him with a dull metallic thud and slammed shut instantly. The car briefly shook from the impact and she let up a little on the gas. Ian was somewhere in her left periphery but she kept her eyes on the widening turn, going way too fast now. Snow banks were high on all sides of the clearing and she knew that if she hit one she would be stuck and they would be on them instantly.

When she was pointed more or less toward the open road, she floored it again. Again the tires spun, then took. The dog was barking and lunging in her direction but fled when the car got closer. She was headed fast toward a bank of plowed snow, and she spun the wheel to avoid it, sending the car too far in the opposite direction. She braked and corrected, feeling the BMW's antilocks rattle beneath. She stepped on the gas again, correcting her turns as she went, until they were well into the road.

"Shit," Jane said between breaths.

Panting, Sarah's eyes darted between the road ahead and the rearview mirror. She heard another shot, but by now Tony and Ian were small figures, getting smaller. She kept the speed as fast as she dared. Gradually the dog fell behind and gave up. Now far behind them, the shrinking figures became impossible to see through the snow.

In control of the wheel but feeling panic with every minor turn in the road, she struggled to keep the center. The narrow road twisted frequently, the snow was deep in places, and she could feel the slipping as she took the curves. More than once the close pines seemed to lunge at them from one side or the other. She had to brake at each turn to make the curves, but after she rounded a bend and the car stopped sliding, she would step on it and pick up speed quickly.

The crack in the windshield made it hard to see, and the speed and the flying snow added to her fear. She kept her eyes directly ahead. She felt that when she did risk looking even slightly to one side or the other that she would start losing control. When she finally caught a glance at the gauge on a straight stretch she was stunned to see she was going close to seventy.

On another straight segment she allowed herself a glance, ever so briefly, at her bleeding leg. The pain was intense. Blood was smeared all over her left thigh and her pants were torn. A splinter of wood was sticking out of her skin, surrounded by blood and purple flesh. She knew she had to take the splinter out and told herself she'd do it when she wasn't thinking about it. It could wait. The dog bite on her right ankle was throbbing, and she couldn't feel the area around the ankle at all. She didn't dare ponder what that meant. Not now. Not yet.

"You've gotta be in a lot of pain," Jane said, staring forward. "You okay?"

"I don't even know," Sarah murmured.

"We can switch. You need to get that out.'"

"I know."

"When we get further up."

"Okay."

"They're going to follow us."

Sarah watched the curves and her speed. "How long is this road?"

"Not sure."

"That guy said it wasn't that far to the fork. So where's this stupid fork? I can barely feel my fingers."

As she drove, keeping it as fast as she could handle, she saw Jane look at the dash, then at her watch. "We have a good head start on them."

"I'm worried if we slip. If we go off the road, we're done." Sarah knew if it happened at this speed and they somehow didn't get hurt, if the car just nuzzled into the deep snow off to the side, the car would probably stall, they'd be stuck, and they would not have a chance.

"Ian was right about the snow. It's deeper than I thought."

"Just stay focused."

Sarah slowed carefully at the turns, and the BMW handled them well.

When she rounded a turn and the road straightened out again, she saw in the distance what almost appeared to be a wider part of the road, like a clearing. As she got closer, she could make out what appeared to be another road.

It had to be the fork.

But as she slowed the car, she realized she was still going too fast—over sixty—and was starting to slide as she stepped on the brakes. Panic gripped her as she felt the car fishtail back and forth in rapid but smooth movement. She allowed herself to imagine this fishtailing getting more pronounced, going all the way until the car slid off the road or turned over.

She let go of the brakes and the car straightened. But she was still moving too fast. She was going to overshoot the fork, if it was the fork. She tapped the brake pedal lightly several times to slow down.

Jane was looking back. "Fuck. They're coming."

Sarah looked in the mirror. She could see the SUV just turning the bend behind them through the snow. They shot past the fork going thirty, slowed to twenty, stopped and skidded to a halt. Sarah slammed it into reverse and looked behind her as she backed up, spinning the tires wildly.

Panic gripped her as they hung there, motionless, suspended, the BMW idling and ready for her next decision. In front of them was not just a fork. It was an intersection. The road went straight, to the left, and to the right. All routes were partially plowed.

CHAPTER 50

At about 10:00 A.M. Brandon sipped the last of the now-cold coffee. Even with the blanket around him, he was starting to feel the cold. His breath escaped in steamy clouds, and his fingers felt the chill through his gloves. Occasional bursts of snow made their way in, since the door wouldn't fully close. He didn't mind any of it. He had warmer gear in the jeep if he needed it, but the cold seemed to help him feel a certain sense of presence. The inability to do anything to advance the cause or alter any chain of events had a sort of calming effect. He had done all the steps, adjusted the levers, spun the gears, and now it was only a matter of waiting. There was nothing he could do now to change the outcome of anything. He was aware of a peaceful sense of tranquility as the large flakes fell silently on the dilapidated timbers and surfaces around him.

By now Mike would be under the impression that the exchange was supposed to happen at 3:00 P.M. He would have read Entry #3 at the Starbucks in Seattle. He would think that Sarah's father had changed the demands: 3:00 P.M. at the abandoned gas station, for less than the requested dollar figure, under the threat of her father going to the authorities with the information that his private investigator had dug up.

Of course, Sarah's father had changed nothing. His understanding of the situation was the same as from day one, based on the videos provided to him, recorded by Sarah. The finer details, in the manila folder in his office, were the same: noon at the gas station. Original amount. There was no private investigator, no different amount, no time changes.

Her father would send the payment, probably via Burke or some other trusted contact, to arrive at the gas station at noon. Marcella would bring Sarah, at noon. The plan was for he and Marcella to split the payment, fifty-fifty. Burke would hand over the payment and get Sarah in return. Marcella would then go east, to the spot they'd chosen. Brandon would go south, back to San Francisco, to play his part as the concerned boyfriend for the next few weeks. Slowly he would detach from California and connect with Marcella in Idaho.

Meanwhile, Mike would scramble to figure out how the victim had escaped. Maybe he'd show up at 3:00 P.M. as per the modified demands dictated to him, hoping to strong-arm the payment. It wouldn't matter. He would arrive alone. Sarah would be long gone, and so would the payment. All he would find, if he looked hard enough, would be a rifle. Maybe he'd find it, maybe not. If he did, maybe he'd touch it. Maybe not. It would be the only thing he would find.

Ah, but Marcella. She'd always had a penchant for drama. Drama by candlelight, drama by fantasy. Cold and calculating by one turn, soft and mellow the next. Her inconsistency would be her downfall. Brandon had even told her that once, and he got the reaction only she could deliver: a line from a Charles Bukowski poem. He chewed on it and spit it back at her with enough innuendo and flair to satiate her ego, and they made love for four hours that afternoon. Sarah would never know the kind of depth he had with Marcella. The standards weren't even comparable.

It would be so ironic that after all these months of planning, he would shortchange Marcella just as Marcella would shortchange him, if she had the chance.

CHAPTER 51

Rearview mirror.

The SUV was fast approaching.

Sarah looked furiously around. The roads in all directions were plowed. She'd been expecting it to be obvious, with one way plowed and the others not. "Oh god," she said. "Didn't he say he ran off into the ditch at the fork? Which way did he come in? One of these has to—"

"Let me drive," Jane said. "You need to deal with that leg."

Sarah looked down at her bloody thigh.

"Now!" Jane began to get up.

"Yeah. Okay."

Jane opened her door and quickly went around while Sarah climbed over into the passenger seat, trying to suppress her screams of pain. The SUV was no more than 200 yards down the road.

With her eyes on the rearview, Jane shifted into drive and the car moved forward. She spun the wheel to the right and went heavy on the gas. Snow flew into the air. As they moved Sarah looked into the side mirror through the broken side window. The SUV would reach the intersection in seconds.

Before she knew it they were going over sixty on a narrow road covered in ice and snow. The side mirror vibrated with the terrain and the speed, and even as the passenger she felt the need to keep her eyes straight ahead. Things in her periphery faded to a blur. Glancing at Jane's tight grip on the wheel she could nearly feel the pressure in her own hands. Whenever she felt the car start to dip to one side or the other, panic stabbed at her. She knew each time it happened it could mean the end. But the car always recovered.

At a turn Jane began applying the brakes slowly, tapping the pedal lightly several times, then increasing the pressure until she'd slowed down to fifty, forty, thirty. She slowly turned the wheel, and with another straight stretch ahead, pushed the pedal down.

After a couple more turns, Sarah saw a road sign ahead. That would mean another road. A larger one. The highway? There may be other cars—maybe people. Someone might stop. They raced toward it but Sarah could tell Jane hadn't braked early enough. The brakes kicked in but the car started shaking, and Sarah could feel the loss of control as it began to slide. The antilocks started clicking, Jane eased up, and the car straightened out but they were still going too fast.

"Jane!"

"Fuck. Hang on!"

She saw the sign pass by her broken window in a blur as they blasted onto a blacktop road. Jane slammed the brakes and clenched the wheel. Sarah caught a glimpse of a semi approaching from one side. The BMW began to spin, and Jane seemed to try to correct with the wheel as they careened and skidded toward the far side of the road. A high-pitched, grinding, scraping sound of steel on steel and the sharp report of the truck's horn filled the air behind them as they crashed into the foliage. The BMW came to a halt and then wobbled slightly with the sudden loss of motion. A massive rush of wind shook the car as the semi passed behind them. They were facing a snowy ravine. The ground dropped away beneath them. Pine boughs, branches, and broken twigs were pressed against the cracked windshield.

A shot rang out from behind them. As Jane frantically reversed Sarah looked behind to see the SUV coming onto the road. Tony was leaning out of the passenger window with a rifle.

"Come on, come on," Jane said, nearly to herself. She spun the wheel in the middle of the road and gunned it.

The road ahead was white. The snow in the center appeared pressed flat by tire tracks, but off to the sides, it got deep. Snow raged across the windows. Jane clutched the wheel with a tight grip. As they progressed there was hardly any traffic but there were signs of accidents, tire tracks that left the road and headed off to the sides. They passed a car that had flipped over on the side of the road. Sarah thought she saw someone in there, upside down.

Out the rear window, through the snow, she could see the headlights of the SUV. They were following and seemed to be gaining. Sarah remained silent.

She looked at the splinter in her left thigh. The pointed piece of wood was sticking out of her jeans. She knew she'd have to remove it but feared the surge of pain and blood that would follow. She leaned over and pulled up her right pants cuff. Blood soaked the sock, was smeared all over her lower leg, and filled the inner part of her shoe around her ankle. Blood-stained snow was crusted in the nooks and crannies. Edging the cuff past the dog bite, she gritted her teeth and held her breath as the torn flesh of her calf came into view in a jagged cacophony of red, purple, and black.

She felt the car begin to slide. Jane was driving fast, hugging the wheel and working the brakes as she slowed for turns. The wipers were on and they were mixing grime from the road with the snow and smearing it all over the glass. Visibility was about fifty yards at most. Even then the only thing to see was white, white on the road, white on the pines on both sides, white swirling in the air.

"Jane," she croaked.

Jane kept her eyes on the road. "Yeah."

"Thanks."

"You okay?"

"I think so. Do you know where we're going?"

There was a moment's hesitation. "No."

"They're back there."

"I know," Jane said, eyeing the rearview.

Sarah looked at the splinter again. It was sticking out, pointing downward. It must have been from knocking the boards loose and was hidden in the snow, sticking up straight, and she hadn't been able to see it from above when she jumped.

"There's some napkins in the glove box," Jane said.

Sarah reached forward and found them, then leaned back and got them ready. She began to pull at the splinter but felt the resistance in her skin. "Shit."

"I can help you."

"How. This thing is—"

"I'll pull it. I'll count to three."

"What?"

Jane reached out with her right hand toward Sarah's leg. "One," she said.

Sarah clenched her eyes and braced herself. A sudden splitting pain in her thigh, and Jane pulled the splinter out.

Sarah bent forward, eyes closed, feeling for the napkins. She still hadn't looked. Feeling her way as she groaned through her teeth, she pressed the wad of napkins into the pain and pressed firmly.

"Fuck," she heard Jane say.

Sarah looked. The splinter was resting on the console. It was at least four inches long, sharply pointed and bloody at one end.

"I don't know how you were able to even move with that in your leg, let alone drive."

They were at the top of a steep downhill. A line of several cars was at the bottom, going around a bend. The brake lights were going on and off through the falling snow. She lifted the napkins and looked at her leg. Blood had soaked through the crumpled mess but the pain was lessened.

"Hang on," Jane said.

She could feel the car skid as Jane tried to brake. The cars down there were crawling along. Jane was able to brake and they edged up against the car in front.

Sarah saw the lights of two patrol cars and an ambulance ahead. She felt an instant sense of relief as soon as she saw the state patrol logo and the troopers directing traffic around the wreck. Two mangled cars were pointed toward each other in a broken disarray of metal and glass in the middle of the road. Four or five people were hovering near the side of the road among crumpled metal as EMTs worked to move two gurneys into the ambulance. Cars coming the opposite direction slowly moved around the accident site.

She looked behind, out the back window. "I don't even know how we're gonna be able to stop."

"What?" Jane said, glancing between the window and the rearview.

"With them coming after us."

"We can't."

"But they're cops."

Jane moved through the scene and beyond as Sarah saw the troopers within shouting distance. They were receding into the background, caught up in the swirling snow and the brake lights.

"Jane!"

"What?"

"We have to stop!"

"We will. When it's safe. Mike and Tony are too close."

"What?"

The wreck and lights and all the cars were fading into the falling snow, getting smaller. Then she saw the headlights of the SUV gaining on them.

CHAPTER 52

In the tiny shed, Brandon was aware of a vague discomfort. He knew objectively that it was just nervous apprehension. He was on alert. The finale of all his planning was drawing near. All the months of intricate deceptions—some to the point that even he had occasionally been uncertain which way a dimly lit path led—were all in the past now. Only the future remained, and it was just out of sight. He'd planned for it, envisioned it; he knew how it was supposed to go. At any moment, the first car would approach, and just as with the flick of a switch, all the months of planning would instantly convert to minutes of action. Things would either go according to script or they would not.

But as he watched the snow falling silently through the narrow crack of the door, he felt the sense of something deeper. The heavy flakes spun in little eddies as the wind blew them around the opening, creating ghostly patterns within the small frame that separated the before and the after. He found himself thinking of Sarah. Not the kidnapped Sarah, or the Sarah in distress, but Sarah the person he had always kept at arm's length. The Sarah he'd trailed along and lied to even as they swore secrets to each other. Sarah, the girlfriend that he'd kept for only one purpose. Sarah, the woman he had deluded into a one-sided love affair. The images floated by like an old movie reel, flickering in tones of black and white and sepia, until they broke and the film began to melt and distort.

They had never done anything with horses or even gone to the stable after that first kiss on Bainbridge, early on. Was it because they never found the time? Because they spent most of their time in the Bay Area? He had lucked out. He'd given her the impression that he kept an Arabian there but he always wondered if she had somehow found out that the horse he'd shown her that day wasn't his. Or that he barely knew how to ride. Had it never come up because she made assumptions based on what he fed her that day? The set pieces of stables and horses and Bainbridge island were enough to set the tone and prevent any followup?

He'd never been able to wear the matching watch from the set he'd bought for them in Geneva. Not until just a few days ago, when drinking the Scotch with Jeff and Dave. He was not superstitious: he was driven by facts. Yet there was something about wearing it that always tore at him. When she'd come over, after that trip, or sometimes when they went out, he would catch the fleeting glance and the searching expression on her face, as she mentally calculated why she was wearing hers and he was not wearing his. She never said anything during those times, and that allowed him, he knew now, to keep her at a comfortable distance. Then, he was happy for those moments. They saved him from explanations. He hadn't had to justify a behavior. But over time, he'd come to see those moments as weakness, a reliance on accidental fortune that only worked because it was easy, not because he'd planned it or was in charge of it. He hated himself for the inaction as much as for the deception.

Or the time at the museum in L.A. It had been such a tiny oversight, and yet something so significant that it had taken him days to reconsider his entire strategy. It was still early days for them, during what he liked to think of as the discovery phase. They were at the museum cafe, talking about one thing or another, and conversation shifted all over, from art to routines and habits to astrology. Lingering on astrology, Sarah asked him about his birthday. By that point, they'd been spending a good deal of time together. Their first kiss on Bainbridge had been weeks ago. Softball questions like this came and went over meals, on verandas, in bed, on the phone, and as soon as it left her lips he felt gripped in a mental vice. It was a perilous split second, during which he could literally see weeks of effort and logistics being undone by a single hollow reply. He had enough time, during that split second, to consider the magnitude of a wrong answer. If he'd spent weeks researching every single detail about her life, finding out where she went, who she'd grown up with, her personal shortcomings, her hopes and aspirations, yet he could not even answer the most basic question about himself, he knew the project was a failure. Scanning the room in a delirious internal frenzy and seeing the date on a poster on the wall, showing the dates of past exhibits, he spit it out: June 7. He was going to ask hers, but he already knew it, so he spent the next microseconds coming up with any knowledge he could regarding Gemini. *Adaptable*, Sarah had said, scrolling through her app. *Intelligent. Afraid of solitude.* He had absorbed each trait that she listed like a sponge, silently calculating how to conform to each one. He later memorized others. He would be ready for anyone if the birthday question ever came up again. But when he'd looked at himself in the mirror that night, it was the first of many times he felt he saw someone else looking back at him.

He heard the sound of a snowplow outside. At least twice one had come by, scraping the road before more snow covered it again. As noon approached, he sometimes thought he could hear a vehicle. But he knew it was overthinking: there wasn't any traffic. They had probably closed the road.

But later, when he did hear the sound of a slowing car, he strained to listen. From his position in the shed, he had only a partial view of one side of the road. From the gap in the door he could see part of the old house in the back of the lot and part of the garage with the gas pumps in front. Unlike the occasional passing car he'd heard earlier in the morning, it seemed to be slowing. Most of the passing cars he'd heard took the gradual curve a little slower, especially with the weather, but their speed was consistent. This one was different. If it was a car slowing down for the station, there was only a small range of possibilities.

He eyed the rifles, the two handguns, and the spent coffee cup. He glanced at the crack in the doorway and the snow swirling its way in. He breathed in deeply, let it out, and focused. He looked at his watch. It was 12:11.

He assumed Burke or whomever Sarah's father would send would come from the west. He would have a partial view through the window. This was coming from the east, so unless it was a total stranger, it would be Sarah. He listened carefully, positioned himself behind the crack in the door, and peeked out. It was a small black BMW. The car had pulled into the space next to the gas pumps and was idling. From his position he could only partly see the front of the car. He leaned back in the dark stillness of the shed and waited.

CHAPTER 53

They continued on for several miles, passing a barricade saying the road ahead was closed. Jane navigated the dangerous twists and turns in the road as fast as she dared to push the BMW. After passing the crash, and especially after the barricade, they saw no cars. Sarah sat in contemplative silence, watching the road ahead, knowing that with each passing mile the obvious chance at help was getting further and further behind them. She had come this far. She had escaped the cabin. Jane had helped her get out. So why was Jane hesitating to take the obvious opportunity?

On a long gradual curve, she saw the hint of something on the right, some kind of building. As they got closer, she could see it was a faded relic of a sign. The wording itself was obscured by snow but from the buildings and sheds it looked like an old gas station. Two antique pumps stood in front of what must have been the service garage. An old house was in the back. A shed was to the left and a tiny shack was in front, closer to the road. All of the buildings were covered in heavy snow, and everything looked faded, aged, and worn out, with some walls sagging or broken and windows boarded up.

"We have to stop," Jane said, looking at the dash.

"What's wrong?"

"Something with the oil pressure."

"What?"

Sarah looked behind them. For now, there was no sign of the SUV. But she knew it wouldn't be far behind.

"We have to check it."

"But we can get to a gas station or something. Tony and Mike'll be here any second. You saw how close they were."

"It—Tony said there's something with the oil in this thing. If you put too much speed on it, it could overheat."

"What?"

"I don't want it to die now, after all this. Look how hard we've been pushing it."

"But they're going to show up any second."

"If this car dies, what're you gonna do then? It's not me they're after."

Sarah pondered that as they pulled into the space between the tiny shed and the gas pumps. Jane opened the trunk lever and went around to the back. Sarah looked at the dash, wondering why Jane was going to the trunk instead of the front. She could see nothing obvious, but Jane had taken the keys out and nothing was lit. The car had seemed fine. They were losing time.

As she waited, she bit her nails and looked around at the collection of buildings, wondering what they were supposed to do now. In front of the house a small set of stairs led up to the front door. The door was boarded over but some of the wood had been pulled off long ago. Graffiti littered some of the surfaces. The windows were broken in several places.

Deciding she could wait no further, she opened her door and stepped out. When she set her weight on her right leg, she had to hold the car door as the pain hit her. The snow was several inches deep, and before she'd taken two steps, Jane closed the trunk. Turning, she saw that Jane was holding the Scream mask in one hand and a handgun in the other. The gun was pointed at her. Momentary confusion quickly gave way to blind panic. She knew the SUV was close. The woman who had helped her escape was now pointing a gun at her. It seemed all she could do was stare blankly at the gun, seeing it but not processing anything. Her mind was numb, and yet she tried to make connections. Trying to find any reason she could.

"If you hurry, it'll make things a lot easier," Jane said. "Like you said, they'll be here any second."

"But you—"

"Just go to the house. Go up the stairs."

Sarah turned and began to limp. Even now, she had what she knew were crazy, fleeting thoughts: that she might overpower Jane somehow and get the car and flee. That she might grab the gun and turn the tables. She knew it was all ridiculous. She stared at the broken boards covering the door and the looming darkness within.

"Hurry!" Jane said. When Sarah allowed herself a quick glimpse behind her, she saw Jane glancing at the road. The SUV was coming, its headlights tearing through the swirling snow.

"Come on, hurry!" Jane said again.

Confused, Sarah limped ahead, shuffling through the snow. She walked up the steps. Jane followed right behind. At the entrance she ducked down and went inside. Dim light from the broken window coverings revealed a small room that must have been the office. A wood stove was in the corner. A counter with a broken cash register on its side. Mostly empty shelves.

Small boxes, containers, canisters, old car parts and supplies lay strewn across the floor.

"Stay here," Jane said. They were a few paces within the entrance, more or less in the middle of the room. Jane stood behind Sarah, both of them facing the front. "Don't move. Don't scream. Don't fuck this up."

Sarah stood still. From her position she could see out into the clearing in front of the steps but not much else. She could hear the sounds of the SUV pulling up. The doors opened and closed. The sounds of feet crunching the snow. Some low conversation, back and forth, then the footsteps went different directions. It sounded to Sarah like one of them was going around to the side of the house.

"Jane!" Ian called from near the front. "No sense fucking this up any further!"

Sarah could hear the sounds at the side of the house, near the partially boarded window. She assumed Jane was trying to figure out what to do, how to handle both threats while using the prisoner as a shield. She held the gun toward the front door while she glanced between the window and the front door.

The footsteps stopped. Tony must be just outside the window, and Ian near the front. In the silence, the falling snow almost seemed to make a sound of its own; or maybe it was her brain filling in, imagining it. She contemplated the move, knew it was foolish to try, but knew she had to. Knew it was now or never. She could tell Jane was distracted, torn between two directions. Tension was high.

Quickly estimating everyone's positions based on her impression of the surroundings, she instantly dropped to the ground, turned, and kicked toward Jane's legs with her splinter leg, sweeping to catch Jane below the knees. Jane was caught up in the sudden move and lost her balance quickly. The gun fell from her grip and she hastily fumbled for it as she went down, falling awkwardly on Sarah's legs as Sarah backed away. The gun slid across the floor and both of them scrambled for it. When they were near the window Jane started to get the handle of the gun. Sarah struck at Jane's extended arm with a metal rod and the gun slid, but Sarah was interrupted by a sudden shattering noise above. She grabbed the gun and quickly covered her eyes as shards of glass fell all around them. Looking up with an arm over her eyes she saw Tony pointing the rifle at Jane.

With only the slightest hesitation, Sarah aimed the gun at Tony, sighted down the barrel, and pulled the trigger. She hadn't aimed well and the gun was smaller than the one from before and she feared the retribution if the shot went wrong, but in the same fraction of a second Tony's rifle went off and he quickly jerked to the side, with his hand covering his chest. Something on the shelf behind her broke into pieces and fell. She heard the sound of Tony dropping to the ground outside the window and a quiet exhalation.

A silence followed. Everything seemed to pause, hanging in a suspended state without sound. Sarah began to turn. The gun was in her hands. From her periphery she saw Ian begin to move, saw his legs coming toward the opening. In an instant she felt the pain in her wrists as the metal rod swung downward. The gun fell from her hands and hit the floor as she screamed. Jane threw the rod down and reached for the gun and aimed it toward the opening.

Sarah quickly got to her feet and staggered toward the back of the room. She crouched just as Ian came through the opening with a gun pointed in her direction. Before he took three steps Jane shot him two times. With a wincing expression of pain Ian looked briefly at Jane as though about to speak. His mouth opened and his gun dropped, and he crumpled to the floor in silence.

Between her heaving breaths Sarah saw Jane with the gun, swinging the barrel away from Ian and pointing it in her direction. It was a vague sort of motion, almost with a sense of reluctance. As she stared back at Jane, she heard a sound outside. A car door was opening. A chime was going off.

Sarah, her mind numb, glanced between Ian, dead on the floor, and Jane, who even now was pointing a gun at her as she cautiously approached the opening. Sarah tried to put pressure on her ankle. The pulsing pain had returned vigorously. Her head was spinning. Her wrists stung.

She watched as Jane paused near Ian's body. One arm was off to his side on the rough wooden floor, and his bracelet was touching it, with the chain attached to his wrist. Jane bent down to tear off the bracelet and open the locket. She smirked to herself and let it fall to the floor, then crushed it underfoot. She picked up the Scream mask that had fallen to the floor. She put it on and adjusted it, then cautiously peeked out through the opening.

"Come on Sarah," she said, waving the gun. Her voice was laced with exhaustion. "This is the last part. This is it."

"What."

"Come on."

"Why are you wearing that again?"

"Mike and Tony would be too if they knew this was the real pickup time."

"What?"

"Hurry up. We don't have time."

Dazed, Sarah slowly got to her feet. She followed as Jane stepped through the opening and went down the steps. Through the falling snow Sarah saw a different scene than the one she had left minutes ago. The SUV that Ian and Tony had arrived in was parked next to the BMW. Behind the SUV was a black Cadillac. And she saw a jeep at the side of the house that she hadn't seen before. It was facing the road.

A figure, she assumed a man, wearing a ski mask over his face, was standing near the tiny shed, holding a rifle in one hand and a handgun in the other. He was pointing the handgun toward the Cadillac. Burke was there, standing just behind the open driver door. He was holding a gas can in one hand and a small blowtorch in the other. The jet of the flame glowed blue in the air.

"Stop there," he called out.

Everyone waited for him. He stepped forward and waved the blue flame around in the air. "I have my cell on right now," Burke called out. "The people on the other end can hear everything happening here. If I'm harmed in any way, if you so much as think about pulling a trigger, it all goes up. If I don't take Sarah back and meet up with them in fifteen minutes, I'll torch everything in this car. The gas is already poured. If you shoot me, this thing drops to the ground and the whole thing goes."

Burke poured some gas on the snowy ground a few feet away and lit it with the torch. The puddle exploded briefly and burned out, causing the snow to hiss. Then he poured some gas around his feet.

"Do we understand each other?"

Burke set down the gas can. Keeping the blowtorch in his left hand he opened the back door on his side and pulled out a metal box about two feet wide. It seemed heavy and he struggled to pull it out enough to let it fall to the ground. It hit the snow and landed at an off angle.

"You can check it out if you want," Burke said. "There's four boxes in all. Everything just like you said."

Jane approached the man in the ski mask. They stood near each other and talked as if they knew each other. Their conversation was brief. He opened the back of the jeep. Jane opened the trunk of the BMW.

The man set down his rifle and went toward Burke to check the contents. He opened the box, took out what looked like bundles of cash, and dug through the box. Burke stood, watching carefully, ready with the torch. Seemingly satisfied with the contents, the man said something to Burke. Burke pulled out another box. They went through all the other boxes as Jane and Sarah watched.

When the man turned and cocked his head for Jane to approach, she went over and they again stood close and exchanged a few words. After a minute or two, Jane looked toward her. "Sarah," she said.

Sarah limped over and waited. The man in the ski mask looked toward Burke.

"Wait here," Jane said.

Together, Jane and the man lifted the first two boxes into the back of the jeep. When they began to lift the third, Sarah assumed they were going to load the others into the BMW, splitting the four boxes between them. Why else would Jane have opened the trunk?

"Put them all in there," she said, nodding to the jeep. The man seemed momentarily confused, but acquiesced and helped her hoist the third box in.

When he went over to get the fourth, he bent down and turned his back briefly to lift one side of the box. Sarah noticed the moment of hesitation as he stood there, bent over the box, holding the little metal handle, waiting for Jane to approach on the other side. It was only a fraction of a second. In a blur, he suddenly spun around, starting to aim his gun at Jane but before he could raise it Jane fired once, then again. He fell to the ground in a distorted position. Burke stepped back, holding the torch and picking up the gas can again, ready.

In a flash, it was over. The man let out a slow moan, and adjusted himself in the snow. Even as his movements began to slow, he seemed to grab at the box, trying, hopelessly, to pull it closer. Sarah could see the blood begin to pool beneath him. She looked away, too shaken to process it any further.

Wasting no time, Jane labored to drag the fourth box into the jeep. She was barely able to hoist it up, and when she did she slammed the hatch shut. She opened the driver door, got in and started the car.

"Marcella," the man on the ground said. Stunned, Sarah turned in his direction. By now he was completely still, but she could see the steam escape from his mouth. He was on his back, and his stomach rose slightly with his fading breaths. Sarah limped toward him, by now feeling so weak she didn't know if she could make it all the way.

Behind her, the jeep left in a rush of spinning tires and kicked-up snow. Sarah looked up to see Jane turn onto the road. She pulled the Scream mask off as she looked back and met Sarah's eyes, then turned away as she headed east. Within seconds she was swallowed up in the swirling snow.

Burke turned off the torch and set it down. Sarah could hear him talking into a phone but didn't catch anything he was saying. She looked down at the man on the ground. By now blood had pooled into the snow in a wide arc on his left side. He had pulled most of his mask off. His arm was positioned just in front of some fallen stacks of cash.

Sarah pulled the rest of the ski mask off. Even before the last of it had left his face she felt as though a small part of her had known all along. When she saw his face, it was the recognition of something she felt she had hidden from herself. A little voice in her told her she should cry or weep—that she should feel sad. But when she looked into his eyes she felt nothing. She just stared at his face, the face of a stranger who had come into her life and was now leaving it. The face of a man she had loved once. The face of someone she realized she had never known. It was the best she could do.

By now, his eyes were staring emptily at the sky. The blood coming out of his mouth had stopped flowing, having trickled down in a clean stripe across his cheek and neck. The pool of blood beneath him was a dark crimson oval against the white snow. The swirling drifts circled around him and collected on his face, his clothes. Gradually, even the blood would get covered up. *No one would know*, she thought to herself.

Burke helped her to her feet.

For an instant, the silence of falling snow captivated her, and she saw the beauty of this place for the first time. Her exhaustion seemed to make her feel light on her feet. She held out her tongue, like she and Tracy had when they were children on snowy days, and stared at the sky with her eyes closed. She could feel the cold, tiny pricks of snowflakes as they landed and melted.

When she heard the cars approaching, she looked up at the white sky. She had no sense of where the sun might be. No sense of how many hours had passed. No sense of the current time. She wondered.

"Burke?"

"Yes?"

She shook her head. "Never mind."

Thank you for reading this *The Kidnapping of Sarah Easton*. If you enjoyed the read—or even if you didn't—please consider taking the time to provide your honest review on the platform where you obtained it. Reader feedback helps others know about your experiences.

If you would like to read more of my work, please follow my newsletter, social media, or whatever works for you to see what I'm writing next. I would love to hear from you! My website has all the info:

www.erikgoddard.com/fiction

Happy reading,
Erik Goddard

Made in the USA
Columbia, SC
12 December 2021

51114623R00243